THE
GREATEST MASTERPIECES
OF
RUSSIAN LITERATURE

LEO N. TOLSTOY

ANNA KARENINA

II

Translated by Rochelle S. Townsend

*Original Illustrations and Frontispiece
by Roland Topor*

Distributed by
HERON BOOKS

Published by arrangement with
J.M. Dent & Sons Ltd.

© *Illustrations, Edito-Service S.A., Geneva*

PART V

I

AT first the Princess Shcherbatsky would not hear of having the wedding before Lent, to which only five weeks remained, as Kitty's trousseau was not yet half finished. But when Levin put it to her that if they waited until after Lent they ran the risk of having it delayed for a very long time, as they might have to go into mourning any day for an old aunt of the prince, who was very ill and expected to die at any moment, she at last agreed, and decided to prepare only a small part of the trousseau at once, leaving the rest until afterwards.

She grew quite angry with Levin because he was not sufficiently interested to say whether he approved of the arrangement or not. It seemed to her a very happy one, as the young people were going into the country directly after the wedding, where Kitty would only need the simple things, and the more elaborate ones could be sent on to her later.

Levin continued in the state of madness in which it appeared to him that he and his happiness formed the chief and only aim of everything in existence, and that now he need not trouble about anything, as others would do everything for him. He made no plans even for his future life, leaving those also to his friends, fully confident that everything would be right. His brother, Sergei Ivanovitch, Stepan Arkadyevitch, and the princess were his principal guides. He agreed absolutely to everything that was proposed to him. His brother borrowed money for him, the princess advised him to go into the country directly after the wedding, while Stepan Arkadyevitch suggested that he should spend his honeymoon abroad. " Do what you like with me, if it amuses you. I am happy, and my happiness can neither be greater nor smaller no matter what you may do," he thought.

When he told Kitty of Stepan Arkadyevitch's advice about

going abroad, he was amazed to find that it did not appeal to her in the least, and that she had her own definite ideas about their future life. She knew that Levin was fond of his work in the country, and though she did not in the least understand it, nor had the slightest wish to understand it, as he could see, still that did not prevent her from considering it very important. Besides, she knew that their home would be in the country and did not wish to waste time abroad, in places where they would not live, but wanted to go straight to that home. Her definiteness surprised Levin. But as it made no difference to him where he went, he despatched Stepan Arkadyevitch down to his house in the country as though it were a positive duty to do so, and asked him to arrange everything there in the good taste for which he was renowned.

"By the way," Stepan Arkadyevitch said to him one day after he had fulfilled his commission of preparing the house for the reception of the young people, "have you a certificate to show that you've been to confession?"

"No; why?"

"Because you can't get married without it."

"Dear me!" Levin exclaimed. "It never occurred to me. I haven't been to confession for about nine years."

"I say!" Stepan Arkadyevitch exclaimed with a smile; "and yet you call me a nihilist! But this won't do; you must prepare yourself at once."

"But when? there are only four days left."

Stepan Arkadyevitch arranged this for him too, and Levin began preparing himself for confession. As an unbeliever, who at the same time respected the belief of others, the participation in all kinds of religious ceremonies was extremely irksome to him. In his present sentimental state the idea of feigning was not only oppressive to him, but seemed next to impossible. Now, in the condition of his glory, of his florescence, he would either have to lie or be sacrilegious. He felt it beyond his strength to do either. But no matter how much he begged Stepan Arkadyevitch to try and get the certificate without his going to confession, Stepan Arkadyevitch insisted that it was impossible.

"What does it matter? It will only take you two days, and he's a dear, intelligent old man and will pull out your tooth before you know where you are."

During the first mass Levin attempted to revive in himself the strong religious emotions he had experienced in his youth, between the age of sixteen and seventeen, but he found it impossible. Then he tried to look at it all as a meaningless, empty custom, something like the custom of paying calls, but he could not do that either. Like most of his contemporaries he was completely undecided in regard to religion. He could not believe, yet did not wholly disbelieve. And so during all the time of his preparation for confession he felt a sense of discomfort and shame for taking part in something he did not understand.

During the service he listened to the prayers, now trying to invest them with a meaning that did not run counter to his views, now condemning them, now trying not to hear them. And gradually he became lost in his own thoughts and paid no further heed to what was going on around him.

Mass, vespers, and evening prayers passed in this way. The following morning, having risen earlier than usual, he went to church to hear matins and go to confession.

There was no one in the church but a mendicant soldier, two old women, and the officiating priests.

A young deacon, his thin long back clearly visible beneath his short cassock, came to meet him, and then going up to a table by the wall he began to read the prayers. As the reading proceeded, especially during the frequent repetition of the words " Lord have mercy upon us," Levin felt that his reason was sealed and that to open it would only result in confusion; so he tried not to listen further and busied himself with his own thoughts.

" What a fund of expression there is in her hand," he thought, recalling how he and Kitty had been sitting in a corner by a table the evening before with nothing to talk about, as frequently happened now. She had placed her hand on the table and began opening and shutting it quickly, laughing at the motion, that seemed to her funny. He remembered how he had kissed that pretty hand and looked at the lines that met on the delicate pink palm. " Again ' Lord have mercy upon us,' " he thought, crossing himself as he watched the deacon prostrating himself before him. " Then she took my hand and examined it. ' What a nice hand you have!' she had said to me." He glanced down at his own hand and then at the short hand of the deacon. " It will soon be over now," he thought. " No, he's going back to the beginning." He turned his attention to the prayers again. " Yes, it is ending now; he is bowing to the ground; that always happens at the end."

3

The deacon took the three-rouble note that Levin had discreetly slipped into his hand, and promising to register him he crossed the flagstones of the empty church with his new boots, and disappeared behind the altar. A minute later he looked out and beckoned to Levin. A thought he had been trying to stifle began to stir in Levin's brain, but he hastened to dispel it. " It will be all right," he said to himself, walking over to the ambo. He went up the steps and turning to the right he caught sight of the priest. He was an old man with a thin beard, that was turning grey, and a wonderfully kind look in his weary eyes. He was standing at the pulpit, turning over the leaves of the missal. He bowed to Levin and began to read the prayers in the usual chant. Having finished, he bowed to the ground and turned his face towards Levin.

" Christ is standing invisible before you to receive your confession," he said, pointing to the crucifix. " Do you believe all that the Holy Apostolic Church teaches us? " he asked, turning his eyes away from Levin and folding his hands under his stole.

" I have doubted and I doubt everything," Levin replied in a voice that sounded unpleasant to his own ears.

The priest waited a moment or two to see if he had anything further to add, and then he began speaking rapidly.

" To doubt is a characteristic human weakness, but we must pray to the merciful God that He may strengthen us. What are your principal sins? " he asked, without the least interval, as though anxious not to lose time.

" My chief sin is doubt. I am nearly always in doubt; I doubt everything."

" To doubt is a characteristic human weakness," the priest repeated. " What is it that you doubt particularly? "

" I doubt everything; I sometimes even doubt the existence of a God," Levin replied in spite of himself, and grew terrified at what he had said. But the words made no impression on the priest.

" How can you doubt the existence of God? " he asked hastily, a scarcely perceptible smile playing about his lips.

Levin was silent.

" What doubt can you have of the Creator when you contemplate His works? " the priest continued. " Who adorned the celestial heavens with stars, the earth with its beauty? How could these things be without a Creator? " he asked, looking at Levin intently.

Levin felt it would be out of place to enter into a philosophical discussion with him, so merely replied directly to his question.

" I do not know."

" You do not know? Then how can you doubt that God created it all? " the priest asked in perplexity.

" I understand nothing," Levin said, flushing red. He felt that his words had no meaning and that they could have no meaning under the circumstances.

" Pray to the Lord and implore Him. Even the holy fathers have doubted and asked God to strengthen their faith. For Satan is mighty and we must not submit to him. Pray to God and implore Him; pray to God," he repeated hastily.

The priest was silent for a while as though in thought.

" I hear that you are about to marry the daughter of my parishioner and spiritual son, Prince Shcherbatsky," he said with a smile. " She is an excellent maiden."

" Yes," Levin replied, blushing. " Why need he ask me about this at confession? " he thought.

And as though in response to this question, the priest went on.

" You are about to enter into the state of matrimony and God may reward you with children. How will you be able to educate them if you do not vanquish within you the temptation of the devil, who is dragging you towards unbelief? " He looked at Levin reproachfully. " If you love your children you will desire for them not only wealth, luxury, honours, but, like a good father, you will be concerned about their spiritual salvation. Is that not so? What will you say to your little ones when they ask you, ' Papa, who made all the lovely things in the world—the earth, the water, the sun, the flowers, the grass? ' Will you reply to them as you replied to me, ' I do not know? ' You cannot help knowing, since the Lord God in His great mercy has revealed it unto you. Or supposing a child of yours should ask you what awaits it after death, how will you answer if you know nothing? What will you say? Will you leave your little one to the mercy of the world and the devil? That would not be well! " He stopped and looked at Levin with his kind gentle eyes, his head leaning a little to one side.

Levin was silent. He was not afraid this time of entering into an undue discussion with the priest; he merely could not reply because no·one had asked him such questions before, and besides there was ample time to consider all these things before his children would be old enough to question him.

"You are entering a period of life," the priest continued, " when a man should choose a path and follow it. Pray to God that He in His goodness may help you and have mercy upon you. May our Lord God, Jesus Christ, in the mercy and bounty of His loving kindness forgive you and succour you, my child." And having finished the absolving prayer, the priest gave him his blessing and took leave of him.

When he returned home, Levin experienced a feeling of joy that the thing was over, which was heightened by the fact that there had been no necessity for him to lie. Besides he had a vague feeling that what the dear old man had said was not at all as stupid as he had supposed, and that there was something that needed investigating.

"Not now, of course!" Levin thought, "but some time later." He felt more conscious than ever that there was something dark and uncertain in his soul, and that his attitude towards religion was exactly the same as that of Sviajsky's and others' whom he had frequently condemned.

He spent the evening with Kitty at Dolly's in the gayest possible mood. He explained to Stepan Arkadyevitch that he felt much like a young dog who had just accomplished the enormous feat of learning to jump through a hoop, and was so delighted that he wanted to leap about on the tables and windows.

II

ON the day of the wedding Levin did not see Kitty, according to the custom, the princess and Dolly having both insisted that all the customary rules should be observed. He dined at his hotel with three bachelors. They were his brother Sergei Ivanovitch, Katavasov, a college friend of his, now a professor of natural history, whom he had run across in the street by the merest accident and brought home with him, and Chirikov, a Moscow justice of the peace, who had accompanied Levin on the bear-hunt, and was now acting as best man. The dinner proved a very merry one. Sergei Ivanovitch was in the happiest of moods and Katavasov's originality amused him. Finding himself so much appreciated, Katavasov began to expand. Chirikov in his gaiety and good-humour agreed with everything and everybody.

"What a clever fellow our friend Konstantin Dmitritch

used to be!" Katavasov said, drawling out his words in his professorial manner. "I am speaking of the past, for he no longer exists. He used to adore science and had many human interests when he left the university; now one half of his ability is directed towards deceiving himself and the other in justifying this deception."

"What a confirmed enemy of marriage you are!" Sergei Ivanovitch said.

"Not at all. I believe in the division of labour. People who can do nothing else must propagate the race, while the others must work for its enlightenment and happiness. That is my opinion. I know a great many people are inclined to confuse these two vocations, but I am not of their number."

"How glad I should be to hear you were in love!" Levin said. "I hope you'll ask me to the wedding."

"I am in love already."

"With a cuttlefish, I suppose. You know," he said, turning to his brother, "Mihail Simionitch is writing a work on nutrition and . . ."

"Oh, never mind what it's about; it makes no difference. The point is that I really am in love with a cuttlefish."

"But the cuttlefish will not interfere with your loving your wife."

"The cuttlefish will not interfere with my wife, but my wife would interfere with the cuttlefish."

"Why?"

"You will soon learn. You are fond of your farming and shooting, but wait and see!"

"Arhip told me to-day that there are lots of elks and two bears at Prudno," Chirikov remarked.

"You will have to hunt them without me."

"That is true," Sergei Ivanovitch observed. "You will have to say good-bye to your bear-hunting, because your wife will forbid it."

Levin smiled. The image of Kitty forbidding him to go out bear-hunting was so sweet that he was prepared to renounce the pleasure for the rest of his life.

"All the same, it is a pity these two bears should be taken without you. It would have been fine sport. Do you remember the last time we were at Hapilov?"

Levin could not very well say that without Kitty nothing would be interesting, so he kept silent.

"There is some good reason in the old custom of bidding

farewell to your bachelor life after all," Sergei Ivanovitch remarked. "No matter how happy you may be, you cannot help feeling a certain amount of regret at the loss of your freedom."

"Confess that you've felt like jumping out of the window, just as Gogol's bridegroom did."

"Of course he has; only he won't own up!" Katavasov said with a laugh.

"Well, the window is open. . . . Let us take the next train to Tver and hunt the she-bear down in her lair. Let them do what they like without you here," Chirikov said with a smile.

"On my honour," Levin replied, also smiling, "I cannot find the least trace of regret in my soul for the loss of my liberty."

"Your soul is so full of chaos just now that you won't find anything in it," Katavasov said. "Wait until you are a little more sober; then you will find it fast enough!"

"No, else I should have had a little feeling of regret in spite of my . . ." (he did not wish to use the word love before Katavasov) "happiness. On the contrary, I rejoice in the loss of my liberty."

"You're a hopeless case I can see!" Katavasov said. "Well, let us drink to his cure, or rather, let us wish him that at least a hundredth part of his dreams may come true. Even that would be a happiness such as never existed on this earth."

Directly after dinner the guests departed to dress for the wedding.

When Levin was left alone he began to probe into his soul to see if he could discover that feeling of regret for his liberty about which they had been talking. "Liberty!" he smiled at the word. "What is the use of it? Happiness consists only in loving, divining her wishes and thinking her thoughts; it does not depend upon liberty!"

"But do I know her thoughts, her desires, her feelings?" he asked himself inwardly. The smile vanished from his face and he grew thoughtful. Suddenly a strange sensation of terror and doubt came over him—he began to doubt everything.

"Supposing she does not love me? Supposing she is merely marrying me for the sake of getting married? Supposing she does not understand what she is doing?" he kept on asking himself. "Supposing she should come to her senses after we are married and realise that she does not love me?" The strangest, meanest thoughts about her presented themselves to his mind. He felt as jealous of Vronsky as he had been a year ago, as though he had seen him with Kitty only the evening before. He suspected her of having kept things from him.

He sprang up. "No, this is impossible!" he said in his despair. "I will go to her, I will say to her for the last time: we are still free; had we not better stop? Anything would be better than eternal misery, disgrace, infidelity!" With despair in his heart and anger against himself, Kitty, and all the world, he left the hotel and drove round to the Shcherbatskys'.

He found Kitty in one of the back rooms. She was sitting on a trunk and giving orders to her maid. Piles of dresses of various colours were hanging over the backs of the chairs and heaped on the floor.

"Oh!" she exclaimed when she caught sight of him, and her face shone with joy. "How did you . . . I did not expect you! I am just sorting out my clothes, so that . . ."

"That's very nice," he said, looking severely at her maid.

"You can go, Dunyasha; I shall call you when I want you," Kitty said. "What is the matter with you?" she asked as soon as the girl had gone. She had observed the strange, severe, agitated expression of his face, and she became alarmed.

"Kitty, I'm in despair! I cannot bear it alone," he began with an entreating look into her eyes. Her loving, trusting face assured him at once, but he longed to hear her dispel his doubts. "I came to tell you that there is still time. It is possible to stop and mend it all."

"What? I don't understand. What is the matter with you?"

"I have told you a thousand times and cannot help feeling it —I am not worthy of you. You can't really wish to marry me. Think it over; perhaps you were mistaken. Consider well; you can't possibly love me. . . . If . . . you had better tell me," he implored without looking at her. "It will make me unhappy. Let people say what they please, anything is better than misfortune. . . . Better now, while there is still time. . . ."

"I don't understand," Kitty said with a look of alarm. "Do you want to withdraw and . . ."

"Yes, if you don't love me."

"You must be mad!" she cried growing red with anger. But his face looked so pitiful that she controlled herself, and throwing some dresses down from a chair she sat down beside him. "What is it? Tell me all."

"It seems to me that you cannot love me. Why should you love me?"

"My God! what can I do?" Kitty exclaimed and burst into tears.

"What have I done?" he cried dropping on his knees before her and kissing her hands.

When the princess entered about five minutes later they were completely reconciled. Kitty had not only assured him that she loved him, but in answer to his questions had even gone into minute details as to why she loved him. She told him that she loved him because she understood him and knew what he liked, and that everything he liked was good. It was all quite clear to Levin and he felt perfectly satisfied. The princess found them sitting beside each other on the trunk, turning over the dresses and disputing about a dress that Kitty wished to give to Dunyasha. She wanted to give her the brown one that she was then wearing, and Levin insisted on her keeping it and giving Dunyasha another instead.

"But you don't understand," Kitty was saying; "she is dark and the blue will not suit her . . . I have planned it all out."

Upon hearing what had brought him there, the princess upbraided him half in jest and half in earnest, and despatched him home quickly to get dressed, as the hairdresser was expected any moment to do Kitty's hair.

"As it is she has not eaten anything the last few days and is beginning to look quite worn. You really should not excite her with your foolishness. Get out, get out, my dear!"

Levin felt guilty and ashamed, but was pacified when he returned to his hotel. Dolly, his brother, and Stepan Arkadyevitch, all dressed for church, were already waiting for him to bless him with the image. There was no time to be lost. Dolly had to rush home afterwards to fetch her little boy, who was being becurled and befrizzled for the duty of carrying the image for the bride. A carriage had to be despatched for the best man, and another, that had brought Sergei Ivanovitch, had to be sent back. There were all sorts of complicated things to do and not much time to do them in, as it was already half-past seven.

The blessing with the image was a ridiculous affair. Stepan Arkadyevitch, in an attitude at once comic and serious, stood beside his wife, grasping the image, and ordering Levin to bow to the ground. He blessed him with a good-natured, playful smile, and kissed him three times. Dolly did the same and immediately hurried away to her carriage. Again there was a confusion about the carriages.

" I'll tell you how we can arrange it; you go for him in our carriage and then if Sergei Ivanovitch would be so kind as to go now, he could send his back again."

" I will with pleasure."

" Then I will bring him straight away. Have your things been sent off? " Stepan Arkadyevitch asked.

" Yes," Levin replied and ordered Kusma to prepare his clothes.

III

A CROWD of people, mostly women, were standing in front of the church that was lighted up for the wedding, pushing each other and quarrelling in their efforts to look through the windows and door.

More than twenty carriages had already been assigned places in the street by the gendarmes. A police officer, disdaining the frost, was standing at the entrance, beaming in his new uniform. Other carriages kept driving up, depositing now ladies with flowers, who held up their trains, now men, who took off their caps or black hats as they entered. The church was brilliantly illuminated with candles. The golden halo against the red background of the iconostasis, the wrought gold of the icons, the silver candelabra and candlesticks, the flagstones, the carpet, the banners above the choir, the steps of the ambo, the old blackened books, the cassocks and surplices—everything was bathed in light. To the right was a gay throng in dress clothes and uniforms, in velvet and satin, amidst a sea of flowers and hair, bare shoulders and arms with long gloves; a repressed though animated conversation was carried on that re-echoed strangely from the high dome. Every time the door creaked there was a hush, and the crowd looked round, expecting to see the bride and bridegroom enter. But the door had been opened at least ten times and admitted either a belated guest, who joined the circle of the invited on the right, or a spectator who had somehow got round the police officer, and joined the crowd on the left. Both relatives and outsiders had already gone through all the phases of expectation.

At first it was supposed that the bride and bridegroom would arrive any minute and no importance was attached to the delay. In a while it began to grow awkward, and relatives and guests tried to look unconcerned and pretend to be absorbed in their conversation.

The archdeacon, as though to remind the company of the value of his time, coughed impatiently once or twice, making the windows rattle. The weary choristers could be heard trying their voices and blowing their noses. The priest kept on sending out the deacon to see if the bridegroom had come, and too impatient to wait, would follow after him in his purple cassock and embroidered girdle. "This is rather strange!" said a lady, glancing at her watch, and all the guests grew uneasy and began to express their surprise and indignation. One of the bridesmen went out to see what had happened.

Kitty meanwhile, in a white gown, long veil, and wreath of orange blossoms, was waiting impatiently in the drawing-room of the Shcherbatskys' house. Her sister, Madame Lvov, and her bridesmother were with her. She kept looking eagerly out of the window, waiting for a bridesman to arrive with the news that the bridegroom had reached the church.

Levin, in his shirt sleeves, was marching up and down his room at the hotel, every now and again looking out at the door and down the corridor. But there was no sign of the person he was waiting for. With a gesture of despair he turned to Stepan Arkadyevitch who was calmly smoking a cigarette.

"Was there ever a man in such a ridiculous position as this?" he exclaimed.

"It is rather stupid," Stepan Arkadyevitch agreed. "But never mind, they'll bring it soon."

"But how?" Levin asked with repressed rage. "These stupid, low-cut waistcoats! Impossible!" he said, looking at his crumpled shirt-front. "Supposing the things have been taken to the railway station?" he asked in despair.

"Then you must put on mine."

"I ought to have done so hours ago."

"You musn't look ridiculous. . . . Better wait; it will all come right in the end."

The trouble was that when Levin had asked Kusma to bring his clothes, the old man had brought him his coat and waistcoat and other necessaries, with the exception of a shirt.

"And the shirt?" Levin had asked.

"You have it on," Kusma had replied with a calm smile.

It had not occurred to Kusma to leave out a clean shirt. Having received orders to pack and send all the luggage down to the Shcherbatskys' from whence the married pair were to depart that evening, he had done so, putting everything away but the dress-suit. The shirt Levin had put on in the morning was too crushed and impossible to wear with a low waistcoat. It was much too far to send to the Shcherbatskys', so a servant was despatched to buy a new shirt. He returned, saying that all the shops were closed because it was Sunday. Some one else was sent off in post-haste to Stepan Arkadyevitch's; a shirt had been brought, but it was too broad and too short. At last they sent to the Shcherbatskys' to have Levin's things unpacked. The bridegroom was expected at church, and here he was pacing up and down his room like a lion in a cage, peering out into the corridor. He recalled with horror what he had told Kitty, and wondered what she would think of him.

At last, the guilty·Kusma rushed into the room panting.

" Just in time. They were packing the luggage into a cart."

In about three minutes, Levin, too sensitive to look at his watch, was tearing down the corridor.

" It won't make much difference now," Stepan Arkadyevitch said with a smile as he walked leisurely after him. " I told you it would all come right."

IV

" HERE they come! Here he is! Which one? The younger looking? And just look at her, my dear, she seems more dead than alive! " was murmured through the crowd as Levin and Kitty met at the door and entered the church together.

Stepan Arkadyevitch began telling his wife the cause of the delay, and the guests, smiling, whispered among themselves. Levin saw nothing, heard nothing—his eyes were fixed on Kitty.

Everybody declared that she had not been looking well the last few days and that under the bridal wreath she did not seem as pretty as usual, but Levin did not find it so. He gazed at her high head-dress with the long white veil and white flowers, at her high standing collar, that in a peculiarly girlish way covered her lovely neck at the sides and left it bare in front; he gazed at her slender waist, and it seemed to him that she was more beautiful than ever. Not because her Parisian gown and flowers and veil added in any way to her beauty, but because in spite of them the same expression of innocence and truthfulness lurked in her glance, her lips, in the whole of her sweet face.

" I was beginning to think you wanted to run away," she said to him with a smile.

" Such a silly thing happened to me; I'm almost ashamed to tell it! " he replied, flushing, and turning to Sergei Ivanovitch who had just come up.

" A fine story that about your shirt! " Sergei Ivanovitch greeted him, shaking his head with a smile.

" Yes, yes," Levin replied, not taking in what his brother was saying to him.

" Well, Kostia," Stepan Arkadyevitch said with a feigned look of alarm on his face, " you have to settle a most important point. You are just in the right state to be able to appreciate its full significance. I was asked if they were to light the burned candles or new ones; the difference is ten roubles," he added, trying not to smile. " I have given the order, but am afraid you will not agree with me."

Levin could see that he was joking, but he was not in a position to smile.

" Well, the burned ones or the unburned ones? that is the question."

" Yes, yes, the unburned ones."

" Delighted. The question is settled! " Stepan Arkadyevitch said with a smile. " How stupid men are under these circumstances," he remarked to Chirikov, when Levin, after looking at him in a confused sort of way, moved up to join his bride.

" Kitty, mind you're the first to step on the carpet," the Countess Nordston said, approaching them. " A nice man you are! " she added turning to Levin.

" Don't you feel frightened? " asked Marya Dmitrievna, an old aunt.

" Are you cold? you look so pale. Wait a moment; bend down a little," her sister Madame Lvov said to Kitty, as she rearranged the flowers on her head with her pretty plump hands.

Dolly came up and was about to say something, but burst into tears, then laughed unnaturally.

Kitty, like Levin, looked at them all absentmindedly.

In the meantime the officiating clergy put on their vestments, and the priest accompanied by the deacon went up to the lectern, placed at the entrance of the sacred doors. The priest addressed a few words to Levin, but the latter failed to understand what he said.

" Take her by the hand and go forward," the best man whispered to him.

For a long time Levin could not make out what was wanted of him, and every one was beginning to lose hope that he would ever be able to understand that he had to take hold of Kitty's right hand with his own right without changing his position. When at last this wonderful feat was accomplished, the priest walked a few steps ahead of them and stopped at the lectern. Amid a murmur of voices and rustling of dresses, the crowd of friends and relatives moved up behind them. Some one stooped down to arrange the bride's train. A silence fell over the church; the drops of wax could be heard falling from the candles.

The old priest in a calotte, his silvery white hair parted in the middle and drawn back behind his ears, drew forth his little wrinkled hands from beneath his heavy silver chasuble, ornamented with a cross of gold, and began turning over the leaves of the service book.

Stepan Arkadyevitch went up and whispered something to him, then made a sign to Levin and walked back again.

The priest lighted two candles decorated with flowers, and holding them sideways in his left hand so that the wax dripped, he turned towards the bride and bridegroom. It was the same priest to whom Levin had confessed. He turned his sad, weary eyes from one to the other, and with a sigh blessed Levin with his right hand, then with a peculiar tenderness he placed his fingers on Kitty's bended head, gave them the candles, and taking the censer he walked away from them.

"Can it be true?" Levin thought as he looked at Kitty. He just got a glimpse of her profile from above, and by the scarcely perceptible tremour of her lips and eyelashes, he knew that she was conscious of his glance. She did not turn, but there was a slight motion of her high collar, which touched her ear. He noticed her breast heave, and the little hand in the long glove, holding the candle, trembled.

The trouble about the shirt, his conversations with friends and relatives, their indignation, the ridiculous position he had been in—all suddenly vanished, and a feeling of joy and terror seized his heart.

The tall handsome archdeacon, in a silver surplice, with his long curly locks combed to either side, stepped quickly forward, and raising his stole he stopped in front of the priest.

" Bless us, O Lord! " he intoned slowly, and waves of sound echoed solemnly through the air.

" The Lord our God be praised now and for ever more," the

old priest replied in a sweet melodious chant, still turning over the leaves of the book. A full chord of the invisible choir answered in response, first filling the whole church with the volume of its sound, then dying slowly away.

Prayers were offered up as usual for peace and salvation from above, for the synod and the emperor, till it came to the turn of the newly betrothed servants of God, Konstantin and Ekaterina.

" Let us pray to the Lord to send them His love, His peace, and His aid." The whole church was filled with the voice of the archdeacon.

Levin was struck by these words. " How could they guess that it was aid we wanted? " he thought, recollecting his recent doubts and fears. " What do I know? What can I do without aid? Yes, it is aid that I need now."

When the deacon had finished the liturgy, the priest turned to the bridal pair with a book in his hand.

" Lord God Eternal, who unitest by an indissoluble bond those who are separate," he read in his melodious voice; " Thou who didst bless Isaac and Rebecca and showest Thy mercy to their descendants, bless now Thy servants Konstantin and Ekaterina and incline their hearts to good. Thou art merciful, O God, and lovest man; to Thee we offer up our praise. For the glory of the Father, the Son, and the Holy Ghost, as it was in the beginning, is now, and ever shall be."

" Amen," the invisible choir rang out through the air.

" ' Who unitest by an indissoluble bond those who are separate.' How profound these words are and how they correspond to what one feels at such a moment! " Levin thought. " I wonder if she feels as I do? "

He turned and their glances met.

By the look in her eyes it seemed to him that she had understood as he had done. But this was not so. She had scarcely comprehended a single word of the service and was paying no attention to the marriage ceremony. She did not hear anything, did not understand anything. Her heart was filled with gladness that the thing she had been longing for, the thing that had caused her so much joy and pain for the last six weeks, was at last realised. From the day on which she had rushed into the drawing-room of their house and had given herself to him, a complete change had taken place in her soul. She had entered a new life, while outwardly she lived the old one. These six weeks had been the most blessed and most painful period of her life. All her hopes and desires were centred on that one man, who was still unintelligible to her, and to whom she was connected by a feeling still more unintelligible than the man, who now attracted her, now repelled her. Though she continued living her former life she was terrified at the change in herself, at her utter indifference to her past, to things, to her habits, to people whom she loved and who loved her, to her mother, who was grieved at this indifference, to her dear kind father, whom she had loved more than anything else in the world. Now she was alarmed at this indifference, now she was glad at the cause of it. She had no thoughts or desires outside the life of this man and the new life that awaited her, though she could not even picture it clearly. She only felt a sense of expectation and fear and joy. And now in a little while the uncertainty, the waiting, the regret at her past life would all be over, and she would be initiated into the unknown in store for her. She could not help feeling frightened, but the present moment was only the consummation of what had taken place in her soul six weeks ago.

Again turning to the lectern, the priest took up Kitty's ring, and with difficulty put it on the first joint of Levin's finger.

"The servant of God, Konstantin, is wedded to the servant of God, Ekaterina." And putting a large ring on Kitty's pink little finger, he repeated the same words.

The wedded pair tried to understand what was expected of them, but kept on making mistakes, till the priest had to correct them in a low voice. At last having done everything that was necessary, he made the sign of the cross over them with the rings and returned the large one to Kitty and the small one to Levin. Again they got confused and changed the ring from hand to hand, not knowing what was required of them.

Dolly, Chirikov, and Stepan Arkadyevitch stepped forward to correct them. A disturbance ensued; there was a whispering and smiling; but the humble, solemn expression on the faces of the married pair did not change. On the contrary, while they got mixed up about their hands, they looked even more solemn than before. The smile with which Stepan Arkadyevitch whispered to them that they should put on their own rings, died on his lips. He instinctively felt that a smile would have offended them.

"From the beginning Thou hast created man, male and female," the priest read on after the rings had been changed; "Thou hast given woman unto man to be his helpmeet and for the procreation of the human race. For Thou, Lord our God, who hast sent down Thy truth for Thine inheritance and Thy promise to Thy servants our fathers, chosen by Thee in each generation, look down upon Thy servant Konstantin and Thy servant Ekaterina; confirm them in one faith and belief, in truth and in love. . . ."

Levin felt more and more that all his thoughts and dreams about marriage had been the merest childishness compared to this. He had never been able to comprehend and could not comprehend now what was happening to him. A lump rose in his throat, his breast heaved, and the rebellious tears came into his eyes.

V

THE whole of Moscow was in the church—acquaintances, friends, and relatives. During the marriage ceremony the throng of gaily dressed women, young girls, men in white ties, dress clothes, and uniforms, were carrying on a conversation among themselves in low tones, mostly started by the men, as the women were too much absorbed in watching all the details of a service so interesting to them.

In the circle nearest the bride were Dolly and her elder sister Madame Lvov, a placid beauty, who had just returned from abroad.

"Why is Mary in purple? It's too dark a colour for a wedding; almost like black," Madame Korsunsky remarked.

"With her complexion it's her only salvation," Madame Drubetsky put in. "I wonder why they had the wedding in the evening? It's the sort of thing shopkeepers do."

"It's more romantic. I was married in the evening," Madame Korsunsky said with a sigh, recalling how nice she had looked on that day, how ridiculously her husband had been in love with her, and how different it all was now.

"They say that if you act as best man more than ten times you will never get married. I was anxious for the post this time, in order to insure myself, having served nine times already, but unfortunately I was too late," Count Sinyavin was saying to the pretty Princess Charsky, who had designs on him.

The princess replied to him only with a smile. She was watching Kitty and thinking that when she, like Kitty, was standing at the altar with Sinyavin, she would remind him of his present joke.

Shcherbatsky was telling an old maid-of-honour that he intended putting the crown on Kitty's chignon for luck.

"The chignon is quite out of place," the maid-of-honour said, having long ago decided that if she could bring a certain old widower to the point of marrying her, she would have a very simple wedding. "I don't like all this show."

Sergei Ivanovitch was talking to Darya Dmitrievna and trying to assure her, in his jesting tone, that the reason newly-married people preferred going abroad nowadays was because they were somewhat ashamed.

"Your brother ought to feel proud; she is wonderfully sweet. Don't you feel a little envious?"

"I have got over that, Darya Alexandrovna," he replied, and his face suddenly assumed a sad, serious expression.

Stepan Arkadyevitch was telling his sister-in-law his pun about the divorce.

"The wreath wants putting straight," she said, not listening to him.

"What a pity Kitty is not looking well," the Countess Nordston remarked. "But all the same he is not worth her little finger. Don't you think so?"

"No, I like him immensely; not merely because he is going to be my *beau-frère*," Madame Lvov replied. "How well he carries himself! So few men know how to carry themselves on these occasions without appearing ridiculous. He does not seem at all ridiculous, nor too stiff, only a little too serious."

"I suppose you expected this?"

"In a way. She has always loved him."

"Let us see which of them will be the first to step on the carpet. I told Kitty to remember it."

"It will not make any difference," Kitty's sister replied. "We are all obedient wives—it runs in our family."

"But I purposely got ahead of Vassily. What did you do, Dolly?"

Dolly was standing close by and heard what they said, but made no reply. She was too full of emotion to speak. The tears stood in her eyes and she could not have opened her lips without giving vent to them. She was glad for Kitty and Levin. A mental picture of her own wedding came back to her; she looked up at Stepan Arkadyevitch, who stood beaming beside her, and forgetting all her present sorrows, she thought only of their early innocent love. She thought not only of herself, but of all the women she knew who, like Kitty, had stood under the wreath with love and hope and terror in their hearts, renouncing their past lives and entering into an unknown mysterious future. Among these many women she thought also of her dear Anna, who was about to be divorced. She, too, had stood there, pure, in her veil and orange-blossoms. " And now? How strange it is! " she muttered.

Not only relatives and friends were eagerly watching the ceremony, but the spectators, especially the women, looked on breathless, not wishing to lose a single expression or gesture of the bride and bridegroom. They grew fearfully angry with the men, who were making jocular, irrelevant remarks.

" Why is she crying? She is not marrying him against her will, surely? "

" Why should she not want to marry him? Such a fine looking man! A prince, I suppose."

" Is that woman in white satin her sister? Just hear the deacon roar ' obey thy husband.' "

" Is he from the Chudovsky monastery? "

" No, from the synod."

" A footman outside told me that he is taking her away to his house in the country. Very rich, I hear. That is why they let her marry him."

" They're a splendid couple! "

" Now, Marya Vassilevna, you would insist that crinolines were worn from the waist! Look at that woman in purple— an ambassador's wife they say. A splendid company, to be sure."

" What a dear little lamb the bride is! Say what you like, women are to be pitied."

Such were the remarks of the spectators who had managed to get into the church.

VI

When this part of the ceremony was over, one of the officiating priests spread a piece of rose-coloured silk down the centre of the church, while the choir began singing an elaborate and beautiful psalm, in which the bass and tenor responded to each other. The priest motioned to the newly-married pair, indicating the silk carpet. Though the familiar saying, that the one who stepped first on the carpet would be the head of the family, was well known to them, both Kitty and Levin had completely forgotten it at this moment. They did not even hear the disputes going on around them, some maintaining that Levin had stepped on it first, whilst others were insisting that they had both stepped on it at the same time.

After the usual questions as to whether they desired to enter into matrimony, or if they had promised themselves to others, and their replies, that sounded so strange to their own ears, another part of the service began.

Kitty listened to the prayers, trying to grasp their meaning, but was unable to do so. The feeling of joy and triumph in her soul increased more and more as the ceremony proceeded, depriving her of the power of attention.

"May they be endowed with the gift of chastity; may their union be fruitful, may they rejoice in the sight of sons and daughters," the priest's voice was heard. Then after a reference to God having created woman from Adam's rib, he continued: "A man shall leave his father and his mother for the sake of his wife, and they twain shall be as one flesh." He then prayed again that God might give them fruitfulness and prosperity and bless them as he had blessed Isaac and Rebecca, Joseph, Moses, and Sephora, and that they might live to see the sons of their sons. "All this is beautiful," Kitty thought as she listened to these words, "and it cannot be otherwise." A glad smile that infected every one in the church lighted up her face.

"Put it on altogether!" was the advice that came from all sides, as the priest produced the crowns and Shcherbatsky, with his gloved hand, was holding Kitty's high above her head.

"Put it on," she whispered with a smile.

Levin gazed at her and was struck by the look of gladness on her face; the feeling communicated itself to him and he felt as she did.

It gave him pleasure to hear the reading of the epistle of the apostle and the archdeacon thunder out his last verse, waited for so impatiently by the spectators. It was a joy to drink the warm red wine and water out of the flat bowl, and a still greater joy when the priest, putting aside his vestment and taking both their hands in his, led them round the lectern, while the choir was singing joyfully, "Rejoice, Isaiah." Shcherbatsky and Chirikov, carrying the crowns, followed them smiling, and nearly stumbled on the bride and bridegroom every time the priest came to a stop. Kitty's joy communicated itself to the whole church. It seemed to Levin that the priest and the deacon must feel as he did, and he could not restrain a smile.

The priest took the crowns from their heads, read the last prayer, and congratulated the young couple. Levin glanced at Kitty, and it seemed to him that he had never seen her like that before. She looked beautiful in her new happiness that shone out in her face. He wanted to say something to her, but was not sure whether the ceremony was over. The priest came to their aid with his kind gentle smile. " Kiss your wife, and you kiss your husband," he said as he took the candles from them.

Levin cautiously kissed her smiling lips, gave her his arm, and walked out of the church with a strange, new sense of nearness for her. He could not believe that it was all true. Only when their bewildered, timid glances met, did he realise what had happened, because he felt that they were one already.

After supper, that very night, the young couple departed for the country.

VII

VRONSKY and Anna had been travelling in Europe for three months. They had visited Venice, Rome, Naples, and had just arrived in a small Italian town where they intended settling for some time.

A handsome waiter, with his thickly pomaded hair parted in the middle, in a dress coat and an expanse of shirt front, was standing with his hands in his pockets, displaying a bunch of trinkets that hung over his rotund abdomen. He was blinking contemptuously and answering the questions of a man standing next to him in a rather off-hand manner. On hearing some one coming up the steps at the entrance, he turned round, and seeing that it was the Russian count, who occupied the best rooms in the hotel, he drew his hands out of his pockets, and bowing respectfully announced that a courier had come and that the palazzo had been taken. The chief agent was waiting for the contract to be signed.

" Ah! glad to hear it," Vronsky said. " Is madame in? "

" Madame was out walking, but has returned now," the waiter replied.

Vronsky took off his soft, broad-brimmed hat and passed his handkerchief over his perspiring brow and hair, that came down as far as his ears, and was combed back to hide the bald patch on the top of his head. He looked vacantly at the man who had been talking to the waiter and was about to walk on.

" This gentleman is a Russian and is asking for you," the waiter said.

With a feeling of annoyance that it was impossible to escape from acquaintances anywhere, mingled with a desire to find some kind of diversion in the monotony of his life, Vronsky turned and looked at the man, who stood at some distance away, and as their eyes met their faces both lighted up.

" Golenishchev! "

" Vronsky! "

It was indeed Golenishchev, a comrade of Vronsky's in the Corps of Pages; a liberal who had left the corps with a civil rank, but had not served anywhere. Since their school days, the two friends had gone each his own way and very rarely met. On one occasion when he had seen him, Vronsky gathered that Golenishchev had chosen some kind of high-flown liberal activity, and was inclined to disdain his own interests and calling. From that day he had given him the cold shoulder, and if ever they came across each other Vronsky's manner seemed to say, " You may like or dislike my way of life; that makes no difference to me, but you must respect me if you wish to know me." Golenishchev, however, had remained supremely indifferent to this tone. It would seem that this meeting could hardly be pleasant to either of them, but they both beamed and shouted with joy when they recognised each other. Vronsky had never dreamt that he would be so glad to meet Golenishchev; he did not know himself how bored and lonely he was. He had completely forgotten their last disagreeable encounter, and as he extended his hand he felt a sincere pleasure in seeing him again. Golenishchev, too, was just as pleased as he was.

" How jolly it is to see you again! " Vronsky said, displaying his fine white teeth in a friendly smile.

" I heard the name ' Vronsky,' but was not certain which one it was. Very glad! "

" Let us go in. Well, what are you doing? "

" I am working here; been here for nearly two years."

" Really? " Vronsky asked with interest. " Come in."

And by force of habit, usual with Russians when they do not wish their servants to understand what they are saying, he continued in French, quite forgetting where they were.

"Do you know Madame Karenina? We are travelling together. I am just going to her." He looked into Golenishchev's face attentively as he said this.

"Oh! I was not aware," Golenishchev said casually, though he knew quite well. "How long have you been here?" he added.

"About four days," Vronsky replied, again giving his friend a searching look.

"He's all right; he looks upon the thing in the right light," Vronsky said to himself, satisfied with the expression of his face and with the way he had changed the subject. "I think I can introduce him to Anna."

During the three months of his travels with Anna, every time he met any new acquaintance Vronsky was a little uncertain as to how they would look upon his relations with Anna. For the most part the men looked upon them in "the right light," but had they been asked what exactly this meant, they would have found it rather difficult to say.

In reality, the men, who in Vronsky's opinion understood the thing in "the right light," did not understand it at all, but like all well-bred people when brought face to face with a delicate complex problem, they forbore to ask any indiscreet questions or to make any unnecessary allusions. They behaved as though they fully comprehended and approved of the situation, yet considered it superfluous to say anything about it.

Vronsky instantly put Golenishchev among this kind and was therefore doubly glad to have met him. And really, Golenishchev's manner towards Anna, when he had been introduced to her, was precisely what Vronsky could have wished for.

Without the smallest effort he seemed to avoid bringing into his conversation anything that might be at all embarrassing.

He had never seen Anna before and was struck by her wonderful beauty, as well as by the extreme simplicity with which she accepted her position. She had blushed when Vronsky brought him in, and that childlike blush, spreading over her frank, lovely face, had pleased him exceedingly. And what pleased him still more was the simple natural way in which she called Vronsky Alexei, and announced that they had taken a house together, which the natives called a palazzo. It seemed as though she wished to avoid any misunderstanding regarding their relations in the presence of a stranger. As he looked at her and compared Vronsky to Alexei Alexandrovitch, it seemed to him that he fully understood her. He thought he understood what she herself had never been able to understand, that is, how she could have abandoned her boy, made her husband wretched, destroyed her reputation, and yet remained gay and happy.

" It is mentioned in the guide book," Golenishchev said, referring to the palazzo that Vronsky had taken. " You'll find a beautiful Tintoretto there; one of his later ones."

" Supposing we go and look at the place again," Vronsky said turning to Anna; " the weather is lovely."

" It would be rather nice; I will get my hat. Did you say it was hot? " she asked from the door, with a questioning look at Vronsky. And again the colour spread over her face.

Vronsky understood by her glance that she did not know what relation he wished to adopt towards Golenishchev, and was afraid that he might not approve of the way she treated him.

He gave her a long affectionate look.

" Not very," he said.

It seemed to her that she comprehended fully, and that he was satisfied with her. She smiled and walked out of the room briskly.

The two friends felt confused when they were left alone. Golenishchev, who evidently admired Anna, wanted to say something about her, while Vronsky wished him to do so, yet was afraid at the same time.

" And so you've really settled here? " Vronsky asked in order to begin some kind of conversation. " I suppose you're still at work on the same thing," he continued, recollecting that Golenishchev was writing some book.

" Yes, I am writing the second part of *The Two Origins*," Golenishchev replied with a flush of pleasure at this question. That is, I am not exactly writing, but collecting material for it. It will be larger and will embrace almost all questions. We Russians refuse to recognise that we are the outcome of Byzantium," and he began a long dissertation.

Vronsky was confused at first, knowing nothing of the early part of *The Two Origins* which Golenishchev seemed to take for granted everybody knew, but later as he began to develop his ideas and Vronsky perceived their drift, his interest was awakened in spite of himself; for Golenishchev spoke well. Vronsky was only grieved and amazed at the agitation Golenishchev displayed in his discourse. The longer he spoke the brighter grew his eyes, the more vehemently did he refute his imaginary opponents, the more injured and agitated grew the expression of his face. Remembering him at school a thin, nervous, kind-hearted little boy, always at the head of his class, Vronsky was unable to understand his present irritation and did not approve of it. What particularly displeased him was that Golenishchev, a man of good social standing, should descend to the level of a set of common scribblers and get angry with them because they criticised him. Was it worth while? Vronsky did not like it, but he felt that Golenishchev was unhappy and so pitied him. His handsome, excited face looked particularly pitiful as, not noticing Anna's entrance, he continued expounding his ideas in the same heated manner.

When Anna, in her hat and cloak, playing with her parasol, came and stood near him, Vronsky, with a feeling of relief, turned from Golenishchev's fixed, feverish gaze, and with a new tenderness looked at his charming companion, so full of life and joy. Golenishchev could hardly regain his composure and was rather depressed at first, but Anna, who was well disposed to the whole world at that time, soon drew him out of himself by her kind, simple manner. After various attempts to speak of other things, she brought the subject round to painting, in which he was very much interested, and listened attentively to what he had to say. They walked as far as the new house and went over it.

" I am glad of one thing," she said to Golenishchev when they returned, " Alexei will have a nice studio. You really must take that room," she said to Vronsky in Russian, using the familiar " thou," as she felt they were likely to see a good deal of Golenishchev in their solitude and that formality would not be necessary.

" Do you paint? " Golenishchev asked, turning quickly to Vronsky.

" Yes, I used to some time ago and am taking it up again now," Vronsky said, reddening.

" He has great talent," Anna said with a proud smile. " Of course, I am no judge, but good judges have said so."

VIII

ANNA, during those early days of her freedom and recovery, felt herself exuberantly happy and full of the joy of life. The memory of her husband's unhappiness did not poison it at all. On the one hand, it was too terrible to think of; on the other, the cause of her husband's unhappiness had brought her too much joy to be the subject of regret. The memory of everything that had followed after her illness, the reconciliation with her husband and their subsequent quarrel, Vronsky's wound, his sudden appearance, the preparations for the divorce, the flight from her husband's home, the parting with her son—all seemed like some horrible dream from which she had awakened abroad, all alone with Vronsky. The wrong she had done her husband evoked in her a feeling of disgust, akin to the feeling a drowning man would have who has shaken off another clinging to him in the water. Of course it was wicked, but it was her only hope of saving herself, and besides it was better not to worry about these details.

There was one soothing reflection in regard to her deed that she could not help remembering whenever she thought of the past. It had occurred to her at the very moment of her departure. " Against my will I have been the cause of this man's unhappiness," she had thought, " but I will not take advantage of it. I too am suffering and shall go on suffering. I give up all that is dear to me—my good name and my son. I have done wrong and for that reason do not want happiness, do not want a divorce. I accept my shame and disgrace and the separation from my son." But no matter how sincere Anna was in her desire to suffer, she did not suffer. Nor was she conscious of any shame or disgrace. With the tact they both possessed to such perfection, they avoided Russian ladies while abroad, never placed themselves in a false position, and only associated with people who pretended to understand the situation much better than they did themselves. Even the parting from her boy, whom she loved, did not worry her at first. Her little girl, Vronsky's child, a dear, sweet little thing, so absorbed her attention, since nothing else remained to her, that she rarely thought of her son.

The desire to live, increased since her recovery, was so strong, and the conditions of her existence were so new and delightful, that she felt immeasurably happy. The more she came to know Vronsky, the more she loved him. She loved him for his own sake and for the love he bore her. The full possession of him was a constant joy to her. His nearness always gave her a sense of pleasure. All the traits in his character that she came to know better and better were inexpressibly dear to her. In his civilian clothes instead of his uniform he was just as attractive to her as if she were a young girl in love for the first time.

In everything he said, thought, or did she saw something unusually fine and noble. Her delight in him frequently frightened her. She sought for some imperfection in him, but in vain. She dared not let him see that she felt her own insignificance in comparison with him. It seemed to her that if he knew it he would cease to love her, and there was nothing she feared more than the idea of losing his love, although there was not the slightest ground for her fear. But she could not help feeling grateful for the way in which he treated her, nor showing him that she appreciated it. She was always filled with wonder that he, who could have had such a brilliant career, had sacrificed everything for her without showing the smallest regret. He was more loving and respectful in his manner towards her than ever before and did everything he could to alleviate the awkwardness of her situation. He, ordinarily such a manly man, not only never contradicted her, but seemed to have no will of his own in relation to her, and was only eager to anticipate her smallest desire. She could not help appreciating it all, though this over-assiduity in his attentions and the atmosphere of care that he surrounded her with sometimes wearied her.

Vronsky, on the other hand, despite the full realisation of the thing he had desired, was not entirely happy. He soon began to feel that the realisation of his desire had only brought him a single grain of that mountain of happiness he had expected. It proved to him the mistake of supposing that happiness consisted in the realisation of one's desires. In the first days when he had cast off his military uniform and donned civilian clothes, he felt a wonderful charm in his freedom generally and in his freedom to love, and he was satisfied, but this did not last long. Soon all sorts of longings and desires rose up in his soul. Unconsciously he began attaching importance to a fleeting caprice, mistaking it for a desire or an aim. The sixteen hours of the day had to be filled somehow, and they were living abroad away from the St. Petersburg social life that had absorbed so much of their time. As for any bachelor amusements he might have indulged in, he dared not even think of them; one attempt in that direction had produced such a feeling of depression in Anna as to counterbalance the pleasure he had derived from a late supper with some friends. Social intercourse with Russians or local people was utterly out of the question on account of their peculiar situation. Sightseeing, even if he had not already seen everything worthy of note, had no attractions for him. As an intelligent Russian he could not ascribe to it the importance that the English did. And as a hungry animal seizes upon everything it can get hold of in the hope that it may be food, so Vronsky seized first on politics, then books, then pictures. Not knowing what to do with his money he began to collect engravings, and having a talent for painting since his childhood, he added that to his store of desires that demanded gratification.

He had a taste for art and a gift for imitating, which he imagined to be the real thing, so after wavering for a while as to whether to choose the religious, historic, *genre*, or realistic school, he began to paint. He understood all schools of painting and could find inspiration in any of them, but he did not know that it was possible not to understand a single one and yet find inspiration within one's own soul. As a result of this, he was not inspired directly by nature and life, but indirectly as they were embodied in art. Thus he accomplished what he set out to do very rapidly and produced something resembling the particular school he was trying to imitate.

The graceful and effective French school appealed to him more than any of the others, and he began to paint a portrait of Anna in an Italian costume in this style, which so far seemed very promising.

IX

THE neglected old palazzo with its high stucco ceilings and frescoes, its mosaic floors, its high windows and heavy yellow curtains, its vases and mantelpieces, its sombre halls lined with pictures—all sustained Vronsky in the pleasant delusion that he was not so much a Russian landed proprietor and ex-colonel, as an enlightened patron of the arts, and a modest artist, who had renounced worldly connections and ambitions for the sake of the woman he loved.

The rôle Vronsky had taken upon himself with his removal into the new house proved to be a success. Through Golenish-chev, he made the acquaintance of several interesting people. Then under the guidance of an Italian master, he began painting studies from nature. At the same time he interested himself in mediæval Italian life, and grew so fascinated by it that he even took to wearing a mediæval hat and to throwing his cloak over the shoulder in the mediæval fashion—a style that was very becoming to him.

" We live and know nothing," he said to Golenishchev, who came in to see him one morning. " Have you seen Mihailov's work? " he asked, handing him a copy of a Russian newspaper with an article on a Russian artist, who happened to live in that very town and had just finished a picture that had been talked about for some time, and had been bought by some one before it had left the easel. The article was full of condemnation of the government and the academy for failing to recognise an artist of such genius.

"Yes, I have," Golenishchev replied. "He has talent certainly, but is working in the wrong direction to my mind. Nothing but the everlasting Ivanov-Strauss-Rénan relation to Christ and religious art."

" What is the subject of this particular picture? " Anna asked.

" Christ before Pilate. Christ is represented as a Jew with all the realism of the new school."

As this was one of his favourite themes, Golenishchev began to expound his views.

" I fail to understand how they can make such coarse blunders. The type of Christ has been well defined by the old masters. If they want to represent a sage or a revolutionist instead of God, why don't they hit upon Franklin, or Socrates, or Charlotte Corday—anybody they please, but not Christ. They take the very person who cannot be used for art and then . . ."

" Is Mihailov really as poor as they make out? " Vronsky asked, feeling that in his character of a Russian Mæcenas he ought to help the artist, irrespective of the quality of his work.

" Hardly. He is a very clever portrait painter. Have you seen his portrait of Madame Vassilkov? But I hear that he's given up portraits, so that he may be in straitened circumstances for all I know. I tell you that . . ."

" Could he be persuaded to paint Anna Arkadyevna? " Vronsky asked.

"Why me? " Anna asked. " I am quite satisfied with your portrait. Let him do Annie's." (This was her little daughter.) " Here she is," she added as she looked out of the window and caught sight of their pretty Italian nurse who was just taking the baby into the garden. This woman, whose mediæval type of beauty Vronsky admired, was the one shadow in Anna's life. Vronsky had made a sketch of her head for his picture, and Anna fearing that she might become jealous was especially kind and attentive to both her and her little boy. Vronsky also approached the window, then catching Anna's eye, he turned to Golenishchev.

" Do you know this Mihail? "

" Oh, yes, I've met him. He's rather a crank and quite uneducated. One of the new savage kind you run across everywhere nowadays. You know, one of those freethinkers who rush headlong into atheism, materialism, universal negation. At one time," Golenishchev continued, completely ignoring Vronsky and Anna who wanted to say something, " at one time, a freethinker was a man who had been brought up in the conceptions of religion, morality, and had arrived at freethought as a result of his own struggles. Now there has sprung up a type of the born freethinker; people who grow up without even knowing that there are such things as religion and morality, people who do not admit the existence of authorities, who have nothing but their negation to fall back upon, in a word utter savages. Mihail is one of them. I believe he was the son of a footman and had absolutely no education. When he had made a reputation for himself in the academy he wanted to remedy this defect, and so he immediately turned to the fountain of culture—journalism. At one time if a man, let us say a Frenchman, had wished to educate himself he would have begun by studying the classics, the theologians, the tragedians, the historians, the philosophers—all the vast scope open before him. But now he immediately turns to journalism, gets some smattering of science, and thinks he's finished. And that is not all. Whereas twenty years ago this same literature bore traces of the struggle against authorities, the conceptions of centuries, whereby a man could see that these things existed; now they no longer trouble to combat the past, but content themselves merely with words—evolution, natural selection, struggle for existence, survival of the fittest, and all that. In my article . . ."

" I have a suggestion," Anna put in. She had been exchanging glances with Vronsky for some time and could see that he was not interested in the education of this artist, but was merely wanting to order a portrait in order to help him. " I have a suggestion . . . " she interrupted Golenishchev with determination. " Supposing we go and see him! "

Golenishchev recollected himself and readily agreed. As the artist lived in a distant quarter they decided to take a carriage.

In about an hour Anna with Golenishchev and Vronsky in the front seat reached the ugly modern house in which the artist lived. The porter's wife came out to meet them at the door and informed them that Mihailov admitted visitors to his studio, but that he was now at his lodgings, a few steps away. They asked the woman to take him their cards with a request to see his pictures.

X

MIHAIL was at work as usual when Vronsky's and Golenish-chev's cards were brought to him. In the morning he had been working in his studio on a large picture, and when he returned home he began quarrelling with his wife because she did not know how to treat an exacting landlady who had asked for money.

" I've told you twenty times," he said to her after they had been disputing for some time, " don't enter into any explanations. You are stupid enough as it is, but when you attempt explaining in Italian you seem three times as stupid."

" Then don't let it go so long; it is not my fault. If I had money . . ."

" Oh let me alone, for Heaven's sake ! " he cried in pain, and putting his hands over his ears he went into the little room where he worked, divided from the other by a partition, and locked himself in. " Absolutely unreasonable ! " he said to himself as he sat down at the table. He opened his portfolio and began working feverishly on an unfinished sketch.

He never worked so quickly or so well as when things were going badly with him, especially after a quarrel with his wife. " Oh, if I could only bury myself somewhere ! " he thought, as he continued his work. He was making a study for the figure of a man seized with an uncontrollable fit of anger. He had already made one sketch, but had not been satisfied with it. " No, the other was better. . . . Where is it ? " He went back to the next room and, without looking at his wife, asked his eldest girl what she had done with the paper he had given her. The piece of paper with the rejected drawing was found, but it was soiled and covered with grease spots. He took it, however, and laying it on his table he walked some distance away from it, and half-closing his eyes began looking at it. Suddenly a joyful smile lighted up his face.

" That's it ! that's it ! " he cried waving his hands about in his delight. He took up a pencil and began working rapidly.

One of the grease spots had the effect of giving the figure a new pose.

As he was drawing this new pose he suddenly recollected the powerful face of a tobacconist with a prominent chin, from whom he bought cigars, and instantly he gave the man in his drawing just such a face and chin. He laughed aloud with joy. The dead figure suddenly became alive. He could not possibly improve on it; he might only alter the position of a leg, an arm, or throw back the hair. In making these slight alterations, he did not change the figure, but only rejected what concealed it. He took off the coverings as it were, so that the thing could be seen as it actually was. Every new line only brought out the force and power that had suddenly appeared to him under the effect of the grease spot. He was just finishing the sketch when the cards were brought to him.

" In a moment, in a moment! "

He went in to his wife.

" It's all right, Sasha, don't be angry," he said to her, with a timid affectionate smile. " You were wrong and I was wrong. Don't worry, I'll see to things." Having made his peace with his wife, he put on an olive-green overcoat with a velvet collar, took his hat, and went to his studio. He had entirely forgotten about the figure he had just finished. He was pleased and excited about these distinguished Russians who had come to see him in a carriage.

About his big picture, the one still standing on the easel, he had but one opinion, and that was, that no one had ever painted anything like it before. It was not that he believed himself superior to Raphael, but he felt in the bottom of his heart that what he had intended to transmit in this painting had never been expressed by any one. He had known that from the very moment he had begun to paint it. But the opinions of others, whoever they might be, were of great importance to him none the less, and he could not help feeling agitated whenever any one came to see it. Every little remark, even the most insignificant, whereby he could see that others saw a small part of the meaning he had intended to convey, stirred him to the depths of his soul. And he nearly always endowed his critics with a depth of insight superior to his own, and expected them to discover some new feature in the picture that had escaped his own observation.

As he hurried along to the studio, despite his agitation, he was struck by the figure of Anna as she was standing in the soft

light of the porch talking to Golenishchev and evidently studying the approaching artist from afar. Unconsciously he stored
up the impression she produced in him for some future use,
just as he had done with the tobacconist's chin.

The visitors, who had been disillusioned about Mihailov
by Golenishchev's description of him, were still further disillusioned when they saw him. He was a thick-set man of
medium height, and his nervous walk, brown hat, olive-green
coat, and tight trousers, that had long gone out of fashion,
produced a most disagreeable impression, that his broad, rather
common face, and the mixture of timidity and pretentious
dignity in his manner did not improve.

" Come in, please," he said, trying to appear indifferent, and
entering the hall he drew a key out of his pocket and opened
the door of his studio.

XI

WHEN they entered the studio, Mihailov once more surveyed
his guests and made a mental note of Vronsky's face, especially
his cheek-bones. Notwithstanding the fact that the artist in
him was at work busy collecting material, and that his agitation increased at the idea that any moment an opinion would
be expressed about his picture, he took accurate store of the
three and placed them correctly in his own imagination. That
one (Golenishchev) was a ˙Russian who lived here. He had
a vague idea that he had seen him somewhere, but could not
remember where, nor his name. He remembered only his face
as he remembered every face he had ever seen. He recalled,
too, that he had put him down as a weak type with an exaggerated idea of his own importance. A high forehead and an
abundance of long hair gave his head a semblance of individuality, while the restless childlike expression concentrated above
the narrow bridge of the nose contradicted it.

Anna and Vronsky he put down as distinguished rich Russians
who imagined themselves connoisseurs and lovers of art. " I
suppose they've done the round of old masters and are now
visiting the modern studios. No doubt they've been to that
German charlatan and to that English idiot of a Pre-Raphaelite,
and have now come to me to finish up." He was familiar with
the manner of the dilettanti (the more intelligent, the worse)
who rushed round from studio to studio for no other purpose

than that they might have the satisfaction of saying that art has declined, and that you had only to compare modern work with the old masters to be convinced of it. He saw all this in their faces and in the careless indifference with which they talked among themselves and wandered about freely among the busts and lay-figures, waiting for him to uncover his picture. But in spite of these thoughts and sensations, as he pulled up the blinds and took down the sheet, his agitation increased; for though all rich Russians were beasts and fools according to his opinion, he had conceived a liking for Anna and Vronsky in spite of himself.

"Here it is," he said, stepping to one side nervously and pointing to the picture. "Christ before Pilate, Matthew, chapter xxvii.," he added, as he felt his lips tremble. He walked away and stood behind them.

During the few moments that the visitors stood looking silently at the picture, Mihailov, too, looked at it, but with the indifferent gaze of an outsider. In those few seconds it seemed to him that the most profound and serious judgment would be expressed by these people whom but a moment ago he had despised. He had completely forgotten all that he had ever thought about the picture during the three years he had been working on it; all its dignity and worth that he had so utterly believed in were gone—he saw the picture from the point of view of the spectator, and it seemed to him that there was nothing good in it. In the foreground was the indignant face of Pilate in contrast to the calm face of Christ, and behind, Pilate's servants and the face of John looking on at the proceedings. Each face that had caused him so much joy and pain and trouble, every shade and tone that he had obtained with so much labour, seen now with the indifferent eyes of a spectator, struck him as common-place and lacking in originality. Even the face of Christ, which he most valued, the centre of the picture, that had nearly sent him wild with joy when he had first obtained it, lost its importance as he looked at it now. He saw only some excellent drawing (and not very excellent in places either) and a repetition of the numberless Christs, soldiers, and Pilates painted by Titian, Raphael, Rubens, and others. It seemed to him poor, badly drawn, gaudy, and weak. They would be justified in saying a few polite things in his presence and then laugh at him when they were gone.

The silence grew too oppressive for him though it had only lasted a minute. To break it he struggled with himself and turned to Golenishchev.

" I think I have had the pleasure of meeting you somewhere," he said with an uneasy look first at Anna and then at Vronsky in his eagerness not to lose a single expression of their faces.

" Oh yes, it was at Rossi's; you remember, when that Italian girl—the new Rachel—recited," Golenishchev replied quite freely, removing his gaze from the picture without the least regret. " Your picture has progressed a great deal since I last saw it," he added, seeing that Mihailov was waiting for him to express an opinion. " I'm immensely struck with the figure of Pilate and remember I was too when I saw it before. As one sees him he does not appear a bad man, but an official to the bottom of his heart, utterly ignorant of what he is doing. But it seems to me . . ."

Mihailov's face suddenly grew animated and his eyes lighted up. He wanted to say something, but was too agitated to speak. No matter what little store he set by Golenishchev's ideas upon art, nor how insignificant was the remark, though a true one compared to the whole magnitude of the picture, still, Mihailov could not help being pleased. Golenishchev had expressed the very idea he had intended to convey. And though it was only one observation in a million that might have been made, Mihailov valued it none the less, and conceived a liking for Golenishchev on the spot. His depression completely left him. The picture seemed to him to be endowed with new life and all the complexities of a living thing. Again he wished to say that that was precisely his idea of Pilate, but his lips trembled disobediently and he could not utter a word. Vronsky and Anna were talking to each other in low tones, partly because of a desire not to offend the artist's ear by some stupid remark about his work. It seemed to Mihailov that the picture had produced a strong impression on them. He walked over to them.

" What a wonderful expression Christ has! " Anna said. Out of the whole work this expression had struck her the most. She felt that it was the centre of the picture and that her mentioning it would be pleasing to the artist. " He seems so sorry for Pilate."

It was another of the million observations that might have been made of the picture generally and of Christ in particular. She had said that there was a look of pity on Christ's face. There was bound to be pity on Christ's face, for there had to be love, resignation, and the consciousness of the vanity of words. Of course there was the expression of the official in

Pilate and of pity in Christ, for the one represented the carnal, the other the spiritual life. All this and much else flashed through Mihailov's brain; and again his face brightened.

"And how that figure is painted! So much atmosphere; you could almost walk round it," Golenishchev said, evidently intending to show by this remark that he did not approve of it.

"Yes, wonderful!" Vronsky said. "A perfect master-piece. See how the figures stand out from the background! This is technique," he added, turning to Golenishchev. In a recent conversation between them, Vronsky had expressed his despair at ever being able to acquire technique.

"Yes, yes, wonderful!" Golenishchev and Anna agreed.

Despite his emotion, Vronsky's remark about technique jarred on Mihailov horribly. He frowned and gave him an angry look. He was always hearing that word "technique," but could never make out what people meant by it. He knew that it meant the mechanical ability to draw, quite apart from the content of the drawing. He had frequently observed, as in the present case, that technique was often opposed to the inner worth of a painting, as no amount of skill could make a bad subject good. He knew that much attention and care were required in removing the coatings so as not to injure the production itself, but to draw well no technique whatever was necessary. A child or the most ignorant person could draw if their observation were strong enough to give out what they saw. And the most skilful artist could not draw with all his technique if the limitations of his subject were not revealed to him first. Besides, he knew that when it came to talking of technique he would not come off very well. In all the work he could see startling defects due to the carelessness with which he had removed the coatings, and they could not be remedied without injuring the whole production. On nearly all the figures and faces there were remnants of coatings that had not been removed that spoiled the picture.

"There is one thing I should like to say if I may . . ." Golenishchev began.

"I should be delighted to hear what it is," Mihailov said with a forced smile.

"Your Christ is a man-God and not a God-man. Of course, I know that that was your intention."

"I cannot produce a Christ that is not in my soul," Mihailov said severely.

"Yes, but in that case, if you will allow me to express my

thought . . . Your picture is so good that anything I can say of it could do it no harm. Your motive seems to me entirely different. . . . Let us take Ivanov for example. It seems to me that if he had to reduce Christ to the level of an historical person, it would have been better for him to have taken a different theme, absolutely new and untouched."

" But this is the greatest theme that presents itself to art."

" If one were to look hard enough one could find others. Art, in my estimation, cannot suffer discussion. And with Ivanov's pictures the question instantly presents itself, 'Is this God or not?' It destroys the unity of the impression."

" Why? With cultured people, I should have thought, doubt was no longer possible," Mihailov observed.

Golenishchev did not agree with him and entered into a long discussion on the unity of impression in art, in which he came off much the best, as Mihailov was unable to say anything in defence of his own ideas.

XII

Anna and Vronsky exchanged glances. They disapproved of their friend's eloquence. At last, leaving the two together, they walked over to a picture hanging some distance away.

" Oh, how charming! how delightful! wonderful!" they cried both in one voice.

" I wonder what has taken their fancy so?" Mihailov thought. He had completely forgotten this picture that he had painted three years ago; forgotten all the joy and suffering it had caused him, all the months of labour he had spent on it—forgotten it, as he forgot all his pictures as soon as they were finished. He hardly liked to look at it now, and had merely put it out because he was expecting an Englishman who wanted to buy it.

" Oh, that's a sketch I made long ago," he said.

" How beautiful it is!" Golenishchev said quite sincerely. He, too, had fallen under its spell.

The picture represented two boys fishing under the shade of a laburnum. The elder had just cast his line and was carefully directing the float past the tree, all absorbed in the work, while the other, the younger, was lying on the grass, with his matted fair head leaning on his arms, looking pensively into the water. What was he thinking about?

The enthusiasm of his visitors brought back to Mihailov his former emotion, but he had no love for sentimentalising over the past, and though their praise gave him a certain amount of pleasure he was eager to draw their attention to another piece of work.

But Vronsky could not tear himself away, and asked if the picture was for sale. At that moment, in the state of excitement he was in, it was very unpleasant for Mihailov to talk of monetary matters.

" It is exhibited for sale," he said with a frown.

When they had gone, Mihailov sat down opposite his picture of Christ and Pilate and went over in his imagination what his visitors had said of it, or rather what they had not said, as they had refrained from expressing everything in words. And, strange to say, what had appeared of such vast importance when they were present, now lost all significance for him. He saw the picture with his whole artistic sense, and the consciousness of its masterfulness and strength came back to him. He needed that feeling of certainty in his work to be able to sustain it above all other interests.

He suddenly saw something wrong about the foreshortening of Christ's leg, and taking up his palette he set to work. As he was working he kept gazing at the figure of John in the background, that seemed to him so absolutely perfect—and his visitors had not even noticed it. When he finished the leg, he wanted to put a few touches to this figure, but felt himself too agitated for that. He could no more work under extreme excitement than he could when he felt himself absolutely cold. There was only one stage in the transition from cold to inspiration when work was possible for him. He was about to cover the picture, but stopped, and holding the sheet in one hand, stood gazing at the face of John with a blissful smile on his face. He tore himself away at last, pulled down the sheet, and went home, tired but happy.

Anna, Vronsky, and Golenishchev were in the best of spirits on their way back. They talked of Mihailov and his pictures. The word " talent," by which they meant an inborn, mechanical skill for drawing, irrespective of mind or heart, occurred frequently in their conversation. It seemed to them that that word covered all the artist's emotions and experiences of which they had not the slightest conception. They admitted that he had talent, but declared that it was not developed to the full, owing to lack of education—the common misfortune of all

Russian artists. But the picture of the boys fishing had made an impression on them; they kept on referring to it again and again. " How charming it was! How well and simply he did it? He does not half appreciate it himself. I must buy it; I really must'nt let it go," Vronsky said.

XIII

MIHAILOV sold his picture to Vronsky and agreed to paint Anna's portrait. He came on an appointed day and began to work.

By the fifth sitting the portrait struck everybody, especially Vronsky, by its accurate likeness as well as its peculiar beauty. It was strange how Mihailov could have discovered that peculiar beauty. " One must know her and love her as I have done to understand that sweet spiritual expression of hers," Vronsky thought, though it was only through this portrait that he himself had discovered it. But the expression was so true that it seemed both to him and others that they had always known it.

" I have been struggling for so long and achieved nothing," he said one day, referring to his own portrait, " but he only looks at her once and the thing is done. That is the advantage of technique! "

" It will come in time," Golenishchev consoled him.

He believed implicitly in Vronsky's talent, and besides Vronsky was a cultured man, and culture gave one a higher view of art. On top of that he needed Vronsky's sympathy and encouragement in his own writings, and seemed to feel that support of that kind should be mutual.

In a strange house, particularly in Vronsky's palazzo, Mihailov was a different man from Mihailov in his own studio. He was unfriendly and respectful in his manner, as though fearing to come too closely in contact with people whom at heart he despised. He called Vronsky " your excellency " and never stayed to dinner, despite Anna's and Vronsky's repeated invitations, nor came at any other time than for a sitting. Anna was kinder to him than to any one else and was very grateful for her portrait. Vronsky was more than civil to him and would have liked to hear his opinion of his work. Golenishchev never let an opportunity slip without impressing him with the proper conceptions of art. But Mihailov remained

supremely indifferent to them all. Anna felt by his glance that he liked to look at her, but he never spoke to her if he could possibly help it. He kept a taciturn silence when Vronsky talked about his art, just as he did when he showed him his pictures, and as for Golenishchev he seemed bored by his incessant chatter and always avoided disputing with him.

On the whole, Mihailov, with his reserved unfriendly attitude, did not please them when they got to know him better, and they could not help feeling relieved when the sittings were over and he ceased coming. Golenishchev was the first to give expression to the thought present in all their minds, that Mihailov was envious of Vronsky.

"Perhaps it isn't envy exactly, because he certainly has *talent*, but he hates the idea that a courtier, a rich man, and a count into the bargain can do so well, or perhaps better, a thing to which he has devoted all his life. And besides you are cultured and he is not."

Vronsky tried to defend Mihailov, but in the bottom of his heart he agreed with what Golenishchev had said; for according to his idea, a man of a lower status in life was bound to envy him.

The two portraits of Anna, his own and Mihailov's, ought to have shown him the difference between them, but he did not see it. He merely concluded that his own was superfluous now that Mihailov's was finished, and he ceased working on it. He still busied himself with his picture of mediæval life, and both Golenishchev and Anna thought it extremely good, because it was more like the old masters than any of Mihailov's.

As for Mihailov, though he had been interested in Anna's portrait, he was even more glad than they when the sittings came to an end and he had no longer to listen to Golenishchev's eloquence and could forget about Vronsky's pictures. He knew that he could not forbid Vronsky amusing himself with art any more than he could any other dilettante, and that every dilettante had a perfect right to paint what he pleased; still he could not help feeling annoyed. A man could not be prohibited from making himself a large wax doll and kissing it, but when the man took his doll and began fondling and caressing it in the presence of a lover, as the latter fondles and caresses the woman he loves, then it became unbearable. It was just such an unpleasant feeling that Mihailov had towards Vronsky's art. He pitied him, was amused, annoyed, and insulted at the same time.

41

Vronsky's interest in painting and the middle ages, however, did not last long. He had too much taste to finish his picture. There was a dim feeling at the back of his mind that its defects, though not very noticeable at this stage, would become perfectly glaring as the work progressed. The same thing happened to him that had happened to Golenishchev, but whereas the latter went on deceiving himself with the idea that his theories had not yet matured and that he was working them out and collecting material, Vronsky did not deceive himself and frankly admitted his failure. Without stopping to give any explanations or justifying himself, he abandoned his painting.

Without this occupation, his own life and that of Anna, who wondered at his sudden loss of enthusiasm, became inexpressibly boring in the little Italian town. The enchanting palazzo now seemed to them old and dirty. The spots on the curtains, the cracks in the floors, the stucco falling away from the cornices were a constant eyesore. And then there was that everlasting Golenishchev, and the Italian professor, and that tiresome German traveller. Yes, a change had become absolutely necessary. So they decided to return to Russia and live in the country. They would stop at St. Petersburg, where Vronsky wished to see his brother to make some definite arrangement about the division of the property, and Anna would see her son. The summer they intended to pass on Vronsky's estate.

XIV

LEVIN had been married for three months. He was happy, but not in the way he had anticipated. At every step he met with some new disappointment and at every other discovered some new delight. Family life was quite different from what he had imagined it to be. He felt rather like a man who, after having admired the gentle motion of a boat on a lake, suddenly finds himself in it. It was not enough to sit still, he had to row and be ever mindful of the course he was taking, for the water was beneath and all around. It was one thing to look on and another to do the work; the unaccustomed action made the hands smart. Still, though it was difficult it afforded a good deal of pleasure.

As a bachelor he had always looked on with contempt at the domestic lives of others, with their petty cares, quarrels, and jealousies. He had assured himself that his own married life would be different, that it would have nothing in common with the lives of others. But not only did it turn out not to be different, but all those petty trifles that he had despised so much assumed an overwhelming importance. He was brought face to face with the fact that it was not so easy to dispose of those trifles as he had supposed.

Although it seemed to him that he had the most exalted ideas of married life, still, like all men, he looked upon it merely as a means of enjoying his love. He was to work and rest from his labours in the happiness of love. His wife was to be loved and that was all. He had completely forgotten that she, too, needed work. And so he marvelled that charming, poetic Kitty could worry about table-cloths, furniture, trays, bedding for visitors, dinners, and so on, not only in the first weeks, but even in the first days of their married life. Yet before their marriage he had been amazed at the decisive manner in which she had refused to go abroad and chose to go into the country, as though she knew there was something to do there outside of her love. He had felt a little hurt then, but now her constant worries and petty cares disappointed him. However, he could see that they were necessary for her, and though he laughed at and ridiculed them, he could not help admiring her all the same. He was amused at the way in which she arranged the furniture brought from Moscow, completely altered his and her own room, re-hung the curtains, got the spare rooms ready for Dolly and a new maid; he laughed at the way in which she gave orders to the old cook about dinner and entered into discussions with Agafia Mihailovna about the larder. He could see how the old cook smiled affectionately at her impossible orders and how Agafia Mihailovna shook her head kindly at her young mistress's notions about the larder. And Kitty looked charming as she came to him in tears one day complaining that Masha, one of the maids, would treat her as though she were still a young lady and not married, and that no one would obey her. It was all very sweet, but strange, and he would have preferred to do without it.

He did not understand the delightful feeling of freedom she was experiencing; she could order what she liked, spend as much money as she pleased, eat as many chocolates as she wanted, without any one to reprove her for it.

She looked forward with joy to Dolly's arrival; thought of how she would let each child have its favourite pudding and how Dolly would admire her new arrangements. She herself did not know why housekeeping had such an irresistible attraction for her. Instinctively she felt the approach of spring. Knowing that there would be stormy days, she was preparing her nest and at the same time trying to find out how to do it in the best way.

These petty cares and anxieties of Kitty's were disappointing to Levin from one point of view, but from another they were a constant source of delight. Their frequent quarrels, too, proved another disenchantment. He had never dreamt that there could be any relation between himself and his wife other than that of tenderness, love, and esteem, but they had quarrelled in the first few days of their honeymoon, when she had wept bitterly in her despair, accused him of being selfish and of not loving her.

The occasion arose from Levin having gone out to inspect a new farm building on a distant part of the estate and coming home half an hour later than he had said he would. Anxious to get back as quickly as possible, he had taken a short cut and missed his way. As he galloped home he was thinking of her, of his love and his happiness, and the nearer he drew to the house the more his tenderness for her increased. He rushed into the room with a feeling akin to the one with which he had proposed to her, but was met by a sad, dejected Kitty, such as he had never seen before. He wanted to kiss her, but she pushed him away.

" What is the matter? "

" You go about enjoying yourself," she began, icily sarcastic, and a torrent of reproachful words of senseless jealousy flowed from her lips. She poured forth all that she had been feeling during the half hour she had stood waiting for him by the window. Though he was hurt, it was no good getting angry with her, for he realised what he had not understood on the day he led her out of the church, that she was so much part of him that he did not know where her personality ended and his own began. He felt rather like a man who, having received a blow from behind, turns round with a desire for revenge on the guilty person and suddenly discovers that there is no guilty person, and that he has somehow struck himself accidentally. He wanted to excuse himself, to point out how wrong she was, but anything he could have said would have irritated her still further and widened the difference between them. It was painful to be under a false accusation, but still worse to pain her by justifying himself. There was nothing else to be done but to go on bearing the pain patiently.

Reconciliation quickly followed. Conscious of her guilt, though not confessing it, Kitty tried to make amends by an added tenderness, and they felt a new happiness in their love.

Unfortunately these differences kept on arising from causes as stupid as they were unexpected, because they had yet to learn what was important and what was unimportant for each of them. These first three months were trying. Either they were both in a bad humour or one of them was. In the latter case it was tolerable, but in the first some stupid senseless quarrel always ensued, causing them to wonder afterwards what it had all been about. Each pulled the chain that bound them in a different direction, and this honeymoon, from which Levin had expected such wonders, in reality left only a heap of painful memories for both. In later life they tried to blot out from their minds all the thousand unfortunate, ridiculous incidents marking that period, when they had rarely been in a natural mood.

It was only after the third month of their marriage, when they returned from Moscow, where they had spent a few weeks, that their life assumed a more even, normal course.

XV

THEY had just returned from Moscow and were glad to find themselves alone once more. Levin was sitting in his study writing. Kitty in a violet dress, the one she had worn in the first days of her honeymoon, that was fraught with such pleasant recollections for them both, was sitting on a leather-covered couch, working on some English embroidery. It was the same old couch that had stood there in his father's and grandfather's time.

Levin went on writing, but was deliciously conscious of her presence. He had not given up his book, the book that was to lay the foundation of a new agriculture, nor had he abandoned his occupations on the farm, but just as they had formerly seemed unimportant and insignificant to him compared to the immensity of his darkness and unhappiness, so now they seemed unimportant and insignificant compared to the light and joy that surrounded him. He continued his occupations, and though he looked at them rather differently because the centre of his interests had been diverted to something else, they were nevertheless more clear and definite. At one time work had been a salvation from a life that would have been hopelessly dull and empty without it; now he needed work so that life might not be too monotonously bright.

When he had returned to his papers and re-read what he had written, he was delighted to find that the work had been worth the time spent over it. Many of his former ideas now appeared to him too extreme and superfluous, whilst those of which he had been but vaguely conscious began arranging themselves clearly in his mind. He was on a new chapter dealing with the causes of the unfavourable condition of agriculture in Russia. He had set out to prove that the extreme poverty of the country was not due so much to the unequal distribution of land, nor to a false economic tendency, as to the rather premature influx of European civilisation, with its railways, producing an exaggerated centralisation in the cities, creating new luxuries and new industries at the expense of agriculture, and further introducing the huge credit system with its concomitant stock exchange gambling. It seemed to him that with a normal development of a country's wealth all these phenomena made their appearance only when agriculture had been raised to a certain standard and had entered upon regular, or at least definite, lines. The wealth of a country must develop evenly, and other branches of wealth should not be allowed to get ahead of agriculture.

Modes of transit ought to be governed by the needs of agriculture. Their present railways, called into existence not by an economic but by a political necessity, were detrimental to agriculture, because they brought in their train the development of industries and the system of credit, fatal to it. Just as the over-development of one particular organ in an animal would be a hindrance to its general development, so all these factors, unquestionably necessary in Europe that was ready for them, were a hindrance to the general development of the wealth of Russia, because it removed the important and pressing question of organising agriculture.

While he was writing, Kitty was thinking of how unnaturally polite he had been to young Prince Charsky, who had paid her ontrageous compliments on the evening before their departure. "He must have been jealous," she thought. "Heavens! what a dear, and how stupid he is! Fancy him being jealous of me! He does not know that they are nothing more to me than Peter the cook," she went on thinking, as she looked with a strange feeling of proprietorship at the back of his head and neck. "It's a pity to make him leave off, but I want to see his face. Oh, he will have plenty of time for work later on. I wonder if he can feel me looking at him? I want him to turn round. . . . He must, must!" She opened her eyes wider, as if to concentrate more strength into her gaze.

"Yes, they take all the sap and give a false lustre," Levin muttered to himself, as he stopped writing, and feeling that she was looking at him he turned towards her.

"What is it?" he asked, rising with a smile.

"He did turn round!" she thought.

"Nothing, I only wanted you to turn round," she said, looking at him and trying to make out whether he was annoyed with her for having disturbed him.

"How happy we are together! At any rate I am," he said, going up to her with a glad smile.

"And I too! I shall never go anywhere, least of all to Moscow."

"What were you thinking about?"

"Oh, I was thinking . . . But never mind, you had better go back to your work," she said, pouting. "And I have to cut out these little holes, do you see?"

She took up a pair of scissors and began to cut.

"Come, tell me what it was," he said, sitting down beside her and following the circular motion of the tiny scissors.

"What was it now? Oh, yes, about Moscow and the back of your neck."

"What have I done to deserve such happiness? It's almost unnatural; too good to be true."

"On the contrary, the happier I am the more natural I find it."

"You have a little stray curl," he said, moving her head round gently.

"Here it is. But leave it alone; you ought to be working!"

But the work was left to take care of itself, and when later Kusma came in to announce that tea was ready they jumped away from each other like a couple of guilty children.

"Have they returned from town?" Levin asked of Kusma.

"They've just got back and are unpacking the things."

"Come along quickly!" Kitty said, "or I shall read all the letters without you. We can play a duet on the piano afterwards." She ran out of the room.

When he was left alone he put away all his notes and papers in a new portfolio that she had bought for him, and washed his hands at the elegant new washstand that had also made its appearance with her. He smiled at his own thoughts and shook his head disapprovingly. A feeling akin to despair had taken possession of him. There was something shameful and effeminate about his life; it was too Capuan, as he expressed it to himself. " It is not good to live like this," he thought. " Three months have gone by and I haven't done a thing. To-day for the first time I set seriously to work, and look at the result! I've even abandoned my ordinary work; I hardly ever go out on the farm. For one thing I hate to leave her, for another I can see that she is lonely without me. And I used to think that life before marriage did not count, that it really began only after marriage. And now, here have I spent three whole months in the most idle fashion possible. No, this won't do; I must turn over a new leaf. Of course, it's not her fault; I can hardly blame her. I ought to have been firmer; I ought to have asserted my manly independence. As it is one can get accustomed to this sort of thing and encourage her to . . . Of course it's not her fault."

But it is difficult for a man not to blame some one else for his discontent, especially the person nearest to him, and as he could not blame Kitty, for she was above blame, he put it down to her frivolous, shallow education. " Take, for example, that fool of a Charsky; I know she wanted to stop him, but did not know how. Besides housekeeping, her clothes, and English embroidery, she has no other interests; no serious interests whatever. She does not care for my book, nor for the farm, nor the peasants, nor reading; not even music, her one strong point. She goes about doing nothing and seems perfectly happy."

Her idleness seemed wrong to him, because he did not understand that she was preparing herself for that period of activity, so soon to arrive, when she would be wife, mother, and housekeeper all in one, when she would need all her strength for the bearing and bringing up of her children. He did not know that she felt this instinctively and consequently did not reproach herself for the moments of idleness and happiness she enjoyed while preparing for her future nest.

XVI

When Levin went upstairs Kitty was sitting at the new silver samovar and new tea service, reading a letter from Dolly, with whom she kept up a constant correspondence. Agafia Mihailovna, with a cup of tea, was sitting near her.

" See where your lady has put me," she said to him when he entered with a kindly smile in Kitty's direction.

In these few words Levin read the sequel to the drama that had taken place between his old nurse and Kitty. In spite of the annoyance and humiliation that her new mistress had caused her by taking the reins of government into her own hands, Agafia Mihailovna had grown to like her.

" I have read this letter of yours," Kitty said, handing him an envelope addressed in an illiterate hand. " I believe it is from that woman who lives with your brother. . . . I only just glanced at it. And this is from home and from Dolly. What do you think? Dolly took Grisha and Tania to the children's ball at the Sarmatskys', and Tania was dressed as a marquise! "

But Levin was not listening. He took Marya Nikolaevna's letter with a blush and began reading it. This was the second letter he had received from her. In the first she had told him that his brother had driven her away for no reason whatever, and though she was in want, she did not ask anything for herself, but was merely afraid that Nikolai Dmitritch would not be able to get on without her and begged Levin to look after him. Now she wrote differently. She informed him that she had gone back to Nikolai Dmitritch, and that together they had left Moscow for a provincial town where he had received an appointment. There he had soon quarrelled with his chief, and on their way back again to Moscow he had fallen ill. " I don't think he will get up again," she concluded. " He keeps on talking of you, and there is no more money."

" Do read this and see what Dolly says of you," Kitty began with a smile, but noticing the change in her husband's face, she stopped.

" What is the matter? What is it, dear? "

" She tells me that my brother Nikolai is dying. I must go to him."

Kitty's face suddenly changed. All her thoughts of Dolly and Tania as a marquise vanished.

" When are you going? " she asked.

" To-morrow." .

" Then I will come with you; may I? " she asked.

" Kitty! really! " he said reproachfully.

" What do you mean? " she asked, hurt at the way in which he had received her suggestion. " Why should I not go? I would not hinder you. I . . ."

" I have to go because my brother is dying," Levin interrupted her, " but why should you . . ."

" Why? For the very same reason that you are going."

" Even at such an important moment her one consideration is that she will be lonely without me," Levin thought. He grew angry.

" But it's impossible for you to go," he said sternly.

Seeing that matters were approaching a quarrel, Agafia Mihailovna put down her cup and went out quietly. Kitty did not even notice her. The tone in which her husband had spoken the last few words had hurt her, particularly as he did not seem to believe what she had said.

" And I tell you that if you go, I will come too. I shall most certainly go," she said quickly and angrily. " Why is it impossible? What makes you think it impossible? "

" Because the Lord knows how I shall get there, nor what sort of hotels I shall have to stop at. You will only be in my way," Levin replied, trying to keep calm.

" Not at all. I don't mind. What is good enough for you is good enough for me."

" And then there is that woman whom you must not meet."

" I don't care who is there and what is there. All I know is that my husband's brother is dying, and that my husband is going to him, and that I am going too, in order . . ."

" Kitty, don't get angry! It's painful for me to see you give way to weakness at such a moment as this, because you don't like being left alone. If you're afraid of being lonely, then you can go to Moscow."

" There! you always ascribe mean, contemptible motives to everything I do! " Kitty burst out, her voice full of pain and anger. " It was not weakness, it was not . . . I felt it my duty to be with my husband in his sorrow, but you wanted to hurt me on purpose, you try not to understand. . . ."

" No, this is unbearable! to be a sort of slave! " Levin cried, rising, no longer able to control his rage, but feeling all the time that he was hurting himself.

" Then why did you marry? You could have remained free. Why, if you regret it . . ." She jumped up and ran out of the room.

He found her sobbing in the drawing-room. He tried to soothe her, but she would not listen to him. He bent down and took her hand; she wanted to pull it away. He kissed her hand, her hair, and again her hand, but still she was silent. At last when he took her face in between both his hands and said " Kitty!" she suddenly regained her composure. After a few more tears they became completely reconciled.

They decided to go together on the morrow. Levin declared that he fully believed that Kitty only wanted to go with him in order to be useful, and that there would be no harm in her seeing Marya Nikolaevna, but in the bottom of his heart he was angry with his wife for not having given way in a matter of such importance. It seemed so strange that he who had so recently doubted the possibility of her loving him was unhappy because she loved him too much and would not even be parted from him for a few days! He was also annoyed with himself that he had not stood his ground better. He hated the idea of her coming in contact with that woman. The very thought of his wife being in the same room with her filled him with disgust and horror.

XVII

THE hotel in which Nikolai Levin lay ill was one of those pretentious, provincial establishments that set out to provide all modern improvements in the shape of cleanliness and elegance, but are speedily converted by the public frequenting them into grubby, dirty inns, worse even than the old-fashioned kind with no pretentions at all. The hotel in question had already reached this stage. A soldier in a dirty uniform, supposed to act as porter, was standing at the entrance smoking a cigarette. An untidy-looking waiter in a greasy dress-coat met them at the door. The common room, with its basket of wax flowers adorning the table, was filthy with dust and had a sort of railway restlessness about it. The staircase was gloomy and dark. The whole thing produced a most depressing effect on Levin.

As usual not a decent room was to be had. There were few

good rooms in the house and one was occupied by a railway inspector, another by a Moscow lawyer, and a third by the Princess Astafev, on a visit from the country. There was only one dirty little room vacant, and the one adjoining it would be vacated by the evening. Levin led his wife to the room assigned to him. He was annoyed with her for having placed him in such an awkward position. Just now, when he was burning to see his brother, he had to busy himself looking after her.

" You can go, you can go," Kitty said, giving him a timid, guilty look.

He left the room without a word. At the door he came upon Marya Nikolaevna. She had heard of his arrival and had come for him, but dared not enter. She seemed just the same as he had seen her in Moscow; she was dressed in the same woollen dress with her arms and neck bare, and had the same stupid, though good-natured, expression on her pock-marked face, that had grown a little fuller.

" Well? How is he? "

" He is very bad; can't get up. He has been expecting you. He . . . Are you . . . with your wife? "

Levin at first failed to understand the cause of her embarrassment, but it was instantly explained to him.

" I will go into the kitchen," she said. " He will be so glad to see you. He has seen her; he remembers meeting her abroad."

Levin realised that she was talking of his wife and did not know what to say.

" Come along, come along! " he said.

But at this moment the door opened and Kitty looked out. Levin blushed with shame and anger that his wife should have placed both him and herself in such an embarrassing situation. Marya Nikolaevna blushed still deeper. She clutched the end of her kerchief in both hands, twisted it about nervously in her red fingers, not knowing what to do or say.

Levin observed an expression of eager curiosity in Kitty's eyes as she looked at this woman, so strange and incomprehensible to her, but it did not last a moment.

" Well? how is he? " she asked, turning first to her husband and then to Marya Nikolaevna.

" We can't stand talking here! " Levin said with an angry look at a man who was walking down the corridor, evidently intent on some business of his own.

" Well, then, come in," Kitty said turning to Marya Niko-laevna; but observing the look of horror on her husband's face, she added quickly, " or perhaps you had better go and send for me afterwards."

She returned to her own room and Levin went to see his brother.

Levin had never expected what he saw and felt in his brother's room. He had imagined that he would find Nikolai in the same condition of self-deception—a common characteristic of consumptives—that had struck him so forcibly during his visit in the autumn. He had thought that he would find him weaker, thinner perhaps, and generally nearer to the end, and that he would experience the same feeling of regret at the loss of his beloved brother, in a higher degree, perhaps, but he found something absolutely different.

In a dingy little ill-smelling room, the walls of which were covered with the expectoration of many travellers, Levin saw a bed standing away from the wall, and a body lying on it, covered with a quilt. The room was separated from another by a thin partition from which issued the sound of voices. The body on the bed had one arm stretched out on the counterpane, as long and thin as a rake, that seemed attached in some impossible manner to the end of a long pipe. The head was lying sideways on the pillow, and the thin hair, bathed in perspiration, was matted over the transparent brow.

" Can it be that this horrible body is my brother Nikolai? " Levin thought, but as he came nearer there was no further room for doubt. It was enough to glance at those piercing eyes that turned towards him as he entered, and at the slight twitching of the mouth under the long moustache, to realise the frightful truth that this seeming corpse was indeed his living brother Nikolai.

Nikolai looked at him severely and reproachfully, and with this glance a living relation was at once established between them. Levin felt the reproach in his gaze and felt ashamed of his own happiness.

When he took his hand Nikolai smiled. It was a faint, scarcely perceptible smile, but, in spite of it, the severe expression of the eyes did not change.

" You hardly expected to find me like this," he said with difficulty.

" Yes . . . No . . ." Levin said, confusing his words. " Why didn't you let me know sooner, before I was married? I made inquiries everywhere."

It was necessary to speak to avoid a silence, but he did not know what to say, particularly as Nikolai made no reply, but kept on looking at him and weighing every word he said. At last he told him that he had brought his wife. Nikolai expressed his satisfaction, but said that he feared his condition would frighten her. A silence ensued. Suddenly Nikolai moved and began to speak. From the expression of his face, Levin thought that he had something very important to tell him, but he merely talked of his health. He complained of the local doctor, saying that he would have liked a certain specialist from Moscow. Levin could see that he still had hopes of recovery.

Wishing to free himself for a moment from the painful sensation, Levin got up at the first moment of silence under the pretext of fetching his wife.

" Very well, and I'll get things cleaned up a little here; it's rather dirty and smelly. Masha! tidy up the room," Nikolai said with difficulty. " And when you've finished, you can go," he added with a searching look into his brother's face.

Levin did not say anything. When he got out into the corridor he stopped. He had said that he would bring his wife, but now he decided that he would not bring her on any account; on the contrary, he would do all he could to persuade her not to come. " Why should she suffer as well? " he thought.

" Well, how is he? " Kitty asked with a look of alarm as he entered.

" Oh, it's terrible, terrible! Why did you come? " he asked.

Kitty was silent for a few seconds, looking timidly and sympathetically at her husband; then she went up to him and put both her hands on his arm.

" Kostia! take me to him, it will be easier for both of us. Take me to him, take me, please, and then leave us," she said. " It is harder for me to see you and not him. I might be useful, perhaps, both to him and to you. Please, let me go! " she implored, as if all her life depended on it.

Levin had to give in. He regained his composure and took Kitty to his brother, entirely forgetting Marya Nikolaevna.

Kitty, walking lightly, her face full of courage and compassion, entered the sick man's room and closed the door noiselessly. She came quietly up to the bed, and placing herself conveniently, so that Nikolai need not turn his head, she took his huge bony hand in her own fresh, youthful one and began talking to him in that kind, inoffensive, compassionate, animated way, so characteristic of women.

" I saw you at Soden, but we were not introduced," she said. " You never dreamt that I should be your sister-in-law."

" I don't suppose you would have recognised me," he said with a smile that had lighted up his face at her entrance.

" Oh, yes, I should. How nice it was of you to let us know. Kostia was always speaking of you; he was very worried not to know where you were."

Nikolai's animation did not last long.

She had scarcely finished speaking when his face again assumed that expression of severe reproach of the dying for the living.

" I am afraid you are not very comfortable here," she said, turning away from his steady gaze and examining the room. " We must ask the landlord for another room," she added to her husband. " He must be nearer to us."

XVIII

LEVIN could not bear to look at his brother, could not even be natural or at ease in his presence. Whenever he came to see him a sort of stupor would come over him; his eyes grew dim and he could not distinguish the details of his brother's condition. He was conscious of the bad odour in the sick man's room, of the filth and dirt, and he could hear the sick man's groans, but he was utterly powerless to do anything to help him. It did not occur to him to find out how his poor limbs were lying under the counterpane, to see if he could ease him in any way, by placing him differently, to do something that would make the unfortunate man more comfortable. A cold shiver would run down his back whenever he thought of these details. He was firmly convinced that nothing could be done either to save the patient's life or to alleviate his suffering. The sick man felt this and was even more irritable in his brother's presence. Levin could see that he felt it and grew more miserable still. It was torture for him to be in the sick-room and still worse to be out of it. He went in and out under all sorts of pretexts, unable to be left alone.

But Kitty felt and acted quite differently. She was sorry for the sick man, and, unlike her husband, she was not seized by a feeling of terror and disgust at sight of him, but saw the need of finding out all the conditions, so that she might know how best to help him. She had not the smallest doubt in her heart that she could help him, and so set to work at once. The very details that terrified her husband immediately attracted her attention. She sent for a doctor and to the chemist's, and got her maid, who had come with her, and Marya Nikolaevna to help her clean and tidy up the room. She ordered various things to be brought up and others taken away. She herself ran several times to and fro to her own room bringing clean sheets, pillow cases, towels, and shirts, paying no heed to the men she met on the way.

A waiter, who was serving dinner to several engineers in the dining-room, came several times in answer to her call with a most surly expression on his face, but she gave her orders with such gentle authority that he could not help obeying them. Levin did not approve of it all; he did not believe that it would make the patient any better; besides, he feared that the commotion might irritate him. But Nikolai seemed more indifferent than annoyed; he watched Kitty moving about the room with a look of shame on his face. When Levin returned from the doctor's where his wife had sent him, Marya Nikolaevna, with the help of a waiter, was changing the patient's clothes, according to Kitty's orders. Nikolai's long white back, with its enormous, prominent shoulder-blades and protruding ribs, was uncovered, while Marya Nikolaevna and the waiter were struggling with a night-shirt, trying to direct his long, limp arms into the sleeves. Kitty, who closed the door quickly after Levin, was not looking in that direction, but when she heard the patient groan she walked over to him quickly.

" Make haste," she said.

" Don't come near ! " the invalid cried angrily. " I can do it myself ! "

" What did you say ? " Marya Nikolaevna asked.

But Kitty understood that Nikolai did not wish her to see him naked.

" I am not looking, I am not looking ! " she said turning his arm. " Marya Nikolaevna go and fix it on the other side," she added.

" Please look in my handbag; you will find a tiny little bottle there; you know, in the side pocket," she said, turning to her husband. " We shall be quite finished here by the time you come back."

When Levin returned with the bottle, the patient was lying back on his pillows, everything around him completely changed. The oppressive, bad odour had given place to the smell of scented vinegar that Kitty was sprinkling around the room. There was not a speck of dust anywhere, and a carpet had been spread under the bed. The medicine bottles and a decanter were neatly arranged on the table, on which were lying some folded underwear and Kitty's embroidery. On another table near the patient's bed stood some sort of beverage, some powders, and a candle. Nikolai himself, washed and combed, was lying on clean bed linen, in a speckless night-shirt, the collar of which made his neck look unnaturally thin. There was a new expression of hope on his face as he gazed steadily at Kitty.

The doctor, whom Levin had discovered at his club and brought along with him, was not the one who had attended the invalid formerly. He examined the patient carefully and shook his head. After writing out a prescription and leaving minute instructions as to how to diet him, he took his departure. He had recommended the patient to be fed on lightly boiled eggs and soda and boiled milk, taken at a certain temperature. When he had gone Nikolai said something to his brother of which the latter only made out the words " your Katya," but from the way he looked at her, Levin understood that he was praising Kitty. The patient called her over.

" I feel better already," he said. " I should have got well long ago if I had had you to look after me. How nice it feels! " He took her hand and was about to raise it to his lips, but fearing that she might not like it, he put it down again and began stroking it gently. Kitty took his hand in both hers and pressed it warmly.

" I should just like you to turn me over on my left side and then you ought to go to bed," he said.

Nobody had heard him, but Kitty understood because she was always on the watch to see whether he needed anything.

" On the other side," she said to her husband; " he always sleeps on that side. Turn him over; I can't and it's unpleasant to call the servants. Can you do it? " she asked turning to Marya Nikolaevna.

" I am afraid," the latter replied.

Though it was terrible for Levin to embrace that terrible body under the counterpane of which he did not wish to know, he submitted to his wife's influence, set his face, put his hands under him, and attempted to turn him over. Despite his great strength, he was amazed at the enormous weight of those emaciated limbs. As he held him and felt his neck embraced by a lean, scraggy arm, Kitty rapidly readjusted the pillows and smoothed the patient's hair as his head sank into them.

Nikolai retained his brother's hand in his own. Levin felt that he wanted to do something with it and was pulling it in some direction; he submitted with a sinking heart.

The invalid with difficulty raised it to his lips and kissed it. Levin was convulsed with sobs, and unable to utter a word he left the room.

XIX

" HE has hidden it from the wise and revealed it unto babes and sucklings," Levin thought as he stood talking to his wife a little later. It was not that he considered himself wise in thus quoting the Gospel. On the contrary, he did not. But he could not help feeling that he was more intelligent than his wife and Agafia Mihailovna, and at the same time could not help knowing that when he thought of death he did so with all the powers of his soul. He knew, too, that the greatest minds had speculated on the question and did not know one hundredth part as much as his wife and Agafia Mihailovna did. Despite the vast differences between his old nurse and his wife, whom his brother called Katya and whom he, too, had taken to calling Katya, in this respect these two women were absolutely alike. Both seemed to know without the least doubt what was life and what was death. Though they could not have answered, nor even comprehended, the questions that presented themselves to Levin, neither the one nor the other had any doubt about the meaning of this phenomenon and looked upon it in the same way as millions of other people. As a proof that they understood what it meant, they were never under an uncertainty as to what to do with the dying and were not afraid of them. But Levin and others like him, though they might be able to say a good many things about death, understood it but little, for they were afraid of it and were utterly at a loss to know what to do in the presence of death. Had Levin been left alone with his brother, he would have looked at him in terror and sat waiting in still greater terror for what was to come, without being able to do anything for him.

The sight of the sick man deprived him of all his faculties. He did not know what to say, how to look, nor how to move about. To talk of indifferent things seemed offensive, impossible; to talk of death was likewise impossible. "If I look at him, he will think I am studying him, or that I am afraid; if I don't look he will think that I am occupied with something else. If I walk on tiptoe it irritates him, if I walk naturally it seems to make too much noise." But Kitty did not consider all these things. She had no time to think of herself, for she was too occupied with the patient. She would talk to him about herself, tell him about their wedding. She would smile and caress him and tell him that he would soon recover. She did all this because she knew and understood. The surest sign that all her activities were not merely instinctive and unintelligent was that, besides attending to the patient's physical comfort, she had managed to persuade him to see a priest to make his confession and receive the last sacrament. In this, too, she resembled Agafia Mihailovna, who, in speaking of the old man-servant's death, had said, "God grant that others die like him. He took the last sacrament and received extreme unction."

On returning from the sick man to their rooms one night, Levin sat down with bowed head, utterly dazed, not knowing what to do. He could not think of supper, nor of getting ready for bed; he could not even talk to his wife; it seemed to him like sacrilege. Kitty, on the contrary, was more active than usual. She ordered supper, arranged the room, helped the maid to make the beds, and did not even forget to sprinkle them with Persian powder. She felt rather like a man on the eve of a battle, or before some important and decisive moment in his life—a moment that was to prove his mettle and show that his past life had not been wasted, but had been a preparation for that supreme moment to come.

It was not yet twelve o'clock when everything was neatly and carefully arranged and the two hotel rooms began to assume a cosy, home-like appearance. On a table near the bed, Kitty had spread a cloth and laid out her combs, brushes, and a mirror.

Levin found it unpardonable in himself to eat, sleep, or even to speak; every movement he made seemed to him inappropriate. Kitty, on the contrary, went about her work in the most business-like way. But neither could eat anything, and it was long before they both got to bed and to sleep.

"I am very glad that I persuaded him to receive extreme unction to-morrow," Kitty said, as she sat in her dressing-jacket before her little travelling mirror, combing her soft, perfumed hair. "I have never seen it, but mamma told me there were prayers about recovery in it."

"Do you really think he will recover?" Levin asked, gazing at the narrow parting on the back of her round head, that disappeared instantly as she drew the comb away.

"The doctor says he cannot last more than three days, but how can he know? All the same, I am very glad that I persuaded him," she said, looking at her husband through her hair. "Everything is possible," she added, with that peculiarly wise expression that always came over her face whenever she talked of religion.

Since the talks on religion that had passed between them before they were married, neither had mentioned the subject again; but Kitty still continued going to church and observing all the rites, with the calm conviction that it was necessary. In spite of his assurances to the contrary, she was firmly convinced that he was just as good a Christian as she herself, if not a better one, and that everything he said about religion was nothing more than one of his masculine vagaries, just like his statement about her English embroidery. He had said that other people darned holes, while she made them, and so on.

"I can see now that that woman, Marya Nikolaevna, would never have known how to arrange it all," Levin observed. "I must confess I'm very glad you've come after all. You are so good and pure, that . . ." He took her hand, but did not kiss it. To kiss her hand in the presence of death seemed unworthy. He merely pressed it and looked into her bright eyes with a guilty expression.

"You would have been so miserable alone," she said, raising her hands to pin up her hair and covering her cheeks that had flushed with pleasure. "She would not have known," she continued; "fortunately I learned a good deal in Soden."

"Were there any people there as ill as Nikolai?"

"Some were worse."

"What is so terrible to me is that I can't help seeing him as he was in his youth. You can't imagine what a fine young fellow he used to be! But I did not understand him then."

"I can quite believe it. He and I would have been such good friends," she said, growing alarmed at her own words as she looked at her husband. The tears came into her eyes.

"Yes, *would have been*," he said sorrowfully. "He is the kind of man of whom we say that he was not born for this world."

"We have a difficult time before us," Kitty said, glancing at her tiny watch; "I think we had better go to bed."

XX

On the following day the sick man confessed and received the last sacrament. During the ceremony he prayed fervently. In his large eyes, fixed on the image, that was placed on a table covered with a coloured cloth, there was so much supplication and hope that Levin could not bear to look at them. He knew that it would only make the parting from life to which he clung still harder in the end. Levin knew his brother through and through. He knew that his unbelief had not been merely the result of a desire to escape from religion in order to lead a freer life. His religious beliefs had been shaken step by step by the theories of modern science. Levin knew, too, that his present return to faith was not genuine, but that his reason had been overmastered by his desire for recovery. Kitty had raised his hopes by her stories of marvellous cures. Levin knew all this and was pained to look at that imploring glance full of hope, that emaciated hand pitifully making the sign of the cross over his brow, the prominent shoulders, the flat, rattling chest, that could no longer hold the life for which he was praying. As an unbeliever, Levin did what he had frequently done before. He addressed himself to God thus: " If Thou existest, I pray Thee make this man well and Thou wilt be saving him and me."

After the anointing the sick man felt himself better. He did not cough once during a whole hour. He lay smiling as he kissed Kitty's hand, thanking her and assuring her that he felt no pain anywhere and that already his appetite and strength were returning. He even sat up without any assistance when his soup was brought to him and asked for a second cutlet. Impossible as his recovery was, Levin and Kitty were happy in that hour. They began to think that perhaps after all they had been mistaken.

" Is he better? "

" Yes, much better."

" Isn't it wonderful? "

" Why wonderful? He certainly seems better," they whispered and smiled at each other.

The delusion did not last long. Nikolai fell asleep calmly, but in about half an hour he was awakened by a fit of coughing. All hope suddenly died out in him and in those surrounding him.

61

The reality of his present suffering destroyed the last glimmer of hope in them all.

Completely forgetting all his thoughts of half an hour ago, or rather trying to put them out of his mind as something embarrassing, Nikolai asked for a bottle of iodine to inhale, and as Levin handed it to him, he looked at him with the same impassioned, imploring gaze with which he had looked at the image, as though beseeching his brother to confirm the doctor's words about the miraculous virtues of iodine.

" Kitty is not here, is she? " he asked above the rattle in his throat, looking round quickly as Levin repeated the doctor's words unconvincingly. " How can I explain . . . I acted the little comedy for her sake; she is so sweet. But you and I cannot deceive ourselves. In this I believe," he said, pressing the bottle in his bony hand as he began to breathe over it.

At eight o'clock in the evening Levin and his wife were drinking tea in their own room when Marya Nikolaevna rushed in breathless. She was pale and her lips were trembling.

" He is dying! " she gasped. " He is dying."

They both ran to him. He had raised himself in bed and was sitting with his back bent and his head low, hanging over his arms.

" How do ycu feel? " Levin asked in a whisper after a short silence.

" I feel that I am going," Nikolai replied, speaking with difficulty, but with extraordinary precision. He did not raise his head, but looked upwards trying to catch his brother's face, but did not succeed. " Katya, go away," he added.

Levin jumped up and in a commanding whisper made her leave the room.

" Yes, I am going," Nikolai said again.

" What makes you think so? " Levin asked in order to say something.

" Because I am going," he repeated as though he had some special affection for the phrase. " This is the end."

Marya Nikolaevna approached the bed.

" You ought to lie down; you would feel easier," she said.

" I shall be lying soon," he said softly; " dead," he added bitterly. " But you can put me down if you like."

Levin helped him to lie down and sat down beside him, gazing into his face and hardly daring to breathe. Nikolai lay on his back with his eyes closed, but the muscles on his brow moved every now and again, as though he were thinking deeply.

Levin tried to imagine what he was passing through, what was going on within him, but he could not. He could see by the stern, calm brow of the dying man that all the doubts and difficulties that were still dark to him were illuminated for Nikolai.

" Yes, that is so," Nikolai said slowly. " Wait a moment." Again he was silent. " That is it ! " he said suddenly, as though something had become clear to him. " O Lord ! " he moaned, and gave a deep sigh.

Marya Nikolaevna felt his legs.

" They are getting cold," she whispered.

For a long, long time, as it seemed to Levin, Nikolai lay motionless, but Levin could see that he was still alive, because he breathed every now and again. Worn out by the mental strain, he felt that he could not understand what his brother had meant by " *That is it !* " It seemed to him that he had somehow been left behind; he could no longer think of the question of death itself; involuntarily the thought of what he would have to do directly, floated through his brain. He could see himself closing his brother's eyes, dressing him, ordering a coffin. And, strange to say, he did not experience any sense of sorrow or loss, still less pity, for the dying man. If he had any feeling at all, it was rather one of envy that his brother now possessed the knowledge that was denied to him.

He sat for a long time waiting for the end, but it would not come. The door opened, and Kitty appeared. Levin rose in order to stop her. But suddenly Nikolai moved.

" Don't go away," he said, extending his hand.

Levin took it in his own and made an impatient gesture for his wife to leave the room.

Thus he sat for an hour or two. He had left off thinking of death and began wondering what Kitty was doing. By degrees all sorts of irrelevant thoughts began crowding in upon him. He wondered who occupied the next room, and whether the house the doctor lived in was his own. An unconquerable desire to eat and to sleep came over him. He drew his hand away gently and felt his brother's legs. They were quite cold, but the dying man still breathed. Levin walked towards the door on tiptoe, but Nikolai stirred again and said, " Don't go away."

.   .   .   .

Day began to break. Levin drew his hand away quietly, and without a look at his brother he went back to his own room and fell fast asleep. When he awoke, instead of hearing the news of his brother's death, he was told that the sick man had returned to his former condition. He was again able to sit up in bed, despite his cough; again he demanded food and expressed his hopes of recovery. But he had grown more morose and irritable than ever, and neither Kitty nor Levin could do anything to pacify him. He was angry with everybody and abused them all; he blamed them for his sufferings, and demanded that the Moscow specialist should be sent for. Whenever he was asked how he felt he replied with the same expression of malice and reproach, " I am suffering terrible, unendurable agony."

And he really did suffer more and more, especially from the bed-sores that were no longer possible of cure. His irritability increased, and he kept on reproaching everybody because the Moscow specialist had not been sent for. Kitty tried her best to make him more comfortable, to pacify him, but in vain, and Levin could see that she was wearing herself out, though she would not admit it. The sadness and emotion they all felt on the night when Levin had been called and Nikolai had taken leave of life had given way to something else. They all knew that he would die soon, that he was half dead already, and had but one desire, that the end might come as quickly as possible; but still they kept on handing him his medicines and trying to discover new ones; deceiving him, themselves, and one another. It was all a most horrible, base, degrading lie, and Levin, both by his peculiar nature and the fact that he loved the dying man more than the others did, was the most pained by it.

Levin, who had long desired to reconcile his two brothers, wrote to Sergei Ivanovitch, and on receiving an answer from him, read it to Nikolai. Sergei Ivanovitch wrote to say that he unfortunately could not come, but begged Nikolai's forgiveness in the most touching terms.

Nikolai did not say anything.

" What shall I say to him? " Levin asked. " You are not angry with him, are you? "

" Not at all! " Nikolai replied, irritated at the question. " Ask him to send me a doctor."

Another three agonising days passed. His death was now desired by every one who saw him, beginning with the landlord, the hotel servants, the people staying in the hotel, the doctor, Marya Nikolaevna, and even Levin and Kitty. But the dying man himself stilled talked of life, continued taking his medicines, and growing angry that the specialist had not been sent for. Only in rare moments, when his pain had been somewhat eased by opium and he was half asleep, did he give expression to the desire that was in him, even stronger than in the others. "Oh, if it would only end! Oh, if it would only end!" he would moan.

His suffering accomplished its work and death was coming on apace. He could not lie in any position without pain, could not for a minute forget himself. The memories, impressions, and thoughts of the past were odious to him; the sight of those who surrounded him and their talk was a constant trial to him. Every one felt it; no one dared move or speak freely in his presence. All his thoughts and feelings were concentrated into the one desire to be free of it all.

The moment had come when he began to look upon death as the greatest possible happiness. Formerly every desire evoked by suffering or privation, like hunger, fatigue, thirst, had given him pleasure when gratified, but now they only gave him pain. He could only hope for deliverance from the source of his woes —his bruised, tortured body. Without finding words to express this desire, he continued from sheer force of habit asking for things that had once given him comfort. "Turn me over on the other side," he would say, and immediately asked to be put back again. "Give me some soup! Take it away! Say something! why are you all silent?" But the moment any one began to speak, he shut his eyes and a look of fatigue, indifference, and disgust came over his face.

On the tenth day after their arrival Kitty fell ill. She had a frightful headache, vomited, and could not leave her bed. The doctor declared that she was run down after the strain and recommended rest. She got up after dinner, as usual, and went into the sick man's room. He looked at her severely when she entered and gave a contemptuous smile when he heard that she had not been well. He had been groaning and moaning the whole of the day.

"How do you feel?" Kitty asked.

"Worse," he said with difficulty. "I have a great deal of pain."

"Where?"

"Everywhere."

"It will be over to-day," Marya Nikolaevna whispered, but loudly enough to be heard by Nikolai, whose sense of hearing had grown acute. Levin motioned her to stop. Though Nikolai had heard what she said, the words produced no impression on him. His gaze remained intense and reproachful.

" What makes you think so? " Levin asked, as Marya Nikolaevna followed him out into the corridor.

" He keeps on trying to pull things off himself," she replied.

" How do you mean? " Levin asked.

" Like this," she said, tugging at the folds of her woollen dress. And indeed Levin noticed that the sick man kept on pulling at himself as though he wished to tear something away.

Marya Nikolaevna's predictions came true. By the evening Nikolai could no longer raise his hands, and only lay staring in front of him with a fixed concentrated gaze. Even when Kitty and his brother bent over him, he took no notice of them, but continued looking in the same direction. Kitty sent for a priest to read the prayer for the dying.

During the reading Nikolai lay with his eyes closed, showing no sign of life. Levin, Kitty, and Marya Nikolaevna were standing by the bed. The prayers were not yet over when Nikolai suddenly stretched himself, sighed, and opened his eyes. Having ended his prayer, the priest put the cross against the cold brow, then wrapped it up in the scapulary. He stood still for a minute or two, then touched the huge, bloodless hand of the dying man.

" He is dead," the priest said, stepping aside, but suddenly the matted moustache of the dying man moved, and from the depths of his chest came the distinct words, that sounded so piercing in the stillness:

" Not yet . . . soon . . ."

A minute had scarcely gone by when his face lighted up and a smile appeared on his lips. He had passed away. The women hastened to dress him.

Levin's horror at the terrible enigma of death came upon him with the same intensity as on that autumn night when his brother had come to see him. Only now, in the very presence of it, he felt worse than ever. His wife's nearness saved him from falling into utter despair; for in spite of his terror he felt the need of loving and living. Love alone had saved him from the despair threatening him and he felt it growing stronger and purer.

The mystery of death had scarcely accomplished itself, when another, just as insoluble, rose up and called him to life and love.

The doctor confirmed his suspicions regarding Kitty. Her indisposition was due to pregnancy.

XXI

FROM the moment that Betsy and Stepan Arkadyevitch had made it clear to him that nothing further was demanded of him other than that he should leave his wife alone and not annoy her by his presence, Alexei Alexandrovitch was at a loss to know what to do. He walked about like one dazed and put himself completely into the hands of those who took so much pleasure in arranging his affairs, agreeing to everything. It was only when Anna left the house and the English governess sent to inquire whether he wished her to dine with him or by herself that he realised what had happened, and grew terrified at his own position.

The most awful part of it was that he was utterly unable to connect the past with the present. It was not the period when he had lived happily with his wife that most troubled him. He had already passed through the transition from his happiness to his wife's infidelity. It had been difficult but comprehensible. Had she left him then, at the time she informed him of her infidelity, it would have been easier to bear than now. The thought of his forgiveness, his humility, his love for a child that was not his own, now seemed to him so strange in his loneliness, disgrace, and shame. He felt that every one ridiculed and despised him and that none needed him.

For the first two days after his wife's departure, Alexei Alexandrovitch received his secretary and petitioners, went to the ministry, and took his dinner in the dining-room as usual. He could not have said why he was doing it all, but during those two days he strained himself to the utmost to try and appear calm and indifferent. In replying to the servants' questions as to what was to be done with Anna's rooms and things, he made a tremendous effort over himself to behave as though he had foreseen these questions and did not betray the slightest sign of despair. On the third day after Anna's departure, Korney brought him a milliner's bill that his wife had forgotten to pay, saying that the clerk from the shop was waiting. Alexei Alexandrovitch asked him to show the clerk in.

"I am sorry to disturb your excellency, but if you wish us to send the bill to her excellency, will you be kind enough to let us have her address?"

Alexei Alexandrovitch stood considering for a few moments, then suddenly he turned away and sat down by the table. He leaned his head on his arms, tried to speak, but could not.

Feeling for his master, Korney asked the clerk to come another time. Left alone Alexei Alexandrovitch realised that he could no longer keep up the semblance of composure and indifference. He gave orders for the carriage to be unharnessed, though it stood at the door waiting for him, told Korney not to receive any one, and did not come out to dinner.

He felt that he could no longer stand the contempt and malice that was poured upon him by everybody, including Korney and the milliner's clerk. He knew that the general hatred was not due to something fundamentally wrong in himself—in that case he might have tried to be better—but because he was offensively, disgustingly unhappy. People were merciless to him for the very reason that his heart was lacerated. He felt that he was being destroyed as one dog destroys another that is howling and whining in its pain. His only salvation had been to conceal his wounds, and he had unconsciously done so for the last two days, but now he could hold out no longer.

His despair was intensified by the consciousness of his utter loneliness. Not only in St. Petersburg, but nowhere had he a single friend to whom he might unburden himself as one man to another.

Alexei Alexandrovitch had grown up as an orphan. He had but one brother. Their father had died before they were old enough to remember him, and their mother when Alexei Alexandrovitch was only ten years old. A small piece of property was left to them. They were both brought up by an uncle, a distinguished official, who at one time had been a favourite of the late emperor.

After leaving school and then the university with honours, by the aid of his uncle Alexei Alexandrovitch started on his official career and gave himself up entirely to his ambitions. He had made no friends either at school or at college, nor had he ever grown intimate with any of his colleagues. His brother had been his only friend, but he had gone in for the diplomatic service that necessitated his living abroad and had died soon after Alexei Alexandrovitch's marriage.

When he had been the governor of a certain provincial town, Anna's aunt, a rich influential lady of that province, had thrown him into the society of her niece and placed them in such a situation that he either had to propose to her or leave the town, For a long time Alexei Alexandrovitch hesitated. There were as many arguments for this step as against it, and so far he had not seen sufficient reason for breaking his rule about never doing anything in a hurry. Anna's aunt, however, impressed upon him through a friend that he had already compromised the girl and was in all honour bound to marry her. So he made his proposal and bestowed on her, both before and after they were married, all the affection of which his nature was capable.

His extreme attachment to Anna took away the last need for seeking intimate friendships; so that now among all his numerous acquaintances there was not a single person near to him. He had a good many of what might be called connections, but no friends. There were a great many people with whom he was on visiting terms, whom he could invite to dinner, and with whom he could discuss things that interested him, from his own work to the higher authorities, or whose influence he could solicit in the matter of finding some one a place, but that was all; with them he could not break those conventional relations that had grown on him by force of habit. There was one college friend with whom he might have talked about his personal affairs, but he was a curator in some province far from St. Petersburg. The only people who were likely to take an interest in him were his secretary and doctor.

Mihail Vassilevitch Sludin, his secretary, was a kind, good-natured man, with quite an attachment for Alexei Alexandrovitch, but their official relationship of five year's standing had placed a barrier between them for anything else. When he had finished signing all the documents on the day of Anna's departure, Alexei Alexandrovitch had looked at Mihail Vassilevitch and made several attempts to speak. He had wanted to ask if he had heard of his misfortune, but ended by making some ordinary request about the work.

As for the doctor, he, too, was kindly disposed towards him, but it had long been agreed between them, though not in words, that they were both so much overwhelmed with work that there was no time for talking.

Of all his women friends, particularly of the Countess Lydia Ivanovna, who might be considered the first of them, Alexei Alexandrovitch did not even think. All women were terrible and loathsome to him now.

XXII

ALEXEI ALEXANDROVITCH had forgotten the Countess Lydia Ivanovna, but she had not forgotten him. At the very moment when he had been seized by despair at his loneliness, she entered his study without being announced. He was sitting in the same position, his head resting on his arms.

" *J'ai forcé la consigne,*" she said, going up to him quickly, and breathing heavily in her agitation. " I know everything! Alexei Alexandrovitch, my poor friend!" She took his hand in both her own and looked at him with her beautiful, dreamy eyes.

Alexei Alexandrovitch frowned, disengaged his hand, got up, and offered her a chair.

" Won't you sit down, countess? I am not receiving to-day, because I'm not well," he said, and his lips trembled.

" My poor friend!" the Countess Lydia Ivanovna repeated, without taking her eyes off him. Suddenly her eyebrows rose and her plain, distorted face grew even plainer still. Alexei Alexandrovitch felt that she was sorry for him and on the point of tears. He was softened; he seized her plump little hand and began kissing it.

" My dear friend," she said in an unsteady voice, " you should not give way to your grief. It is great, I know, but you must seek consolation."

" I am broken, crushed, completely unmanned!" Alexei Alexandrovitch said, dropping her hand, but still looking into her eyes that were full of tears. " And the worst of it is that I can find no support, no guide anywhere, either in myself or outside of myself."

" You will find it," she said with a sigh. " Do not look for it in me, though I want you to believe in my friendship. In love alone do we find our support—in the love that He has enjoined upon us. His burden is light," she continued, with that look of ecstasy in her eyes that Alexei Alexandrovitch knew so well. " He will help and sustain you."

Though Alexei Alexandrovitch had disapproved of this new mystic exaltation prevalent in St. Petersburg, her words comforted him.

" I am crushed and weak; I did not foresee anything and cannot understand anything."

" My poor friend! " Lydia Ivanovna repeated.

" It is not so much the loss," Alexei Alexandrovitch continued, " I am not grieving so much over that; I cannot help being ashamed of the position I am in. I know it is wrong, but I cannot help it."

" It was not you who committed that noble act of forgiveness that astonished us all, but He who dwells in your heart," the Countess Lydia Ivanovna said, raising her eyes to heaven; " and so you cannot be ashamed of your deed."

Alexei Alexandrovitch frowned and cracked the joints of his fingers.

" You ought to know all the details," he began in a thin voice. " There are limits to a man's strength, countess, and I have reached the limits of mine. The whole of to-day has been wasted in domestic details, arising " (he laid special stress on the word) " from my new and lonely situation. First the servants, then the governess, and then bills. . . . It was like going through fire; I couldn't endure it any longer. At dinner . . . Yesterday I nearly left the dinner table; I could not bear to look at the boy. He did not ask for any explanation, but he wanted to and his gaze was like torture to me. He was afraid to look at me; but that is nothing. . . ." Alexei Alexandrovitch was about to mention the milliner's bill, but his voice shook and he stopped. He could not think of that account, for a hat and some ribbon, without a feeling of pity for himself.

" I understand, my friend," the Countess Lydia Ivanovna said. " I understand everything. I know I cannot give you help and consolation, but still, I came to see if there was anything I could do. If I could relieve you of the burden of these petty cares . . . I understand you need a woman's word, a woman's hand. . . . Will you entrust them to me? "

Alexei Alexandrovitch was silent, but pressed her hand gratefully.

" We can look after Serioja together. I am not very great in practical matters, but I will do my best; I will be your housekeeper. Don't thank me, please. I am not doing this alone. . . ."

" I cannot help expressing my gratitude."

" No, my friend, you must not abandon yourself to your feelings—you must not be ashamed of what is the highest degree of perfection in a Christian. ' He who humbles himself shall be exalted.' And there is nothing to thank me for. Thank

Him and pray for His guidance. In Him alone can we find peace, consolation, salvation, and love." She raised her eyes to heaven and Alexei Alexandrovitch could tell by her silence that she was praying.

Alexei Alexandrovitch listened to her, and those very words that would formerly have seemed to him affected and superfluous, now appeared natural and consoling. He had never liked this new ecstatic spirit. He was a believer and was interested in religion mainly from a political point of view, and these new doctrines that permitted new interpretations were distasteful to him on account of their danger of opening the door for discussion and analysis. He had always been hostile to this new doctrine, though the Countess Lydia Ivanovna was one of its strong adherents, and had always forborne to talk of it in her presence. Now for the first time her words gave him pleasure and he could not even criticise them inwardly.

" I am grateful both for your deeds and your words," he said, when she had finished praying.

The Countess Lydia Ivanovna again pressed his hand in both her own.

" I am going to begin at once," she said with a smile, wiping the tears from her face; " I must see Serioja. I shall only turn to you when absolutely necessary." She rose and left the room.

The Countess Lydia Ivanovna went to Serioja's rooms, and while she bathed the scared boy's cheeks with her tears, she told him that his father was a saint and that his mother was dead.

. . . .

The Countess Lydia Ivanovna fulfilled her promise; she really did take upon herself the care of Alexei Alexandrovitch's house, but she had not exaggerated when she declared that she was incapable in practical matters. Her orders were impossible, so they were not executed, and the management gradually fell into the hands of Korney, the valet. While dressing his master he would employ all the tact at his command in letting him know such things as he considered essential. But the Countess Lydia Ivanovna's help was none the less valuable. Her devotion and esteem were a moral support to Alexei Alexandrovitch. To her great consolation she had succeeded in converting him to Christianity; that is, to the new interpretation of the Christian teaching then current among a certain set in St. Petersburg. The conversion had been an easy one. Like Lydia Ivanovna and other people who shared her views, Alexei Alexandrovitch was lacking in that depth of imagination, that spiritual force, that gets to the reality of things. He saw nothing impossible or inconsistent in the conception that death existed for unbelievers and not for himself, and that being in possession of the fullest faith his soul was free from sin, and that he had attained complete salvation on this earth.

It is true Alexei Alexandrovitch was dimly conscious that there was something wrong about this theory, and that when he had abandoned himself to those feelings that led him to forgive Anna he was happier than now, when he was constantly thinking about Christ dwelling in his soul and that in signing documents he was fulfilling His will. But it was necessary for Alexei Alexandrovitch to delude himself. In his humility he needed that height, even though it was only an imaginary one, from which he could despise those people who despised him; and so he clung to his imaginary salvation.

XXIII

WHEN quite a young girl, full of enthusiasm, the Countess Lydia Ivanovna had been married to a rich, distinguished man, who was very friendly and good-natured, but a great debauchee. Two months after the marriage he left her, and to all the ecstatic assurances of her love for him he replied only by ridicule and even cruelty. Knowing his kindness and seeing no defect in the romantic Lydia, outsiders were astonished at his behaviour. Since then, though they had never been divorced, they lived apart, and whenever the husband met his wife he treated her with that bitterness, the cause of which no one had ever been able to explain.

The Countess Lydia had long ceased to love her husband, but she was always in love with somebody or other; sometimes with several people at a time, both men and women indiscriminately, and generally with people of note. She was in love with all the royal princes and princesses who married into the imperial family. She had been in love with a bishop, a vicar, and a priest; she had in turn been in love with a journalist, three Slavs, and Kornisarov; with a minister, a doctor, an English missionary, and with Karenin. All these loves, that were constantly flaming up and dying out again, did not in the least hinder her from keeping up the most complex relations both at court and in society. But since she had taken Karenin under her protection after his misfortune, working in his house and looking after his welfare, she had come to feel that all her former loves were illusory and that she really loved Karenin alone. The sentiment she felt for him seemed to her stronger than any she had ever experienced before. It was now perfectly clear to her that she could not have loved Kornisarov had he not saved the emperor's life, nor Rititch-Kudjitsky had there not been a Slavonic question. She felt that she loved Karenin for himself, for his noble soul, that no one understood, for his thin voice, his slow manner of speech, his weary eyes, his soft white hands with the swollen veins. She was not only glad to meet him, but was always studying his face to see what kind of an impression she produced upon him. She wanted to please him not only by her speech but by her person. For his sake she began taking more pains over her toilet. She would find herself dreaming as to what might have been had she not been married and he had been free. She would blush whenever he entered the room, and could not repress a smile of pleasure when he happened to say something agreeable or pleasant to her.

For several days the Countess Lydia Ivanovna had been in the greatest state of excitement; she had heard that Anna and Vronsky were in St. Petersburg. Alexei Alexandrovitch had to be saved from the danger of meeting her; he had even to be saved from the knowledge that this awful woman was in the same town with him, and that he ran the risk of meeting her at any moment.

Lydia Ivanovna made inquiries among her acquaintances to find out what those " disgusting people," as she called Anna and Vronsky, were doing, in order to so guide the movements of her friend that he should not meet them.

A young adjutant, who knew Vronsky and hoped to receive a commission through the Countess Lydia Ivanovna, informed her that they had finished their business and were leaving St. Petersburg on the following day. The Countess Lydia was beginning to feel reassured, when the next morning she received a letter, the handwriting of which she recognised with horror. It was Anna's. The envelope was of thick paper and on the yellow, scented sheet inside was a large monogram.

" Who brought it? "

" A servant from the hotel."

For a long time the Countess Lydia Ivanovna could not read the letter. The excitement and agitation gave her an attack of asthma, to which she was subject. When she calmed down a little, she read the following, written in French:—

MADAME LA COMTESSE,—Knowing the Christian sentiments that fill your heart I take the unpardonable liberty of turning to you. I am unhappy at being separated from my son, and I beg you to let me see him once before my departure. I am sorry to trouble you, but I did not wish to pain Alexei Alexandrovitch, that noble generous man, by reminding him of my existence. Knowing your friendship for him, I feel that you will understand. Will you send Serioja to me, or shall I come to the house at an appointed hour? Or if it seems best, I could meet him outside the house if you would let me know when and where. I know you are too kind to refuse me. You do not know how I long to see him and so cannot imagine how grateful I shall be for your help. ANNA."

The whole letter annoyed Lydia Ivanovna. She did not like the reference to either hers or Karenin's generosity, and thought the whole tone was too free and easy.

" There is no answer," she said, and immediately sat down and wrote a note to Alexei Alexandrovitch saying that she hoped to see him at court at one o'clock, where every one would be going to congratulate the emperor on his birthday. " I have to speak to you about an important, painful matter and we can arrange where we had best meet. It would be better at my house, where I shall have tea ready as *you* like it. It is essential for me to see you. He gives the cross and the strength to bear it," she added in order to prepare him a little.

The Countess Lydia Ivanovna was in the habit of writing to Alexei Alexandrovitch two or three times a day. She liked this process of communication with him, because it had a sort of romantic mysteriousness about it that was lacking in their personal relations.

XXIV

THE congratulations were over. The departing guests were discussing the events of the day and those who had received promotions and honours.

"I think the Countess Marya Borisovna ought to be made the minister for war and the Princess Vatkovsky a general," a grey-haired old man in a gold-embroidered uniform remarked jestingly to a tall handsome maid of honour who happened to be talking to him.

"And you ought to make me an adjutant," she said with a smile.

"But I have another appointment for you—in the ecclesiastical department, with Karenin to help you."

"How do you do, prince?" the old man asked, shaking hands with another man who joined them.

"What was that you were saying about Karenin?" the prince asked.

"He and Putyatov have received the order of Alexander Nevsky."

"I thought he had it already."

"Oh, no. Just look at him," the old man said with a gesture in the direction of Karenin, who was standing by the door in his court uniform, with a red ribbon across his shoulder, talking to an influential member of the Imperial Council, "he seems as pleased as anything." He turned to press the hand of a fine athletic looking chamberlain who had just come up.

"He looks much older," the chamberlain observed.

"From care. He spends his days writing projects. He won't let that unfortunate man off until he has explained to him everything, point by point."

"I don't think he looks old. *Il fait des passions.* It appears the Countess Lydia Ivanovna is jealous of his wife."

"Please don't say anything bad about the Countess Lydia Ivanovna!"

"Is there anything bad in her being in love with Karenin?"

"Is it true that Madame Karenina is here?"

"Not here at court, but in St. Petersburg. I met her arm in arm with Vronsky on the Morsky."

"*C'est un homme qui n'a pas . . .*" the chamberlain began, but stopped to bow to a royal personage who passed him.

76

While they were discussing him thus Alexei Alexandrovitch was doing his best to engage the attention of the member of the Imperial Council whom he had buttonholed. He was explaining some new financial project at great length.

Almost at the same time that his wife left him, there happened to Alexei Alexandrovitch that most grievous of all events for an official—the cessation of his upward progress in the service. Possibly he was the only person who did not see that his official career was ended. Whether it was the conflict with Stremov, or his trouble with his wife, or simply that he had reached his limits, the fact remained that every one saw clearly that his official race was over. He still occupied an important position, was a member of many committees and commissions, but people had ceased expecting anything from him. No matter what he said or proposed he was always listened to with the indulgence accorded to a man who had grown out of date. But Alexei Alexandrovitch did not feel it; on the contrary, being removed from the direct participation in governmental activity, he saw the mistakes and blunders of others more clearly and considered it his bounden duty to indicate the means of remedying them. Soon after the separation from his wife he began his pamphlet on the new judicial courts, the first of a long string of utterly useless pamphlets, dealing with all branches of administration, that he was fated to write.

Quite unconscious of his hopeless position in the official world and consequently not grieved by it, Alexei Alexandrovitch was more than ever satisfied with his activities.

" He that is married careth for the things that are of this world, how that he may please his wife. He that is unmarried careth for the things that belong to the Lord, how he may please the Lord," says the Apostle Paul, and Alexei Alexandrovitch, who now directed his life in all respects according to the epistle, often had occasion to quote this text. It seemed to him that ever since he was left without his wife, by these very projects he was serving the Lord more than ever.

The obvious impatience of the man he was talking to did not in the least embarrass Alexei Alexandrovitch, but he stopped a moment as a member of the imperial family passed by and his victim chose this opportunity of making his escape.

Left alone, Alexei Alexandrovitch lowered his head and tried to collect his thoughts; he looked absently about him and turned to the door in the hope of meeting the Countess Lydia Ivanovna.

"How well and strong they all are," he said to himself with a passing glance at the powerful form of the chamberlain with his well-groomed perfumed whiskers, and at the red neck of the prince coming out above his uniform. "There is some foundation for the saying that everything in the world is evil," he thought, with another look at the chamberlain's calves.

Alexei Alexandrovitch bowed to this group as he passed them slowly, with his habitual look of fatigue and dignity, and passed his eyes over the crowd to see if he could distinguish the Countess Lydia Ivanovna.

"Ah! Alexei Alexandrovitch!" the old man exclaimed, with a mocking light in his eyes, as Karenin drew near him and inclined his head coldly. "I have not yet had the pleasure of congratulating you." He pointed to the new ribbon.

"Thank you," Alexei Alexandrovitch replied. "What a splendid day we are having," he added with special emphasis on the word splendid. He knew that they were laughing at him, but he did not expect anything else; he had grown accustomed to it by now.

Catching sight of the yellow shoulders of the Countess Lydia Ivanovna soaring out of her corsets as she was walking towards the door and beckoning to him with her beautiful dreamy eyes, Alexei Alexandrovitch gave a smile that showed his white teeth and went across to join her.

The Countess Lydia's toilet had cost her a great deal of trouble, like all her toilets of late, for her aim was a very different one to that she had set herself thirty years ago. Formerly, she thought only of adorning herself as much as possible and nothing had been too extravagant for her taste, but now she was particularly careful to dress more in keeping with her age and figure, so that the contrast between her finery and her looks should not be too glaring. She was successful as far as Alexei Alexandrovitch was concerned, for she seemed attractive to him. She was like an island of friendship and love amidst the sea of hostility and ridicule that surrounded him.

As he passed between the rows of sarcastic glances, he was attracted by her affectionate gaze as a plant is attracted to the light.

"Accept my congratulations," she said as she indicated the ribbon with her eyes.

Restraining a smile of pleasure, he shrugged his shoulders, affecting indifference. The Countess Lydia knew that it afforded him great joy, though he was not willing to admit it.

" How is our little angel? " she asked, meaning Serioja.

" I can't say that I'm altogether pleased with him," Alexei Alexandrovitch replied, raising his eyebrows. " And I don't think Sitnikov is either." (Sitnikov was a pedagogue who was engaged to superintend Serioja's education.) " He does not seem to take any interest in those questions that ought to touch every man and child alike." Alexei Alexandrovitch began to express his views about the boy's education—the only thing that interested him, apart from his official activities.

When Alexei Alexandrovitch returned to life and activity under the influence of Lydia Ivanovna, he felt it his duty to look after the education of his son. As he had had no experience in educational matters, he began to study the question from a theoretical point of view. He read several books on anthropology, pedagogics, and didactics, and having decided on a system he engaged the best pedagogue in St. Petersburg to help him and set to work. Later it proved a constant source of interest to him.

" But he has a good heart, like his father's, and with such a heart a child cannot be very bad," Lydia Ivanovna said enthusiastically.

" Perhaps. . . . I do my duty by him; I cannot do more."

" I want you to come home with me," the Countess Lydia said after a pause; " we must talk about that sad affair of yours. I would give anything to free you of certain reminiscences, but other peeple think differently. I've received a letter from *her*. *She* is in St. Petersburg."

Alexei Alexandrovitch shuddered at the mention of his wife, but instantly his face assumed that death-like rigidity that expressed his utter helplessness where she was concerned.

" I expected it," he said.

The Countess Lydia Ivanovna gave him a look full of ecstasy; tears came into her eyes at the grandeur of his soul.

XXV

WHEN Alexei Alexandrovitch entered the Countess Lydia's cosy little boudoir decorated with pictures and delicate porcelain, the hostess herself was not there. She was changing her dress.

On a round table covered with a cloth stood a Chinese tea-service and a silver tea-pot with a spirit lamp. Alexei Alexandrovitch cast his eyes vacantly over the numerous portraits adorning the walls, and seating himself by the table took up a copy of the New Testament that was lying on it. The rustle of a silk dress diverted his attention.

"Well, now we can sit down quietly," the Countess Lydia Ivanovna said as she hurriedly made her way between the couch and the table with an agitated smile on her lips, "and have a good talk over our tea."

After a few words of preparation, the countess, breathing heavily, handed Alexei Alexandrovitch Anna's letter, with a blush.

Having read the letter he kept silence for a long time.

"I suppose I have no right to refuse her," he said timidly, raising his eyes.

"My dear friend! you see no evil in anybody!"

"On the contrary, everything seems to me evil. But is it just . . . ?"

His face expressed indecision. It seemed as though he were asking for guidance and support in a matter incomprehensible to him.

"No," the Countess Lydia interrupted him; "there is a limit to everything. I can understand immorality," she continued, though this was not sincere, for she never had been able to understand what it was that led women astray, "but I cannot understand cruelty. And to whom? to you! How could she bring herself to come to the same place you are in? One has to live and learn. Day by day I learn to understand your greatness and her littleness."

"And who shall cast the stone?" Alexei Alexandrovitch asked, evidently satisfied with the part he was playing. "I have forgiven her everything and therefore cannot deprive her of that which is a necessity to her—her love for her child."

"But is it love, my friend? Is it sincere? Granted you have forgiven and still forgive, does that give us the right to disturb the soul of that little angel? He considers his mother dead. He prays for her and asks God to forgive her her sins. . . . That is much better to my mind. But what will he think when he sees her?"

"I had not thought of that," Alexei Alexandrovitch said, evidently agreeing with her.

The Countess Lydia covered her face with her hands and was silent. She was praying.

"If you ask me," she began, having finished her prayer and

uncovering her face, " I should advise you not to let her see the boy on any account. I can see how you suffer, how all your wounds have been opened afresh, but of course you never think of yourself! In any case what can it possibly lead to? To further suffering on your part and the child's. If she had a spark of human feeling left in her she would not desire this. No, I have not the remotest doubt that a meeting would be undesirable. If you like I will write to her."

Alexei Alexandrovitch agreed, and the Countess Lydia Ivanovna wrote the following letter in French:—

" DEAR MADAME,—The mention of you to your son might lead to all sorts of questions on his part, to which it would be impossible to reply without creating in him a spirit of condemnation for what he ought to hold sacred; under the circumstances, I beg you to take your husband's refusal in the spirit of Christian love and charity in which it was given. May the Almighty have mercy upon you. COUNTESS LYDIA."

The letter achieved the end desired, that the Countess Lydia Ivanovna would not even have admitted to herself. It wounded Anna to the depths of her soul.

When Alexei Alexandrovitch returned home he was unable to devote himself to his usual occupations or to find that spiritual calm he had formerly experienced in the consciousness of his salvation.

The memory of his wife, in comparison with whom he was such a saint, as the Countess Lydia had said, ought not to have troubled him, but he could not be at peace. He did not understand a word of the book he was reading, and could not rid himself of the painful mémories, the fearful mistakes he had made in his relations with her. He recalled how she had told him of her infidelity after the races and the letter he had written her. He should never forgive himself for that letter nor for having asked her to observe the proprieties instead of challenging Vronsky. And then the thought of his forgiveness and his care for a child that was not his own tore his heart with shame. And with the same sense of shame and regret he reviewed all his past relations to her, recalled the awkward way in which he had proposed to her after months of indecision.

" But where am I to blame? " he asked himself, and this question set him wondering whether all those other men, those Vronskys and Oblonskys, handsome chamberlains with fat calves, felt differently, loved differently, and married differently. And a whole crowd of dashing, handsome, self-confident men rose up in his imagination. He tried to banish these thoughts and to assure himself that he was not living for the present temporal life, but for the life eternal, and that his soul was full of peace and love. But the fact that he had made a few insignificant mistakes in that temporal life tormented him as though the eternal did not exist.

But this state did not last long. Soon Alexei Alexandrovitch felt a return of that height and calmness that made him forget what he did not wish to remember.

XXVI

" WELL, Kapitonitch? " Serioja greeted the porter merrily, as he returned from a walk on the day preceding his birthday and handed his cloak to the tall old man who stood smiling down at him, " did that muffled-up man come to-day? And did papa see him? "

" Yes. As soon as the seeretary had gone I announced him," the porter replied with a merry twinkle in his eye. " Let me take it off."

" Serioja! " Slavyanin, the tutor called, as he stopped at the door leading to the inner apartments, " take it off yourself! "

But Serioja, though he had heard his tutor's feeble voice, paid no attention. He stood holding on to the porter's girdle and looking up into his face.

" Did papa do what he wanted him to? "

The porter nodded.

The muffled-up man who had called several times to petition Alexei Alexandrovitch about something or other, interested both Serioja and the porter. Serioja had found him in the hall one day begging the porter in most pitiful tones to announce him and saying that otherwise his children would have to starve.

" Well, was he pleased? " he asked.

" Of course he was. He nearly danced for joy."

" Has anything come for me? " Serioja asked after a pause.

" Yes, sir," the porter replied in a whisper, shaking his head, " something from the countess."

Serioja understood that it was a birthday present from the Countess Lydia Ivanovna.

" Where is it? "

" Korney took it to papa. I think it's something nice."

" How big? So? "

" No, smaller, but good."

" Is it a book?"

" No, a toy. You had better run along now; Vassily Lukitch is calling," the porter said as he heard the tutor's approaching footsteps. He opened the boy's gloved hand that was holding on to his girdle and nodded to Vunitch.

" Coming in a minute, Vassily Lukitch! " Serioja said with that merry affectionate smile of his that always won the tutor's heart.

Serioja was too happy not to share with his friend, the porter, the piece of good news he had learnt from the Countess Lydia Ivanovna's niece in the Summer Garden. The pleasure he had received at hearing that his father had received the muffled-up man and that a new toy awaited him had put him in a general good humour. It seemed to him that every one must be happy on a day like this.

" I say, do you know that papa has received the Alexander Nevsky? "

" Of course I do! People have been calling to congratulate him."

" Is he pleased? "

" Of course he is pleased at an imperial favour. He has deserved it, no doubt," the porter said solemnly.

Serioja stood thinking for a moment as he gazed into the porter's face, every detail of which was known to him, at his chin between his grey whiskers that no one had ever seen except Serioja, because he looked at him from below.

" Is it long since your daughter came to see you? "

The porter's daughter was a ballet dancer.

" She can't come on week-days, because she has to study. You, too, have to study, sir, so you had better go."

When Serioja got to his room, instead of sitting down at his lessons, he began talking to his tutor about the toy the countess had sent him, saying that he thought it must be an engine. " What do you think? " he asked.

But the tutor was only thinking that he ought to be preparing his grammar lesson for the master, who was due at two o'clock.

" Tell me, Vassily Lukitch," he said suddenly, when he was already sitting at his desk with a book in his hand, " what is higher than the Alexander Nevsky? You know papa has received it, don't you? "

Vassily Lukitch told him that the Vladimir was higher.

" And what is higher than that? "

" The Andrei Pervosvany."

" And higher than the Andrei? "

" I don't know."

" You don't know? " Serioja asked in astonishment, and putting his elbows on the table he became lost in thought.

His reflections were of the most complex and varied character. He tried to imagine that his father had suddenly received the Vladimir and the Andrei and that as a result of it he would be much more lenient when he came to hear his lessons to-day, and that when he grew up he would receive all the orders, even those higher than the Andrei, if they invented them; they would no sooner invent a new order than he would earn it.

These thoughts made the time pass quickly, and when his master arrived the grammar lesson was not prepared, much to the master's pain and annoyance. Serioja was sorry that his master was grieved, but could not feel sorry for not having learnt his lesson. No matter how hard he tried to, he simply could not learn it that day. So long as the master explained it to him he seemed to understand more or less, but directly he was left alone it all became perfectly unintelligible to him.

" Mihail Ivanovitch, when is your birthday? " he asked suddenly when his master happened to be looking at a book.

" You had much better think of your work. Birthdays are stupid things to sensible people; they are no different to other days, and one must work on them just the same."

Serioja looked fixedly at his master, at his thin beard and spectacles, that had dropped down low on his nose; he fell to thinking and no longer heard what he was saying to him. He knew that his master was not thinking of the thing he was trying to explain; he could tell that by the tone of his voice. " But why do they all talk of the same thing, in the same way, when it's so dull and useless? " Why does he try to keep me at a distance? Why does he not love me? " he asked himself sadly, but could find no answer.

XXVII

AFTER the master came the lesson with his father. Before his arrival Serioja seated himself at the table, playing with his knife and thinking. When out walking, one of his favourite occupations was to try and find his mother. He did not believe in death in general, least of all in her death, though both the Countess Lydia Ivanovna and his father had told him that she was dead. It seemed to him that every graceful woman with dark hair whom he happened to meet must be his mother. At the sight of such a woman his emotion would grow so strong that the tears came into his eyes. He would wait for her to come up to him and lift her veil and disclose her face, and smile and embrace him. Once more he would smell the delicious scent about her, feel the tender clasp of her hand, and cry with joy. He would be as happy as on one evening when he had lain at her feet and she had tickled him and he had roared with laughter and bitten her white hand laden with rings. Later, when he had learned from his nurse that his mother was not really dead, but that his father and the countess had told him so because she was bad, he went on looking and waiting for her just the same; he could not believe that she was bad because he loved her. That morning in the Summer Garden he had seen a lady with a violet veil and had waited with a sinking heart for her to approach him, thinking that it was she, but she had disappeared without coming to him at all. To-day Serioja seemed to love his mother more than ever, and he sat there thinking of her, with beaming eyes, cutting the edge of the table with his pen-knife absently.

" Papa is coming ! " Vassily Lukitch said suddenly, bringing Serioja to himself.

Serioja jumped up, went to his father, and kissed his hand, looking searchingly into his face for any signs of joy at having received the Alexander Nevsky.

" Did you enjoy your walk ? " Alexei Alexandrovitch asked, seating himself in an arm-chair, and taking up a copy of the Old Testament he opened it. Though he had frequently impressed upon Serioja that every Christian ought to have a thorough knowledge of sacred history, yet Serioja noticed that his father often had recourse to the Old Testament to refresh his memory.

" Very much," Serioja replied, sitting down sideways on a

chair and rocking it, a thing that was forbidden him. " I saw
Nadenka " (Nadenka was a little niece of the Countess Lydia's,
whom she was bringing up), " and she told me you had received
a new order. Are you glad, papa? "

" In the first place, please don't rock," Alexei Alexandrovitch
said; " and in the second, it is work that gives pleasure not the
reward. I should like you to understand that. If you are
merely going to learn your lessons and work for the sake of the
reward, it will seem hard to you " (he recalled how the consciousness of his duty had sustained him throughout the morning in
the monotonous work of signing one hundred and eighteen
documents), " but if you work for the love of it, you find your
reward in the work itself."

The sparkling, affectionate light in Serioja's eyes died out
under his father's gaze. It was the same, old, familiar tone
that he always adopted towards him, to which Serioja had long
become accustomed. It seemed to him that his father treated
him like some imaginary boy out of a book, utterly unlike him,
and he involuntarily tried to imitate that boy.

" I hope you understand," his father said.

" Yes, papa," Serioja replied as the boy in the book would
have done.

The lesson consisted in his learning several verses from the
Gospel by heart and in repeating the beginning of the Old Testament. He knew the verses from the Gospel fairly well, but just
as he was reciting them, he became lost in the contemplation
of his father's frontal bone, which turned so abruptly at the
temples, that he got mixed up in what he was saying and went
on to the second verse before he had finished the first. Alexei
Alexandrovitch could see that he did not understand a single
word he was saying and was irritated.

He frowned and began explaining. Serioja had heard him
explain the same thing dozens of times, but could never
memorise it, because he understood it too well, just like the
statement that " suddenly " was an adverb. Serioja was
frightened as he looked at his father, but he could only wonder
whether he was going to make him repeat the same thing again
or not. He was so terrified at the thought that he could not
understand anything, but fortunately he was saved this time, for
his father went on to the Old Testament. Serioja narrated the
various events accurately, but when it came to explaining certain
of them, he was utterly unable to do so, though he had frequently
been punished for this very lesson. The most difficult part of all,

where he most wriggled and cut the table in his nervousness, was when they came to the antediluvian patriarchs. He could not remember a single one besides Enoch, who had been taken alive to heaven. At one time he had been able to remember them all, but now he could think of no other than Enoch, because Enoch happened to be his favourite personality in the whole of the Old Testament. The idea of his being taken alive to heaven brought up a long procession of ideas, to which he surrendered himself as he stood gazing at his father's watchchain and the buttons on his waistcoat.

He could never be brought to believe in death. It seemed to him absurd that people he loved could possibly die, least of all himself. He had often questioned those in whom he had a certain amount of confidence and found that even his nurse believed in death, though perhaps not quite so firmly as the others. But Enoch had not died, and so it was possible for others not to die.

" Why can't everybody be so good that God will take them up alive to heaven? " Serioja thought. " Bad people, that is, people whom He did not like, might die, but all the others would be like Enoch."

" Well, what patriarchs are there? "

" Enoch, Enos."

" You have said that before. This is very bad, Serioja, very bad. If you can't be interested enough to learn the things that a Christian ought to know, what will interest you? I am not pleased with you," his father continued, rising, " and Peter Ignatitch is not pleased with you." (This was his chief pedagogue.) " I am afraid I shall have to punish you."

Both his father and the pedagogue were dissatisfied with Serioja, and indeed he was very poor at his lessons. It was not that he was stupid; on the contrary, he was a good deal more intelligent than other boys whom the pedagogue set up as an example for him. According to the father, he did not wish to learn, but in reality he could not, because his soul was full of other more urgent demands than his father and the pedagogue made on him. These demands were in direct opposition to theirs, and he could do nothing but fight against them.

He was only nine years old, only a child, but he knew his own soul and guarded it as the eyelid guards the eye; without love no one could penetrate to that soul of his. His teachers complained that he would not learn, yet his soul was thirsting for knowledge. He learned from Kapitonitch, from his nurse, from Nadenka, from Vassily Lukitch, but not from them. The very waters that his father and the pedagogue had hoped would turn their mill-wheels had flown away from them and were working in another direction.

As a punishment he was forbidden to go to Nadenka's, but this turned out quite happily for Serioja. Vassily Lukitch happened to be in a very good humour and showed him how to make a wind-mill. He spent the whole evening trying to construct one, and dreaming of a wind-mill you could turn round on, either by catching hold of the sails or tying yourself to it. He never once thought of his mother till he got to bed, when he prayed that she might leave off hiding herself and come and see him to-morrow, on his birthday.

"Vassily Lukitch, do you know what I've been praying for?"

"To learn your lessons better."

"No."

"For toys."

"No; you can't guess. It's a lovely secret! If it comes true I will tell you. Have you guessed?"

"No, I haven't. You had better tell me," Vassily Lukitch said with a smile; he smiled very rarely. "Well, make haste and get into bed; I'm going to blow out the candle."

"The thing I've been praying for I can see better in the dark. There! I've nearly told you!" he said laughing merrily.

When the candle was taken away, Serioja heard and felt his mother. She was bending over him with a caressing light in her eyes. But soon a wind-mill appeared and then a penknife; everything became confused and he fell asleep.

XXVIII

WHEN they got to St. Petersburg, Anna and Vronsky put up at one of the best hotels; Vronsky separately on the lower floor, Anna upstairs with the child, the nurse, and her maid, in a large suite consisting of four rooms.

The day after his arrival Vronsky went to see his brother. He found his mother there, who had come up from Moscow on some business. Both she and his sister-in-law greeted him in the usual way, questioned him about his journey abroad, but did not refer to Anna. His brother, however, who came to see him

on the following day, was the first to ask about her. Vronsky informed him that he looked upon their union as a marriage and considered Anna his wife, and that he would make her his legal wife as soon as they could get a divorce. He begged him to tell his mother and Varia as much.

" I don't care what the world thinks or does," Vronsky said, " but if my relatives want to be on friendly terms with me, they must behave decently to my wife."

The elder brother, who always respected the judgment of the younger, was not sure whether he was right or wrong as society had not yet expressed an opinion. Nevertheless, he saw no objection to his going with Alexei to see Anna.

In his brother's presence Vronsky addressed Anna as " you " and treated her as an intimate friend, though it was understood that he knew of their relations. They mentioned her going to Vronsky's estate.

In spite of his experience as a man of the world, Vronsky was living in a strange state of delusion. He ought to have known that society was closed for him and Anna, but he kept on deceiving himself and imagining that people might have become more broad-minded. In any case the question was not yet settled. " Of course," he said to himself, " they would hardly receive us at court, but with intimate friends it is different; they ought to understand the thing in the right light."

It may be possible for a man to sit in one position with his legs under him for several hours at a time, if he knows there is nothing to prevent him moving if he wishes to, but the moment he thinks he is compelled to stay in that position, he will begin to feel cramped and want to move about. This was Vronsky's attitude towards society. Though in the depths of his heart he knew that its doors were closed to them, he kept on trying to see if there might not be some way in. He soon observed, however, that though society was prepared to welcome him personally, it was not at all anxious to welcome Anna. As in the game of cat and mouse, the hands that were raised for him immediately fell before her.

One of the first society ladies he happened to meet was his cousin Betsy.

" At last! " she greeted him joyfully. " Where is Anna? I am so glad you're back! Where are you staying? I can imagine how horrible St. Petersburg must seem to you after your beautiful time abroad and your lovely honeymoon in Rome. How about the divorce? Is it over? "

Vronsky noticed that Betsy grew less enthusiastic when she heard that there had been no divorce.

" I know I shall be condemned for it," she said, " but I'm going to see Anna. I really must. How long shall you remain here? "

Betsy called on Anna that very day, but her manner towards her had changed. She seemed to be proud of her boldness, and behaved as though Anna ought to appreciate the loyalty of her friendship. She did not stay more than ten minutes and merely spoke of society news.

" You have not told me yet when you expect the divorce," she said, just as she was leaving. " Of course I've ignored the conventions, but you'll find that others will give you the cold shoulder until you're married. But that is so simple to arrange now-a-days. *Ca se fait.* Are you going on Friday? What a pity we shall not be able to see each other again! "

From Betsy's tone Vronsky might have known what he had to expect from society, but he made yet another attempt in his own family. He had no hopes of his mother. He knew that though she had been enthusiastic during her early aquaintance with Anna, she was now merciless to her, because she considered her to have been the wreck of her son's career. But he placed great hopes in Varia, his brother's wife. It seemed to him that she would not condemn Anna, and would go and see her and receive her in her own house in that simple, determined way of hers.

On the day after his arrival he called to see her, and finding her alone, told her plainly what he wanted.

" You know how fond I am of you, Alexei," she said after having listened to what he had to say, " and that I would do anything I could for you, but I have been silent because I know that I can be of no use to either you or Anna Arkadyevna." She pronounced the name " Anna Arkadyevna " very distinctly. " You must not think that I sit in judgment upon her. I have never done so; I should probably have acted exactly the same in her place. I cannot go into details," she continued, gazing timidly into his face, " but I like to call things by their proper names. You want me to call on her and receive her—to get her into society again—but you know I can't possibly do it. My daughters are growing up and I am obliged to mix in society, if only for my husband's sake. Supposing even that I go and see Anna Arkadyevna, I should have to let her understand that I could not receive her here, at any rate not when she is likely to meet other people, and I'm sure she would be hurt. I cannot lift her up. . . . "

" But I don't consider that she has fallen any lower than numbers of other women whom you receive! " Vronsky interrupted her severely. He rose, seeing that his sister-in-law's decision was final.

" Alexei, don't be angry with me! Please try to understand that it's not my fault," Varia said, looking at him with a timid smile on her face.

" I am not angry," he said solemnly, " but I am doubly pained. It grieves me because this breaks our friendship—weakens it at any rate. Of course you understand that it can't be otherwise for me."

With these words he left her.

Vronsky now saw that all further attempts would be futile, and that he must try and avoid all communication with his former world for the rest of their stay in St. Petersburg, so as not to be subjected to unpleasantness and insult. The thing that annoyed him most of all was that his name and that of Alexei Alexandrovitch were on everybody's lips. It was impossible to begin a conversation without its turning on Alexei Alexandrovitch, or to go anywhere without meeting him. At any rate, so it seemed to Vronsky, just as a man with a sore finger keeps on thinking that he is fated to knock it against something.

The stay in St. Petersburg was the more oppressive because he noticed a strange, new mood in Anna that was utterly incomprehensible to him. One moment she would be affectionate, the next cold and distant. She seemed to be tormented by something she was trying to hide from him, and paid no attention to those slights and insults that poisoned his life. With her sensitiveness this puzzled him.

XXIX

ONE of Anna's aims in returning to St. Petersburg had been to see her son. From the day she left Italy the thought of a meeting with him had not ceased agitating her. And the nearer she drew to St. Petersburg the greater did the joy and significance of the meeting appear to her. She did not stop to consider how it could be brought about; it seemed such a simple and natural thing to see her boy when she should be in the same town with him. But as soon as she arrived in St. Petersburg, she suddenly realised her present position in society and saw that a meeting would be difficult to arrange.

She had now been in the town for two days. The thought of her son never left her for a moment, but she had not yet seen him. She felt she had no right to go straight to the house where she ran the risk of meeting Alexei Alexandrovitch; besides they might insult her and not let her in. The thought of writing to her husband was too painful to entertain; she could only be at peace so long as she did not think of him. She might have got to know when Serioja went out for his walks and tried to see him then, but this was not enough for her; she had so long been looking forward to this meeting, and had so much to tell him, and wanted to kiss and hug him to her heart's content. The only person likely to help her in this matter was Serioja's old nurse, but she was no longer living in Alexei Alexandrovitch's house. Thus two days passed in uncertainty and in hunting for the nurse.

On the third day, having heard of the close intimacy between Alexei Alexandrovitch and the Countess Lydia Ivanovna, she decided to write to her. The letter, in which she purposely appealed to her husband's magnanimity for permission to see her son, had cost her a good deal of labour. She knew that if he saw it he would continue his rôle of the magnanimous husband and not refuse her request.

She was frightfully pained when the hotel servant returned and informed her that there was no reply. She had never felt herself so humiliated as at the moment when the man gave her a detailed account of how he had waited, and been finally told that there would be no answer. She was humiliated, insulted, but she could not help seeing that, from her point of view, the countess was right. Her grief was all the stronger, because she felt herself so utterly alone; she did not wish to, nor could she have shared it with Vronsky. She knew that though he had been the cause of her unhappiness the question of her seeing her son was a secondary one for him. She knew that he would never be able to understand the depths of her sufferings, and that she would get to hate him for his indifferent tone were she to mention it to him. And as she feared this more than anything else in the world she concealed from him all her thoughts and feelings concerning her son.

She remained at home the whole of that day trying to think

out a means of seeing him, and finally decided to write to her husband. She was already composing the letter in her mind, when the Countess Lydia Ivanovna's was brought to her. The countess's silence had humbled her, but her letter, especially the things she read between the lines, infuriated her. This malice and spite seemed to her so little in comparison with her passionate love for her son, that she was filled with a feeling of anger against others and began to justify herself.

" This coldness is nothing but hypocrisy! " she said to herself. " They only want to insult me and torment the boy, but I will not give in! Not for anything! She is worse than I am; at any rate I do not stoop to lies." She decided at once that she would go straight to her husband's house to-morrow and see Serioja on his birthday. She would bribe the servants, do anything, so long as she could see her boy once more and destroy the monstrous lies with which they had surrounded him.

She went to a shop and bought some toys, then made out a plan of action. She would go early in the morning at about eight o'clock, before Alexei Alexandrovitch was up. She would have some money prepared in her hand for the porter and footman, and would say that she had come from Serioja's god-father to congratulate him, with strict orders to leave the toys on the boy's bed. At eight o'clock on the following morning Anna got out of a hired cab and rang the bell at the front door of her former home.

" Go and see what she wants. It's some lady," Kapitonitch said as, still undressed, in an overcoat and goloshes, he looked out of the window and caught sight of a lady, closely veiled, standing at the door. A young lad, the porter's assistant, whom Anna had never seen before, had no sooner opened the door than she stepped in, and taking a three-rouble note out of her muff hurriedly, she thrust it into his hand.

" Serioja . . . Sergei Alexaevitch," she said and turned to the stairs. Having glanced at the note the lad rushed after her and stopped her at the glass door.

" Whom do you want? " he asked.

She did not hear him and made no reply.

Observing the unknown lady's strange confusion, Kapitonitch himself came out and asked what she wanted.

" From Prince Skorodumov to Sergei Alexaevitch," she said.

" He is not up yet," the old porter said looking fixedly into her face. Anna had not expected that the unchanged aspect of the home in which she had lived for nine years, would affect her so powerfully. One after another, first happy then painful memories rose up in her soul, so that for a moment she forgot what she had come for.

" Will you be kind enough to wait a little? " Kapitonitch said, taking off her fur coat.

He looked closely into her face, and recognising her, bowed low.

" This way, your excellency," he said.

She wanted to say something, but her voice refused to utter a sound; she gave the old porter an entreating look and rushed up the stairs. Bending forward and doing his best not to catch his goloshes on the steps, Kapitonitch ran after her, trying to get ahead.

" The tutor is there; perhaps he's not yet dressed. Let me announce you."

Anna walked on without understanding a word the old man was saying to her.

" This way; to the left, please. I am sorry it is not very clean. He has been put into the little sitting-room," the porter said, panting. " Please wait a moment, your excellency; I will just look in." He got in front of her, opened the door, and disappeared behind it. Anna stood waiting.

" He has just awakened," the porter said coming out again.

But at this moment Anna heard the sound of a child yawning, and by this sound alone she recognised her son and seemed to see him standing before her.

" Let me in, let me in; go away! " she said and entered through the high door-way. To the right stood a bed, and on it sat a little boy with his night-shirt unbuttoned, stretching himself and yawning. He gave a happy smile as his lips came together again, and he fell back on the pillows.

" Serioja! " she called in a whisper, walking quietly up to the bed.

During the whole of her separation from him and during her recent outburst of love and longing she had imagined him as a boy of four, the age at which she had loved him most; now he was even bigger than when she had left him. How thin he looked, and what long arms and short hair he had! How changed he was! But it was he! There were the same lips, the same shaped head, soft cheeks, and broad shoulders.

" Serioja! " she called again, almost into the boy's ear.

He raised himself on his elbows, turned his tangled head from side to side as though looking for something, and opened his eyes. For a moment he looked in wonder at his mother, standing motionless before him, then a glad smile lighted up his face. He closed his eyes again and threw himself into her arms.

"Serioja! my dear boy!" she murmured, scarcely able to breathe, as she put her arms about his chubby little body.

" Mamma!" he said, moving about in her arms and trying to get closer to her.

Smiling sleepily, with his eyes still shut, he threw his little arms about her shoulders, and pressing close to her began rubbing his face against her neck and shoulders, exhaling that sweet odour of warmth and sleep that only children have.

" I knew it! I knew you would come on my birthday! I'll get up at once!" And saying this, he began to doze off again.

Anna devoured him with her eyes; she could see how much he had changed during her absence. His long bare legs that stretched under the bed-clothes, his thin cheeks, his short closely cropped curls on the back of his neck, that she used to be so fond of kissing, appeared to her now familiar, now strange. She passed her hand all over him, but could not utter a word; the tears choked her.

" Why are you crying, mamma?" he asked, completely awake by this time. " Mamma, why are you crying?" he repeated in a tearful voice.

" I? I won't cry any more . . . I am crying for joy. It's so long since I've seen you. But I won't cry, I won't," she said, swallowing her tears and turning away from him. " Well, you must get dressed now," she said, when she had regained her composure, and not letting go his hand, she sat down on a chair beside the bed on which his clothes were lying.

" How do you manage to dress without me? How . . ." She wanted to talk to him simply and naturally, but could not and had to turn away again.

" I don't wash in cold water; papa won't let me. And you haven't seen Vassily Lukitch, have you? He'll be here in a minute. Why, you're sitting on my clothes!"

Serioja burst out laughing. She looked at him and smiled.

" Mamma! you darling!" he cried, throwing his arms round her again, as though her simle had made him realise for the first time what had happened. " You mustn't keep that on," he said, taking off her hat, and at sight of her without it, he began hugging and kissing her again.

" What did you think about me? You did not think I was dead, did you?"

" I never believed it."

" You didn't? you darling! "

" I knew, I knew you would come! " he repeated, and taking her hand that was stroking his hair, he pressed the palm against his lips, and began showering kisses upon it.

XXX

MEANWHILE Vassily Lukitch, who did not know who the lady was, having come to the house after Anna had left, suddenly realised from their conversation that it was Serioja's mother, and could not make up his mind whether to go in or to inform Alexei Alexandrovitch. Finally, having come to the conclusion that it was his duty to wake Serioja at a given hour, no matter who happened to be there, whether his mother or any one else, he dressed, walked over to the door, and opened it.

But the scene within made him stop and reflect. He shook his head with a sigh and closed the door. " I'll wait another ten minutes," he said to himself as he gave a cough and wiped the tears from his face.

In the meantime a great commotion was going on in the servants' quarters. The news had spread like wild-fire that the mistress had come, that Kapitonitch had let her in, and that she was now in the nursery. They knew that the master was in the habit of going there at nine o'clock in the morning, that a meeting between husband and wife was impossible, and had to be prevented at all costs. Korney, the valet, went down to remonstrate with the porter for having admitted her, saying that he ought to be dismissed for it, at which Kapitonitch jumped up and shook his fist in his face.

" So you would not have let her in, would you! " he said. " I have lived here for ten years and have known nothing but kindness from her, and you would have me show her the door! You're very clever, aren't you? You had much better mind your own business and not rob master of his fur coats! "

" Shut up, you old fool! " Korney said contemptuously and turned to the old nurse who was just coming in. " Now what do you think of it, Marya Yerfimovna? He lets her in without saying a word to anybody and Alexei Alexandrovitch will be going into the nursery in a minute! "

" Oh dear, oh dear! " the nurse exclaimed. " You must

96

detain the master somehow, Korney Vassilitch, and I'll try to get her away. What a misfortune!"

When the nurse entered Serioja was telling his mother how he and Nadenka had fallen down a hill and rolled over and over, turning three somersaults. She could hear the sound of his voice, could see the play of his features, feel the touch of his hand, but could not understand a word he was saying. She had to go away, to leave him, that was the only thought that possessed her mind. She heard Vassily Lukitch's cough and footsteps and the nurse entering the room; she sat as though turned to stone, unable to move or to speak.

"My dear mistress!" the nurse exclaimed, going up to Anna and kissing her hands and shoulders. "What a joy the Lord has sent for our boy's birthday! You have not changed a bit."

"Why, nurse darling, I didn't know you were in the house," Anna said, coming to herself for a moment.

"I don't live here; I am living with my daughter; I only came to congratulate Serioja. Anna Arkadyevna, my dear!"

The nurse suddenly burst into tears and again began kissing her hand.

Serioja, beaming and smiling, stamped his bare little feet on the floor in his joy at seeing the nurse's tenderness for his mother.

"Mamma! nurse often comes to see me, and when she does . . ." he began, but stopped as he noticed the nurse whispering to his mother, and an expression of fear and shame coming over her face, so strange and unlike her.

She came up to him.

"My darling!" she said.

She could not say "good-bye," but the expression of her face said it and he understood. "My little Kutik!" she murmured. She had called him by this name when he was a baby. "You won't forget me? You . . ." but she could not utter another word.

How many times did she not think afterwards of all the things she might have said to him! But now she was quite unable to say anything. Serioja understood her. He understood that she was unhappy and that she loved him. He even understood what it was the nurse had whispered to her. He caught the words "regularly at nine o'clock," and he knew they referred to his father and that his father and mother must not meet. The only thing that puzzled him was that her face should express fear and shame. "It is not her fault; she has nothing to be afraid and ashamed of." He wanted to ask a question, to have it explained to him, but he dared not; he could see that his mother was suffering, and he was sorry for her. He could only press close to her and whisper, "Don't go away, he is not coming yet."

She pushed him from her a little, to look into his face, to find out if he understood what he was saying, but by the frightened expression of his face she could see that he was not only speaking of his father, but as it were asking her how he ought to behave towards him.

"Serioja, my dear," she said, "you must love him always. He is a thousand times better than I am and I have been much to blame before him. When you grow up you will understand."

"There is no one better than you!" he cried through his tears, and putting his arms about her shoulders he pressed her close to himself, his little arms trembling from the tension.

"My dear little one!" Anna murmured, and burst out crying in the same childlike way that he had done.

At this moment the door opened and Vassily Lukitch entered. Steps were heard from the other door, the nurse whispered, "He is coming!" and handed Anna her hat.

Serioja threw himself on the bed and burst out sobbing, covering his face with his hands. Anna took them away, and kissing him once more on his tear-stained face she walked quickly towards the door. Alexei Alexandrovitch was just coming in. He stopped when he caught sight of her and lowered his head.

Though she had declared but a moment ago that he was a thousand times better than she was, yet the look that she cast at him, taking in all the details of his figure, was full of loathing and hatred for having deprived her of her son. With a quick gesture, she lowered her veil and almost ran out of the room.

She had entirely forgotten the toys that she had bought with so much love and care on the day before, and took them back with her to the hotel.

XXXI

THOUGH Anna had been preparing herself for this meeting, she had never imagined that it would affect her so deeply. When she returned to her rooms at the hotel, she felt so dazed that she could not make out how she had got there. "Yes, it's all over and I am alone," she said to herself, dropping into a chair by the fireplace without removing her hat. She remained in that position, thinking, her eyes fixed vacantly at a bronze clock that was standing on a table between the windows.

A French maid, whom she had brought from abroad, came in to ask if she would like to change her dress, but Anna gazed at her in surprise. " Later," she said. A footman offered her coffee, but she took no notice of him.

The Italian nurse came in, bringing the baby, whom she had just dressed. The little one smiled when she saw her mother and stretched out her tiny chubby hands. Anna could not resist her. She could not help kissing her pink cheeks and pretty shoulders, nor giving her a finger that the child caught hold of with delight, nor pouting her lips that the little one took into her small toothless mouth. She danced her up and down on her knee, but the sensation the child produced in her was not the same as that she had felt for Serioja. Everything about the little thing was sweet, but she could not fill the wants of her heart. All the strength of her affection had been centred on her first-born, though he had been the child of a man whom she did not love. The little girl was born under the most painful circumstances and had not received a hundredth part of the care she had bestowed on Serioja. Besides, she was such a tiny mite, all hopes in her lay in the future, and Serioja was almost a man, with thoughts and feelings of his own. He understood, he loved, and even judged her, she thought, recalling his looks and words. And now she was separated from him for ever, not only physically, but morally, and nothing could ever be done to help it.

She gave the child back to the nurse, dismissed her, and opened a locket containing a portrait of Serioja, done when he had been about the same age as the little girl herself. She rose, removed her hat, and going over to the table took up an album in which were several photographs of Serioja, taken at different ages. She wanted to compare them all, and began by taking them out of the album. Only one remained, the last and best. It represented him sitting astride on a chair in a white shirt, with knitted brow and smiling lips. This was his most characteristic expression. She gave a nervous tug at the photograph with her small white fingers, but it refused to move from its place. There was no paper-knife on the table, so she took out another photograph (one of Vronsky's, taken in Rome, in a round hat and long hair) and pushed her son's out with it. " Here he is!" she said, glancing at Vronsky's photograph, and suddenly recalling that he had been the cause of all her trouble. She had not thought of him once that morning. But now, as she looked at that manly, noble face, so familiar and dear to her, a feeling of love and longing for him came over her.

"But where is he? Why does he leave me alone in my grief?" she asked herself, full of reproach, completely forgetting that she had purposely hidden from him everything concerning her son. She sent word to ask him to come to her, and sat waiting with a beating heart, thinking of how she would tell him all and how he would love and console her. The messenger returned saying that he had a visitor and had asked for permission to bring him along too. It was Prince Yashvin, who had just arrived in St. Petersburg.

"He is not coming alone, though he has not seen me since dinner yesterday," she thought. "Yashvin will be here and I shall not be able to tell him anything." And suddenly she began to wonder if he had ceased loving her. All the incidents of the last few days seemed to confirm her in her suspicions. He had insisted that they should occupy separate apartments; yesterday he had not dined at home; now he was coming with somebody, as though to avoid being alone with her.

"He must tell me; if I know the truth, then I shall know how to act," she said to herself, though she could not for a moment have imagined what she should do. It seemed to her that he had grown indifferent to her, and she was on the verge of despair. She rang for her maid and went into her dressing room. She took more pains over her toilet than usual, as though hoping to win him back by a becoming gown and head-dress.

There was a ring at the door before she was ready.

When she entered the drawing-room, not he, but Yashvin, met her gaze. Vronsky was standing by the table looking at Serioja's photograph that she had left lying there and did not immediately turn round.

"Give it me!" she said, snatching the photograph out of Vronsky's hand and giving him a significant look with her flashing eyes. Then turning to Yashvin, she said, "I think we've met before," putting her tiny little hand into his enormous one, as he stood there in a state of embarrassment, that seemed so out of keeping with his powerful form and rough face. "It was at last year's races I believe. This year we saw the races in the Corso at Rome. You don't like life abroad, do you?"

she added with a sweet smile. " You see, I know all your tastes and habits, though we've met so little."

" I am sorry to hear that, because my tastes are mostly of the bad kind," Yashvin said, biting his left moustache.

After they had sat talking for a few minutes, Yashvin observed that Vronsky was glancing at his watch, and asking Anna if she intended staying long in St. Petersburg he rose and took up his cap.

" Not long I think," she said, slightly confused, with a glance at Vronsky.

" Then shall I not see you again? " Yashvin asked, turning to Vronsky. " Where are you dining? "

" Come and dine with me," Anna said resolutely, as though annoyed with herself for her confusion. She blushed as she always did whenever she had to admit her situation for the first time to a stranger. " The cooking here is not very excellent, but you will have the consolation of seeing Alexei. Of all his regimental friends, he loves you the best."

" I shall be delighted," Yashvin said with a smile, from which Vronsky gathered that Anna had pleased him.

Yashvin took leave of her and went out, Vronsky remained behind.

" Are you going too? " Anna asked him.

" I am rather late already," he said. " All right; I'll soon catch you up," he called after Yashvin.

She took his arm, and not losing sight of his face for a moment, kept casting about in her mind for something to say that would detain him.

" Don't go yet, I have something to tell you," she said, taking his hand and pressing it against her neck. " You don't mind my having asked him to dinner, do you? "

" I'm very glad," he said with a calm smile that showed all his teeth. He kissed her hand.

" Alexei, you have not changed towards me, have you? " she asked, pressing his hand in both her own. " Alexei, I can't bear being here; when shall we go away? "

" Oh, quite soon. You can't think how difficult it has been for me, too," he said, drawing his hand away.

" All right, go, go! " she said, hurt and indignant, as she walked away from him quickly.

XXXII

WHEN Vronsky returned home, Anna was not there. The servants informed him that she had gone out with some lady, who had called soon after he left. Her disappearance now and the fact that she had gone out in the morning without telling him a word about it, coupled with the strange manner in which she had snatched away Serioja's photograph from him in Yashvin's presence, caused him to reflect. He decided that an explanation with her was absolutely essential, and he sat down to wait for her in the drawing-room. She came in shortly, but not alone; her old maiden aunt, the Princess Oblonsky, was with her. It was she who had called in the morning and had accompanied Anna to do some shopping. Anna tried not to notice the worried, beseeching expression in Vronsky's face, and began telling him gaily about all the purchases she had made. He felt there was something strange and unusual about her. There was an uneasy look in her sparkling eyes, something forced about her speech, and her quick, graceful movements, that had so fascinated him in the early days of their intimacy, were unnaturally nervous and alarming.

Dinner was laid for four. They were all assembled and were just about to go into the small dining-room when Tushkevitch called with a message from the Princess Betsy. She begged Anna to excuse her for not having called to bid her good-bye as she had not been well, and asked her to come and see her between half-past six and nine o'clock. Vronsky cast a look at Anna at this specified time, obviously fixed so that she should not meet any one there, but Anna did not seem to notice it.

" I'm sorry I cannot come between half-past six and nine," she said with a faint smile.

" The princess will be sorry too. Are you going to hear Patti? " Tushkevitch asked.

" Patti? Not a bad idea. I should like to go if I could get a box."

" I could get one for you," Tushkevitch said gallantly.

" Thanks," Anna said. " Won't you have some dinner with us? "

Vronsky gave a slight shrug of the shoulders. He simply failed to understand Anna's actions. Why had she brought back this old princess? Why had she asked Tushkevitch to stay to dinner? And, most surprising of all, why did she want him to get her a box? How could she think of going to hear Patti when she knew she would be bound to meet all her former friends and acquaintances there. He gave her a searching look, but she replied to him with that defiant, half desperate glance of hers that he had been unable to fathom. At dinner she was rather over gay and merry, and seemed to flirt with Tushkevitch and Yashvin. When they rose from table Tushkevitch went to see about the box, while Yashvin retired with Vronsky to his own rooms to smoke. In a short while Vronsky ran upstairs again. Anna was already dressed for the theatre in a light-coloured silk dress, trimmed with velvet and cut low in the front, that she had bought in Paris. The costly white lace on her head set off her beauty to advantage.

" Are you really going to the theatre? " he asked, trying not to look at her.

" Why do you ask in such a frightened tone? " she said, hurt that he did not look at her. " Why should I not go? "

She did not seem to understand the meaning of his words.

" Of course there is no reason why you should not," he said with a frown.

"Exactly," she said, ignoring the irony of his tone and calmly turning over her long perfumed gloves.

" Anna, for Heaven's sake, what is the matter with you? " he exclaimed in his effort to bring her to her senses, just as her husband had once done.

" I don't understand what you mean."

" You know you can't go there."

" Why? I am not going alone; the Princess Varvara is coming with me; she has gone home to dress."

He shrugged his shoulders in despair and amazement.

" But don't you know . . ." he began.

" I don't want to know! " she almost shouted; " I don't want to. I cannot repent of what I've done; never, never, never! If I had my time now, I should do it all over again. The only thing that matters to us, to you and to me, is whether we love each other. All other considerations have not the slightest importance. Why do we live apart here and not see anything of each other? Why can't I go? I love you, and everything else is a matter of indifference to me, so long as you have not changed," she said in Russian, looking at him with a strange, incomprehensible light in her eyes. " Why don't you you look at me? "

He turned and looked at her. He saw her in all her beauty

and elegance, but now that very beauty and elegance irritated him.

"You know quite well that my feelings for you cannot change, but I beg you, I implore you not to go," he said in French with a tender note of entreaty in his voice, but with coldness in his gaze.

She did not hear his words, she only saw his cold glance.

"But tell me, why can't I go?" she asked irritably.

"Because it may cause you . . ." He hesitated.

"I don't understand. Yashvin *n'est pas compromettant*, and the Princess Varvara is no worse than others. And here she is."

XXXIII

FOR the first time in his life Vronsky experienced a feeling of anger and annoyance towards Anna. He failed to understand how she could thus purposely ignore her situation. His annoyance increased by the very fact that he could not tell her the cause of it. Had be been able to tell her frankly what he thought, he would have said, "For you to appear at the theatre in that costume, with the princess, who is notorious to every one, is like throwing down the gauntlet to public opinion, acknowledging yourself a lost woman, and renouncing all hopes of ever getting into society again." But he could not say that to her.

"How can she fail to see it? What is the matter with her?" he asked himself, with a feeling that his respect for her was diminishing, while the consciousness of her beauty was increasing.

He went back frowning to his room, where he found Yashvin with his long legs stretched out on a chair, drinking brandy and soda.

He ordered the same for himself.

"You were talking of Landovsky's Mighty; a fine horse that; I should advise you to buy him," Yashvin said, looking into Vronsky's scowling face. "He has slanting haunches, but his head and legs are splendid."

"I think I shall have him," Vronsky replied.

He was interested in their talk about horses, but he did not for a moment forget Anna, and kept on listening to the sounds in the corridor and looking at the clock on the mantelpiece.

" Anna Arkadyevna asked me to inform you that she has gone to the theatre," a servant announced.

Yashvin drank another glass of brandy and soda, got up, and began buttoning his coat.

" Well, shall we go? " he asked with a faint smile beneath his moustache, showing that he understood the cause of Vronsky's depression, but did not attach any importance to it.

" I am not going," Vronsky said darkly.

" But I must; I promised. Well, good-bye. Why not come to the stalls? Take Krasinsky's place," he added, as he walked towards the door.

" I won't come; I have some work to do."

" With a wife there is trouble; with a woman who is not a wife, it is worse still," Yashvin thought as he left the hotel.

When Vronsky was left alone he got up and began pacing the room.

" What is to-day? It will be the fourth performance I think. . . . Yegor and his wife will be there, and mother perhaps; the whole of St. Petersburg. She has probably got there by now, taken off her cloak and entered her box in the blazing light. Tushkevitch, Yashvin, and the Princess Varvara. . . ." He pictured the scene to himself. " But what am I doing? Am I afraid, or have I transferred the guardianship to Tushkevitch. Whichever way you look at it, it's stupid, ridiculous. . . . Why on earth did she place me in such a position? " he asked himself with a wave of the hand.

With this motion he accidentally struck the table on which stood a bottle of brandy and soda water, and almost knocked it over. He made an effort to steady it, but merely struck it again, and in his anger he kicked it over and rang the bell.

" If you want to stay with me," he said to his valet who entered, " you must understand your business. Mind this doesn't happen again! clear it up! "

Feeling himself innocent the valet wanted to justify himself, but seeing from his master's face that all that was required of him was to keep quiet, he got down on his hands and knees and began picking up the pieces of broken glass.

" That is not your work! Send a servant to do it and get my dress clothes ready! "

.   .   .   .

Vronsky got to the theatre at half-past eight. The performance was in full swing. The attendant, taking off his fur

coat, recognised him and addressed him as " your excellency."
In the brilliantly lighted corridor there were only the theatre
attendants and two footmen, with cloaks over their arms,
listening at the door. From within issued the sounds of the
orchestra and a woman's voice. The door opened and the
sounds grew louder, but it instantly closed again, and Vronsky
knew from the applause that the song had come to an end.
When he entered the brightly illuminated hall the noise and
commotion still continued. On the stage the prima donna,
glittering with her bare shoulders and diamonds, was bowing and
smiling, and with the help of the tenor, who was holding her
hand, she collected the numerous bouquets that came flying
over the footlights. She walked over to a man with shining
hair, who stretched out his long arms in his efforts to hand her
something across the footlights. The whole house rose, shouting
and clapping their hands. The conductor of the orchestra came
to their assistance, and adjusted his white necktie. Vronsky
stopped and began surveying the audience. That night he was
less interested than ever in the stage, the noise, and the crowd of
spectators filling the theatre.

There were the same ladies in the boxes, with the same
officers in the background, the same gaily dressed women, the
same dress coats, the same dirty crowd in the gallery. In all
that mass, in boxes and stalls, there were only about forty
people that represented *society*, and to these Vronsky turned
his attention.

The act had just ended when he came in, so he did not go to
his brother's box, but walked down the first row of the stalls
towards Serpuhovsky, who was standing near the footlights
and beckoning to him from a distance.

Vronsky had not seen Anna, and purposely did not look for
her, but he knew from the direction in which all eyes were
turned where she was to be found. He gazed around, expecting
the worst; he sought Alexei Alexandrovitch with his eyes, but
to his joy he was not in the theatre that evening.

" How little of the soldier there is left in you," Serpuhovsky
said to him. " One would take you for a diplomat, an artist,
or something of the sort."

" Yes, I've begun wearing these clothes since my return from
abroad," Vronsky said with a smile, taking out his opera-glasses.

" That is where I envy you. When I return from abroad and
put on these " (he pointed to his epaulets) " I cannot help
regretting my lost liberty."

Serpuhovsky had long washed his hands of Vronsky's military career, but he still liked him, and was particularly nice to him that evening.

" What a pity you missed the first act."

Vronsky, while listening with one ear, turned his opera-glasses to the dress circle, then began examining the boxes. Anna's proud, beautiful head, in a frame of lace, caught his eye. She was sitting in the fifth box within twenty paces of him, near a lady in a sort of turban, and a bald-headed old man with an angry expression on his face. Anna was in front of the box, slightly turned from them, talking to Yashvin. The poise of her shapely head on her lovely round shoulders, the restrained, animated expression of her eyes and face, reminded him of what she had looked like at the ball in Moscow, but now the sense of her beauty impressed him differently. There was no longer any mysteriousness in his feelings towards her, and though she attracted him more than ever, her beauty at that moment offended him. He was not looking at her, but he felt that she had seen him.

When he turned his glasses towards her box again, he noticed that the Princess Varvara was unusually red in the face, that she laughed unnaturally, and kept on glancing into the next box. Anna was beating her folded fan on the plush edge of the box and trying to look indifferent. Yashvin looked as though he had just lost heavily at cards. He sat scowling, biting his left moustache, and casting side-long glances in the direction of the neighbouring box.

In that box, on the left, were the Kartasovs. Vronsky knew them, and knew too that Anna was acquainted with them. Kartasov's wife, a small, thin woman, was standing with her back to Anna, putting on a cloak that her husband had handed to her. Her face was pale and angry and she was speaking in an excited tone of voice. Kartasov, a stout bald man, kept on looking at Anna, evidently wishing to bow to her, and trying to calm his wife. Anna did not look in their direction. She was sitting back, talking to Yashvin, whose closely cropped head was bent down to her. Kartasov eventually went out without bowing and the box was left empty.

Vronsky could not make out what had happened, but he felt that it was something humiliating for Anna. He could tell that by the proud look on her face as she sat there gathering up her last forces to try and appear indifferent. And she succeeded. Those who did not know her and her circle, who had not heard all

107

the expressions of indignation and surprise on the part of the women at her daring in appearing before the world in all her beauty and gorgeous attire, would never have dreamed that she was experiencing the feelings of a criminal placed in the pillory.

Though he did not know what had happened, Vronsky was troubled and decided to go into his brother's box to see if he could find out. As he walked towards the door he caught sight of his old colonel, who was standing near by talking to some friends. Vronsky heard Karenin's name mentioned, and noticed that his colonel was motioning him to come up, with a significant look at the two men beside him.

" Ah, Vronsky! When will you come to the regiment? We must have a banquet in your honour. You know you belong to us through and through," the colonel greeted him.

" Sorry I shall not be able to this time; some other day I hope," Vronsky said. He left them instantly and ran up to his brother's box.

The old countess his mother, with her iron grey curls, was in the box; Varia and the young Princess Sorokin were walking about in the lobby. Varia led the princess back to the box, and coming out took her brother-in-law's arm and instantly began talking about the thing that interested him. Vronsky had never seen her in such a state of agitation.

" I think it was mean and revolting, and Madame Kartasova had no right whatever to behave as she did. Madame Karenina . . ." she began.

" What has happened? "

" Haven't you heard? "

" Of course I should be the last to hear anything."

" I don't think there could be a more spiteful woman than that Kartasova creature! "

" But what has she done? "

" My husband told me. . . . She has insulted Madame Karenina. Kartasov said something to her across the box and his wife made a scene. They say she said something offensive in a loud voice and went out."

" Count, your mother wishes to speak to you," the Princess Sorokin said, appearing at the door of the box.

" I have been waiting for you all the time," his mother said, with a sarcastic smile, as he entered. " We hardly ever see you now."

Vronsky saw that she could hardly contain her joy.

" Good evening, mother; I was just coming to you," he said coldly.

" Why don't you go and *faire la cour à Madame Karénine ?* " she added when the Princess Sorokin had withdrawn a little. *Elle fait sensation. On oublie la Patti pour elle.*"

" Mamma, I have asked you not to speak of her," he said with a frown.

" I am merely saying what every one is saying."

Vronsky made no reply, and after exchanging a few words with the Princess Sorokin he went out. At the door he came across his brother.

" Oh, Alexei," his brother greeted him; " how awful! The woman is a fool, nothing more . . . I was about to go to Anna Arkadyevna; let us go together."

Vronsky did not hear him. He ran downstairs as fast as he could. He felt as though he had to do something, but did not know what. He was indignant with Anna for having placed them both in such a false position, yet was full of pity for her suffering. When he got to her box, Stremov was standing there talking to her.

" There are no more tenors. *Le moule en est brisé.*"

Vronsky bowed to her and exchanged greetings with Stremov.

" I think you came late and missed the best aria," Anna said with a sarcastic look at Vronsky.

" I am a poor judge," he said, returning her gaze sternly.

" Like Prince Yashvin," she said with a smile. " He finds that Patti sings too loud. Thank you," she added, as Vronsky picked up the programme she dropped and handed it back to her. At this moment her beautiful face twitched. She got up and went to the back of the box.

Noticing during the next act that her box was empty, Vronsky left the theatre, much to the disgust of the people near him, whom he had to disturb, and went home.

Anna was already there. When he came in he found her sitting in the same attire she had worn at the theatre, staring straight before her. She must have dropped into the first chair that came to hand. She looked up as he entered and instantly assumed her former attitude.

" Anna," he said.

" It is you, you who are to blame! " she cried angrily, as she stood up.

" I begged you, I implored you not to go. I knew it would be unpleasant. . . ."

"Unpleasant!" she shouted. "It was awful! As long as I live I shall never forget it. She said it was a disgrace to sit next to me!"

"The words of a foolish woman," he said; "but why risk and provoke . . ."

"I hate that self-possession of yours. You should not have brought me to this. If you had loved me . . ."

"Anna! what has my love got to do with it?"

"If you had loved me as I love you, if you had suffered as I suffer. . . ." She looked at him with an expression of fear.

He felt sorry for her, but he was angry all the same. He began assuring her of his love, as he could see that that was the only thing that would calm her. He did not reproach her in words, but he reproached her in his heart. And those assurances of his love, that seemed to him so hackneyed and commonplace that he was ashamed to utter them, she drank in greedily. They were like balm to her soul.

On the following day, completely reconciled, they left for the country

PART VI

I

DARYA ALEXANDROVNA and her children were spending the summer at Pokrovsky with her sister, Kitty Levin. The house on her own estate had completely fallen to pieces, so that Levin and his wife persuaded her to come and stay with them. Stepan Arkadyevitch only too readily approved of the arrangement. He regretted that his official duties prevented him from passing the summer with his family in the country, but said that he would be delighted to run down and see them for a day or two from time to time. Besides the Oblonskys, their children and governess, the old princess was at the Levin's too, for she considered it her duty to look after her inexperienced daughter in the condition she was in. Then there was Varenka, Kitty's friend from abroad, who had fulfilled her promise and come to see her.

All these people were relatives and friends of Levin's wife, and though he liked them all, he nevertheless could not help regretting his old Levin world and order, that had become submerged by the influx of the " Shcherbatsky element," as he put it to himself. Sergei Ivanovitch was their only guest from among his own relatives, but as he was more a Kosnishev than a Levin, the Levin spirit was completely suppressed.

Levin's old house, so long deserted, had now scarcely an unoccupied room. Each day, before seating herself at table, the old princess would count the guests to make sure they were not thirteen, and would invariably remove some grandchild to a separate table. And Kitty, who attended carefully to her household, had no end of trouble about procuring chickens, ducks, and turkeys, of which a large number were consumed, for though it was summer, the appetites of both young and old were excellent.

The whole family were at table. Dolly's children, their governess, and Varenka were planning to go out picking mushrooms. Sergei Ivanovitch, who was worshipped by everybody alike on account of his wit and learning, surprised the whole company by his interest in the mushroom expedition.

" Let me come too; I am very fond of gathering mushrooms,"
he said, looking at Varenka. " An excellent occupation I
think."

" We shall be delighted," Varenka said with a blush.

Kitty and Dolly exchanged glances. That Sergei Ivanovitch
should want to go mushroom gathering with Varenka was a
further confirmation of a suspicion they had both entertained
regarding them. Kitty hastened to make some remark to her
mother lest their glances should be observed.

After dinner Sergei Ivanovitch sat down in the drawing-room
by the window with his cup of coffee, and while continuing a
conversation with his brother, kept on watching the door for
the children to appear on their mushroom expedition. Levin
sat down by the window near his brother. Kitty stood beside
him. She was evidently waiting for their rather uninteresting
conversation to come to an end in order to say something to her
husband.

" You have changed in many things for the better since you
married," Sergei Ivanovitch said with a smile at Kitty, evidently
taking little interest in their conversation, " but you have
remained true to your passion for defending the most paradoxical
ideas."

" Katya, you mustn't stand," Levin said to his wife with a
significant look, as he moved up a chair.

" However, I've no time to talk any more now," Sergei
Ivanovitch added, as the children came running out.

Tania came at full gallop towards Sergei Ivanovitch, waving
his hat in her hand. She approached him boldly, with her
sparkling eyes, so like her father's, and made a motion as though
she wished to put it on for him, softening her daring with a
timid smile. " Varenka is waiting," she said, putting the hat
on his head carefully, having concluded from his smile that she
might do so.

Varenka was standing at the door in a yellow print dress with
a white kerchief on her head.

" I'm coming, I'm coming, Varvara Andraevna," Sergei
Ivanovitch said, finishing his coffee quickly and putting his
handkerchief and cigar-case into his pockets.

" Isn't Varenka charming!" Kitty said to her husband the
moment Sergei Ivanovitch rose, loudly enough for the latter
to hear. " She is perfectly lovely, I think. Varenka!" she
called, " shall you be in the mill wood? We will come for you."

" You forget your condition, my dear," the old princess

remonstrated, coming in quickly. " You really must not shout like that."

Hearing Kitty's call and her mother's reproach, Varenka rushed up to Kitty with a light, rapid step. The colour in her face, her rapid movements—everything about her showed that something unusual was taking place in her. Kitty knew what it was and scrutinised her friend closely. She had called her for no other reason than that she might bless her mentally for the important event that she felt was about to take place in the wood.

" Varenka, I shall be very happy if a certain thing happens," she whispered as she kissed her.

" Are you coming too? " Varenka asked Levin, confused, and pretending not to have heard Kitty's words.

" Only as far as the threshing-barn."

" What have you to do there? " Kitty asked.

" I must examine the new carts and see what the men are doing," he replied. " Where will you be? "

" On the terrace."

II

ALL the ladies were assembled on the terrace. They usually liked sitting there after dinner, but to-day there was an extra special reason for their doing so. In addition to the making of baby garments with which all were occupied just now, jam-making was going on in a method entirely new to Agafia Mihailovna, which consisted in not adding water to the fruit. Kitty introduced this new method which had been practised in her own home. Agafia Mihailovna, to whom the jam-making was entrusted, though she considered that a Levin could not possibly do anything bad, nevertheless had little faith in the new method and put water into the strawberries, insisting that it was impossible to do them otherwise. Now the raspberry jam was to be made in the presence of all, and Agafia Mihailovna was to be convinced that it would come out right without water.

Agafia Mihailovna, flushed, with dishevelled hair and sleeves tucked up, exposing her lean arms, was stirring the pot over the fire, with a cross gloomy expression on her face, wishing in her heart of hearts that the jam would thicken before the raspberries were done. The princess, who felt that Agafia Mihailovna's anger was no doubt directed against herself, as the principal advisor in the matter of jam-making, was trying to look unconcerned, as though the raspberries did not interest her, but kept on casting stealthy glances at the fire.

" I always give my maids cheap dresses," the princess was saying. " Hadn't you better take off the scum, my dear? " she added, turning to Agafia Mihailovna. " You mustn't do it, Kitty; it's too hot."

" I will," Dolly said. She got up and began skimming the jam carefully. " How the children will enjoy it with their tea," she thought, as she looked at the plate of frothy mixture with streaks of red syrup that she had skimmed off, and recalled how she used to love it as a child.

" Stiva thinks it is much better to give them money," Dolly remarked " (they had been talking about the best kind of presents to give to servants), " but . . ."

" How can you give money! " both the princess and Kitty exclaimed in one voice. " They appreciate a little present much more."

" Last year I remember buying a dress for Matriona Simionovna . . . not poplin, it was something like this," the princess said.

" Oh, yes, she wore it on your birthday."

" It was a dear little pattern, so simple and nice. I should have had a dress of it myself if she had not already got one. It was something like Varenka's; cheap and pretty."

" I've finished now," Dolly said, letting the syrup drip off the spoon. " Boil it a little longer, Agafia Mihailovna. When the bubbles come then it will be ready."

" These awful flies! " Agafia Mihailovna said angrily. " It won't be any better," she added.

" Oh, how sweet! don't frighten it! " Kitty exclaimed suddenly as a sparrow alighted on the balustrade and began pecking at the stalk of a raspberry that was lying on it.

" You had better move away from the fire," her mother cautioned her.

" *A propos de* Varenka," Kitty said (they had been talking in French all the time so that Agafia Mihailovna should not understand them), " you know, mamma, what I am expecting to-day, don't you? It would be so nice if it would come to pass! "

" Really, you're getting quite a match-maker! " Dolly said. " How cleverly she brings them together! "

" Well, what do you think, mamma? "

" What is there to think? He " (she meant Sergei Ivanovitch) "could have made the best match in Russia at one time, but of course he is not so young as he was. Still, I know that even now he could. . . . She is very nice, but he could have . . ."

"No, mamma, they couldn't be better suited for one another. In the first place she's sweet!" Kitty said, beginning to enumerate Varenka's qualities on her fingers.

"He certainly likes her," Dolly put in.

"And then the position he occupies in society is such that he needs neither fortune nor social position from his wife. All he wants is a nice, quiet girl . . ."

"Yes, he could be quiet with her," Dolly confirmed.

"And a girl that loves him as I'm sure Varenka does. It would be so nice if it came off! I am longing for them to come back from the wood. I shall be able to tell by their eyes if anything has happened. I should be so glad? What do you think, Dolly?"

"You mustn't excite yourself; you really mustn't, dear," her mother said.

"I'm not, mamma. I feel certain he'll propose to her to-day."

"How strange it is when a man proposes . . . there seems a sort of barrier and then it breaks down," Dolly said, smiling pensively, as she recalled her past with Stepan Arkadyevitch.

"Mamma, how did papa propose to you?" Kitty asked suddenly.

"Nothing very unusual happened; it was all very simple," the princess replied, but her face lighted up at the recollection.

"But how did he do it? You must have loved each other before you were permitted to speak."

Kitty experienced a special charm in being able to talk about these important feminine questions to her mother, as to an equal.

"Of course he loved me. He used to come and see us in the country."

"But how was it decided, mamma?"

"You seem to think that you've invented something new, but I assure you it was always the same. It was decided by looks and smiles . . ."

"You've expressed it exactly, mamma!" Dolly said. "Looks and smiles . . ."

"But what did he say?"

"What did Kostia say to you?"

"He wrote it down with a piece of chalk. It always struck me as very wonderful that," she added.

And the three women began musing about the same thing. Kitty was the first to break the silence. She recalled the winter before her marriage and her strange infatuation for Vronsky.

"There is just one thing, that old love affair of Varenka's—I had meant telling Sergei Ivanovitch in order to prepare him," she remarked, by some natural connection of ideas. "You know men are so jealous of our past."

"Not all men," Dolly said. "You are judging by your own husband. I suppose he is still bothered about Vronsky, is he not?"

"Yes," Kitty replied pensively, a smile shining in her eyes.

"But I can't understand what it is that troubles him," the princess put in, defending the maternal cares she had spent on her daughter.

"Is it that Vronsky paid you attentions? That happens to every girl."

"We were not talking of that," Kitty said with a blush.

"And when I wanted to speak to him," the princess continued, "you yourself would not let me. Do you remember?"

"Mamma!" Kitty implored, with a pained expression on her face.

"Nowadays girls take things into their own hands, but we should never have let him go farther than was proper; otherwise I should have challenged him myself. But, my dear, you mustn't excite yourself; do try and keep calm."

"I am quite calm, mamma."

"What a good thing it was for Kitty that Anna arrived on the scene," Dolly observed; "and how unfortunately it turned out for her. The tables have turned," she added, struck by a certain thought. "Anna considered herself happy then and Kitty unhappy; now it is exactly the opposite. I often think of her."

"A nice person to think of! She is a mean, contemptible, heartless woman," the princess said. She could never forgive Anna for having carried off Vronsky.

"Why speak of it?" Kitty asked with annoyance. "I never think of it and don't want to think of it . . . don't want to think of it," she repeated as she listened to her husband's steps coming up the terrace.

"What is it you don't want to think of?" Levin asked as he drew near them.

No one ventured to reply and he did not repeat his question.

"I am sorry to have disturbed you," he said, taking them all in at a glance and realising that they had been discussing something they would not have cared to talk about in his presence.

For a moment he sympathised with Agafia Mihailovna in her dislike of the Shcherbatsky influence down to the new method of making jam. He smiled though, and went up to Kitty.

" Well, how do you feel? " he asked in a tone in which every one spoke to her now.

" I'm all right, thanks," Kitty replied with a smile. " How did you get on? "

" The new carts hold twice as much as the old ones. Shall we go for the children? I have ordered the trap to be harnessed."

" Do you mean to drive Kitty in a trap? " the princess asked reproachfully.

" We can drive very slowly, princess."

The princess was hurt that Levin did not call her mamma, as he should have done, but though he liked her, he could never bring himself to call her that, out of respect to the memory of his dead mother.

" Why not come with us, mamma? " Kitty said.

" It annoys me to see your carelessness."

" Very well, then, I'll walk. It will do me good."

Kitty rose and took her husband's arm.

" Yes, but you must take it gently," the princess cautioned her.

" Well, Agafia Mihailovna, is the jam done? " Levin asked with a smile, wishing to cheer her up. " How did it come out in the new way? "

" I suppose it's all right, but we should think it over-boiled."

" It will keep better like that, Agafia Mihailovna. You know our ice is melted and we have no suitable place to keep it in," Kitty said. She had understood her husband's intention and turned to her with the same feeling that he had done. " Your pickles, now, are so good that mamma says she has never eaten any like them," she added with a smile, trying to adjust Agafia Mihailovna's kerchief.

Agafia Mihailovna looked at her angrily.

" You needn't console me, madame. When I look at you and him together, I am happy," she said.

Kitty was touched.

" Come and help us gather mushrooms; I am sure you know all the good places," she said.

Agafia Mihailovna smiled and shook her head, as much as to say, " I should like to be angry with you, but I can't."

" Please take my advice and soak the paper in rum before you tie it down," the princess said. " It will keep perfectly like that even without ice."

III

KITTY was very glad to be left alone with her husband. She had not failed to observe the expression of grief that came over his face when, coming on to the terrace, he had asked what they were talking about and received no reply.

When they started out on foot, ahead of the rest, and got out of sight of the house, on the beaten, dusty road, strewn with ears of rye, she leaned more heavily on his arm and pressed it closely against her side. He had already forgotten the unpleasant impression of a moment ago and experienced that delicious sensation of her proximity, entirely free from sensuality, now that the consciousness of her pregnancy was always with him. There was nothing to talk about, but he wanted to hear the sound of her voice, that had changed with her new condition, just as her glance had done. There was a gentle seriousness in the one and in the other, such as is often seen in people who constantly dwell upon one particular theme.

" You're not tired, dear, are you ? Lean on me more heavily," he said.

" No thanks; I am so glad of an opportunity to be alone with you. I confess that though I like having them all with me, I regret the lovely winter evenings we had all to ourselves."

" It was jolly then, but this is better. It is all better," he said, pressing her hand.

" Do you know what we were talking about when you came in ? "

" About the jam, no doubt."

" The jam and something else too. We were talking about how men propose."

" Oh ! " Levin said, listening more to the sound of her voice than her words, and carefully noticing the road through the wood, so as to avoid any uneven places where she was likely to stumble.

" And also about Sergei Ivanovitch and Varenka. Have you noticed anything ? I should be so glad if they fixed it up between them," she continued. " What do you think of it ? " She looked into his face.

" I really don't know," Levin replied with a smile. "Sergei is a marvel to me in that respect. I told you about . . ."

" Oh, yes, about his having been in love with a girl who died."

" I was quite a child then, but I've heard about it. I remember him well in those days; he was awfully nice. But since then, as far as I can make out, he does not seem to care for women. Of course he is always amiable and likes some that he meets, but you somehow feel that he does not look upon them as women."

" Yes, but with Varenka . . . It seems to me there is . . ."

" Perhaps, but you ought to know him; he is a very peculiar man. His life is entirely a spiritual one. His soul is too pure and high to . . ."

" But do you think this would lower him? "

" Oh, no; but he has grown so accustomed to his spiritual life that he would never be able to adjust himself to a material existence, and Varenka is material after all."

Levin had long become used to expressing his thoughts boldly, without taking the trouble of clothing them in precise words. He knew that, loving him as she did, his wife would understand him by mere hints. Just now she had fully grasped his meaning.

" There is not the same materialism about her that there is about me, for instance. I know he would never have been able to love me, but she is so spiritual. . . ."

" My dear, he loves you very much; I am glad to think that all my people love you."

" Of course he is nice to me, but . . ."

" It is not the same as with Nikolai though . . . you and he took a liking to each other at first sight. I can't help reproaching myself sometimes for forgetting him," he added. " What a tragic man he was! and yet he had so many good qualities and possibilities in him. . . . What were we talking about? " he asked after a pause.

" Then you think that Sergei Ivanovitch cannot fall in love? " Kitty asked interpreting what he had said in her own language.

" That was not exactly my meaning," Levin replied with a smile. " He has not the weakness that is necessary. . . . I've always envied him, even now, happy as I am."

" Do you envy him for not being able to fall in love? "

" I envy him because he is better than I am," Levin said smiling. " He does not live for himself; his life is guided by duty. That is why he can be so serene and contented."

119

"And you? Kitty asked with a playful irony, looking at him with an affectionate smile.

She could not have explained the course of ideas that produced that smile, but she felt somehow that her husband was not altogether sincere in his excessive praise of his brother and depreciation of himself. She knew that this insincerity arose from the great love that he bore him, from the fact that he reproached himself for being too happy, and from an ever-present desire to become better. She liked all this about him, and that was why she smiled.

"And you? What makes you discontented? " she asked with the same smile.

Her lack of faith in his discontent amused him, and unconsciously he tried to get her to express her reasons for it.

"I am happy, but dissatisfied with myself . . ." he began.

"How can you be dissatisfied if you're happy? "

"How shall I explain? In my heart of hearts I desire nothing more than that you should not stumble against anything . . . you mustn't jump like that, dear," he said reproachfully, cutting short his remarks as she made a rapid motion in stepping over a branch that lay across the road; "but when I look into myself and begin comparing myself with others, especially with my brother, it makes me feel that I am no good."

"But why? " Kitty persisted, still with the same smile. "Don't you do things for others too? What about the farm and your book? "

"No, that is not the thing," he said, "and it's your fault, you know," he added, pressing her hand. " I don't take it seriously enough. Now if I could love my work as I love you . . . but lately I've been doing it as a sort of lesson."

"And what about papa? " Kitty asked; "do you think him bad too, because he does nothing for the general good? "

"Oh, no. But you want to have his simplicity and kindness of heart, and I haven't. I do nothing and am conscience-stricken. It is your fault, my dear. Before I had you and *this* was not " (he gave a glance at her figure and she understood), " I used to put all my energies into my work; now I can't. I look upon it as a sort of task, a lesson, a pretence. . . ."

"Would you like to change places with Sergei Ivanovitch? " Kitty asked. "Would you prefer to be able to work for the common good, and love that task of yours as he does, and nothing more? "

"Of course not," Levin replied. "I am so happy that I

understand nothing. Do you really think he'll propose to-day? " he asked after a pause.

" I do and I don't; only I should like him to. Stop a moment." She bent down and picked a daisy from the side of the road. " Now count and let us see if he will," she said handing him the flower.

" He will, he will not," Levin began, pulling off the little white petals one by one.

" No, no! " Kitty cried excitedly, seizing his hand; " you've pulled off two at once."

" Very well, we won't count this tiny one," Levin said, tearing off a little half-grown petal.

" But I say, here comes the trap."

" Aren't you tired, Kitty? " the princess called.

" Not a bit."

" Get in, if the horses are quiet and we'll drive slowly."

But it was not worth while. They were quite near their destination and all walked the rest of the way on foot.

IV

VARENKA, with her white kerchief over her black hair, surrounded by the children to whom she was talking merrily, and apparently agitated by the possibility of a declaration from a man whom she loved, looked exceedingly attractive. Sergei Ivanovitch was walking beside her and kept glancing at her with admiration. As he gazed at her and recalled all the sweet things she had said and all the good things he had heard about her, he became more and more conscious of the fact that the sentiment he was feeling towards her was like something he had already experienced in his youth, a long time ago. The joy of being near to her increased step by step. He bent down and picked a mushroom which he threw into her basket, and in doing so their glances met. A joyous flush overspread her face. He grew embarrassed and smiled with a smile that spoke too much.

" If that's the case," he said to himself, " I must think it over and make up my mind. I am not a boy to abandon myself to the infatuation of the moment."

" I am going off to gather mushrooms on my own account," he said, " otherwise my contributions will be unnoticed." And he walked away from the edge of the wood where they were, over the soft low grass between the sparse trees, until he entered a thicket, where between the silvery birch trunks the grey stems of aspens and hazel-bushes could be seen. After he had gone about forty paces he stopped by a furze bush in full bloom, whence he could not be seen. Around him everything was quiet. Only above the tops of the birches, under which he was standing, the buzzing of flies and humming of bees could be heard, and now and again the voices of the children were borne to him. Suddenly, Varenka's contralto voice was heard not far away calling Grisha, and a joyous smile lighted up Sergei Ivanovitch's face. Becoming conscious of this smile, he shook his head disapprovingly and took out a cigar. He attempted to strike a match on the trunk of a tree, but for a long time he was unable to do so, as the soft bark stuck to the phosphorus and would not let it catch fire. He succeeded at last and the fragrant smoke of his cigar rose high above the drooping branches of the birch-trees. Watching the stream of smoke, Sergei Ivanovitch strolled on slowly, meditating upon his condition.

"And why not?" he thought. "If it were only a burst of passion, if I felt that this attraction (I suppose I may say mutual attraction) ran counter to the whole composition of my life, if I felt that in abandoning myself to it I was renouncing my calling and duty . . . but there is nothing of the kind. The only thing to be said against it is that I vowed to be true to Marie's memory. That is an important factor though," he said to himself. He did not feel its importance personally, but was reluctant to destroy the poetry that people surrounded him with on account of it. "Besides this, nothing can be said against my sentiment. Had I chosen with my reason alone I could not have found anything better!"

Of all the women and girls of his acquaintance he could not recall a single one who possessed all the essential qualities that he desired to see in a wife to the same degree that Varenka did. She had all the charm and freshness of youth, but was not a child; and if she loved him, she did so consciously as a woman ought to love. She was not worldly, obviously despised society, yet was at home in it and had the manners of a woman of good society, without which a wife for Sergei Ivanovitch was unthinkable. She was religious, not childishly so, like Kitty, for instance; her life was based on religious convictions. Even in trifles he found in her everything that he wanted in a wife. She was poor and lonely, and consequently would not bring a crowd of relatives to her husband's house as in Kitty's case. She would be for ever grateful and look up to her husband, a thing he had also desired for his future domestic life. And this girl who combined all these qualities loved him. He was modest, but he could not help seeing it. And he loved her too. The one consideration against it was his age, but he came from a long-lived stock, had not a single grey hair in his head, and nobody would have taken him for forty. He remembered how Varenka had said that it was only in Russia where people regarded themselves as old at fifty. In France a man of fifty considered himself to be *dans la force de l'age,* while a man of forty was *un jeune homme.* But what did his age matter since he felt himself as young at heart as he had been twenty years ago? Was it not youth he was experiencing now as he stepped out on to the edge of the wood on the other side and saw Varenka's graceful figure in the sunlight, passing an old birch with the basket on her arm? Was it not the sensation of youth that made her form blend with the beauty of the yellow corn-fields, bathed by the slanting rays of the sun, and the golden tints on the wood that mingled with the azure distance? His heart stood still. A feeling of meekness came over him. He felt that his decision was made. Varenka, who had just bent down to pick a mushroom, got up quickly and looked about her. Sergei Ivanovitch threw away his cigar and walked towards her with a determined step.

V

" VARVARA ANDRAEVNA, as a young man I formed an ideal of the woman I was to love and whom I should be happy to call my wife. Many years have gone by, and now for the first time I find in you the thing I was seeking. Will you marry me? "

Sergei Ivanovitch was saying this to himself when he was within ten paces of Varenka. She was down on her knees trying to defend a mushroom from Grisha and calling Masha.

" Here, little ones! come here! There are lots of them! " she called in her full, mellow voice. When she caught sight of Sergei Ivanovitch she did not rise, or change her position, but he could see that she was conscious of his approach and was glad of it.

" Well, have you found any? " she asked from behind her white kerchief, as she turned her beautiful, smiling face towards him.

" Not one," Sergei Ivanovitch replied. " Have you? "

She did not reply, as she was occupied with the children who surrounded her.

"There's another one next to that little twig," she said to Masha, pointing to a tiny mushroom that was trying to force its head up through the grass. Varenka rose when Masha picked it and broke it in half. "This reminds me of my childhood," she said as she walked away from the children by Sergei Ivanovitch's side.

For a short time they were silent. Varenka saw that he wanted to speak; she divined what it was that he wished to say to her, and her heart was filled with joy and terror. They were already out of earshot, but still he did not speak. For Varenka it was better to keep silent. After a silence it would have been easier for them both to say what they wished than if they had been talking about mushrooms.

"So you have not found any?" she asked against her will. "They are rather scarce in the middle of the wood."

Sergei Ivanovitch heaved a sigh and said nothing. He was annoyed to hear her speak of mushrooms; he wanted her to go on talking about her childhood, but he replied to her words involuntarily.

"I've heard that the boleti are to be found at the edge of the wood, though I cannot tell a boletus when I see one."

A few more minutes went by. They were alone, completely out of sight of the children. Varenka could hear the beating of her own heart. She felt herself growing red, then pale, and red again.

To be the wife of a man like Kosnishev, after her position at Madame Stahl's, presented to her the height of happiness. Besides, she was sure that she loved him. And any moment her fate was to be decided. She was mortally afraid. She feared what he might say and what he might not say.

Now or never was the moment of explanation, and both felt it. Everything about Varenka, her flushed cheeks, drooping eyes, showed an unnatural nervous excitement. Sergei Ivanovitch saw it and pitied her. He even felt that not to speak now would be insulting to her. He quickly turned over in his mind all the arguments in favour of his decision, and even repeated to himself the words in which he wished to propose to her, but instead of saying them, by some perversity of fate he returned to the mushrooms again.

"What is the difference between a boletus and an agaricus?" he asked.

"There is hardly any difference in the head, but their stalks are different."

Her lips trembled as she said this.

No sooner were these words spoken than they both felt that everything was over and their agitation began to die down.

"The stem of a boletus looks rather like the growth on a dark man's face who has not shaved for a couple of days," Sergei Ivanovitch remarked, calmly.

"So it does," Varenka replied with a smile.

They instinctively changed their course and began walking towards the children. Varenka was pained and ashamed, but she experienced a feeling of relief.

When Sergei Ivanovitch returned home and examined all his arguments, he found that his conclusions had been incorrect. He could not be untrue to Marie's memory.

．　　　．　　　．　　　．　　　－　　　．　　　．

"Gently, gently, children!" Levin cried, almost angrily, as he stood before his wife in order to shield her from the children who were making a wild rush towards her, screaming with delight.

After them came Sergei Ivanovitch and Varenka. Kitty had no need to ask; she could see by the calm and somewhat abashed expressions of both their faces that what she had hoped for had not been realised.

"Well?" her husband asked on their way back home.

"It didn't come off," Kitty replied with a smile and a shake of the head that reminded Levin of her father.

"Why not?"

"I don't know," she replied, taking his hand and raising it to her lips. "That is how you kiss the bishop's hand."

"With whom does the fault lie?" he asked with a smile.

"With both. It ought to be done like this . . ."

"Some peasants are coming . . ."

"They can't see us."

VI

DURING the children's tea the elders were sitting on the veranda talking among themselves as though nothing had happened, though all knew, especially Sergei Ivanovitch and Varenka, that a very important event had taken place, or rather had not taken place. They both felt rather like children who had failed in an examination and would be compelled to remain in the same class or perhaps be turned out of the school altogether. The others, under the shadow of the event, tried to carry on a conversation about indifferent things. Kitty and Levin were particularly happy in each other that evening. They could not, however, help feeling a little ashamed of their happiness; it was rather an unpleasant hint at the others who had failed in getting what they possessed.

" I don't think Alexandre will come," the old princess remarked.

Stepan Arkadyevitch was expected by the evening train, and the old prince had written to say that he might come with him.

" Of course I know why," she continued; " he will insist that a young couple ought to be left alone."

" Papa seems to have abandoned us altogether; we never see him at all," Kitty observed. " And we're not a young couple any longer, we're quite old now."

" If he doesn't come, I shall have to say good-bye to you, my dears," the princess said with a sigh.

" But why, mamma? " both daughters fell on her at once.

" Just think how awful it must be for him alone. You see, now . . . "

And suddenly without any why or wherefore her voice trembled. Kitty and Dolly exchanged glances.

" Mamma is sure to find something to worry over," they seemed to say. They did not know that though the princess was happy at her daughter's and felt that she was needed there, she had not ceased grieving both for herself and her husband since the moment that Kitty, their favourite, had been married and the family nest became deserted.

" What is it, Agafia Mihailovna? " Kitty asked, as the old housekeeper stopped near her with a most mysterious, solemn expression on her face.

" What about supper? "

" Capital! " Dolly said; " you can go and see about supper and I'll give Grisha his lesson; otherwise he will have done nothing to-day."

" That is a lesson to me! " Levin exclaimed, jumping up. " Let me go, Dolly."

Grisha, who already went to school, had to review his lessons during the summer vacation, and his mother, who had studied Latin together with him in Moscow, had made it a rule on her arrival at Levin's to go over the most difficult lessons with him, both in Latin and arithmetic. Levin had offered to teach the boy himself, but Dolly noticed during the very first lesson that he taught in a manner different from that in which the teacher in Moscow had done, and so thought it best to attend to them herself. Levin was indignant with Stepan Arkadye-vitch for not watching over the boy's instruction himself, but for leaving it to the mother who knew nothing at all about it. Eventually he promised his sister-in-law to conduct the lessons as she wanted him to, though he had little faith in the method. And so he continued to work with Grisha in the approved way, according to the book, but did so reluctantly, and frequently forgot the time of the lesson.

"No, Dolly, I will go and you stay here," he said. "We'll do everything properly according to the book. As soon as Stiva comes, I shall not be able to, because we shall be out hunting."

And Levin went in search of Grisha.

Varenka, too, said something similar to Kitty. Even in her friend's orderly, well-managed house, she knew how to make herself useful.

"Let me see about supper and you sit still," she said, getting up to go with Agafia Mihailovna.

"Very well. They probably haven't been able to get any chickens; if so take . . ." Kitty began.

"Agafia Mihailovna and I will see to all that," Varenka interrupted her, and she disappeared with the old housekeeper.

"What a sweet girl she is!" the princess said.

"She's more than sweet, mamma; she's perfectly wonderful. There are few like her nowadays."

"So you're expecting Stepan Arkadyevitch?" Sergei Ivano-vitch asked, not very eager to go on talking of Varenka. "It would be difficult to find two men less like each other than he and Kostia. The one is always moving about and at home in society like a fish in water; the other is quick, alive to every-thing, but when it comes to society, he's like a fish out of water and has not a word to say for himself."

"Yes, he is very thoughtless," the old princess remarked, turning to Sergei Ivanovitch. "I wanted you to try and persuade him to let her go to Moscow," she continued, referring to Kitty. "She cannot possibly stay here, though he talks of engaging a doctor . . ."

"Mamma, Kostia will do anything you want him to," Kitty

put in, annoyed that her mother should have appealed to Sergei Ivanovitch in this matter.

Just then the sound of horses and the rumbling of wheels was heard down the avenue. Dolly had scarcely time to rise when Levin sprang out of the window of the room in which he had been teaching Grisha, and lifted the boy out after him.

" It's Stiva," he called. " We've finished, Dolly; don't be afraid," he added, and started running towards the carriage like a boy.

" *Is, ea, id, ejus, ejus, ejus,*" Grisha shouted, rushing down the avenue.

" There is some one else; papa, no doubt," Levin said as he stopped at the entrance of the avenue. " Kitty, don't come down the steep staircase; walk round the other way."

But the other man in the carriage was not the old prince as Levin had imagined. When he drew nearer he saw a handsome young man in a Scotch cap with long ribbons behind, who was sitting beside Stepan Arkadyevitch. It was Vasenka Veslovsky, a second cousin of the Shcherbatskys, a dashing young man of Moscow and St. Petersburg drawing - rooms, " a jolly good fellow and a splendid sportsman," as Stepan Arkadyevitch introduced him.

Not in the least embarrassed by the look of disappointment on Levin's face at not finding the old prince, Veslovsky greeted him gaily, reminded him of their former acquaintance, and picking up Grisha, he lifted him into the carriage over the head of the pointer that Stepan Arkadyevitch had brought with him.

Levin did not get into the carriage; he walked behind it. He was annoyed that instead of the old prince, whom he grew to love more and more, a perfect stranger had arrived, who was not wanted by anybody. And his annoyance increased when he got to the porch, where the whole crowd of children and elders were gathered, and saw Vasenky Veslovsky kissing Kitty's hand in a most amiable and gallant manner.

" Your wife and I are cousins and old friends," Veslovsky said, giving Levin another shake of the hand.

" Well, is there any game? " Stepan Arkadyevitch asked, turning to Levin before he had even had time to exchange greetings all round. Veslovsky and I have come here with the most murderous intentions. But, mamma, they haven't been to Moscow since . . . Tania, I've got something for you; fetch it from the back of the carriage," he turned first to one and then to the other. " How well you look, Dolly dear! " he said, turning to his wife and kissing her hand again. He retained it in his own and patted it with his other one.

Levin, who a moment ago had been in the best of spirits, stood looking gloomily at them all. Everything about them annoyed him.

" I wonder whom he kissed yesterday with those lips of his," he thought, as he noticed Stepan Arkadyevitch's tenderness towards his wife. He looked at Dolly, and she too annoyed him.

" She doesn't believe in his love; then why should she be so pleased to see him? It's disgusting! " he thought.

He glanced at the old princess, who had been so dear to him a minute ago, and was displeased at the way in which she welcomed this Vasenka with his ribbons, as though she were in her own house. Even his brother, Sergei Ivanovitch, irritated him, as he came out and met Stepan Arkadyevitch cordially, since he knew that he did not like or respect him. And Varenka, too, was hateful as she shook hands with the darling young man with the air of a *sainte nitouche*, when all she thought about was how to get married.

But Kitty annoyed him most of all. He was furious at the way in which she fell in with Veslovsky's merriment, who seemed to look upon his arrival in the country as a holiday for everybody else as well as himself, and the manner in which she replied to his amiable smiles.

The whole company walked into the house talking gaily, but no sooner were they seated than Levin went out again.

Kitty could see that something was wrong with her husband and wanted to snatch a moment to talk to him, but he hurried away from her, saying that he had some work to do in the office. His farm affairs suddenly assumed an overwhelming importance. " It's all holiday for them," he thought; " but there's not much holiday about this; these things can't wait and you can't live without them."

VII

LEVIN returned home only when he was sent for to come to supper. On the staircase he came across Kitty and Agafia Mihailovna in consultation about the wine.

" What is all this fuss about? Give them the usual kind."

" Oh, no, Stiva won't like it. . . . Kostia, wait a moment, what is the matter with you?" Kitty asked, hastening after him. But he was merciless. He took no notice of her and walked into the dining-room with long strides, where he instantly began taking part in an animated conversation that was going on between Vasenka Veslovsky and Stepan Arkadyevitch.

" Well, shall we go out shooting to-morrow?" Stepan Arkadyevitch asked.

" Do let us go, please," Veslovsky said, seating himself sideways on another chair and tucking his fat legs under him.

" Certainly, I shall be delighted. Have you done any shooting this summer?" Levin asked him, staring at his leg. He spoke with the feigned politeness that Kitty knew so well and that did not suit him. " I doubt if we shall find any snipe, but there are plenty of woodcocks. We must go out early though. You won't be tired? Stiva, you're not tired, are you?"

" Tired! I never get tired. I don't mind if we stay up all night. Supposing we go for a walk?"

" Capital idea! It's absurd to go to bed!" Veslovsky assented.

" We quite believe that you are able to stay up and keep others from sleeping," Dolly remarked in the slightly sarcastic tone that she always adopted towards her husband. " But I think it's time we were all in bed. I am going now; I shall not wait for supper."

" No, Dolly, don't go yet," Stepan Arkadyevitch said, walking over to her. " I've heaps of things to tell you."

" I don't suppose they're very important."

" Do you know, Veslovsky has been to Anna's and he's going there again. They are only about seventy miles away from here. I shall certainly go too. Veslovsky, come here!"

Vasenka came over to the ladies and sat down beside Kitty.

Levin remained at the other end of the table, and while talking to the princess and Varenka, noticed that a very animated, mysterious conversation was going on between Stepan Arkadyevitch, Dolly, Kitty, and Veslovsky. And not only that, Kitty was looking seriously into the young man's handsome face and talking to him in a very earnest manner.

" It's very nice at their place," Vasenka was saying, referring to Vronsky and Anna. " Of course, it's not my place to judge them, but one always feels so at home in their house."

" What are they going to do?"

" I think they intend spending the winter in Moscow."

" How nice it would be for us to go there together! When shall you go? " Stepan Arkadyevitch asked Vasenka.

" I shall spend the whole of July with them."

" Will you come too? " Stepan Arkadyevitch asked, turning to his wife.

" Certainly; I've long wanted to," Dolly replied. " I am so sorry for her, and I know her well. She's such a fine woman. But I'll go alone, when you're no longer there, so that I shall not be in anybody's way. Besides, I shall prefer it without you."

" Very well," Stepan Arkadyevitch said. " And you, Kitty? "

" Why should I go there? " Kitty said, flushing red, and looking round at her husband.

" Do you know Anna Arkadyevna? " Veslovsky asked her. " She's a very attractive woman."

" Yes," she said, flushing still deeper, as she rose and walked over to her husband.

" Are you going out shooting to-morrow? " she asked.

The twinge of jealousy that had come over him when he had seen her blush while talking to Veslovsky had increased amazingly. As he listened to her, he construed her words in his own way. Though he was ashamed to think of it later, just then it seemed to him that she had merely asked the question because of Vasenka, with whom she was already in love.

" Yes, I am," he replied in an unnatural voice that grated on his own ear.

"Why not stay at home to-morrow? Dolly has scarcely had a chance of seeing Stiva; you could go the day after," Kitty said.

It seemed to Levin that his wife was pleading not to be parted from the young man to whom she had taken such a fancy.

" Oh, we can stay at home if you like," he replied with a forced amiability.

Meanwhile, Vasenka, perfectly ignorant of the suffering he was causing, rose and followed Kitty. He watched her with a particularly kind smile in his eyes.

Levin noticed that glance. He grew pale and held his breath. " How dare he look at my wife like that! " he thought.

" We're going to-morrow, aren't we? " Vasenka asked,

dropping into a chair and arranging his legs in his habitual fashion.

Levin's jealousy had grown beyond bounds. He already saw himself as a deceived husband, whom the guilty pair looked upon merely as a convenience, to furnish them with the comforts and pleasures of life. But in spite of it all he was very affable to Veslovsky, questioned him about his gun, his boots, and agreed to go out shooting in the morning.

To his great joy the old princess put an end to his sufferings by advising Kitty to retire to bed. He still had another pang in store for him. On bidding the hostess good-night, Vasenka bent down to kiss her hand, but Kitty, with a naïveness for which her mother reprimanded her later, pulled it away from him.

"That is not customary with us," she said.

According to Levin she was to blame for having permitted such relations, and still more so for the clumsy way in which she showed him that she disapproved of them.

"What a pity it is to go to bed now!" Stepan Arkadyevitch said. He was in an exceedingly poetic mood after the few glasses of wine drunk at supper.

"Look here, Kitty!" he exclaimed, pointing to the moon that was rising behind the trees. "How beautiful! A lovely night for a serenade, Veslovsky. Oh, by the way, he has a splendid voice; he and I were singing all the way down. He has brought some songs; two new ones. It would be rather nice for Varvara Andraevna to sing them with him."

* * * * * * *

Stepan Arkadyevitch and Veslovsky wandered up and down the avenue long after the others had retired. They could be heard practising a new song.

Levin was sitting in his wife's room, scowling as he listened to their voices, and to all Kitty's questions as to what was the matter with him he kept a stubborn silence. When at last it dawned upon her that Veslovsky might have something to do with his mood, and she hinted her thought timidly, all his fury broke loose, and he told her all that was in his mind. His words sounded offensive to his own ears, and he grew even more irritable than before.

He was standing before her with flashing eyes, scowling heavily and pressing his powerful arms against his breast as though trying to restrain himself. The expression of his face was hard and even cruel, but there was a shade of suffering about it that touched her. His jaws quivered, and there was a tremor in his voice.

" Don't suppose for a moment that I'm jealous; it's a disgusting word. I can't be jealous and believe that . . . I can't tell you what I feel, but it's awful. . . . I am not jealous; I only feel insulted, humiliated, that any one should dare look at you with eyes like . . . "

" Like what? " Kitty asked, trying to recall everything that had happened that evening.

In the bottom of her heart she felt that there had been something suggestive in the way Veslovsky had followed her from the table, but she was not even willing to admit it to herself, least of all to him in his present mood.

" How can I possibly be attractive to any one in my condition? "

" Oh! " he exclaimed; " you had much better not have spoken! I suppose if you had been attractive . . . "

" But, Kostia dear, listen! " she implored, looking at him compassionately. " How can you think that, when you know that I don't care for men? . . . Would you have me see no one at all? "

In the first moment his jealousy had offended her. She was annoyed to think that the slightest distraction, even of the most innocent character, was forbidden her. But now she would gladly have sacrificed all that and everything for his peace of mind, in order to free him from the pain he was suffering.

" I know my position is a ridiculous one," he continued desperately, in a whisper. " He is my guest, and has really done nothing improper. I don't like his free-and-easy manner and the way he has of tucking his leg under him. Still, he considers it good form, so I shall have to be amiable to him."

" But, Kostia dear, you exaggerate," Kitty said, feeling proud in the bottom of her heart that the strength of his love would allow him to be jealous of such trifles.

" It seems so dreadful, now that you are so sacred to me, and we are so happy, so wonderfully happy, that this fool . . . I won't abuse him; he is nothing to me. But why should our happiness . . . "

" I think I can guess the cause of the trouble," Kitty began.

" What was it? "

" I saw you watching us when we were talking at supper."

" Yes, well? " Levin asked in a frightened tone.

She told him the subject of their conversation, and as she did so she was breathless with excitement. Levin gazed at her in silence, then suddenly seized his head in both his hands.

" Kitty, darling, forgive me; I've nearly worn you out! What madness! It was my fault throughout. How dreadful to worry you with such trifles! "

" I'm so sorry for you, dear."

" For me? I'm an utter madman! How cruel I was to you! It is terrible to think that a mere stranger can come and spoil our happiness."

" Of course, it is not nice to think . . . "

" No, I shall invite him to spend the whole summer with us, and be as pleasant to him as possible," he said, kissing her hand. " You shall see! To-morrow. . . . Oh, yes, we're going out shooting."

VIII

EARLY the next morning, when the ladies were still asleep, two conveyances were standing at the door, and Lasca, who had instinctively felt that something was on foot, and had barked her fill, was sitting beside the coachman on the box, waiting impatiently for the sportsmen to come out. The first to appear was Vasenka Veslovsky, in high boots that came up to the middle of his stout thighs, a green blouse with a new leather girdle round the waist, and the Scotch cap with ribbons down the back. He was carrying a new English hammerless gun. Lasca made one bound towards him, jumped all over him, asked him in her own way when the others were coming, but receiving no reply, she resumed her post of waiting, and sat there motionless with one ear pricked up. At last the door opened with a mighty sound, and out flew Stepan Arkadyevitch's spotted yellow pointer, Krak, followed by his master himself, with a gun in his hand and a cigar in his mouth.

" Gently, gently, Krak," he said to the dog, who was pawing him all over and clutching at the game-bag.

Stepan Arkadyevitch had on a common pair of leggings, shabby trousers, and a short coat. He had some sort of a hat at the back of his head, but his gun was a beauty, of the very latest fashion, and his game-bag and pouch, though a little worn, were of the very best quality.

Vasenka Veslovsky had never realised that a sportsman looked best when he paid little attention to his clothes and a great deal to his appliances. He understood it now as he looked at Stepan Arkadyevitch in his shabby clothes, with his beaming face, the best possible figure of a gentleman, and he decided that he would get himself up like that for the next shoot.

" Well, where is our host? " he asked.

" He has a young wife," Stepan Arkadyevitch replied with a smile.

" And such a charming one, too."

" He was quite ready, but I suppose he has run in to her again."

Stepan Arkadyevitch had guessed aright. Levin had run back to his wife to ask her once more if she had forgiven him for last night's stupidity, and to beg her to take care of herself as much as possible, insisting that she should keep away from the children, who might possibly push her by accident. And once more receiving her assurances that she was not angry with him for deserting her for two days, he begged her to send a messenger with a note to him to-morrow morning, if only to let him know how she was.

Kitty was sorry to part from her husband for so long a time as two whole days, but when she saw his handsome figure, that looked unusually large in top boots and a white blouse, and his animation and gaiety before the shoot, so incomprehensible to her, she could not help rejoicing with him. She forgot her grief and bade him good-bye merrily.

" I'm sorry, gentlemen! " he said as he ran out at the door to join the others. " Have they put in our lunch? Why is the chestnut on the right? Never mind, though. Get down Lasca! go to your place! "

" Turn them in with the heifers," he said, turning to a man who had come out to ask some question about the young bullocks. " Excuse me, here comes another rascal."

Levin jumped out of the carriage and went up to the contractor who was approaching the house with a measure in his hand.

" You didn't come to the office yesterday, and now you're detaining me! What do you want? "

" Can I make another turn and add three more steps, sir' It will come out all right and be more comfortable."

" You ought to have carried out my orders," Levin said, annoyed. " I told you to fix the string-boards first and then cut out the steps. It can't be done now; you'll have to make a new staircase."

In the new wing that was being added the contractor had spoiled a staircase, having constructed it quite irrespective of the elevation, so that when it was put in its place, the steps were all slanting. To put it right the man merely suggested adding another three steps.

"It will be much better, sir."

"But where will your three steps lead to? '

"Why, sir," the contractor said with a disdainful smile, "it will be just the thing. It will be raised from beneath," he continued with a convincing gesture, "and go on until it gets there."

"But three steps will add to the length; where is it going to get to? "

"If it begins from the bottom it must get there," the contractor said stubbornly.

"Yes, it will probably get to the wall or the ceiling."

"Excuse me, sir; it will begin from the bottom and go on until it gets there."

Levin took out the ramrod and began drawing a plan of the staircase in the dust. "Do you see what I mean? "

"As you please, sir," the carpenter said, his eyes beaming, having at last understood the point in question. "I see that a new staircase will be required."

"Very well, make one! " Levin called to him, as he took his seat in the carriage again. "You can go! Hold the dogs, Fillip! "

Freed from domestic and farm cares, Levin experienced such a joyful sensation that he did not feel like talking. Besides, he was full of that excitement and expectancy that every sportsman feels as he approaches the scene of action. If anything interested him at all just then it was merely such trifles as to whether they would find anything in the Kolpensky swamp, how Lasca would come out in comparison with Krak, or what sort of a shot he would make that day. The idea of making a good show before a stranger and not letting Oblonsky beat him also flashed across his mind.

Oblonsky experienced a similar feeling and was also not inclined to be talkative. Vasenka Veslovsky was the only one who kept on talking merrily all the time. Listening to him now Levin was ashamed to think how unjust he had been to him the night before. Vasenka was indeed a jolly good fellow, simple, frank, and kind-hearted. Had Levin met him before his marriage, he would probably have become close friends with him. He was a little displeased at the way in which Vasenka treated life as a perpetual holiday and also at his rather free and easy elegance. It seemed as though he looked upon himself as of immense importance because of his long nails, cap, and everything else corresponding to them, but all these things were excusable on the ground of his extreme good-nature. Levin liked him for his good breeding, his manner of speaking French and English, and also because he was a man of his own class.

Vasenka went into raptures over the left side horse, a Cossack horse from the Don. " Wouldn't it be jolly to gallop through the steppes on a Cossack horse? " he said. The idea presented something wild and poetical to his mind, though there really was nothing in it, but his naïveté, his handsome face, sweet smile, and grace of gesture were very attractive. Levin, either because he found him sympathetic or he wished to atone for his sins of the previous night, tried to see nothing but good in him, and took great pleasure in his company.

When they had gone about three miles Veslovsky suddenly thought of his cigars and his pocket-book; he could not tell whether he had lost them or left them behind on the table. The pocket-book contained some three hundred and seventy roubles, so it could not very well be left.

" I say, Levin, let me ride back on this Cossack horse. It will be very jolly; eh? " he said, getting ready to mount.

" Oh, no, why should you? " Levin replied, calculating that Vasenka could not weigh less than twelve stone; " I will send the coachman."

The coachman rode back on the off-horse and Levin drove the other two himself.

IX

" WELL, what route are we going to take? " Stepan Arka-dyevitch asked.

" I thought we would go by Gvosdevo. On this side of it there is a snipe bog, and beyond some splendid bogs full of snipe and woodcocks. It's rather hot now, but we shall get there by the evening, as it's only twenty miles away. We can do some shooting, spend the night there, and take the large bogs to-morrow morning."

" Is there nothing on the way? "

" Oh, yes, but we should only lose time and it's too hot. There are two fine little spots, but there's hardly anything there."

Levin was not quite sincere when he said this, but as these two spots were so near home and he could take them at any time, and there was not enough room for three to shoot there, he was reluctant to go. But the experienced eye of Stepan Arkadyevitch detected a small marsh from the side of the road.

" Do let us get down! " he said, pointing to it.

" Oh, yes, please," Vasenka implored. Levin could do nothing but give in.

They had barely time to pull up when the two dogs leapt down and began chasing each other into the marsh.

" Krak! Lasca! "

The dogs turned back.

" I shall stay here; there is not enough room for three," Levin said, hoping that they would find nothing but plovers, who, disturbed by the dogs, were crying piteously over the bog.

" Oh, do come too, Levin! Let us go together! " Veslovsky called to him.

" It will be too crowded, really. Lasca, here! You don't want another dog, do you? "

Levin remained by the carriage, looking enviously at the others. They found nothing but a wild hen and some plovers, of which Vasenka killed one.

" You see, I was not trying to save the swamp," Levin said. " It was only a waste of time."

" It was jolly all the same. Did you see how nicely I killed this one? " Vasenka asked as he climbed awkwardly into the conveyance with the gun and plover in his hand. " How soon shall we be at the real place? "

Suddenly the horses started, Levin hit his head against the barrel of somebody's gun, and a shot was heard. At any rate so it seemed to Levin, but the report came first. Vasenka was uncocking his gun and discharged it by accident. The shot went into the ground without harming any one. Stepan Arkadyevitch shook his head and gave a reproachful smile at Veslovsky. But Levin had not the heart to reprimand him. In the first place, it would have looked as though he were annoyed at the danger he had just escaped and at the bump on his forehead; secondly, Veslovsky was so genuinely sorry and laughed so good-naturedly at the general commotion, that he could not help laughing with him.

When they reached the second swamp, a much larger one, Levin tried to persuade them not to get out as he was afraid they would lose too much time, but Veslovsky again implored him to let them go. As the swamp was narrow, Levin, as a hospitable host, remained behind again.

Krak immediately made for the knolls and Vasenka Veslovsky was the first to follow him. Stepan Arkadyevitch had scarcely time to come up when a snipe flew out. Veslovsky fired and missed, and the bird alighted in the uncut field. Krak found it again, and this time Veslovsky killed it, and came back to Levin.

"You go now and I'll stay with the horses," he said.

Levin was beginning to feel envious. He handed the reins to Keslovsky and went into the swamp.

Lasca, who had been whining piteously against the injustice of keeping off the swamp, made straight for a promising spot that Levin was familiar with, into which Krak had not yet gone.

"Why don't you stop her?" Stepan Arkadyevitch shouted.

"She won't startle them," Levin replied, hastening after the dog joyfully.

The nearer Lasca drew to her favourite spot, the more solemn did she get. A small swamp bird distracted her attention for a moment. She made a circuit round the knolls, began a second, when suddenly she trembled and stopped still.

"Come along, Stiva!" Levin shouted, his heart beating violently. He felt as though something had been lifted from his ears; his sense of sound lost all proportion of distance. Stepan Arkadyevitch's step seemed to him like the distant tramp of horses, the squashing of the earth beneath him seemed to him like the flight of a bird. Not far off there was a splashing in the water, of which he could give himself no account.

Choosing a spot for his foot he moved up towards the dog.

"Go!"

It was not a snipe, but a woodcock that rushed out past the dog. Levin raised his gun, but just as he was aiming the splashing sound in the water drew nearer and mingled with Veslovsky's voice, saying something in a strange, excited manner. He felt that he was aiming behind the woodcock, but fired nevertheless.

When he had convinced himself that he had missed the bird, he turned round. The carriage and horses were no longer on the road but in the swamp. Anxious to see the shooting Veslovsky had driven them there, and they had stuck fast.

"What the devil brought him here?" Levin muttered to himself as he walked up to the vehicle. "What made you come here?" he asked brusquely, and calling to the coachman he turned his attention to the horses.

Levin was annoyed at being disturbed in his shooting, the more so as neither Stepan Arkadyevitch nor Veslovsky had the slightest idea about harness and could not help him to take out the horses. He disregarded Vasenka's assurances that the ground was quite dry there, but continued extricating the horses by the help of the coachman. Later, when he saw with what zeal Veslovsky was tugging at the wing of the vehicle, so that he even pulled it off, he reproached himself for his brusqueness and tried to be particularly amiable to him. When the carriage was safely in the road again, he ordered lunch to be brought out.

"*Bon appétit—bonne conscience ! le poulet va tomber jusqu'au fond de mes bottes,*" Veslovsky said as he finished his second chicken. "All our troubles are over; now everything will go well. Only as a punishment for my sins, I shall have to sit on the box. Isn't that so, eh? I'm a perfect Automaton. You'll see how I can drive!" He took the reins out of Levin's hand, the latter having asked him to hand them to the coachman. "No, I must atone for my sins, and I'm quite comfortable on the box." And he drove on.

Levin was at first afraid that he would wear out the horses, especially the left chestnut, whom he did not know how to manage, but he involuntarily abandoned himself to his merriment, enjoyed his singing, and laughed at the way he imitated the English fashion of driving four-in-hand. After lunch they reached the Gvosdevo bog, all three in the happiest of moods.

X

VASHA had driven so fast that they came to the bog too early, before the cool of the evening. When they reached the large bog, the main object of their journey, Levin involuntarily began thinking of how best to rid himself of Vasenka so as to go about unhampered. Stepan Arkadyevitch was evidently possessed by the same desire, as Levin could see from the worried look on his face and a certain good-natured cunning, so characteristic of him.

"Are we walking? The bog is an excellent one. Here are

some hawks," Stepan Arkadyevitch said, pointing to two large birds that were circling above the reeds. "Where there are hawks there is sure to be game."

"Well, gentlemen," Levin said, pulling up his boots with a dejected expression, and examining the caps on his gun, "do you see those reeds?" He pointed to a dark green patch in a large, swampy, half-mown meadow, on the right side of the river. "The bog begins here just in front of us, where it looks green. To the right where the horses are, among the knolls, there are snipe, and also by the reeds as far as the elder-tree and the mill. You see that swampy place over there? I once killed seventeen woodcocks on that spot. We can scatter in various directions with the dogs and meet again at the mill."

"Well, who goes to the right and who to the left?" Stepan Arkadyevitch asked. "It is much broader to the right, so you two had better go there, and I'll turn down to the left," he added quite casually.

"Capital! We'll get ahead of him. Come along, Levin!" Veslovsky exclaimed.

Levin could do nothing but assent, and they separated.

The moment they entered the bog the two dogs made for the moor. Levin knew what that cautious, indefinite search of Lasca's meant; he knew the spot too and was expecting to see a flock of woodcocks come flying out.

"Veslovsky, walk beside me, beside me!" Levin said to Veslovsky, who was trudging on behind him, in trepidation. Since the accident of the morning, Veslovsky's gun had a curious interest for him.

"No, I shall only be in your way; don't bother about me."

But Levin involuntarily thought of the words Kitty had said to him at parting. "Take care you don't shoot each other."

The dogs came nearer and nearer, passing one another, each on a different scent. Levin's excitement was so great that the squashing sound of the swampy ground appeared to him like the cry of a woodcock and he cocked his gun.

"Bang! bang!" Vasenka had fired at a flock of ducks which had made their appearance at an unpropitious moment. Levin had scarcely time to look round when a woodcock soared up into the air, followed by a second, a third, and eight more rose from the ground.

Stepan Arkadyevitch aimed at one just as it was beginning to zigzag in the air, and the bird fell with a thud into the swamp. He turned his gun leisurely to a second that was flying towards the reeds, and as the shot rang out the woodcock dropped down and could be seen running along the mown reeds, flapping its unhurt wing, white at the edge.

Levin was not so fortunate. He aimed at a bird at too close a range and missed it; he aimed at another as it was beginning to rise in the air, but at that moment a third flew out from beneath his feet, distracting his attention, and he missed again.

While they were reloading, Veslovsky fired two shots over the water. Stepan Arkadyevitch looked at Levin with sparkling eyes.

" Now we shall separate," Stepan Arkadyevitch said, whistling to his dog as he walked down one side with the gun in his hand. Levin and Veslovsky went down the other.

Whenever Levin made a bad start, he invariably got cross and annoyed, and shot badly for the rest of the time. It happened to be his fate on that day. There were woodcocks in abundance; they kept rising from under the dogs, under the sportsmen's feet, and Levin might have improved had he not been so angry with himself and ashamed before Veslovsky. The latter kept on firing merrily at random, and was not in the least embarrassed that he did not kill anything. Levin was too hasty, and his excitement grew until it reached the point when he gave up all hope of ever hitting anything. Lasca seemed to understand his master's condition; she scented less eagerly, and looked at the hunters in perplexity and with reproach. Shot followed after shot, but in the roomy game-bag there were only three little woodcocks, and one of these had been shot by Veslovsky, who also had a hand in the killing of the second. From the other side of the bog came the frequent report of Stepan Arkadyevitch's gun, then shouts of " Fetch it, Krak! "

This excited Levin still more. The woodcocks kept on circling above the reeds; there was an incessant sound of croaking on the ground and in the air. Instead of two, dozens of hawks rose high, screeching over the bog.

Having tramped down the whole of one side, Levin and Veslovsky came to a spot where some peasants had been mowing. Though he knew they could not possibly find as many birds on the unmowed spots, Levin, having promised to meet Stepan Arkadyevitch, trudged by the side of his companion over the mowed and unmowed strips alike.

" Hi there, sportsmen! " a peasant called to them, who was

sitting near a cart. " Come and have some dinner with us and a drink! "

Levin looked round.

" Come along! " another shouted, a jolly peasant with a red beard, displaying his white teeth in a grin, and holding up a greenish bottle that shone in the sun.

" *Qu'est ce qu'ils disent ?* " Veslovsky asked.

" They want us to come and have a drink with them. They've probably been mowing the field. I think I should rather like a drink," he said, not without a certain hope that he might rid himself of Veslovsky in that way.

" What makes them so hospitable? "

" Oh, they're only doing it for fun. Come along; you'll find it interesting."

" *Allons, c'est curieux.*"

" Supposing you go alone? you can find your way to the mill," Levin said, and turning round he saw to his great joy that Veslovsky was dragging his tired feet out of the swamp towards the peasants, with his gun in his hand.

" You come too! " the peasants shouted to Levin. " We'll give you a piece of our pie! "

Levin would very much have liked a little vodka and a piece of bread. He was fatigued, and dragged himself along the bog with difficulty. For a moment he was in doubt whether to go or not, when suddenly his dog stopped and all his fatigue vanished. A woodcock rose from under his feet; he fired and killed it, but the dog remained standing still. A second rose from under her, he fired again and missed. It was indeed an unlucky day. He went to look for the dead bird, but could not find it; he crawled among the reeds, but to no purpose. He sent Lasca to hunt for it, but she only pretended to do so, not really believing that her master had killed the bird.

Even without Vasenka, whom Levin had blamed for everything, matters did not improve. There were many woodcocks, but he missed one shot after another.

The slanting rays of the sun were still hot; his clothes, soaked through and through with perspiration, stuck to his body; his left boot, full of water, was heavy and made a squashing sound as he walked; the perspiration came down in drops over his face; there was a bitter taste in his mouth, and in his nose the odour of gunpowder and stagnant pools. His ears were filled with the sound of woodcocks; the barrels of his gun were so hot that he could not touch them; his heart beat violently, his hands trembled, and his weary legs stumbled over the tufts and boggy places. Finally, after a disgraceful miss he threw his hat and gun on the ground in disgust.

" I must stop till I feel myself again! " he said aloud, and calling Lasca, he picked up his gun and hat and left the bog. When he got to a dry place, he sat down on a little mound, took off his boots, emptied the water out of them, then walking back to the swamp, he drank some water that had a rusty taste, wetted the heated barrels, and washed his face and hands. Once more refreshed he moved up to a place where he had seen a woodcock fly out, with the firm determination of keeping cool.

He wanted to keep calm, but could not. His finger pressed the trigger before he aimed at the bird. Matters grew from bad to worse. There were only five pieces in the game-bag when he left the bog and walked towards the spot where he was to meet Stepan Arkadyevitch.

Before the latter appeared he caught sight of his dog. Krak jumped out from the old root of an elder-tree, filthy from the ill-smelling swamp, and sniffing at Lasca with the air of a victor. He was followed by the stately figure of Stepan Arka-dyevitch himself, who came towards Levin, looking red and perspiring, his collar unbuttoned, and limping a little as before.

" Well, have you had good luck? " he asked gaily.

" And you? " Levin asked in his turn; but there was no need to do so! he could see that his game-bag was full.

" Oh, it wasn't bad."

He had killed fourteen birds.

" A fine swamp this! I dare say Veslovsky was in your way. It's awkward for two people with one dog," Stepan Arkadyevitch said, anxious to tone down his own success.

XI

WHEN Levin and Stepan Arkadyevitch got to the peasant's hut, where Levin usually put up, Veslovsky was already there. He was sitting on a bench in the middle of the room, laughing with his merry, infectious laugh, while a soldier, the host's brother, was trying to pull off his filthy, soaked boots.

" I've only just come. *Ils ont été charmants*. Think of it! they gave me something to eat and to drink. Such bread!

delicieux ! And as for the vodka, I have never tasted anything better! And they wouldn't take any money, though I insisted on it!"

"Why should they take money? They were treating you. They don't sell vodka, you know," the soldier put in, having at last pulled off the boot and the stocking as well.

In spite of the dirty condition of the hut, not improved by their hunting boots and the smelling, filthy dogs, who were trying to lick themselves clean; in spite of the powder smoke with which they were saturated, and the absence of knives and forks, the sportsmen drank their tea and ate their supper with an appetite that only a day's shooting can produce. Having washed themselves they went into the newly-swept hay-barn, where the coachman had prepared their beds.

Though it was getting dark, none of them felt inclined to sleep. They lay talking about all sorts of things, the day's shooting, the dogs, former escapades, until the conversation at last drifted into a theme in which all were interested. Inspired by Vasenka's frequent expressions of delight at the manner in which they were spending the night, at the delicious scent of the hay, the charm of the broken cart (it seemed to him broken, because it was taken off its front wheels), at the good-natured peasants who had given him vodka, and at the dogs, which lay stretched each at his master's feet—inspired by all this rapture, Oblonsky followed on in a similar strain with stories of the shooting on the estates of a man called Maltus, a rich railway magnate. He described the bogs that Maltus had bought in the government of Tver, how he preserved them, and gave the minutest details of the horses and carriages that had taken the sportsmen there, and the large lunch-tent that had been pitched for their use.

"I can't understand," Levin said, raising himself on his bed of hay, "how it is these people don't disgust you. I can enjoy Lafitte at lunch as well as anybody, but I think this excessive luxury is revolting. All these people, like our former mono-polists, make their wealth in such a manner as to earn the contempt of all decent folk. They ignore the contempt and try to live it down with their ill-gotten gains."

"That's perfectly true!" Vasenka Veslovsky put in; "perfectly true! Of course we know that Oblonsky merely does it out of *bonhomie*, but others say that he goes there . . ."

"Not at all," Oblonsky said, with a smile. "I do not consider him more dishonest than any other rich merchant or nobleman; they have all earned their wealth by their wits and labour."

"What kind of labour? Do you call it labour to get a concession and then sell it to some one else? "

"Of course it is! And labour in the best sense of the word too; if it were not for him or others like him, we should have had no railways."

"But it is not labour in the sense in which a peasant or a learned man understands it."

"I dare say; but it is labour nevertheless, for it yields fruits in the shape of railways. But I forgot, you don't approve of railways anyhow."

"That's quite another question; I am prepared to admit that railways may be useful, but every gain that is not proportionate to the labour involved must be dishonest."

"Who is to determine the proportion? "

"The acquisition of wealth by dishonesty, by sharp practice," Levin said, at a loss to know how to define the difference between what was honest and dishonest in this matter, " is an evil, just like the acquisition of banking-houses. The amassing of enormous fortunes without labour is always an evil, no matter what form it may take. *Le roi est mort; vive le roi !* We had no sooner abolished the monopolies than railways and banks sprang up in their place, and they, like the others, set out to acquire wealth without labour."

"That's all very fine. . . . Lie down, Krak! " Stepan Arkadyevitch shouted to his dog, who was scratching himself and turning about in the hay; he was so convinced of the justice of his theme that he spoke calmly and leisurely; " but you have not drawn the line between honest and dishonest labour. Is it dishonest for me to get a larger salary than my manager does, though he probably knows more about our work than I do? "

"I don't know."

"Then I'll tell you. Your getting, say, five thousand roubles a year for the labour you spend on your farm, while our independent peasant gets about fifty, no matter how hard he works, is just as much dishonest as my getting more than my manager and Maltus more than a navvy. It seems to me that the attitude of society to such men is extremely unjust, and I dare say that envy . . . "

"That is not fair," Veslovsky objected. " Envy has nothing to do with it; there is something dirty about the whole business."

"Excuse me," Levin continued; " what you said just now

about the injustice of my getting five thousand roubles a year from my farm, while a peasant gets only fifty, is perfectly true. It is unjust, and I feel it, but . . ."

" It is really awful when you think of it. Why do we eat, drink, shoot, and go about idle while the peasant is eternally working? " Vasenka Veslovsky interrupted him, quite sincerely, having been struck by the fact for the first time in his life.

" Yes, you feel it, but at the same time you do not give him your estate," Stepan Arkadyevitch observed as though on purpose to tease Levin.

Of late a sort of secret hostility had arisen between the two brothers-in-law. Being married to sisters there was a constant rivalry going on between them as to who had arranged his life better, and now this hostility found its expression in the personal tone the conversation was beginning to assume.

" I don't give it up because no one demands it of me, and even if I wanted to, I couldn't," Levin replied. " Besides, there's no one to give it to."

" Try the peasant here; he won't refuse it."

" But how can I give it to him? Shall I make him out a bill of purchase? "

" I don't know how it could be arranged, but it seems to me that if you are convinced, then you have no right . . ."

" I'm not at all convinced. On the contrary, I feel that I have no right to give it away. I owe certain duties both to the land and to my family."

" If you admit the inequality, I can't see how you can help acting according to your convictions."

" I do act according to my convictions in a negative sort of way, in the sense that I do not try to increase the difference that exists between me and the peasants."

" Isn't that rather a paradox? "

" A sophistical explanation, I agree," Veslovsky put in. " Halloa! " he exclaimed as the door creaked and the host entered the barn. " Why aren't you sleeping? "

" Sleep indeed! I thought you were asleep, but as I came along I heard you talking. I've come to fetch a sickle. She won't bite, will she? " he asked, treading cautiously with his bare feet past the dog.

" Where are you going to sleep? "

" We're not going to sleep; we're going to watch the cattle."

" What a glorious night! " Veslovsky said, as he looked through the frame of the open door at a corner of the hut and some unharnessed carts standing out in the half-light. " Listen, some women are singing; how jolly! Who is that singing? " he asked of the host.

" The serf girls, close by here."

" Supposing we go for a walk, Oblonsky? We shan't sleep in any case. Come along."

" How nice it would be if I could remain lying like this and go at the same time," Oblonsky said, stretching himself. " I think I'll stay as I am."

" Then I'll go alone," Veslovsky said, starting up and seizing his boots. " If it's jolly, I'll come and fetch you."

" What a nice fellow he is! don't you think so? " Oblonsky remarked as soon as Veslovsky had gone and the peasant had shut the door behind him.

" Yes, he is," Levin replied, as he turned their recent conversation over in his mind. He was hurt that he had been accused of sophistry by two sincere, intelligent men, when it seemed to him that he had expressed his ideas and feelings so clearly.

" Yes, yes, my friend, it must be either the one thing or the other," he said to himself. " Either you accept the present social order as a just one and defend your rights, or you acknowledge that you are enjoying unjust privileges—privileges you have no right to. Yet if they were unjust you would not be able to enjoy them, at any rate I could not. The most important thing for me is to feel that I am not in the wrong."

" What do you say to going out? " Stepan Arkadyevitch asked, evidently tired of the mental strain. " We probably should not sleep in any case."

Levin did not reply. The remark he had made during their conversation about his acting justly in a negative sense occupied his attention. " Is it possible that one can be just only negatively? " he asked himself.

" How strong the hay smells! " Stepan Arkadyevitch said, sitting up. " I wouldn't go to sleep for anything. Vasenka has something on there. Do you hear them talking and laughing? Come along, let us see what it is."

" I don't want to go," Levin replied.

" Is it also a point of principle? " Stepan Arkadyevitch asked with a smile, searching round in the dark for his cap.

" It is not a question of principle; why should I go? "

" You will get into trouble yet," Stepan Arkadyevitch remarked, getting up as he discovered his cap.

" Why? "

" Can't I see how things are between you and your wife? You make a mountain even about going away for a couple of days' shooting. All that is very nice and idyllic, but it won't last for ever. A man must be independent; he has his own interests. A man should be manly," Oblonsky added, opening the door.

" You mean he should go and make love to peasant girls," Levin retorted.

" And why not? It's very jolly. *Ça ne tire pas à consequence.* My wife will not be any the worse off because of it, and I shall enjoy myself immensely. So long as you keep up the sanctity of the home, it doesn't matter; you can do what you like."

" Perhaps," Levin replied dryly. " To-morrow we have to go early; I will not wake anybody, but will start out at day-break."

" *Messieurs, venez vite !* " Veslovsky said as he put his head in at the door. " *Charmante !* It was I who discovered her. *Charmante ;* a perfect Gretchen, and we're quite good friends already. She's awfully pretty, really," he added in a tone of approval, as though she had been made pretty especially for his benefit.

Levin pretended to go to sleep; Oblonsky put on his slippers, lighted a cigar, and went out. Soon their voices died away.

Levin lay awake for a long time. He could hear his horses chewing the hay, and the peasant and his eldest son getting ready for the night watch. He could hear the soldier lying down to sleep in another part of the barn, with his nephew, the peasant's youngest boy, who kept questioning him about the dogs, saying they were enormous and terrible. He could hear the boy asking whom they were going to catch, and the soldier in a sleepy voice replying that the sportsmen were going to take them to the swamp in the morning, where they would. fire off their guns, and then advising him to go to sleep. The two began to snore and all grew quiet, except for the neighing of the horses and the croaking of the woodcocks.

" Negatively," Levin thought. " Well, and if so? It's not my fault." And he began thinking of to-morrow.

" I shall turn out early and try not to get excited. There are woodcocks in abundance and snipe too. When I come back there will probably be a note from Kitty. Yes, Stiva is right; I am not manly enough with her; I've grown too effeminate. But what can I do? Something negative again ! "

As he was dropping off to sleep he could hear the voices of Stepan Arkadyevitch and Veslovsky talking and laughing. He opened his eyes for a moment. The two were standing by the open door in the full light of the moon. Stepan Arkadyevitch was saying something about the freshness of a girl, whom he compared to a newly-opened hazel-nut, while Veslovsky was laughing with his merry laugh and saying, " Get your own if you can! " evidently repeating a peasant's phrase.

" Gentlemen, we have to go out at daybreak! " Levin said, and dozed off again.

XII

LEVIN rose at daybreak and tried to wake his comrades. Vasenka was lying face downwards with his legs stretched out, sleeping so soundly that it was impossible to make any impression on him, and when Oblonsky was roused, he declined to go out so early. Even Lasca, who was curled up in the hay, got up reluctantly and stretched her hind legs lazily one after another. Levin put on his boots, took his gun, opened the door cautiously, and went out into the open air. The coachmen were asleep near the vehicles, the horses were dozing. Only one was chewing some oats in an indolent manner, scattering them about in the trough. The light was still grey.

" What made you get up so early, my dear? " the old hostess asked him in a friendly tone from the door of the hut.

" I am going out shooting, auntie. Can I get to the swamp from here? "

" By the back, past the threshing-floors, my dear. You see that hemp slip? You'll find a footpath there."

The old woman conducted him to the threshing-barn, treading carefully with her bare sunburnt feet, and opened the gate.

" That will take you straight to the swamp. Our boys went there last night."

Lasca bounded merrily down the path, Levin followed with light rapid steps, every now and again looking up anxiously at the sky. He wanted to get to the marsh before sunrise, but the sun would not wait. The moon grew fainter, the morning-star, so brilliant a short time ago, now looked indistinct, the objects on the distant fields became more visible. The dew among the tall fragrant hemp drenched Levin as far as his waist. The minutest sound could be heard in the calm stillness of the

morning. A bee buzzed past his ear. He looked up and saw
a second and a third. They came out of a yard and were flying
over the hemp-field straight in the direction of the swamp. As
he drew nearer, he could see the vapours rising from it like
a mist, through which the willows and reeds appeared like little
islands. A crowd of peasants and boys, who had been watching
the cattle during the night, were now lying at the edge of the
swamp by the road, asleep under their coats. Near by three
hobbled horses were walking about, their chains jangling as
they went. Lasca was trotting by the side of her master on
the alert, and every now and again casting a beseeching look
at him, as though asking to be let off. As soon as he passed
the sleeping peasants, Levin examined the caps and let the dog
go. One of the horses shied at the sight of Lasca, flicked its
tail, and snorted. The others were startled too, and began
jumping about in the swamp, splashing in the water and making
a clanging sound with their chains. Lasca stopped and gazed
at them disdainfully, then turned to Levin with a questioning
look. He patted her and gave a whistle as a sign to start.

Lasca ran merrily over the marsh, looking about her. Amidst
the familiar odour of the vegetation and horse-dung, she soon
scented the birds that excited her most. In places, amongst
the moss and swamp-sage, the scent was particularly strong,
but it was still impossible to tell in what direction it grew
stronger or weaker. To find it, it was necessary to go further
under the wind. Inhaling the air with her dilated nostrils, she
instantly felt that before her were not only the traces, but the
birds themselves, and a great many of them. Lasca checked
the rapidity of her motion. They were there, but she was not
certain of the exact spot. To find it she began circling round,
when suddenly her master's voice diverted her attention.
" Here, Lasca! " he called, pointing to the other side. She
stopped as though asking him to let her be where she was, but
he repeated the command in an angry voice, pointing to a tufty
place under the water. She obeyed, pretending to be on the
scent in order to satisfy him, but she soon returned to her
former place. Now that he left her in peace, she knew exactly
what to do. Without so much as looking under foot, she began
the magic circle that was to explain everything to her, stumbling
over tufts and falling into the water. The scent grew stronger
and more definite, and it suddenly became clear to her that
one was there, behind that knoll, within five paces of her. She
stopped still. On her short legs she could see nothing ahead of

her, but she was certain it was there, quite close. She stood still inhaling the scent and enjoying the sensation of expectancy. Her tail was erect, quivering at the end; her mouth was open and her ears pricked. She breathed heavily, but cautiously, and turned her eyes still more cautiously towards her master. With his familiar face and terrible eyes, he was stumbling along over the knolls very slowly, as she thought, but in reality he was running fast.

When Levin observed that peculiar look of Lasca's, as she bent down to the ground with her mouth open, he knew that she scented snipe and prayed inwardly for success, especially with the first bird. When he came up to her and looked around, he saw from his height what she had perceived with her nose. In a sort of little lane between two rows of tufts, he caught sight of a snipe. It had its head turned and was listening. Suddenly it opened its wings slightly, closed them again, and disappeared round a corner.

" Go, Lasca, go! " Levin cried, pushing her behind.

" But how can I go? Where shall I go? " Lasca thought. " I can smell them from here, but as soon as I move, I don't know where they are or what they are." But again he pushed her with his knee and said in an agitated whisper, " Go, Lasca, go! "

" I suppose I must if he wants me to," she thought, darting in between the knolls, " but I shall not be responsible for myself." She was no longer on the scent and walked about aimlessly.

Within ten paces of the former spot a snipe rose with a wild cry, making a peculiar hollow sound of its wing. Levin fired, and the bird fell heavily with its white breast against the wet ground. Another, without waiting for the dog, flew up behind Levin. When he turned it was already some distance away, but the shot hit. It flew on about twenty paces, rose straight in the air, and rolling over and over fell to the ground like a ball.

" This looks like business! " Levin thought, putting the two birds into his game-bag. " Eh, Lasca, what do you think? "

When Levin reloaded his gun and moved on, the sun had already risen, though it was still invisible behind the clouds. The moon had lost all its splendour and looked faint and pale; not a single star could be seen. The puddles, that a short time ago had looked silvery in the dew, were now golden. The grass too, that had appeared bluish before, now assumed a yellow-green tint. The swamp-birds were chirping about in

the bushes, sparkling with dew, and casting long shadows. A hawk was sitting on a rick, wagging its head from side to side, and looking discontentedly over the marsh. Jackdaws were flying about in the meadow; a barefooted boy was leading the horses up to the old man, who raised himself from under his coat and began scratching different parts of his body. The smoke from the shot lay like a white mist on the green grass.

A boy came running towards Levin.

" There were wild ducks here yesterday! " he shouted from a distance as he tried to catch him up.

And Levin experienced a double pleasure in killing three more woodcocks in the presence of this boy.

XIII

THE sportsman's saying, that if the first shot is not missed the day will be a propitious one, proved true.

After tramping for many miles, Levin returned home, tired, hungry, and happy, with nineteen small birds and a duck, that he had stuck into his belt, there being no more room left in the game-bag. His companions had been up for some time, and feeling hungry had already breakfasted.

" Wait a moment, I know there are nineteen," Levin said, counting the birds a second time. They were twisted and clotted with blood and did not look so inspiring as they had done when they had risen high in the air.

There were indeed nineteen in all, and Stepan Arkadyevitch's envy added to Levin's pleasure. He was still happier when he discovered that a messenger was waiting with a note from Kitty.

" I am quite well and happy," she wrote. " Don't be worried about me. I have a new body-guard in the person of Marya Vlasevna." (Marya Vlasevna was a midwife, an important addition to Levin's household.) " She came to see how I was and we've made her stay until you come back. Everybody is well and happy. If you are enjoying the hunt, don't hurry back, but stay another day."

The joy he experienced on reading Kitty's note, added to the delight of the successful hunt, was so great that the two unpleasant incidents that occurred later passed by almost unnoticed. One was that the chestnut off horse had evidently been overworked the day before; it was out of form and refused to eat anything.

"The poor thing was driven too hard yesterday, Konstantin Dmitritch," the coachman said. "We drove about ten miles across the fields!"

The other piece of unpleasantness that somewhat impaired his happy frame of mind was that out of all the provisions they had brought from home absolutely nothing was left, though it had seemed to them they had brought enough to last them a whole week. On his way back from the swamp, weary and hungry, Levin was mentally consuming little pies, and as soon as he got to the hut he ordered Fillip to bring him some. It turned out that all the pies and even all the chickens were gone.

"You should have seen what an appetite he had!" Stepan Arkadyevitch said with a smile, referring to Vasenka Veslovsky. "I did not suffer from lack of appetite myself, but his was marvellous."

"What is to be done?" Levin asked with a surly look at Veslovsky. "You had better bring me some beef, Fillip."

"The beef has been eaten up, sir, and the bones were given to the dogs."

"They might have left me something!" Levin said in his anger and annoyance. He felt like crying.

"Get one or two of the birds ready," he said to Fillip in a trembling voice, trying not to look at Vasenka, "and ask them to let me have some milk."

When he had somewhat appeased his hunger by a good draught of milk, he grew ashamed at having betrayed his annoyance before a stranger, and began to laugh at his own rage.

They went out shooting again in the evening, when Veslovsky had the good luck to kill several birds, and at night they set out for home.

They were just as gay and merry as they had been on the way out. Veslovsky now sang, now went over his experiences with the peasants who had treated him to vodka, now the delightful time he had spent with the peasant girls. He related one thing that had amused him more than anything else. A young peasant had asked him if he was married, and on hearing that he was not, had said, "Then don't ogle other men's wives, but try and get one of your own!"

"We did have a jolly time, didn't we? Don't you think so, Levin?" he asked.

"I enjoyed it immensely," Levin replied, quite sincerely. He was delighted that the hostile feeling he had experienced towards Veslovsky at home had vanished, and he was now more than amiably disposed towards him.

XIV

AT ten o'clock on the following morning, after having been the round of the farm, Levin knocked at the door of Vasenka's room.

"*Entrez*," Vasenka called. "Excuse me, I have only just finished my ablutions," he greeted Levin with a smile, as he stood before him in his shirt sleeves.

"Don't mind me, please!" Levin seated himself at the window. "Did you sleep well?"

"Splendidly! What is the day like for shooting?"

"Do you take tea or coffee?"

"Neither, thanks; I shall wait till breakfast. I really feel ashamed of myself; the ladies I suppose are already up. It would be delightful to go out, and I should like to see your horses."

After they had walked round the garden, visited the stables, and even practised together on parallel bars, Levin brought his guest back to the house and entered the drawing-room.

"The shooting was splendid, and so was everything else!" Veslovsky said, going up to Kitty, who was sitting at the samovar. "What a pity it is that ladies are deprived of these pleasures!"

"I suppose he must talk to his hostess sometimes," Levin thought. And again he detected something unpleasant in the smile and the victorious expression with which Vasenka turned to his wife.

The princess, who was sitting at the other end of the table with Marya Vlasevna and Stepan Arkadyevitch, called to Levin, and began questioning him about their removal to Moscow for Kitty's confinement. Just as the preparations for the wedding had been offensive to Levin on account of their pettiness, so now were the preparations for the coming important event.

For weeks past he had been trying not to listen to their talk about the proper method of swathing the new baby, nor to see those mysterious endless garments they had been working at with such care. The birth of a son (he was convinced that it would be a son) seemed to him such an extraordinarily mysterious event, that he could scarcely believe in the possibility of it, and here they were preparing for it in the most unheard of, commonplace way!

But the princess did not understand his feelings and gave him no peace, putting down his reluctance to speak of it to sheer indifference. She had commissioned Stepan Arkadyevitch to find them rooms in Moscow, and now wanted Levin to fix a definite time for going.

" I don't know, princess; you had better do what seems to you best."

" You ought to decide about going to Moscow."

" I'm not in a position to judge, but I know that millions of babies are born out of Moscow and without doctors . . . then why . . . "

" If that is what you think . . . "

" I don't know. Let Kitty decide."

" Kitty mustn't be worried with these things! Do you want me to frighten her? Only this spring Nataly Golitsin died in child-birth as a result of poor attendance."

" I will do whatever you want me to," he said dejectedly.

The princess continued talking to him, but he was no longer listening to her. Though their conversation had annoyed him, it was not on that account that he was depressed; he was disturbed at the scene he had witnessed at the samovar.

" No, this can't go on," he thought, casting a look at Vasenka every now and again, as he was bending over Kitty and talking to her with that sweet, winsome smile of his, and at Kitty herself, who was blushing and looking agitated.

There was something offensive and suggestive about Vasenka's pose, about his glance and his smile. Even Kitty's pose and smile were offensive to Levin. The light in his eyes died out, and, as before, he felt himself cast down from his height of happiness, peace, and dignity into the depths of despair, anger, and humiliation. Again everybody and everything became loathsome to him.

" Do just as you please, princess," he said, looking round the room.

" The cap of Monomachus weighs heavily on you!" Stepan Arkadyevitch said to him jestingly, referring not only to the conversation with the princess, but to Levin's agitation, the cause of which he had observed. " How late you are, Dolly!"

All rose to greet Darya Alexandrovna. Vasenka got up for a moment, and with a lack of civility to the other sex, characteristic of modern young men, bowed to her in an off-hand way, and continued his conversation.

"Masha was very restless during the night; I feel quite worn out," Dolly said.

Vasenka and Kitty were again discussing Anna, and debating whether love should be held higher than the conventions. On the whole the conversation was disagreeable to Kitty, by its contents as well as by the tone in which it was carried on, and especially because she knew how it would affect her husband. She was too naïve to know how to break it off, or how to put a stop to the young man's pleasantries. She felt that whatever she might do would be noticed by her husband and misinterpreted. And indeed when she questioned Dolly about Masha, and Vasenka stood looking on indifferently until she should turn to him again, it seemed to Levin nothing more than a cunning ruse.

"Shall we go out to gather mushrooms to-day?" Dolly asked.

"I should love to," Kitty replied with a blush. She felt as though she ought to ask Vasenka to come too, out of sheer politeness, but could not bring herself to do so. "Where are you going, Kostia?" she asked with a guilty expression on her face, as her husband walked resolutely past her. This expression confirmed all his suspicions.

"The engineer came while I was away and I haven't seen him yet."

He went downstairs and had barely got to his study when he heard his wife's footsteps hurrying after him with heedless rapidity.

"What is it?" he asked her, coldly. "We are busy."

"Excuse me," she said, turning to the German engineer. "I should like a few words with my husband."

The German was about to go out, when Levin stopped him.

"Is the train at three o'clock?" the German asked; "I should not like to miss it."

Levin did not reply, but went out to his wife.

"Well, what do you want to say to me?" he asked her in French.

He was not looking at her. He did not wish to see that she was agitated in a way unsuited to her condition, and that she looked pitiful.

" I wanted to say . . . that we cannot live like this . . . it is nothing but torture," she said.

" The servants are in there," he said angrily; " don't make a scene."

" Then come in here."

They were standing in the hall; Kitty wanted to go into the room at the side, but the English governess was there giving Tania her lessons.

" Let us go into the garden."

In the garden they ran against a peasant who was sweeping the path, and without considering the fact that he saw Kitty's tear-stained, agitated face, and that they both looked like people who were escaping from some calamity, they walked on quickly, anxious to unburden themselves from the suffering they were experiencing.

" It is impossible to live like this! I am tormented, and you are tormented; and what for? " she began, when they got to a lonely seat at the bottom of a linden avenue.

" Now tell me, was not his tone disgusting, horrible? " he asked, standing before her with his hands folded on his breast as he had done on the night of Vasenka's arrival.

" Yes, it was," she replied in a trembling voice. " But, Kostia, don't you see that I am not to blame? I wanted to snub him, but you know these men. . . . Why did he come here? when we were so happy together! " she said, convulsed with the sobs that shook her whole body.

The gardener saw them returning to the house with pacified, beaming faces and wondered what they had found so particularly cheerful about the bench.

XV

LEVIN conducted Kitty to her room and went in to see Dolly. Darya Alexandrovna was very much upset that day. She was pacing up and down the room, scolding a little girl who was crying in a corner.

" I shall make you stand in that corner the whole day," she was saying. " You shall have dinner all by yourself, and won't be allowed to play with your dolls, and I won't buy you a new dress." She could not think of any other punishment for her.

" She's a bad, bad girl! " she said to Levin as he entered. " I don't know where she gets her nasty habits from."

" What has she done? " he asked indifferently, for he wanted to consult her about his own affair and was annoyed to have come at such an unpropitious moment.

" She went with Grisha to pick raspberries and . . . I can't tell you what she did there! You would be immensely sorry for Miss Elliot. She does not think of anything . . . a perfect machine. *Figurez-vous, que la petite . . .*"

And Darya Alexandrovna began telling him what Masha had done.

" Oh, it's nothing. It doesn't prove that the child is bad; she's simply mischievous," Levin said, trying to calm her.

" But what is the matter? You look upset. What is going on there? " Dolly asked.

From her tone Levin knew that it would not be difficult for him to tell her what he had come to say.

" I was not in there; I was alone with Kitty in the garden. We've quarrelled twice since . . . since Stiva came."

Dolly looked at him with her intelligent eyes.

" Now tell me frankly, don't you think there was something disgusting in the tone of that young man to Kitty? Something that might be offensive to a husband? "

" Well, I don't quite know how to express it. . . . Stand in the corner! " she said, turning to Masha, who having observed a faint smile on her mother's face, had come forward a little. " Most people would think that he was behaving like all young men. *Il fait la cour à une jeune et jolie femme,* and a man of the world would only be flattered by it."

" Oh, yes," Levin said solemnly; " have you noticed it? "

" Not only I, but Stiva has, too. ' *Je crois que* Veslovsky *fait un petit brin de cour à* Kitty,' he said to me this morning."

" Very well; I am perfectly satisfied. Now I can tell him to go."

" What do you mean? Are you mad? " Dolly asked in a fright. " Really, Kostia, you must consider what you're doing," she added, laughing. " You can run away to Fanny," she said to Masha. " If you like I'll speak to Stiva; he can take him away. We might say that you are expecting other visitors. Anyhow, I don't think he quite fits in with us."

" No, I must tell him myself."

" But you'll quarrel with him! "

" No, I won't. I shall rather enjoy it," he said, his eyes sparkling. " Why don't you forgive her, Dolly? She won't do it again," he added as he saw Masha, who had not gone to

Fanny's, standing before her mother irresolutely with a beseeching expression on her face.

The mother looked at her. The child burst out sobbing and buried her face in her mother's skirts. Dolly stroked her head with her dry, bony hand.

"What is there in common between him and us?" Levin thought as he went in search of Veslovsky.

As he walked through the hall he ordered the carriage to be harnessed to drive to the station.

"One of the springs got broken yesterday," the servant replied.

"Then the cart will do; only be quick. Where is our visitor?"

"Upstairs in his room."

Vasenka had just unpacked his portmanteau, and his clothes and music lay strewn about the room. He was putting on his boots to go out riding when Levin entered. Whether there was something peculiar about Levin's face or he felt that *ce petit brin de cour* was somewhat out of place in that family, Vasenka was a little embarrassed when he saw Levin, in so far as a man of the world can be embarrassed.

"Do you ride in gaiters?"

"Yes, it's much cleaner," Vasenka replied, as he placed his leg on a chair and fastened the bottom buttons, smiling with his good-natured smile.

He was indeed a jolly good fellow, and Levin began feeling sorry for him and ashamed of himself as he noticed the timidity in his face.

There was a piece of cane on the table that they had broken that morning over the gymnastic exercises, trying to raise the parallel bars. Levin took it up and began peeling pieces off it, not knowing how to begin.

"I wanted . . ." He stopped, but suddenly thought of Kitty and everything that had happened. "I've ordered the carriage for you," he went on, looking resolutely into Vasenka's eyes.

"I don't understand," Vasenka said in surprise; "are we going anywhere?"

"You have to go to the station," Levin replied, gloomily, breaking little pieces off the end of the stick.

"Are you going away or has anything happened?"

"I'm expecting some visitors," Levin replied, attacking the stick more nervously with his powerful fingers. "No, I am not expecting any visitors and nothing has happened, but I ask you to leave. You may explain my incivility as you please."

Vasenka straightened himself up.

"But I ask *you* to explain," he said with dignity, having understood at last.

"That I cannot do," Levin said softly and slowly, trying to stop the trembling of his jaws; "and it would be better for you not to insist."

And as the split end of the stick was completely broken off, Levin took hold of the thick end, snapped it in half, and quickly caught the falling piece.

No doubt the sight of those arms in tension and the muscles he had felt that morning during their exercises, together with the trembling jaw and sparkling light in Levin's eye, did more towards persuading Vasenka to ask no further questions than mere words would have done. He shrugged his shoulders, gave a contemptuous smile, and made a low bow.

"Can I see Oblonsky?"

Neither the shrug of the shoulders nor the smile produced any effect on Levin. "What else can he do?" he thought.

"I'll send him to you at once."

"What nonsense is this I hear?" Stepan Arkadyevitch began, when he found Levin in the garden, waiting for the departure of his guest, after the latter had told him the whole tale. "*Mais c'est ridicule!* Have you been bitten by a mad dog? *Mais c'est du dernier ridicule!* What harm is there if a young man does . . ."

But the spot the dog had bitten was evidently still sore, for at Stepan Arkadyevitch's words Levin grew pale and pulled him up abruptly.

"Please don't go into my reasons! I'm sorry, but I couldn't do otherwise. I'm sorry for him and for you. But I don't think it will be such a great grief for him to go away, and my wife and I don't want him here."

"But it's so insulting to him! *Et puis c'est ridicule.*"

"It's insulting and painful for me, too! It's not my fault; I don't see why I should suffer."

"Really, I should not have expected it of you! *On peut-être jaloux, mais à ce point, c'est du dernier ridicule!*"

Levin turned away from him quickly and began walking up and down the avenue alone. Soon he heard the rumble of wheels and through the trees caught a glimpse of Vasenka in his Scotch cap sitting on some hay in the cart, for unfortunately there was no seat, bumping up and down as he drove down the avenue.

"What is this?" Levin thought, as a servant came running out of the house and stopped the cart. The engineer, whom Levin had entirely forgotten, bowed to Veslovsky, said a few words to him, climbed into the cart, and both were driven off.

Stepan Arkadyevitch and the princess were very much annoyed at Levin's act, and he felt himself not only ridiculous in the highest degree, but guilty and utterly disgraced. But as he thought of the suffering that he and his wife had gone through, he assured himself that if he had to do it all over again he would behave precisely in the same way.

In spite of it all, every one, with the exception of the princess, who could not forgive Levin for his deed, became exceedingly animated and happy, like children who had escaped a punishment, or adults after a tiresome, official reception. In the evening when the princess had retired, the event was spoken of as though it had happened long ago. Dolly, who had her father's gift of being able to tell funny stories, made Varenka roar with laughter, when for the third or fourth time she related, with little humorous additions, how she had put on a new pair of shoes for Vasenka's benefit and was coming into the drawing-room, when she heard the rumble of a ramshackle cart, and looking out she saw Vasenka himself sitting on the hay, with his Scotch cap, songs, gaiters and all. "They might have ordered the carriage! When I heard someone call 'Wait,' I began to think that they had taken pity on him, but no, they put the fat German in with him and drove them off together. And my new shoes were wasted."

XVI

DARYA ALEXANDROVNA fulfilled her intention and went to see Anna. She was sorry to displease Kitty and Levin, for she felt that they were right in refusing to have anything to do with Vronsky, but she considered it her duty to visit Anna, in order to show her that her feelings had not changed, in spite of the altered circumstances.

Dolly did not wish to be dependent on the Levin's for this journey, and so sent to the village to hire some horses, much to her brother-in-law's annoyance when he heard of it.

"What makes you think that I disapprove of this visit? If

I disapprove of anything at all, it is that you do not wish to take my horses," he said to her. "You have not once told me that you really intended going. It is not very nice for me to have you hiring horses in the village. Besides, they probably won't take you all the way. I have plenty of horses, and if you don't wish to hurt me, please make use of them."

Dolly had to give in, and on the appointed day Levin had a team of four horses and relays prepared for her, consisting of field and riding horses, not a very imposing affair truly, but one that would take her to her destination in a day. It was rather awkward for Levin, as he needed the horses for the princess and the midwife, who were both leaving, but his sense of hospitality would not permit him to allow Dolly to hire horses when she could use his. Besides, he knew that the twenty roubles it would have cost her would come in in good stead, her financial affairs not being in the most flourishing condition.

Acting on Levin's advice, Dolly started before daybreak. The road was good, the carriage comfortable, and Levin had sent his bailiff, in addition to the coachman, to help look after her. Dolly went to sleep and only awoke when they drew up at an inn where the horses had to be changed.

She took tea at the house of the same rich peasant with whom Levin had put up on his way to Sviajsky's, and after telling the woman all about her children and chatting with the old man about Vronsky, whom he seemed to think a good deal of, she proceeded on her journey at about ten o'clock. At home her many domestic cares never gave her a spare moment in which to think, but now, feeling perfectly free, all manner of thoughts began crowding into her brain. She began reviewing her life as she had never done before, and her strange musings astonished her. At first she began thinking and worrying about the children, though the princess and Kitty had promised to look after them. "I hope Masha won't be naughty again," she thought, "and that Grisha will not go near that horse that always kicks him. Poor Lily! I hope she won't get ill!" Soon present difficulties gave way to questions of the future. She began thinking of their financial affairs, and saw clearly that they would have to move to a cheaper house this winter, and then they must buy new furniture for the drawing-room, and Tania must have a new fur coat. She looked still further ahead and wondered how she would make men and women of her little ones. "The difficulty will not be with the girls," she thought, "but what about the boys? Fortunately I am free

163

to work with Grisha just now, but supposing I were to have another baby? Stiva, of course, is not to be depended upon. I may be able to bring them up with the help of good people, but if others come . . ." And it suddenly seemed to her unjust that a woman should have to bring forth children in sorrow. " Giving birth to a child is not so bad; it's the period of pregnancy that is so dreadful," she thought, as she recalled her last pregnancy and the death of the child afterwards. A conversation she had had with a young woman at the inn came back to her. She had asked the woman if she had any children, and the woman had replied merrily: " I had a little girl, but the Lord took her from me; I buried her last Lent."

" Did you grieve for her? " Dolly had asked.

" Why should I? The old man has enough grandchildren as it is. They are only a trouble. You can't work or do anything; they only tie you hand and foot."

At the moment the young woman's words had seemed horrible to Dolly, but now, thinking it over, she could not help seeing that there was a particle of truth in them.

" What is there in it after all? " she asked herself, as she looked back on her fifteen years of married life. " Nothing but the bearing and rearing children, and constant worries and cares. Your mind gets dull and you become indifferent to everything. Even Kitty, young and pretty as she is, looks awful in her condition, and when I'm like that, I'm positively hideous, I know. Then there is the excruciating suffering at childbirth, then the nursing and sleepless nights and terrible pain . . ."

Dolly shuddered at the very thought of the pain she had experienced in nursing her infants with cracked nipples.

" Then come their ailments—one eternal anxiety; then education and signs of evil tendencies " (she recalled Masha's last deed among the raspberries), "their lessons . . . Latin . . . It is all so difficult. And worst of all is the constant fear of losing them." And a vivid picture of the death of her last boy rose up before her. Again she saw herself standing by his little pink coffin, heart-broken, amidst the universal indifference; again she felt the anguish as she gazed at the little brow and curly hair and open mouth—the last thing she had seen as the pink lid with the embroidered cross was closed over him.

" And what is it all for? What will come of it? Here am I, now pregnant, now nursing, always cross and ill-tempered, a worry to myself and everybody else, and my husband no

longer loving me. So I shall live for the rest of my life, for no other purpose than launching into the world a lot of beggared, badly brought up children. Even now, I don't know what we should have done if the Levins had not invited us to spend the summer with them. Of course, Kitty and Kostia are so nice that we haven't felt uncomfortable about it, but it can't go on for ever. They will have children of their own soon, and won't be able to help us any longer. Besides, they are crowded enough as it is. And there's nothing to hope for from papa; he has scarcely enough for himself. How awful not to be able to bring up your own children, but to have to depend on others to help one! At best, supposing I have the good fortune not to lose any more of them, I may manage to educate them somehow or other, so that they may not be utterly useless. That is the highest I can hope for. And how much suffering, how much labour will have been spent just on that! My whole life has been ruined!" And again she thought of the young woman's words, and could not help admitting that there was a brutal truth at the back of them.

"Have we far to go yet, Mihail?" she asked the bailiff, anxious to drive away these oppressive thoughts.

"Seven miles from this village."

The carriage drove down the village street and over a small bridge. They came across a crowd of peasants with bound sheaves on their backs, who were talking and laughing merrily as they walked along. They stopped and looked curiously at the carriage as it passed them. All their faces seemed to Dolly happy, healthy, and brimming over with the joy of life. "Every one seems alive except I," she thought as she left the women and the village behind her and was swaying pleasantly on the soft springs of the old carriage as it drove up the hill. "I am like a prisoner let out for a moment from a world of cares to collect my thoughts. Every one enjoys life; these women, my sisters, Varenka, and Anna, but not I. Why do they all condemn Anna? What for? Am I better than she is? At any rate, I have a husband whom I love, not in the way I should have liked, but still, I love him, and Anna never loved her husband. It was not her fault; she wanted to live. We were born with that desire in our souls. In her place I should probably have done the same. Even now I am not sure whether I did right to listen to her when she came to me in Moscow during that terrible time. I ought to have left Stiva then and begun life anew. I might have loved and been loved. And what sort of a position am I in now? I do not respect him; I need him," she thought, referring to her husband, "and so I put up with everything. Is that better? At that time I was still attractive. . . . I had not lost all my beauty." She was suddenly seized with a desire to see her own face. She had a little travelling mirror in her handbag, and wanted to take it out, but fearing that the coachman or the bailiff might turn round and see her, she forebore from doing so.

But even without the mirror it occurred to her that it might not be too late even now. She recalled how amiable Sergei Ivanovitch always was to her, and thought of Stiva's friend, Turovtsin, who had helped her nurse the children during the scarlet fever. She felt certain he was in love with her. Then she thought of another young man who always declared that she was prettier than her sisters, as Stiva had told her. All sorts of absurd, impossible romances presented themselves to her mind. "Anna acted quite rightly and I don't blame her," she continued. "She is happy, and is making another happy. She is not crushed as I am. She is probably just as fresh and alive as ever, and ready for anything." A smile played about her lips as she tried to imagine herself in the same position as Anna, with some ideal man who was in love with her. She saw herself making a clean breast of it to her husband as Anna had done, and tried to picture Stepan Arkadyevitch's surprise and mortification when she told him the news.

With such thoughts as these she reached the turn in the road that led to Vosdvejensky.

XVII

THE coachman stopped the horses and looked towards a field of rye on the right in which some peasants were sitting near a cart. The bailiff was just on the point of getting down from the box when he changed his mind and called to one of the peasants, motioning him to come up. The slight breeze they had felt on the journey died down as soon as the carriage came to a standstill; the flies buzzed round the sweating horses, who tried to switch them off with their tails. The sound of some one sharpening a scythe near the cart ceased, and one of the peasants got up and came towards the carriage.

"Hi, make haste!" the bailiff shouted impatiently, as he saw the peasant coming slowly towards them, treading gingerly with his bare feet over the rough, uneven ground. "Are you coming or not?"

The old man, his curly hair bound round with a piece of bass, his bent back dark with perspiration, quickened his steps, and coming up to the carriage, put his sunburnt hand on the wing.

"You want Vosdvejensky, the count?" he repeated. "Just go right up the hill and turn to the left; you can't miss it. Is it the count himself you want?"

"Are they at home?" Dolly asked, not knowing how to inquire about Anna even of a peasant.

"I think so," the peasant replied, leaving a distinct trace of his bare feet in the dust as he moved along. "I should think so," he said again, evidently wishing to strike up a conversation. "Some visitors arrived yesterday—such fine visitors too. What do you want?" he asked, turning to a lad who was calling him from the cart. "They passed here on horseback a short time ago to look at the mowing, so they must be at home now. And who may you be?"

"We come from a distance," the coachman replied, climbing on to the box. "So you say it is not very far?"

"Quite close here, as you get round the bend," he replied, passing his hand over the carriage-wing.

Just then a sturdy young fellow came up.

"Is there any work to be had over the harvesting?" he asked the old man.

"I don't know."

"If you turn to the left you can't miss it," the old peasant repeated, reluctant to be parted from the travellers.

"Ili! hi!" two voices shouted, as soon as they had started. The coachman pulled up again.

"Here they come! look!" the old peasant shouted, pointing to four riders and two people in a waggonette, who were coming down the road.

The party consisted of Vronsky, his jockey, Veslovsky, and Anna, all on horseback, and the Princess Varvara and Sviajsky in the waggonette. They had gone out to inspect the new reaping machines that had just arrived.

When the carriage stopped, the riders slowed down to a walk. Anna and Veslovsky were in front. Anna was on a powerful English cob with closely-cropped mane and short tail. Dolly was struck by Anna's beautiful head, with the black hair peeping out from beneath her tall hat, her full round shoulders, slender waist in a black riding habit—by the whole of her graceful pose.

In the first moment it had seemed to her not the proper thing for Anna to be on horseback. The idea of a lady riding was associated in her mind with something youthful and coquettish, ill-becoming to Anna's position, but as she drew near Dolly forgave her on the spot. She looked so simple and dignified in her elegant attire that nothing could have suited her better or been more natural.

By the side of her, on a grey, mettlesome, cavalry horse, rode Vasenka Veslovsky, in his Scotch cap and streaming ribbons, looking well pleased with himself. Dolly could hardly repress a smile as she recognised him. Behind them came Vronsky on a thoroughbred chestnut, pulling at the reins to curb it. At the back of him was a little man dressed like a jockey. Sviajsky and the princess, in a new waggonette, brought up the rear.

Anna's face lighted up with joy as she recognised the small figure of Dolly sitting in a corner of the old carriage. She gave a cry, trembled in her saddle, and sent the horse forward at a gallop. When she got to the carriage, she jumped down unaided, and raising her habit she rushed up to Dolly.

" I hoped it would be you, yet I dared not think it! What joy! You can't think how glad I am! " And she pressed her face against Dolly's and kissed her again and again; then stood back to have a good look at her.

" What joy, Alexei! " she said, turning to Vronsky, who had dismounted and was approaching them. He raised his tall grey hat and went up to Dolly.

" You can't think how pleased we are to see you," he said significantly, disclosing his fine white teeth in a smile of welcome.

Vasenka Veslovsky, without dismounting, greeted Dolly gaily, and waved his cap joyously in the air.

" You know the Princess Varvara," Anna said, with a questioning look at Dolly, as the waggonette came up.

" Ah! " Dolly said, and a shade of displeasure spread over her face.

The princess was an aunt of her husband's; she had long known her and did not respect her. She knew that the Princess Varvara spent the whole of her life as a hanger-on at the houses of rich relatives, and her presence in the house of Vronsky, a perfect stranger to her, offended her family pride. Anna observed Dolly's expression and blushed. She dropped her riding-habit and stumbled over it.

Dolly walked over to the waggonette to exchange greetings with the Princess Varvara. Sviajsky, too, was known to her. He asked after his eccentric friend and his young wife, and casting a glance at the badly-matched horses and at the old carriage in which Dolly had come, he suggested that the ladies should drive the rest of the way in the waggonette.

" And I will get into that vehicle," he said. " You need not be afraid, the horse is a quiet one and the princess drives well."

" Oh, no, do stay where you are! " Anna implored, coming up, and taking Dolly's arm she led her away.

Dolly could not help looking at the smart conveyance, the fine, handsome horses, and at the smiling, elegant people about her. She was struck by the immense change that had taken place in her beloved Anna. A woman less observant than Darya Alexandrovna, one who had not known Anna as she had done, would not have noticed anything particular about her. But Dolly, full of the thoughts that had come to her on her journey, saw in her that rare beauty that comes to women when they are in love. Everything about her, the dimples on her cheeks and chin, her lips, the smile that flitted across her face, the sparkling of her eyes, the grace and rapidity of her movements, the rich sound of her voice as she gave a curt, though not unkind reply to Veslovsky, who had asked for permission to ride her cob in order to teach him to gallop from his right leg—everything was charming and attractive, and it seemed as though she herself was deliciously conscious of it.

When the two women seated themselves in the carriage they did not know what to say to each other. Anna was embarrassed by Dolly's close, scrutinising gaze, while Dolly felt ill-at-ease after Sviajsky's remark about the " vehicle," and was ashamed of the shabby old carriage as Anna sat down beside her. The coachman and the bailiff were undergoing a similar sensation. To hide his embarrassment, the bailiff bustled about, helping the ladies to get in, while Fillip assured himself inwardly that he would not allow their external superiority to crush him at any rate. He gave a disdainful smile as he glanced at the black trotter harnessed to the waggonette, and decided that it was only good for *promenade*, and could never go forty miles in the heat.

The peasants at the cart had all risen and stood looking curiously at the whole company.

" They seem pleased; I suppose they have not seen each

other for a long time," the old peasant with the curly hair remarked.

" Uncle Gerasim, if that black stallion were to haul the sheaves we should soon get the work done! " another said.

" Look here, is that one in trousers a woman? " a third asked, pointing to Vasenka Veslovsky, who had mounted Anna's horse.

" No, didn't you see the way he jumped up? "

" Well, boys, aren't we going to sleep? "

" Not to-day," the old man said; " it is getting late. Take the sickles and start. "

XVIII

ANNA gazed at Dolly's emaciated, worried face, dusty from the journey, and was about to remark that she looked thinner, when she recollected her own appearance as Dolly looked at her; she heaved a sigh and began talking about herself.

" I suppose you are wondering if I am happy in my position," she said. " How shall I explain? I am ashamed to confess it, but I . . . I feel unpardonably happy. I am living in a sort of enchanted world after having awakened from a horrible dream. You know, one of those terrific nightmares, when you wake up and wonder what it is that has frightened you so. Of course, I have gone through the most agonising moments, but now it is all over, and I am happy, especially since we came down here." She looked at Dolly with a timid questioning smile.

" I am very glad," Dolly said returning her smile, with one somewhat colder than she had intended it to be. " I am glad for your sake. Why didn't you write to me? "

" I? I did not dare to . . . You forget my position. . . ."

" Fancy your not daring to write to me! If you only knew how I . . . I consider . . ."

Dolly wanted to tell Anna her thoughts of the morning, but for some reason or other it seemed to her inappropriate just then.

" However, we can talk of these things later. What are all those buildings? " she asked, in order to change the subject, as she pointed to the red and green roofs that could be seen through the acacias and lilacs. " It looks quite like a little town."

But Anna did not reply to her words.

" No, no; tell me what you think of me," she implored.

" I think . . ." Dolly began, but just then Vasenka Veslovsky, having achieved the feat of making the cob gallop from the right leg, rushed past them, bumping up and down on Anna's saddle as he went. " I've got him to do it, Anna Arkadyevna! " he shouted. Anna did not even look at him.

" I don't think anything," Dolly said, again feeling that the carriage was hardly the place to start a long explanation in and anxious to be as brief as possible, " but I've always loved you, and if you love any one it is only for what they are and not what you want them to be."

Anna turned away and half closed her eyes, a habit that Dolly had not noticed in her before. She was trying to grasp the full significance of those words.

" If you had any sins," she said after a moment or two, " they would be forgiven you for this visit, and for what you have just said."

Her eyes filled with tears, and Dolly pressed her hand silently.

" What are these buildings? " she asked again after a pause. " There are so many of them! "

" Those are the servants' cottages and the stables," Anna replied. " And the park begins from here. It was all very much neglected, but Alexei has worked wonders since we came here. He is fond of the place and is very much interested in farming, a thing I should never have expected of him. He's so full of ideas and can do anything he sets his mind on. He is passionately fond of the work and has no time to get bored. It is wonderful to think that he, of all men, should have turned out such a capital farmer. And he's so economical, too, almost mean, but only with the farm I'm glad to say; when it comes to a question of thousands he is generosity itself." She gave an affectionate wise smile, the sort of smile with which women often speak of the man they love. " Do you see that large building over there? It is a new hospital. It will have cost more than a hundred thousand roubles. It is his special hobby just now. And do you know how he came to build it? I once accused him of meanness, because he refused to let the peasants have the land at a lower rent when they asked him to, and so he built it to prove that I was wrong. Of course it was not altogether because of that; there were other reasons as well. *C'est une petitesse* if you like, but I love him all the more for it. You will soon see the house. It was built by his grandfather, and it has not been altered at all on the outside.

"How lovely!" Dolly exclaimed as she caught a glimpse of a beautiful house with columns standing behind the old trees.

"Isn't it! We get a most magnificent view from upstairs."

They drove into a gravel court-yard, adorned with flower-beds, in which two workmen were bordering the shrubbery with rough, porous stones.

"Oh, they've got here before us!" Anna said, as she looked at the horses that were being led away from the porch. "That cob is my favourite. Bring it here and give it some sugar. Where is the count?" she asked of two footmen in livery, who rushed out to meet her. "Here he is!" she said, as she saw Vronsky and Veslovsky coming towards them.

"What room will you put the princess in?" Vronsky asked Anna in French, and without waiting for a reply, he turned to Darya Alexandrovna, welcomed her a second time, and kissed her hand. "The large room with the balcony would be rather nice."

"Oh, no, that is much too far off! I am going to put her in the corner room, to be near me. Come along," Anna said, giving her favourite horse the sugar that a footman had brought her.

"*Et vous oubliez votre devoir,*" she said to Veslovsky as he came out of the porch.

"*Pardon, j'ai eu tout plein les poches,*" he said with a smile, feeling in his waistcoat pockets.

"*Mais vous venez trop tard,*" she said, wiping her hand on her handkerchief after the horse had licked it in taking the sugar. She turned to Dolly.

"How long shall you stay? Don't say it is only for one day!"

"I promised to get back soon, as the children . . ." She stopped, feeling ill at ease because she had to take her shabby little bag out of the carriage, and also because she felt that her face was dusty.

"No, Dolly, you mustn't go so soon. . . . We'll talk it over. Come along."

Anna led her to her room.

It was not the gorgeous room that Vronsky had suggested, but a smaller one, about which Anna was very apologetic. And even this was furnished with a luxury such as Dolly had never known in her own home, and that reminded her of some of the best hotels on the continent.

"I'm so glad you've come, dear," Anna said, sitting down beside Dolly in her riding-habit. "Tell me all about yourself. I saw Stiva for a moment, but you know he can't tell you much about the children. How is my favourite, Tania? She's quite a big girl now, I suppose."

"Yes, she has grown a great deal," Dolly replied, surprised to hear herself talk so coldly of her children. "It is very jolly at the Levins," she added.

"Had I known that you did not despise me," Anna said, "you might all have come to stay with us. Stiva is quite an old friend of Alexei's, you know," she added with a blush.

"We are quite comfortable. . . ." Dolly said, confused.

"I know I am talking nonsense, dear, but that's because I'm so glad to see you!" Anna said, kissing her again. "You haven't yet told me what you think of me, and I want to know everything. It is nice to have you see me such as I really am. I don't wish to pose or prove anything; I simply want to live and do no harm to any one but myself. I have a perfect right to do that, haven't I? However, we can talk things over later; it will take us a long time to explain everything. I will go and change my dress now and send a maid to help you."

XIX

LEFT alone, Dolly surveyed the room with the expert eye of a housekeeper. Everything she had seen both inside and outside the house, as well as in her own room, gave her the impression of abundance and luxury, the new European kind of luxury she had often read about in English novels, but had never seen in Russia, least of all in the country. Everything in her room, beginning with the French wall-paper and ending with the carpet, that covered the whole floor, was perfectly new. The bed had a spring mattress with a separate headpiece, and the pillows were covered with fine embroidered pillow-cases. The marble washstand and toilet-table, the couch, the chairs, the bronze clock on the mantel-piece, the curtains and draperies were all new and of the best and most expensive quality.

The smart maid who came in to help her was better dressed and had her hair arranged more fashionably than Dolly herself. Dolly liked her polite manners and neatness, but was ill-at-ease in her presence because, to her great discomfort, she had brought a patched blouse with her. Those very patches and darns, of which she had been so proud at home, made her feel uncomfortable among these surroundings. She was immensely relieved when Annushka, whom she knew well, came in to take the place of the smart maid, who was wanted by her mistress.

Annushka was evidently glad to see her and chatted incessantly. Dolly could see that she was anxious to express an opinion about her mistress's position, and to talk of her devotion to the count, so stopped her discreetly.

" I grew up with Anna Arkadyevna, and I am more fond of her than of any one else in the world," she said. " It is not for us to judge. She loves him so . . ."

" Please get this washed if possible," Dolly interrupted her.

" Yes, madame. We have two laundresses, and all the washing is done by machinery. The count likes to see to everything himself. He is such a considerate husband and . . ."

Dolly was glad when Anna came back and put a stop to her chattering.

Anna had put on a very simple muslin dress. Dolly scrutinised it carefully; she knew at what price such simplicity was attained.

" Quite an old acquaintance of yours," she said, referring to Annushka.

She was not in the least embarrassed now, but quite calm and at her ease. The emotion produced in her by Dolly's arrival had completely left her, and she had assumed that light, superficial tone, through which it was impossible to get at her real feelings.

" Well, and how is your little girl, Anna? " Dolly asked.

" Annie? Oh, she is quite well, thanks—has improved wonderfully. Would you like to see her? Come into the nursery. We had such a bother with our nurses," she went on. " We have an Italian wet-nurse. She is very nice, but so stupid! We were anxious to get rid of her, but the child is so used to her that we decided to let her stay in the end."

" But how did you manage about . . ." Dolly stopped. She had wanted to ask about the child's name, but observing the frown on Anna's face, she pulled herself up. " How did you manage about weaning her? " she asked.

But Anna had understood.

" It was not that you wished to ask; you wanted to know about her name, isn't that so? She has no name; that is, she is Karenin," she said, closing her eyes. " However," she

added, her face brightening, " we can talk of that later. Come
and see her. *Elle est très gentille.* She crawls about now."

The luxuriousness of the nursery struck Dolly even more than
what she had observed in the rest of the house. There were
little English carts and walking stools; there was a huge couch
arranged like a billiard-table for the child to crawl on, and
swings and novel kinds of baths. All these things were of
English make and of the very best quality. The room itself
was large, light, and airy.

When they entered the child was sitting in a chair, with
nothing on but a little shirt, eating some soup that she was
spilling all down the front of her. A Russian maid, whose duty
it was to wait in the nursery, was feeding her and at the same
time eating herself. Neither the nurse nor wet-nurse were
there; they could be heard carrying on a French conversation
in the adjoining room, the only language in which they could
talk to each other.

On hearing Anna's voice a tall, smart Englishwoman with
an exceedingly disagreeable, unsympathetic face came in
quickly, and shaking back her fair curls instantly began excusing
herself, though Anna had not in any way reproached her. To
every word of Anna's she kept on saying, " Yes, my lady."

The black-haired, ruddy little girl, with her fat, chubby little
body, produced a favourable impression on Dolly, though she
looked rather severe at the sight of a strange face. She seemed
so robust and healthy that Dolly almost envied her. She was
particularly taken with the way the little one crawled; not one
of her own children had ever crawled like that. She looked
wonderfully sweet as she was put down on the carpet with her
little dress tucked up behind. She peeped at them mischiev-
ously, like some little animal, with her sparkling black eyes,
delighted to be admired.

But the general tone of the nursery, especially the English
woman, displeased Dolly very much. She could not understand how Anna, with her knowledge of the world, could have
engaged such an unsympathetic girl, of such low character, to
look after her child. She concluded that it must have been
owing to the difficulty of getting any one else to enter such an
irregular family. Dolly could see at a glance that both this
woman, the wet-nurse, and the child did not get on together,
and that a visit to the nursery on the mother's part was an
unusual thing. Anna wanted to give the child one of its toys,
but did not know where to find it. And when Dolly asked her

how many teeth the child had she was not quite certain of the number, and apparently knew nothing whatever about the two last ones.

"Sometimes it gives me pain to think what a superfluous person I am here," Anna said, lifting up her train to get it out of the way of some toy as they left the room. "It was not like that with my first."

"I should have thought, on the other hand . . ." Dolly began timidly.

"You know, I saw Serioja," Anna interrupted her, half closing her eyes, as though looking far into the distance. "But I will tell you about that later. Would you believe it? I feel like some starved creature before whom a sumptuous feast has been placed, and who does not know what to start on first. I have so much that I want to tell you, and don't know what to begin upon. There is no one else to whom I could talk as I can to you. *Mais je ne vous ferai grâce de rien.* I must tell you everything."

"I suppose I had better give you some idea of the company here," she went on. "I will begin with the ladies. There is the Princess Varvara, whom you know of course. I know quite well what you and Stiva think of her. He maintains that the whole aim of her life consists in proving her superiority over Aunt Katerina Pavlovna, and it may be true. But she is a good soul all the same, and I am very grateful to her. In St. Petersburg there were moments when a chaperon was very useful to me, and she turned up quite unexpectedly. She is a good-natured thing really. She did much to make my position more bearable. I can see that you don't understand the difficulty of my position . . . in St. Petersburg," she added. "Here I am quite happy and contented, but I'll talk about that later. I must get on to the others. There is Sviajsky, our marshal, a very nice man; he seems to want Alexei to do something for him. With his fortune, you know, now that we've settled down, Alexei can have a great deal of influence. Then there is Tushkevitch—you know him, I think. He was rather gone on Betsy. She has given him up now, I believe, and so he has come to us. He is one of those men, Alexei says, who are extremely nice if you take them for what they wish to appear; *et puis, il est comme il faut,* as the Princess Varvara puts it. Then Veslovsky; but of course you know him. A very nice boy." A mischievous smile began playing about her lips. "What is this wild story about Levin? Veslovsky told

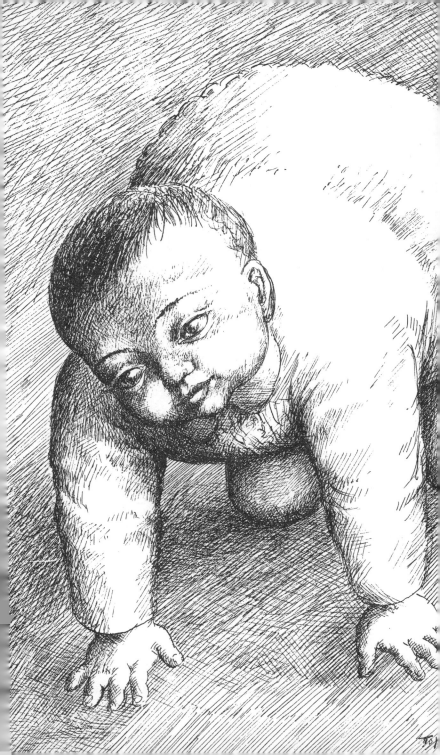

Alexei, but we couldn't believe it. *Il est très gentil et naif,"*
she added with the same smile. " Alexei likes to have lots of
people about him; that is why I enjoy them all. I wouldn't
have him be dull for the world. Then there is our manager,
a German, a most excellent man, and understands his business
well. I had nearly forgotten our young doctor; quite a young
man, not exactly a Nihilist, but he eats with his knife, you know.
He's a very clever doctor for all that. Then there is our architect—quite *une petite cour."*

XX

" I've brought you Dolly, princess; I know you wanted to
see her," Anna greeted the Princess Varvara, as she was sitting
on the stone terrace at an embroidery frame, working on a
chair-cover for Count Alexei Kirillovitch. Dolly was with her.
" She declares that she doesn't want anything before dinner,
but will you please see that she gets some lunch and I'll go and
find Alexei and the others."

The princess received Dolly kindly, but was a little patronising.
She hastened to explain that she had settled in Anna's house
because she was more fond of her than her own sister, Katerina
Pavlovna, with whom Anna had been brought up, and that
now that everybody had turned against her, she considered it
her duty to help her in her difficult situation.

" As soon as her husband divorces her, I shall return to my
solitude, but so long as I can be useful, I shall stand by her, no
matter how hard it may be for me to do so. I shall not give
her the cold shoulder as others have done. It was very good
of you to have come, my dear! They get on together like the
best of married couples; it is for God to judge them, not us.
And when you think of Birusovsky and Aveneva . . . and
Nikandrov himself, and Vasillev and Mamonova, and Liza
Neptunova, why nobody says anything against them now;
they are received by everybody. And then, *c'est un interieur
si joli, si comme il faut. Tout-à-fait à l'anglaise. On se réunit
le matin au* breakfast *et puis on se sépare.* You can do what
you like until dinner, which is usually at seven. Stiva did very
wisely to send you. He ought to stick to them. You know,
he can do anything through the influence of his mother and
brother. And then they do so much good. Has he told you

about his hospital? *Ce sera admirable*—everything is from Paris."

Their conversation was interrupted by Anna, who had discovered the men in the billiard-room and was returning with them to the terrace. It was still two hours before dinner, and as the weather was fine several proposals were made for passing the time. There were ways of doing this at Vosdvejensky such as were never dreamt of at Pokrovsky.

" Let us play tennis," Veslovsky suggested with his sweet smile. " Will you be my partner again, Anna Arkadyevna? "

" It's too hot for tennis. Let us walk about in the garden, or go on the river; I'm sure Darya Alexandrovna would like it," Vronsky said.

" I will do anything you wish," Sviajsky said.

" I think Dolly would prefer walking; would you not, Dolly? We can go on the river afterwards," Anna remarked.

They walked down the path in couples, Anna with Sviajsky and Dolly with Vronsky. Veslovsky and Tushkevitch went down to the river to bathe, promising to prepare a boat. Dolly felt ill at ease in the new surroundings in which she found herself. Theoretically, she not only justified but approved of what Anna had done, as frequently happens in the case of a blamelessly moral woman, who, tired with the monotony of a moral life, not only excuses another who has fallen away from it, but even envies her. At the bottom, however, though she loved Anna with all her heart, when she saw her among all these strange people with their *bon ton*, she felt extremely uncomfortable. She could not help feeling disgusted with the way the Princess Varvara forgave them everything in order to enjoy the comforts they could offer her.

Though in the abstract Dolly approved of Anna's deed, she could not bear to look on the man for whom it had been committed. She had never liked Vronsky, considered him proud, and saw nothing about him to be proud of, except perhaps his wealth. But here, in his own house, he impressed her in spite of herself, though she could not be at ease with him. She experienced the same sort of sensation towards him that the smart maid had aroused in her over the patched blouse. She had been ashamed before the maid on account of her blouse; before him she was ashamed on account of herself.

As they walked along she was at a loss to know what to say to him. Though she felt that with his pride he might be displeased to hear her praise his house and garden, still, not finding anything else to pick upon, she told him how much she admired his house.

"Yes, it is a beautiful building, in the good old style," he replied.

"I like the court-yard by the entrance. Has it always been like that?"

"Oh, no!" he said, his face beaming with pleasure. "You should have seen it in the spring!"

By degrees he grew quite enthusiastic in pointing out to her the various improvements in the house and garden. Having spent so much time and labour over his estate, he seemed to be glad to have a new person to whom he could talk about it, and was sincerely pleased with Darya Alexandrovna's praises.

"If you are not too tired and would like to see the hospital, it is quite near here. Shall we go there?" He looked into her face to see if he was not boring her.

"Will you come too, Anna?" he asked, turning to her.

"You won't mind, will you?" Anna said, turning to Sviajsky. "*Mais il ne faut pas laisser le pauvre* Veslovsky *et* Tushkevitch *se morfondre là dans le bateau.* We must send word to them."

"Yes, Alexei will leave it behind him like a memorial," she said, turning to Dolly with the same wise smile with which she had spoken of the hospital before.

"It is certainly an excellent thing," Sviajsky said, and not wishing to appear to be humouring Vronsky too much, he coupled this with another remark not quite so complimentary.

"I fail to understand, count, how it is that you, who have done so much for the people in the sanitary direction, are not interested in their schools."

"*C'est devenu tellement commun les écoles,*" Vronsky said. "It was not for the reason you suggested. I simply became infatuated. We go this way to the hospital," he added to Dolly, turning down a side-path.

The ladies opened their parasols. After a few turns they passed through a gate, and Dolly had a full view of a large, quaint building, not quite completed, that was standing on a hill in front of her. The corrugated iron roof, not yet painted, gleamed brightly in the sunlight. Near this building another was being erected. It was surrounded by timber, and workmen in aprons were standing on the scaffolding busily engaged.

"How quickly they've got on!" Sviajsky said. "When I was here last there was no sign of the roof."

"It will be quite finished by the autumn. Inside they have nearly finished already," Anna remarked.

"What is this new place?"

"The doctor's quarters and dispensary," Vronsky replied. Just then he saw the architect, in a short overcoat, coming towards him, and asking the ladies to excuse him he went over to meet him.

He walked round a trench where the workmen were getting their mortar and entered into a heated conversation with him.

"The façade seems to come out lower," Vronsky said to Anna when she asked him what the trouble was.

"I said all along that the foundation should have been higher," Anna remarked.

"It might have been better, Anna Arkadyevna, but it's too late now," the architect observed.

"Yes, I am very much interested in architecture," Anna said to Sviajsky, who had expressed his surprise at her knowledge of the subject. "The new building should have had some relation to the hospital itself, but it was thought of later and begun without any definite plan."

Having disposed of the architect, Vronsky joined the ladies and took them into the hospital.

Though they were still working on the cornices outside and painting on the lower story, the upper part was completely finished. They went up a broad iron staircase on to a landing, and entered a large room. The walls of it were plastered in imitation of marble; the large windows were all in; only the parquetrie was not yet finished, and the men busy on it stopped their work to greet the company.

"This is the waiting-room," Vronsky said. "There will be nothing but a desk, a table, and cupboard in the way of furniture."

"Come this way, please, but don't go near the windows," Anna said, putting her hand on one to see if the paint was still wet. "Alexei, the paint is dry already!" she added.

They passed out into a corridor, where Vronsky pointed out the new system of ventilation he had introduced. Then he showed them the marble baths and beds with spring mattresses. Next they visited the wards, the store-room, the room for linen; they examined the new-fashioned stoves and the noiseless trucks for carrying things along the corridor. Sviajsky, who understood modern improved appliances, appreciated all these things; whilst Dolly was simply overwhelmed with everything

she saw and asked Vronsky to explain to her every detail, much
to his delight.

"I dare say it will be about the only perfect hospital in
Russia," Sviajsky remarked.

"Will there be a lying-in ward?" Dolly asked. "It is so
necessary in the country; I've often thought . . ."

"This is not a lying-in establishment, but a hospital intended
for all kinds of diseases, except those of an infectious character,"
Vronsky interrupted her, contrary to his habitual politeness.

"Just look at this!" he said, pushing a new invalid chair
towards Dolly. "Isn't it nice?" He seated himself in the
chair and began rolling it along. "Supposing a man can't
walk . . . is too weak or has some disease of the legs and wants
the fresh air he just sits in this and pushes himself along."

Dolly was interested in everything, but in Vronsky most of
all. She was charmed with his naturalness and simplicity.
"Yes, he is a very nice man," she thought without listening to
his words, as she scrutinised him closely and tried to put herself
in Anna's place. As she watched his boyish enthusiasm, she
began to understand how it was that Anna had fallen in love
with him.

XXI

"I THINK we had better not; the princess is tired and horses
do not interest her," Vronsky said to Anna, who had proposed
walking down to the stables where Sviajsky wished to see a new
stallion. "You two can go, of course, and the princess and I
can walk home together and have a chat. That is if you would
like to," he added, turning to Dolly.

"I should be delighted; I know nothing whatever about
horses," she replied with some surprise.

She saw by Vronsky's face that he had something to say to
her and she was not mistaken. The moment they entered the
garden he turned in the direction of Anna, and having convinced
himself that she was out of earshot, he began.

"I suppose you've guessed that I wanted to talk to you,"
he said, with a laughing look in his eyes. "I am sure you are
Anna's friend." He removed his hat and passed his handkerchief over his head that was beginning to turn bald.

Dolly did not reply, but gave him a frightened look. Now
that she was left alone with him she was afraid; his laughing

eyes and the severe expression of his face alarmed her. The most varied thoughts of what he wished to say to her flashed through her mind.

" Supposing he asks me to come to his place with the children? I shall have to refuse, of course. Or may be he wants me to try and get Anna into Moscow society, or to talk about Vasenka Veslovsky and his relations to Anna; or perhaps he is going to tell me how sorry he was about Kitty! " She had a sort of feeling that it would be something unpleasant, but what it was she could not exactly tell.

" Anna is very fond of you, and you have such a great influence over her that I wish you would help me," he began.

Dolly cast a timid, searching look into his manly face, visible now in patches in the glaring sunlight, now altogether in the shade of the lindens. She waited for him to continue, but he walked silently beside her, dragging his cane along the gravel path.

" You are the only woman of all Anna's former friends who has visited us—not counting the Princess Varvara. Of course, I understand that you have not done so because you regard our position as a normal one, but because you love Anna, and knowing the difficulty she is in, wish to help her. Isn't that so? " he asked, looking into her face.

" Yes," Dolly replied, shutting up her parasol; " but . . . "

" No," he interrupted her, and forgetting that he was thus placing his interlocutor in an awkward position, he stopped instinctively, so that she too had to stop. " No one feels the gravity of Anna's situation more than I do. It is only natural since I was the cause of it; I want you to believe that I have some heart."

" I quite understand," Dolly said, admiring the firm, sincere manner in which he had said this; " but just because you feel it so strongly, it probably seems harder to you than it really is. Her position in society must be hard, I admit . . . "

" In society it is hell! " he said savagely, frowning heavily. " You can't imagine what torture she had to go through during the two weeks we spent in St. Petersburg."

" Yes, but here, since neither of you have any need of society . . . "

" Society! " he said contemptuously. " What need can I have of society? "

" So long as you feel like that . . . it may be for the rest of your life, you can be perfectly happy and contented. I can see that Anna is perfectly happy; in fact, she told me so," Dolly added with a smile, and as she said this a doubt came into her mind as to whether Anna really was happy. But Vronsky did not question it.

" Oh, yes," he said. " I know she has recovered from the effects of her terrible sufferings and is happy. She can be happy in the present, but I am afraid of what lies in store for us. I am sorry. Would you like to go in? "

" No, thanks."

" Then let us sit down here."

Dolly sat down on a garden-seat at the end of the avenue; he stood in front of her.

" I see that she is happy," he repeated, and again the doubt struck Dolly more powerfully than before. " But can it possibly last? Whether we have acted rightly or wrongly is another question; the die has been cast," he said, passing from the Russian to French, " and we are united for life, united by the most sacred ties of love. We have a child and may have others. But the law and our situation are of such a character that thousands of complications are always arising that Anna refuses to face. I know it is quite natural after all her trials and sufferings, but I cannot help seeing them. My little girl by law is not mine but Karenin's. I can't bear the idea of it! " He made an energetic gesture of the hand and gave Dolly a solemn, questioning look. She returned his gaze, but made no reply.

" Supposing we were to have a boy; by law he would be a Karenin. and would not inherit my name or my property. No matter how happy we might be in our family, nor how many children we might have, there would be no connection between them and me; they would always remain Karenins. Consider the horror of such a position! I try to speak of it to Anna, but it only irritates her. She does not understand, and I cannot tell *her* everything. Of course, there is another side to the question. I am happy in her love, but I must have some occupation. I have found it, I am glad to say, and am proud of it. I look upon it as far more important than the occupations of my former comrades at court and in the service, and wouldn't exchange with any of them. I work and am quite happy and contented here; we need nothing further. . . . *Cela n'est pas un pis-aller ;* on the contrary . . . "

Dolly could see that he was wandering off the main point, and was at a loss to understand the meaning of it. She felt, however, that having once begun to speak he was making a clean breast of everything, and that his activities in the country were in some way connected with the question of his relations to Anna.

"I must continue," he said, as though coming to himself. "The point is, you see, that in order to work I must have the conviction that what I am doing will not die with me, that I have heirs to whom I shall leave it, but I know I have not. magine the position of a man who knows beforehand that his wn children from a wife whom he adores will belong to some-)ody else, and to a person who hates them and does not wish to recognise them. It is terrible!" He stopped in his emotion.

"I quite understand," Dolly said; "but what can Anna do?"

"This brings me to the main object of our talk," he said, mastering himself with an effort. "Anna could . . . it depends entirely on her. . . . Even to petition the emperor to legitimise one's children it is necessary to get a divorce. It all depends on Anna. Karenin was quite prepared to grant a divorce; you know your husband had almost arranged it. I feel certain he would not refuse now. It's only a question of writing to him. Of course," he added severely, "only a heartless man would be capable of behaving like that. He knows quite well what torture it is for her even to think of him, and knowing this he demands a letter. I know how painful it would be for her to write, but the reasons that necessitate it are so great that I feel one ought to *passer par dessus toutes ces finesses de senti-ment. Il y va du bonheur et de l'existence d'Anne et de ses enfants.* I am not speaking of myself, though the position is hard enough for me, very hard," he added with a set expression. "I seize upon you, princess, as I would to an anchor of safety. Help me persuade her to write to him and demand a divorce."

"Yes, of course," Dolly said pensively, recalling her last meeting with Alexei Alexandrovitch. "Yes, of course," she repeated, as her thoughts went back to Anna.

"Try and use all your influence with her and get her to write. I can't speak to her about it myself."

"Very well, I will. But how is it she does not think of it herself?" Dolly asked, suddenly recalling Anna's strange, new habit of half-closing her eyes when anything touching her life was raised. "It seems as though she closes them on her life so as not to see the whole of it," she thought. "I shall be pleased to speak to her for my own sake as well as hers," Dolly replied in response to his expressions of gratitude.

They rose and walked back to the house.

XXII

WHEN Anna met Dolly on her return to the house her eyes seemed to question her about her conversation with Vronsky, but she did not ask about it in so many words.

"It will soon be dinner-time," she said, "and I've scarcely seen anything of you. Perhaps there will be more opportunity in the evening. I must go and change my dress now and suppose you would like to do so as well; we got so grubby in the building."

Dolly felt amused as she went to her room. She had nothing to change into as she was already wearing her best dress, but just to show that she had done something in honour of dinner she got the maid to brush it for her, put on clean cuffs, a different ribbon, and a piece of lace on her head.

"This is all I could do," she said with a smile as Anna came in, wearing a beautiful gown, the third Dolly had seen her in that day.

"Yes, I suppose we are rather too ceremonious here," she said as though excusing herself for her splendour. "Alexei is more pleased with your visit than he ever is with anything. He is positively in love with you! You're not tired, are you?"

There was no time to talk before dinner. When they entered the drawing-room the Princess Varvara was already there with the men, the latter in dress clothes. Vronsky introduced his manager and the doctor to Dolly; the architect she had already met at the hospital.

A portly footman, beaming with his round, clean-shaven face and starched white necktie, announced that dinner was ready. The ladies rose. Vronsky asked Sviajsky to take in Anna, and he himself went up to Dolly. Veslovsky offered his arm to the Princess Varvara, and Tushkevitch followed behind with the doctor and the manager.

The dining-room, the dinner, the dishes, the wine, the food, the servants, not only corresponded to the general tone of luxury in the whole house, but seemed, if anything, more luxurious still. Darya Alexandrovna, with the practised eye of a housekeeper, wondered at this luxuriousness, and instinctively noticing every detail, she tried to imagine how it was all done. Not that she hoped to introduce any of the things she saw into her own house; they were far above her means and manner of life; she merely wondered how the establishment was run. People like Vasenka Veslovsky, her husband, and even Sviajsky, took it for granted that the business of a host was to make his guests as comfortable as possible, never thinking of the immense amount of pains and labour it involved. They somehow imagined that everything went on of its own accord. But Dolly knew that the porridge for the children's breakfast would not get made unless there was some one to see to it, and from Vronsky's glance as he scanned the table and made a sign to the footman, who asked her if she would prefer thick or clear soup, she understood that everything was done and sustained by the cares of the host himself. On Anna it evidently depended no more than it did on Veslovsky. She was like a guest in the house, just like Sviajsky, the princess, and the others, and enjoyed everything that had been prepared for her.

Anna was the hostess only in so far as she directed the conversation. And she did it remarkably well too, considering the presence of the architect and the manager, two people belonging to an entirely different world, who tried not to appear embarrassed by the sight of so much luxury. She conducted it in a most simple and natural manner, and seemed to take a certain pleasure in it herself, as Darya Alexandrovna observed.

Tushkevitch and Veslovsky were talking about boating, and the former began telling them of the last races of the St. Petersburg Yachting Club. Anna waited for an opportunity to draw the architect out of his silence.

" Nikolai Ivanitch was surprised to see how much the building had progressed since he was there last," she said when a favourable moment arrived, referring to Sviajsky. " It surprises me, too, though I see it every day."

" It is a pleasure to work with his excellency," the architect said with a smile. He was a quiet, respectful man, conscious of his own dignity. " It is so different from having anything to do with government officials. Things that would take them reams of paper to report about, the count and I manage in two or three words."

" American methods," Sviajsky remarked with a smile.

" Perhaps. There buildings go up in a rational manner . . . "

The conversation passed on to the abuse of power in the United States, but Anna, now anxious to break the manager's silence, drew round to a theme that would be of interest to him.

" Have you ever seen a reaping-machine? " she asked Dolly. " We went to examine one just before we met you this morning; I had never seen one before."

" How does it work? " Dolly asked.

" Something like a pair of scissors. There is a board and a number of small scissors . . . like this."

Anna demonstrated her description with the aid of a knife and fork that she held in her beautiful hand, covered with rings. She must have known that no one would be able to understand her explanation, but conscious that her voice sounded pleasant and that her hands looked beautiful, she persevered.

" More like a penknife, I should think," Sviajsky remarked, jestingly, not taking his eyes off her.

Anna gave a scarcely perceptible smile, but did not reply.

" What do you think, Karl Fedotitch? Does it not work like a pair of scissors? " she asked, turning to the manager.

" *O ja*," the German replied. " *Es ist ein ganz einfaches Ding*," and he began to explain the construction of the machine.

" What a pity it does not bind the sheaves. I saw one at the Vienna exhibition that did," Sviajsky said. " It would be much more useful."

" *Es kommt drauf an . . . Der Preis vom Draht muss ausgerechnet werden. Dass lässt sich ausrechnen Erlaucht*," he said, turning to Vronsky now that the ice was broken. He was about to hunt in his pockets for a pencil and note-book in which he entered all kinds of calculations, when he noticed Vronsky's cold glance and recollected that it was dinner-time. " *Zu kompliziert, macht zu viel Klopot*," [1] he added.

" *Wünscht man Dochots* [2] *so hat man auch Klopots*," Vasenka Veslovsky said, making fun of the German. " *J'adore l'allemand*," he turned to Anna with a smile.

" *Cessez*," she said to him with mock reproach. " We had hoped to find you in the field, Vasilly Simionitch," she remarked, turning to the doctor, a sickly-looking man. " Were you there? "

" I was, but I evaporated," he replied, somewhat gloomily, though he had meant to be jocular.

" Did you have a good walk? "

" Capital! "

" How did you find the old woman to-day? I hope it is not typhoid."

" It's not typhoid, but I'm afraid she's a bad case."

" Poor thing! " Anna said, and having paid her tribute to

---

[1] A corruption of the Russian word " hlopot," which means bother or trouble.

[2] A corruption of the word " dohod," which means income.

the inmates of the house she turned her attention to the guests.

" It would be extremely difficult to construct a reaping-machine to your description, Anna Arkadyevna," Sviajsky said to her, jestingly.

" Why? " Anna asked with a coquettish smile that Dolly found disagreeable.

" In architecture, Anna Arkadyevna's knowledge is quite sound, though," Tushkevitch remarked.

" It was only last night that I heard Anna Arkadyevna talking of plinths and . . . " Veslovsky put in.

Dolly could see that Anna did not like the playful tone that Veslovsky adopted towards her, but she involuntarily fell into it herself.

Vronsky acted quite differently to Levin. He not only ascribed no importance to Veslovsky's jests, but even encouraged them somewhat.

" Come, tell us, Veslovsky, how are the stones set together? " he asked.

" By cement, of course."

" Bravo! And what is cement?

" It's a sort of paste or putty," Veslovsky replied, amid a general roar of laughter.

The whole company went on talking incessantly, with the exception of the doctor, the architect, and the manager, who maintained a solemn silence. One thing that was mentioned touched Dolly to the quick. It was when Sviajsky, in speaking of Levin, ridiculed his strange ideas about machinery being harmful to Russian agriculture.

" I have not the pleasure of knowing Mr. Levin," Vronsky remarked, " but I should think he could never have seen the machines since he condemns them. Or if he has, it must have been some home-made kind, not the imported ones. What ideas can he have of the subject? "

" Turkish ones, generally," Veslovsky said, turning to Anna with a smile.

Dolly flushed red.

" I cannot defend his ideas, because I know nothing about them," she said, " but he is a cultured man, and were he here I feel sure he would be capable of defending them himself."

" We are great friends and I am very fond of him," Sviajsky said with a good-natured smile. " *Mais pardon, il est un petit peu toqué.* For instance, he declares that the county council and the justices of the peace are of no use, and won't have anything to do with them."

" Our usual Russian indifference," Vronsky remarked, filling a glass with iced water. " We refuse to recognise the duties that our privileges impose on us, and so deny their very existence."

" I know of no man who is more strict in the performance of his duties than he is," Dolly said, irritated by Vronsky's tone of superiority.

" On the contrary," Vronsky continued, for some reason touched to the quick by this conversation, " I am proud of the honour of having been elected a justice of the peace, thanks to Nikolai Ivanitch." He made a gesture in the direction of Sviajsky. " To me the duty of attending the sessions, of deliberating on a peasant's horse, is as important as anything I may do. I should consider it as the greatest honour to be elected a member of the county council. It would afford me an opportunity of repaying in some measure for the advantages I enjoy as a landowner. I regret that the large landowners do not take a more important part in the affairs of the country."

It seemed strange to Dolly to see him so calm in his righteousness at his own table; she recalled that Levin, too, who held exactly opposite views, was just as determined in his own judgments. But she loved Levin and so was on his side.

" May we rely on you for the next session, count? " Sviajsky asked. " We shall have to leave earlier to get there by the eighth. You will come and stay with me, won't you? "

" I am a little of your brother-in-law's opinion, though for different reasons," Anna said to Dolly. " Of late too many of these public duties have sprung up to my mind. Formerly we were beridden by officials and now by public men. Alexei has been here for about six months and is already a member of at least five or six public institutions. He is a curator, a judge, a county councillor, a juryman, and I don't know what else. *Du train que cela va*, he spends his whole time at it. With such a multiplicity of duties, I am afraid they must be reduced to mere form. Of how many institutions are you a member, Nikolai Ivanitch? " she asked, turning to Sviajsky. " More than twenty, I believe."

Though Anna had spoken in jest, there was a note of irritation at the back of what she said. Dolly, who had been watching both her and Vronsky carefully, could not help noticing it. Coupling that with the fact that the Princess Varvara hastened to change the subject round to St. Petersburg acquaintances, and with the way Vronsky had dragged in the question of his public activity into their talk in the garden, she felt there was some sort of disagreement between them over this matter.

The dinner, the wines, the service were all excellent, but Dolly felt it was too much like a state dinner-party or a ball; there was too much affectation and formality about it. On an ordinary day, among a small circle of friends, it seemed to her out of place.

After dinner they sat out on the terrace for a while, and then played tennis. Dolly tried to play too, but for a long time could not make out the game, and when she was at last beginning to understand it, she felt so tired that she gave up and joined the Princess Varvara. Her partner, Tushkevitch, gave up too, but the others continued playing for a long time. Sviajsky and Vronsky played well and Veslovsky very badly, but he was perfectly cheerful all the time, and his good-humour never abated. With the permission of the ladies the men had taken off their coats, and Vasenka looked very impressive with his fine, handsome figure and excited face. When Dolly closed her eyes that night she kept seeing a picture of Vasenka Veslovsky flying over the tennis-court.

Dolly did not feel happy during the game. She did not like the tone of frivolity that existed between Anna and Vasenka, but not to act as a wet blanket she joined them after a rest and pretended to be amused. It seemed to her that she had been play-acting all day with better actors than herself and had spoiled the whole show. She had come with the intention of staying two days, but now decided to leave in the morning. Those very maternal cares that she had wanted to escape from on her way down now appeared to her wonderfully attractive.

After the evening tea they went out on the river, and as soon as they returned Dolly retired to her own room. She experienced a feeling of relief as she took off her garments and began dressing her hair for the night. She did not even like the idea of Anna coming in to her; she wanted to be alone with her own thoughts.

XXIII

Dolly was just about to get into bed when Anna came in, dressed for the night.

During the day whenever she had happened to touch upon any of her intimate affairs she had ended by saying, " Later when we are alone," but now that they were alone, she did not know what to say. It seemed to her that everything had been said already.

" How is Kitty? " she asked with a sigh, casting a guilty look at Dolly. " Is she still angry with me? "

" Angry? No," Dolly replied with a smile,

" Then she probably hates and despises me."

" Oh no! but of course one can never forgive those sort of things."

" I know," Anna said, looking away from her through the open window; " but it was not my fault."

" Whose fault was it? And was it a fault."

" Could it have been otherwise? Can you imagine yourself as not being Stiva's wife? "

" I don't know; but tell me, Anna . . ."

" We haven't finished about Kitty yet. Is she happy? I hear that Levin is a very nice man."

" Nice is hardly the word to describe him. There isn't a better man than he in the whole world."

" I'm glad to hear it. He must be wonderful if nice doesn't describe him! "

Dolly smiled.

" But tell me about yourself; there is such a lot I want to know about. I had a long talk with . . ." Dolly did not quite know what to call Vronsky; count or Alexei Kirillovitch seemed awkward to her.

" Oh, yes, I know you have been talking to Alexei," Anna said. " But I want you to tell me plainly what you think of me and of my life."

" How can one say all at once? I really don't know."

" Do tell me! You see the sort of life I am leading. Of course you see us in the summer, when we are not alone. When we came here in the spring we were quite alone. I don't ask for anything better than to live alone with him always, but I fear it will not be. He is already away from home a good deal and will probably be more so as time goes on. I shall hate to be without him."

She rose and seated herself nearer Dolly. Dolly was about to say something, when she interrupted her. " Of course I shall not hold him back by force. For instance, there are some races to-day in which he is taking part. I don't grudge his going there, but think of me, imagine my position. . . . But what use is there in talking of it? " She smiled. " Well, what was it he talked to you about? "

" About something I had myself intended mentioning to you, so it is easy for me to be his attorney. I had wanted to ask if it were not possible to . . . to . . ." Dolly hesitated, " to improve your position. . . . You know how I look upon it, but still, if possible, I think you ought to marry . . ."

" You mean I ought to try and get a divorce? " Anna said. " Do you know that the only woman who came to see me in St. Petersburg was Betsy Tversky? You know what she is like, don't you? *Au fond c'est la femme la plus dépravée qui existe.* She was Tushkevitch's mistress and deceived her husband in the most disgraceful way. And she told me that she would have nothing to do with me so long as my life was irregular. Don't imagine for a moment that I'm making comparisons . . . I know you, my dear, but I just happened to think of it. Well, and what did Alexei say? "

" He said that he suffers for you as well as for himself. You may call it egoism if you like, but it is a noble kind of egoism. He wants to legitimise his daughter and be your husband; he wants to have some claim over you."

" Could any wife be more of a slave than I am in my position?" she interrupted her dejectedly.

" The main thing is . . . that he does not want you to go on suffering."

" It is hardly possible for me to do anything else."

" And the most natural thing . . . he wants your children to bear his name."

" What children? " Anna asked, half-closing her eyes and not looking at Dolly.

" Annie and any others that may come . . ."

" He can be at ease on that point; I shall not have any more children."

" But how can you say that? How do you know you will not? "

" Because I don't want to."

And in spite of her emotion, Anna could not help smiling as she saw the look of curiosity, surprise, and horror depicted on Dolly's face as she said this.

" The doctor told me after my illness. . ."

" Impossible! " Dolly exclaimed, opening her eyes very wide. She felt that it was one of those discoveries the results of which were far too important to grasp at a moment's notice. She wanted time to consider it. She understood at last why it was that some families had no more than one or two children, but the feelings it evoked in her were so conflicting that she was unable to say anything and only looked at Anna with wide open eyes. It was precisely what she had been longing for, but now that she discovered that the thing was not only a dream, but a possibility, she was terrified. It seemed to her too simple a solution for so complicated a problem.

" *N'est ce pas immoral ?* " was all she could say after a pause.

" Why? I have a choice of two things, either to be always pregnant and sickly or to be my husband's companion. He is my husband in every sense," Anna added in a light superficial tone, that she had adopted on purpose.

" You may be right," Dolly said, with lack of conviction, for though she had used similar arguments to herself, they had now lost all their force and meaning.

" For you and others like you it may be different," Anna said, as though divining Dolly's thought, " but for me . . . You know I am not his wife, or rather I am his wife only for as long as he loves me, and how shall I keep his love if my body is not attractive? "

All sorts of ideas and recollections began crowding into Dolly's head? " When I no longer attracted Stiva," she thought, " he sought another, but she, too, did not keep him, in spite of her pretty looks and cheerful disposition; he abandoned her and took up a third. And can Anna really keep Vronsky in that way? If that is all he cares for he will find dozens of other women more jolly and handsome and better dressed than she is. Though she looks lovely with her stately figure, beautiful bare arms, and black hair, he can find lovelier ones still, as my reprobate of a Stiva finds them."

Dolly sighed, but did not say anything. Anna knew that the sigh expressed disapproval and brought up other arguments to prove her case.

" I can see you don't approve of it, but just consider," she continued. " You forget my position. How can I wish for children? It is not the suffering I was thinking of, I am not afraid of that. But think of me bringing children into the world, unfortunate beings, who will bear a stranger's name! They are bound to be ashamed of their birth, ashamed of their father and mother."

" That is the very reason why you should get a divorce."

Anna was not listening to her; she was anxious to bring out all the arguments with which she had so frequently been trying to persuade herself that she was right.

" Why should I bring unfortunate beings into the world when my reason tells me that it is wrong? " She looked at Dolly, but continued without waiting for a reply.

" I should always feel guilty towards them," she said. " There will be so many less unhappy people in the world, at any rate."

Dolly had used those very arguments to herself, but now they did not impress her. " How can one feel guilty towards a child that does not exist? " she thought. " Would Grisha have been any better off if he had not existed? " This idea seemed so wild and strange to her that she shook her head as though to drive away such a tangle of insane thoughts.

" I don't know, but it doesn't seem to me right," she said with a look of disgust on her face.

" But you must take into consideration what you are and what I am . . . Besides," Anna added, for in spite of the wealth of her arguments and the poverty of Dolly's, she had a feeling at bottom that the latter was right, " you must not forget the difference in our positions. For you it is only a question of whether you wish to have more children or not; for me it is a question of whether I wish to have them at all. I could not possibly desire to in my condition."

Dolly did not reply. She suddenly felt an immense gulf between her and Anna. She could see that there were questions upon which they would never agree, and decided that it was best not to talk about them.

XXIV

" ALL the more reason why you should alter it if possible," Dolly remarked.

" Yes, if it is possible," Anna said in an entirely different, sad tone of voice.

" Is a divorce out of the question then? I was told that your husband would be willing to give you one."

" Dolly, I don't want to talk of it! "

" Very well, we won't," Dolly said hast'ly, as she noticed an expression of pain on Anna's face. " But I see that you look sad."

" I? Not in the least. I am quite happy and contented. Why, *je fais des passions*, Veslovsky. . . ."

" To tell you the truth, Anna, I dislike Veslovsky's tone," Dolly said, anxious to change the subject.

" Oh, it's nothing. It amuses Alexei, that is all. He is such a boy, and entirely in my hands; I can do what I like with him. He is no more than a child, like your Grisha. . . . Dolly! " she said suddenly; " you say that I look sad, but you can't understand how terrible it is. I try not to think about it."

" But you ought to. You should do everything possible . . ."

" But what is possible? Nothing, it seems to me. You suggest my getting legally married to Alexei, as if I were not always thinking of it! " she said, and the colour spread over her face. She rose with a sigh, straightened herself, and began walking up and down the room with a light step. " As if I were not always thinking of it! " she repeated. " Not a day, not an hour passes when the thought is not in my mind, and I am not upbraiding myself for brooding over it. It nearly drives me mad! drives me mad! When I think of it I can never go to sleep without the use of morphia. I must try and be calmer. People talk about a divorce. In the first place, I know he will not divorce me. He is under the influence of the Countess Lydia Ivanovna."

" You can but try," Dolly said softly.

" Supposing I do; what will be the result? " she said, as though giving expression to a thought that had long been in her mind. " It is so revolting to think that I who hate him and consider myself guilty towards him should humiliate myself and appeal to his magnanimity. I shall either get an insulting reply or his consent. Supposing at best that I get his consent." She was in a remote corner of the room and stopped to arrange one of the curtains. " What about my s . . . son? He will never let me have him. And so the boy will grow up despising me for having abandoned his father. You must understand that I love Serioja as much as Alexei; they are both dearer to me than life."

She had stopped in the middle of the room before Dolly,

pressing her hands against her breast. In her white dressing-gown she looked unusually tall and large. She bent her head and looked up at Dolly, her eyes glistening with tears. Dolly was trembling with emotion, and appeared thin and small and pitiful in her patched night-dress and cap, beside her.

"These are the only two beings I love, and the one excludes the other. I cannot possess them both, and that is the only thing I need. Everything else is a matter of indifference to me. It will end some way or other; that is why I do not like to speak of it. Don't condemn me, don't judge me. You, with your purity of soul, cannot understand what I am suffering."

She sat down beside Dolly, took her hand, and peered into her face timidly.

"What do you think? What do you think of me? Don't despise me; I am not worth it. I am very unhappy; there is not a more unhappy creature in the world than I am." She turned away, for she could no longer hold back her tears.

When Dolly was left alone she said her prayers and got into bed. She had pitied Anna from the bottom of her soul when she was speaking to her, but now that she was gone she could not bring herself to think of her. The thought of her own home and children now seemed to her invested with a strange, new charm. That world of hers from which she had longed to escape suddenly appeared to her so sweet and precious that she longed to return to it as soon as possible, and definitely decided to leave on the morrow.

In the meantime Anna went back to her boudoir, and filling a wineglass with some sort of drug, principally composed of morphia, she drank it and sat down for a while motionless. When she had regained her composure she proceeded to her bedroom in a calm and cheerful mood.

As she entered Vronsky scrutinised her carefully. He tried to find some traces of the conversation that he knew she must have had with Dolly, since she had remained so long in the latter's room. But in her animated though reserved expression he could see nothing but her wonderful beauty, so familiar to him and so captivating. He felt that she was consciously trying to charm him now. He did not wish to question her about her talk with Dolly, but hoped she would tell him of her own accord.

"I am glad you like Dolly; you do, don't you?" was all she said.

"I've known her for some time you know. She is a good

creature, *mais excessivement terre-à-terre*. But still I was very glad to see her."

He took her hand and looked questioningly into her eyes. But she interpreted his glance differently and smiled at him.

.   .   .   .

The next morning, though she was pressed to stay, Dolly got ready for her journey. Levin's coachman, in an old coat and shabby hat, drove the shabby old vehicle into the courtyard.

Bidding good-bye to the Princess Varvara and the men was distasteful to Dolly. After one day all mutually felt that they did not fit well together, and that it was best to separate. Anna was the only one who felt sad at her going. With Dolly's departure she knew that the feelings she had aroused in her would never be stirred again. All these feelings were painful to her, but she was conscious that they belonged to the better part of herself, which was fast becoming submerged in the life she was leading.

Dolly experienced a feeling of relief when she reached the open fields, and was about to ask the coachman how he had enjoyed his stay at the Vronskys', when he turned to her of his own accord.

"They are rich enough, but they gave us only three measures of oats. They were all gone by cock-crow. What are three measures? Just a bite. And nowadays you have to pay forty-five kopeks for oats at an inn. When we have visitors we let the horses eat as much as they like."

"Very mean I call it," the bailiff agreed.

"Did you like their horses?" Dolly asked.

"The horses were good and the food was good, but I was homesick, Darya Alexandrovna. I don't know how you felt?" He turned his good-natured, kindly face towards her.

"I was too. Shall we be back by the evening?"

"We shall have to be."

When she returned home and found everything quite all right, and every one particularly sweet and charming, she told them about her journey with great animation, said how well she had been received, described the luxuriousness of the Vronskys' house and amusements, and would not allow any one to say a word against them.

"One must know Anna and Vronsky to understand how touching it all was. He is so nice, quite different from what I had imagined him to be," she said.

197

She meant this sincerely, having already forgotten the un-defined feeling of dissatisfaction and awkwardness she had experienced when she was with them.

XXV

VRONSKY and Anna spent the whole of the summer and part of the autumn in the country without taking any measures for securing a divorce. They had decided not to go anywhere, but the longer they remained alone, especially in the autumn, when the visitors had all departed, the more they felt that they could not endure the life and that some change was necessary.

It would have seemed that the life ought to have satisfied them both. They had an abundance of everything, good health, the child, and plenty to do. Anna took as much pains over her toilets as when the guests were there, and spent a good deal of her time reading. She ordered all the books favourably re-viewed in foreign papers and periodicals—novels and more serious literature—and applied herself to them with a concen-tration only possible in solitude. And besides she made a special study of all subjects in which Vronsky was interested, so that he frequently turned to her with questions on agricul-ture, architecture, and even on sport. He was amazed at her knowledge and memory, and admired the way in which she sometimes confirmed her statements by showing him passages from some book or article, written by an authority on the par-ticular subject. The hospital, too, interested her. She not only helped in its organisation, but even arranged and invented many things herself. Nevertheless her principal care was her-self—herself, in so far as she was dear to Vronsky. She wanted to take the place of everything he had left behind him in his old life. Vronsky could not but appreciate that desire of hers, over-ruling every other interest of her life—a desire not only to please him, but to be of use to him as well; at the same time he chafed at the love-nets in which she tried to ensnare him. The more he felt those nets close around him the more he longed not so much to get out of them, as to try and see whether they interfered with his freedom. But for his ever-present desire to be free, and the scenes he was compelled to go through every time he had to absent himself from home for the sessions or the races, Vronsky would have been perfectly contented and happy.

The rôle he had chosen for himself, that of the benevolent, rich landowner, was completely to his liking, and though the newness had somewhat worn off, still he felt an ever-increasing sense of pleasure in it. His affairs were progressing excellently. In spite of the large sums he had spent on the hospital, machinery, cows imported from Switzerland, and other things, he was convinced that he was not wasting his fortune, but adding to it. Where it was a question of rents, the sale of timber, grain, wool, etc., Vronsky was as firm as a rock and knew how to hold his own. In farming, both on that estate and his others, he stuck to the simplest, least risky methods, and was very economical and calculating in every detail. He would not allow himself to be misled by the wily German who tried to draw him into all sorts of purchases that proved afterwards unnecessary. He would agree to heavy expenditure only when there was a surplus of capital, and always took care to get the best for his money.

The elections of the gentry of the government of Kashin were to be held in October. Vronsky's estates were in that district, and so were Sviajsky's, Kosnishev's, Oblonsky's, and a small part of Levin's.

These elections attracted the general public attention, both on account of the people who were taking part in them, as well as for other reasons. A great deal had been talked about them and a great many preparations had been made. People from Moscow and St. Petersburg, and even from abroad—people who never voted, flocked to record their votes.

Vronsky had promised Sviajsky that he would be there in good time, and just before they were to take place the latter came to fetch him.

The day before his departure a quarrel had almost ensued between Vronsky and Anna. It was that gloomy part of the autumn, so oppressive in the country, that made the event seem worse than it really was. He prepared himself for the struggle, and with a stern, cold expression, such as he had never adopted towards her before, he informed her of his journey. To his great astonishment she received the information quite calmly, merely asking when he would be back. He watched her closely, utterly unable to understand the meaning of it. She smiled when she noticed his eyes fixed upon her. He was familiar with that capacity of her for receding into herself and knew that she had decided upon something that she would not communicate to him. He was somewhat alarmed, but his anxiety to avoid a scene was so strong that he pretended to believe in her good sense, and perhaps partly actually did so.

" I hope you won't be lonely."

" I hope so too," she said. " But I don't think I shall be; I received a box of new books from Gauthier's yesterday."

" If she wants to assume that tone, so much the better," he thought. " It's all the same to me."

He left without coming to an understanding with her. It was the first time such a thing had happened since they had known each other. In one way it disturbed him, in another he was satisfied. " She will probably behave like that for some time, but in the end she will get used to it. I don't mind giving up anything for her sake but my independence," he thought.

XXVI

In September the Levins removed to Moscow for Kitty's confinement. Levin had already spent a month there, doing absolutely nothing, when Sergei Ivanovitch suggested that he should come with him to the government of Kashin for the elections. Levin had a vote in the Selesnevsky county and had one or two things to see to in connection with his sister's property, of which he was the trustee, as she was living abroad. He had also to receive a certain sum of money for some land that had been sold. For all that he was undecided about going, until Kitty, who could see that he was getting tired of Moscow, begged him to go, and unknown to him got a tailor to make him a new uniform, such as the nobility wear on public occasions, costing eighty roubles. It was the fact of these eighty roubles that eventually decided Levin, and he accompanied his brother to Kashin.

Levin had now been about six days in Kashin attending the assembly and trying to get his sister's affairs settled. As all the marshals were at the elections it was very hard to get anything done, even in so simple a matter as the trusteeship. The other matter about the money presented equal difficulties. After an immense amount of trouble about removing an injunction, the money was ready to be paid over, but the notary could not give him a receipt because it needed the signature of a certain marshal, still in office, who was attending the sessions. All this bother, this perpetual walking from one place to another, holding endless conversations with well-disposed, kindly men, who fully sympathised with his unpleasant situation, but were unable to aid him, all the wasted effort, produced a helpless, oppressive sensation in Levin, similar to the sensation a man experiences in sleep, when he wants to do something, exercise physical force, and is unable to move. This feeling was emphasised in his dealings with the good-natured attorney. The poor man seemed to be doing his best to get Levin out of his difficulty. " Try this," he would say, or, " Go to such and such a place. But all the same they will delay matters," he would add. And Levin acted upon his various suggestions, walked and drove from place to place. Every one was just as good and kind as the attorney, but endless obstacles stood in the way. Levin was at a loss to know with whom he was struggling; in fact nobody knew that, not even the good little attorney himself. If Levin could have understood it as he understood the reason why it was people had to stand in a line at a railway booking-office in order to get a ticket, he would not have felt so annoyed.

Levin had changed much since his marriage. He was more patient, and refrained from passing judgment, saying to himself that there were probably good reasons why it had to be done in that way. This attitude kept his indignation in abeyance.

Similarly, he refrained from criticising the elections, but did his best to try and understand what it was that all these good honest people, whom he knew and respected, were so eager about. Since his marriage he had discovered a meaning in many sides of life that had formerly appeared to him insignificant and worthless. Thus it was that, even in the matter of the elections, he tried to find a serious meaning behind it all.

Sergei Ivanovitch hinted at the enormous changes that were expected as a result of these elections. It appeared that the marshal for that government, who had the control of a great many public affairs and funds, by right of his office, was a man of the old type, and though good and honest in his own way, was quite unable to understand the requirements of the times. He was on the side of the gentry almost in everything, opposed popular education, and gave a class character to the council. It became necessary to put a new, more up-to-date man in his place, one who would conduct matters in such a way as to derive all the advantages of self-government and make use of the privileges granted to the gentry, not as such, but as part of the county council. The rich influential government of Kashin, that always led all the other governments, was now full of such forces that, if matters were properly conducted, it would be in a position to serve as a model for the whole of Russia. It would be seen then that this election was of the very greatest importance. Sviajsky was proposed as marshal in the place of Snetkov, who was then holding the office, and an even better man was suggested—Nevyedovsky, a retired professor, very clever and a great friend of Sergei Ivanovitch.

The assembly was opened by the governor, who made a speech to the gentry urging them to elect their officers, not through favouritism, but for the sake of the country's good and the merits of each individual candidate. He expressed the hope that the Kashin gentry would do their duty as in former elections, and justify the high confidence that the sovereign had placed in them.

When he had finished, the governor left the hall and was immediately surrounded by a great many of the nobles present, who talked among themselves with great enthusiasm. The governor went up to the marshal, and Levin, who was standing in the crowd anxious not to lose a thing, overheard him saying, " Please tell Marya Ivanovna that my wife is very sorry that she is going to the asylum." In a short while they all put on their fur coats and proceeded to the cathedral.

During the service Levin raised his hands with the rest and repeated the words of the bishop, taking the most terrible oaths to perform everything that the governors expected of them. The church service always affected Levin, and as he pronounced the words " I kiss the cross," and cast a look at the crowd of old and young about him, he was touched.

On the second and third day, certain funds belonging to the gentry and a girls' school were under discussion, and as Sergei Ivanovitch explained that they were matters of no importance, Levin did not follow them, but spent the time looking after his own affairs. On the fourth day the government funds were audited, bringing the old and new party into conflict for the first time. The commission entrusted with the auditing of the accounts reported them to be correct. The government marshal rose with tears in his eyes to thank the gentry for the trust they placed in him. He was received with loud acclamations and pressures of the hand. But just at that moment, an adherent ·of Sergei Ivanovitch's party got up and announced that it had come to his knowledge that the commission had not audited the accounts at all, considering it a personal insult to the marshal. A member of the commission confirmed this statement in an off-hand way. Then a small, very young, but exceedingly sarcastic man began to speak, saying that the marshal would no doubt be pleased to give an account of the sums expended, but that the excessive delicacy of the commissioners deprived him of that moral satisfaction. The commissioners at once retracted their statement, and Sergei Ivanovitch pointed out in very logical terms that the accounts had either to be regarded as audited or as not audited. A man from the opposite party replied to him, then Sviajsky spoke, and after him the sarcastic young man again. The discussion lasted for a long time and ended in nothing. Levin marvelled to see them debating the matter for so long, especially when, asking Sergei Ivanovitch if he considered that the sums had been squandered, he replied, " Oh, no! he is an honest man. But it's necessary to put an end to that antiquated, patriarchal way of managing the affairs of the gentry."

On the fifth day the elections of the district marshals took place. Sviajsky was elected for Selesnevsky by a unanimous vote and gave a dinner on the same day.

XXVII

On the sixth day the government elections took place. The large and smaller halls were full of noblemen in different kinds of uniforms. Many had come down especially for that day. There were men from the Crimea, from St. Petersburg, and from abroad, whilst acquaintances who had not met for a long time ran across each other in the halls. Debates were going on at the government table, beneath the portrait of the emperor.

The gentry grouped themselves according to the parties, and from the hostile, suspicious glances that were cast at a stranger approaching any given group, and the whispering going on in the corridors, it could be seen that each party had secrets from the other. They were divided largely into two camps, the old and the new. The former were mostly dressed in old-fashioned uniform of the nobility with swords and hats, except those who were clad in the uniforms of the navy, the cavalry, or the infantry. All these uniforms were cut short in the waist and looked too tight and small, as though the persons wearing them had outgrown them. Some of the younger men wore uniforms, cut low in the waist and broad at the shoulders, which were unbuttoned, exposing their white waistcoats. Others had on uniforms with black collars, embroidered with laurel leaves in gold—the uniforms of the ministry of justice. Those in court uniforms also belonged to the new party.

The old party did not necessarily consist entirely of old men, nor the new of young ones, for, as Levin could see, there was a sprinkling of both kinds in each party.

Levin was standing in one of the small halls, where some were smoking and others were taking refreshment. He was listening intently to a group of his own people, vainly trying to grasp what it was they were talking about. Sergei Ivanovitch was the centre of this group. He now turned his attention to Sviajsky, now to Hlustov, the marshal of another county, yet a staunch adherent of their party. Hlustov declared that he could not go with his party in asking Snetkov to stand as candidate, while Sviajsky and Sergei Ivanovitch were trying to persuade him to do so. Levin could not understand the desire on their part for a man of the opposite camp to stand when all the time they intended voting against him.

Stepan Arkadyevitch, who had just finished his lunch, was wiping his mouth with a perfumed handkerchief as he walked over to them dressed in the uniform of a chamberlain.

"Our position is unshakable, Sergei Ivanovitch," he said, stroking his whiskers.

As soon as he got into the conversation he supported Sviajsky's views.

"One district is enough and Sviajsky is in open opposition," he remarked. These words were plain to every one except Levin.

"Well, Kostia, so you're beginning to like it," he added, turning to Levin and taking his arm.

Levin was quite prepared to like it, but he could not understand what it was all about. When they had walked away a few paces he expressed his astonishment about the government marshal being asked to stand.

"O sancta simplicitas!" Stepan Arkadyevitch said, and began explaining to Levin the reasons for this move.

"If, as in former elections, all the districts had accepted him as candidate he would have been elected by a large majority, a thing we don't want. Eight districts have already consented to his standing, and if two back out Snetkov may refuse to do so, in which case his party will put up some one else, thus spoiling all our plans. If, however, only one district refuses to accept him, and we intend this to be Sviajsky's, Snetkov is bound to stand. He will be voted for by everybody, perhaps two or there times over, so that when his votes are counted his party will be nonplussed, and when our candidate's turn comes, the same trick will be played upon him."

Levin only partly understood, and was about to ask a few more questions when there was a general noise and bustle, and all began to move into the large hall.

"What's the matter? What is it? Whom? Confidence? To whom? What? Do they deny it? Not the confidence. Flerov is not admitted. Is he under trial? In that case they may refuse to admit any one! That's too bad! The law!" Levin heard on all sides, and following the stream, who were hurrying and pushing past people as though anxious not to lose anything, he reached the government table where Sviajsky, the marshal, and other dignitaries were disputing something in a very heated manner.

XXVIII

LEVIN was standing at some distance off. He could not hear distinctly as one man near him was breathing heavily and another's boots creaked as he moved about. He could just catch the quiet voice of the marshal, the squeaky voice of the sarcastic man, and finally Sviajsky's voice. As far as he could make out they were disputing the legal meaning of the words " one who is under trial."

The crowd moved aside to allow Sergei Ivanovitch to pass through. Waiting for the sarcastic man to finish, he suggested that the best thing to do would be to refer to the article of the law, and asked the secretary to find it. It turned out that in case of a disagreement a ballot had to be taken.

Sergei Ivanovitch read the article and then began explaining its meaning. Just then he was interrupted by a tall stout man with stooping shoulders and a dyed moustache who wore a tightly fitting uniform with a collar that stuck into the nape of his neck. He went up to the table and striking it with his fist called out, " A ballot! It's no use talking! A ballot! "

Several voices began speaking all at once. One man wearing a signet ring tried to make himself heard above the rest, but it was impossible to make out what he was saying.

He was trying to endorse Sergei Ivanovitch's proposal, but evidently hated him and the party he represented. He spoke in such terms as to arouse the general hatred of all present. For a moment there was a general hubbub; everything was so confused that the government marshal was compelled to rise and call for order to be restored.

"A ballot; a ballot! Only a nobleman understands! We would give our last drop of blood. . . . The confidence of the monarch. . . . Don't count the marshal, he is not a clerk. . . . That is quite another thing. . . . A ballot, please! Disgusting!" loud angry voices shouted on all sides. Their faces were even more enraged than their cries; there was an expression of undying hatred in each. Levin marvelled at the passion displayed over so simple a matter as voting on this question or not. He did not understand until Sergei Ivanovitch explained it to him later that it was a matter of importance to secure the right for Flerov to vote, as every man they could add to their numbers made it more possible for them to defeat the marshal.

"One vote may turn the balance," Sergei Ivanovitch concluded, "and we might as well be consistent."

Levin, who did not know this at the time, was pained to see all these excellent men whom he respected in such a deplorable state. To rid himself of the oppressive sensation he did not wait for the end of the debate, but went into one of the smaller halls, just then quite deserted except for a few waiters at the buffet. Levin experienced a sensation of relief as he saw the men calmly wiping the dishes and arranging the plates and glasses. He felt as though he had escaped from some oppressive atmosphere into the fresh air. He began walking up and down the room with a sense of pleasure. He took special delight in watching an old waiter with grey whiskers teaching the younger ones, who were making fun of him, the proper way of folding napkins. Levin was just about to make some remark to the old man when the secretary of the gentry trusteeship, an old man whose special quality was to know all the gentry of the government by their Christian names and patronymics, distracted his attention.

"If you please, Konstantin Dmitritch, your brother wants you," he said to him. "The ballot is about to be taken."

Levin went into the large hall where he was given a white ball, and following his brother Sergei Ivanovitch, he approached the table. Sviajsky was standing close by, tugging at his beard with a grim, ironical expression on his face. Sergei Ivanovitch put his ball into the box and stepped aside to make way for Levin. The latter came up, but was so embarrassed that he did not know what to do, and asked his brother where he should put his ball. He spoke softly, hoping that in the general noise he would not be heard, but as luck would have it, there was a momentary lull and his question was heard distinctly by every one. Sergei Ivanovitch frowned.

" That is a matter of personal conviction," he said sternly.

A few of the men smiled. Levin blushed, stuck his hand in hurriedly under the cloth, and put his ball on the right, it happening to be in his right hand. He suddenly recollected that he should have stuck in his left also and was about to do so, but realising that it was too late, he grew even more confused than before and hastened away to the back of the hall.

" One hundred and six for, and ninety-eight against! " the secretary's voice was heard. There was a general laughter as some one announced that two buttons and two nuts had been found in one of the boxes. The nobleman was admitted, and the new party was victorious.

The old party, however, did not consider itself vanquished. A crowd of men surrounded Snetkov, begging him to stand as their candidate. Levin approached them. He overheard Snetkov thanking them for the confidence they placed in him, and for the love they bore him, saying that he was not worthy of so much honour, and that his only merit was his extreme devotion to them. " I have served you for twelve years to the best of my ability," he was saying, but could go on no further for the tears that choked him. He rushed out of the hall. Whether these words were due to a sense of injustice towards him, or to his love for the gentry, or to the awkward situation in which he found himself, was difficult to say, but his emotion communicated itself to the crowd. The majority of those present were touched, and Levin was overcome by a feeling of tenderness towards him.

The marshal stumbled against him at the door.

" I beg your pardon," he said, and on recognising Levin, gave a timid smile. It seemed to the latter that he wished to say something, but was too agitated to do so. The expression of his face and his whole bearing reminded Levin of some hunted creature who realises that things are hopeless. He looked pitiful in his uniform, crosses, and white trousers. Levin could not help feeling sorry for him. He recalled how he had seen him at his house only the night before, over the matter of the trusteeship, and how kind and dignified he had looked, surrounded by his family. He remembered the large house, the old furniture, the respectful old servants, evidently former serfs who had refused to leave him, his stout, good-natured wife in a lace cap and Turkish shawl, who sat caressing her grandchild, his son who had just come home from school and kissed his father's large hand reverently as he entered the room. He had looked so impressive in that sphere that Levin's sympathy was aroused.

"So I hear you are going to be our marshal again," he remarked, anxious to say something agreeable to the old man.

"That is hardly settled," he replied, looking around nervously. "I am tired and old. There are younger and better men than I. Let them have a turn." He disappeared through a side door.

The solemn moment had arrived. They were about to begin the voting. The leaders of both parties were counting the white and black balls on their fingers.

The technical point that had arisen about Flerov gave the new party not only his vote, but a gain of time in which they could send for three more supporters who, by a ruse of the other party, had been deprived of the possibility of attending the elections. Two of these men had been made drunk by Snetkov's henchmen and the third had had his uniform stolen.

During the debate about Flerov they managed to find a uniform for the latter, and the two drunken ones were brought to the assembly in a cab.

"I've brought one," a certain landed proprietor whispered to Sviajsky. "I had to pour some cold water over him, but he's all right now."

"Isn't he too drunk? Won't he fall down?" Sviajsky asked with a shake of the head.

"Oh, he is steady enough; if only they don't give him anything here. I told the waiters not to do so on any account."

XXIX

THE narrow hall in which they smoked and ate was full of men. The general agitation increased, and anxiety was expressed on every face. Most excited of all were the leaders who knew every detail and kept count of all the balls. They held the full

responsibility for the battle; the rank and file, though preparing for the fray, were in the meantime trying to amuse
themselves. Some ate standing, others sitting at tables, whilst
others smoked and walked up and down the room, talking to
acquaintances whom they had not seen for a long time.

Levin did not feel like eating and did not smoke. He had
no wish to be with his own people, that is, with Sviajsky, Sergei
Ivanovitch, Stepan Arkadyevitch, and others, for they were
engaged in an animated conversation with Vronsky, dressed in
the uniform of an equerry. Levin had seen him at the elections
the day before and had carefully avoided him, as he had no
desire to have anything to do with him. He sat down by a
window, watching the various groups and listening to what was
being said around him. He felt depressed. Every one around
was animated and busy except for an old toothless man in a
naval uniform, who sat near him and kept mumbling something
with his lips. They seemed to be the only two who had no
interest and no business there.

" I told him so, the scoundrel, but no! Of course, he could
not collect it in three years," a short, stooping man was saying.
His pomatumed hair was hanging over the embroidered collar
of his uniform, and he was clattering the heels of his new boots,
evidently put on for the occasion. He cast an angry look at
Levin and turned round sharply.

" I must say it's a dirty business," another little man said
in a thin voice.

A crowd of men who were surrounding a portly general
hurriedly moved up towards Levin. They were apparently
looking for a quiet spot in which to talk undisturbed.

" How dare he say that I stole his trousers! He's probably
spent them in drink. Damn his princely title. Just let him
open his mouth, the pig! "

" My dear man, they will fall back on the article of the law,"
some one was saying in another group. " The wife has to be
inscribed as belonging to the nobility."

" To the devil with their article! What I say is perfectly
true. That is what the nobility are for. We must have faith."

" Come along, your excellency, there's some fine champagne."

" I've always advised Marya Simionovna to let her estate,
because she hardly ever covers expenses," a man with a grey
moustache was saying in a pleasant voice. He was dressed in
the uniform of a colonel, and Levin immediately recognised him
as the old man he had met at Sviajsky's. As he cast a look in

his direction, he too recognised him and they exchanged greetings.

"Very glad to see you; I remember you well. I saw you at the Nikolai Ivanovitch's last year."

"How are matters on your farm?" Levin asked.

"Still working at a loss," the old man replied with a humble smile, as though he had a firm conviction that it could not be otherwise. "How do you come to be in our government? Are you going to take part in our *coup d'état ?*" (He pronounced the French words badly.) "The whole of Russia seems to have congregated here; there are chamberlains and ministers too." He pointed to the handsome figure of Stepan Arkadyevitch, in white trousers and the uniform of a chamberlain, engaged in talking to a certain general.

"I confess I understand very little of these elections of the nobility," Levin remarked.

"There is nothing to understand. The thing has lost all its meaning. It is an institution kept alive merely by the force of inertia. You can see it by the very uniforms. There are a good sprinkling of justices of the peace, permanent members, and so on, but very few of the real nobility."

"Then why do you attend them, if I may ask?"

"From force of habit, I suppose. One must keep up one's connections, and to a certain extent there is a moral obligation as well. But to tell you the truth, I have a little interest of my own. My brother-in-law is anxious to be elected a permanent member; he is not very well off, so I must see him through it. I wonder why these people come here?" he asked, indicating the sarcastic man who stood talking to some one at the government table.

"That is the newer generation of the nobility."

"It is new without doubt, but there is not much nobility about it. They are merely landowners; it is we who are the nobility. As noblemen they are merely putting an end to themselves."

"But you say yourself that it is an obsolete institution."

"That may be, but still it would not hurt people to treat it with more respect. Take Snetkov for instance. . . . Whether we are any good or not is another question, but we have been growing for a thousand years. Supposing you had to lay out a garden in front of your house, and on the very spot there was a tree that had stood there for a thousand years. You would not cut it down for the sake of the flower beds though it was old and twisted, would you? You would arrange them so as to make use of the tree. You can't grow a tree like that in one year. And how is your farm? " he asked suddenly to change the subject.

" Not at all well; it yields about five per cent."

" You don't count yourself though; you must be worth something too. Before I took to farming I used to receive three thousand roubles a year from the service, now I work harder than I did in the service and only make about five per cent. As for my own labours they count for nothing."

" Then why do you do it if you consider it a direct loss? "

" For the sake of doing it I suppose. What would you have? It's a sort of habit and you know it can't be otherwise. There is another thing," he continued, leaning against the window, " my son does not care for farming; he has more taste for learning, but still I keep on, even though I know there will be no one left to carry it on after me. I planted an orchard this year."

" That is true enough," Levin said. " It is just the same with me. I always feel that there is no real profit in farming, yet go on working. . . . It seems a sort of duty one owes to the land."

" That reminds me," the old man went on; " a neighbour of mine, a merchant, came to see me one day and I took him over my estate and garden. 'Everything seems all right, Stepan Vassilevitch,' he said to me, 'but your garden is very much neglected. If I were you I would cut down those lindens. There are at least a thousand of them, and the bark would fetch a high price just now.' "

" He would have bought cattle for that money, or got hold of some land for a mere nothing and let it to the peasants." Levin smiled as he said this, having come across that sort of man before. " He will make a fortune for himself no doubt, but you and I will be thankful if we can only keep what we have to leave to our children."

" I hear you are married," the old man remarked.

" I am," Levin replied with a sense of pride and pleasure. " It is strange," he continued, " that it should be ordained for us to work without profit. We are like the Vestals of old who kept the 'sacred fire burning."

The old man smiled.

" There are some among us—like our friend Nikolai Ivanitch and Count Vronsky, who has lately settled here—who want to introduce an agronomic industry; I am afraid it will lead to nothing but wasting capital."

" Why don't we take example by the merchants? Why don't we cut down our trees for the sake of the bark? " Levin asked, returning to a thought that had struck him before.

" Because we are too intent on watching the sacred fire, as you have just said. That is no work for the nobility. Our class instinct tells us what is fitting. Even the peasant feels as we do. Every good peasant will hold as much land as he can, and no matter how poor he may be, he will plough it, though he knows there is no profit in it; in fact only loss."

" Yes, we are like that," Levin said. " I am very glad to have met you," he added as he caught sight of Sviajsky coming towards them.

" We have just met for the first time since we became acquainted at your house," the old man said to him, " and we have had a nice talk together."

" Have you been abusing the new order? " Sviajsky asked with a smile.

" Of course we have."

" We have opened our hearts."

XXX

Sviajsky took Levin's arm and led him towards their friends.

It was now impossible to avoid Vronsky. He was standing with Stepan Arkadyevitch and Sergei Ivanovitch, looking straight at Levin as he approached.

" Glad to see you. I believe I had the pleasure of meeting you at the Princess Shcherbatsky's," he said, extending his hand to Levin.

" Yes, I remember our meeting quite well," Levin said. He flushed red, and immediately turning away, he began talking to his brother.

Vronsky gave a slight smile and continued his conversation with Sviajsky, evidently having no desire to say anything further to Levin. But the latter kept looking at him and wondering what to do to make up for his rudeness.

" What is it all about now? " he asked, looking from Sviajsky to Vronsky.

" About Snetkov; he has either to decline or accept," Sviajsky replied.

" Has he not accepted? "

" The trouble is that he will do neither the one nor the other," Vronsky said.

" And who will stand if he refuses? " Levin asked, looking at Vronsky.

" Any one who likes," Sviajsky said.

" Will you? "

" Anybody but I," Sviajsky said in some confusion, casting a nervous look at the sarcastic man who was standing near Sergei Ivanovitch.

" But who will then? Nevyedovsky? " Levin asked, feeling that he had made a mistake.

This was worse still. Nevyedovsky and Sviajsky happened to be the two candidates proposed.

" I wouldn't stand under any condition," the sarcastic man put in.

It was Nevyedovsky himself.

" Are you, too, excited over it? " Stepan Arkadyevitch asked, with a wink at Vronsky. " It affects one rather like racing; makes you want to bet on it."

" It is rather exciting," Vronsky said; " when you once take the matter up you feel as if you must carry it out. There is going to be a struggle," he added with a frown, pressing his jaws together.

" How businesslike Sviajsky is! He does things so precisely and clearly."

" Oh, yes," Vronsky said absentmindedly.

There was a pause. Since it was necessary to look at something, Vronsky's eyes wandered over to Levin. He gazed at his uniform, his feet, his face, and becoming aware that Levin in his turn was looking at him solemnly, he turned about in his mind for something to say.

" How is it you are not a justice of the peace since you always live in the country? " he asked. " I see you are not wearing the uniform."

" Because I consider it a stupid institution," Levin replied. He had been waiting for an opportunity to speak to Vronsky in order to cover over his former rudeness.

" I don't agree with you; on the contrary . . ." Vronsky began in some surprise.

" It is nothing more than a toy," Levin interrupted him. " We have no need of justices of the peace. I never had a single case in eight years. The little I had to do has not been worth it. In some dispute over two roubles I had to send an attorney who cost me fifteen."

He began relating a story about a peasant who had stolen a bag of flour from a miller and afterwards sued him for slander when the latter complained about him.

" He is altogether too eccentric! " Stepan Arkadyevitch said, coming up with his habitual smile. " We had better go, though; I think the voting has begun."

They separated.

" I can't understand how one can be so devoid of political tact," Sergei Ivanovitch said to his brother. Levin's awkward sally had not escaped his notice. " We Russians are hopeless in that respect. The government marshal is our adversary and you are *ami cochon* with him and ask him to stand as candidate. And then Count Vronsky . . . I should not choose him for my friend myself; he asked me to dine with him, but I shall not go . . . still, he is on our side, so why make an enemy of him? And on top of all you go and ask Nevyedovsky whether he will stand! These sort of things are not done."

" I understand nothing about it! It is all the merest nonsense," Levin replied dejectedly.

" You say it is nonsense, yet when you have anything to do with it, you make a mess of things."

Levin did not reply, and both entered the large hall.

The government marshal, in spite of the fact that there was treason in the air and that all had not asked him to stand, nevertheless offered himself as a candidate. There was a momentary hush, and the secretary proclaimed in a stentorian voice that the captain of the Horse Guards, Mihail Stepanovitch Snetkov was to be voted on.

The county marshals approached the government table with the plates containing the balls, and the balloting began.

" Put it in on the right," Stepan Arkadyevitch whispered to Levin as he and his brother followed the marshal to the table. Levin had already forgotten the calculation that had been explained to him, and was afraid that Stepan Arkadyevitch must have made a mistake as Snetkov was an adversary. He held the ball in his right hand as he approached the box, but transferred it to the left and deposited it on that side. An expert standing by the box, who could tell from the mere motion of the elbow where a ball had been placed, frowned involuntarily.

There was perfect stillness in the hall except for the counting of the balls. Soon a voice announced the number of ayes and noes.

The marshal had been elected by a large majority. There was a wild excitement and all rushed headlong towards the door. They surrounded Snetkov who had just entered, and began showering congratulations upon him.

" Is it all over? " Levin asked of his brother.

" It is only the beginning," Sviajsky replied for Sergei Ivanovitch with a smile. " Our candidate may get a larger number of balls."

Levin had a vague recollection that there was some subtle point in it all, but was too tired to think what it was. A longing to get out of the crowd took possession of him.

As no one paid any attention to him or seemed to want him, he directed his steps to the smaller hall, where refreshments were served, and again felt a sense of relief at sight of the waiters. The old man who had attracted his attention before offered him something to eat, and he gladly accepted it. He chatted to the old waiter while eating his cutlet and beans, then, not wishing to return to the large hall where he felt ill at ease, he went up into the gallery.

The galleries were full of ladies in gay attire, who were leaning over the balustrades, trying to catch every word that was passing below. There were also elegant lawyers, masters from the gymnasium in spectacles, and officers in uniform. Every one was talking about the elections; some were saying how tired the marshal looked and how magnificent the speeches were. Levin overheard one lady saying something in praise of his brother to a lawyer beside her.

" I am so glad I have heard Kosnishev! It was worth going without one's dinner for that alone. How wonderful he was! He spoke so clearly that you could hear every word. Nobody speaks like that at your courts except Maydel perhaps, and he isn't nearly so eloquent."

Levin discovered an unoccupied seat in front, and leaning over, he, too, began to listen. The noblemen were all sitting behind small partitions at the tables of their respective districts. A man in a uniform was standing in the middle of the hall, proclaiming in a loud voice—

" Captain Yevgeny Ivanovitch Apuhtin is to be voted on as candidate for the government marshal of the nobility! "

A silence ensued.

" Declines! " a feeble old man's voice was heard to say.

"The imperial councillor Peter Petrovitch Bol is to be voted on . . ." the voice began once more. "Declines!" a youthful squeaky voice was heard.

The same process was repeated for about an hour. Levin stood looking on from the gallery and listening. At first he was rather bewildered and wanted to understand what it all meant, but later when he realised that he could not grasp it, he began to feel tired. He recalled all the excitement and anger he had seen on all the faces during the course of the day, and feeling depressed he went downstairs. As he was walking through the lobby he came across a dejected looking youth pacing up and down. On the staircase he met a lady who was running up as fast as she could with a dashing lawyer coming behind her.

"I told you we should be in time," the lawyer was saying just as Levin stepped aside to let the lady pass.

Levin was already on the staircase leading out to the street, and was taking the ticket out of his pocket to get his fur coat, when the secretary caught him up.

"Konstantin Dmitritch, do come, please; the voting has begun."

The candidate was Nevyedovsky, who had so emphatically declined to stand a short time ago.

Levin went to the door of the large hall and found it locked. The secretary knocked; the door was opened and two flushed men darted out past him.

"I can't stand it any longer!" one of them was saying.

The government marshal put his head through the door. The look of fear and exhaustion on his face was terrible to behold.

"I told you not to let any one out!" he shouted to the door-keeper.

"I was letting some one in, your excellency!"

"O Lord!" The marshal heaved a deep sigh and walked away towards the large table with bowed head.

Nevyedovsky was elected by a bigger majority and he was now marshal. A great many were satisfied, a great many dissatisfied. Snetkov could not conceal his disappointment. When Nevyedovsky left the hall he was followed by an enthusiastic crowd, just as Snetkov had been when he had opened the elections, and when he had secured the first majority that day.

XXXI

THE newly - elected marshal and many adherents of the triumphant party dined with Vronsky that day. Vronsky had gone to the elections partly because he felt bored in the country and wanted to assert his independence before Anna, and partly to repay Sviajsky for all the trouble he had taken in getting him elected a member of the county council. The idea of performing his duties as a landowner and nobleman may also have been an important factor in deciding him to go. He was an entirely new man in that circle, but every one liked him and he was not mistaken in supposing that he had already gained some influence among the local nobility. His popularity may have been aided by his wealth, his splendid quarters in the town that had been lent to him by a friend, his excellent cook, whom he had brought from the country, his friendship with the governor who had been a friend and *protégé* of his, but perhaps, above all, his simple, natural manner, that compelled the majority of people to change their opinion about his supposed haughtiness. Apart from the eccentric man married to Kitty Shcherbatsky, who had treated him rather rudely, every one was enthusiastic about him and loud in his praises. He was flattered to think that others held him largely responsible for Nevyedovsky's success. He could not help feeling the triumph for the chosen man as he sat at his own table. He was completely fascinated by the elections and decided that he would himself stand as candidate three years after he and Anna were legally married, just as after winning a race through his jockey he was seized by a desire to race himself.

The dinner was somewhat like the celebration of a successful race. Vronsky was sitting at the head of the table. On his right sat the young governor, a general of the suite. For every one present, except the host, he was the head of the government, who had opened the elections in all solemnity, had made a great speech and evoked awe and respect in many; for Vronsky he was "Maslov Katka," as he had been nicknamed in the corps, who felt shy in his presence and whom he had to be constantly putting at his ease. On his left sat Nevyedovsky with an undaunted, sarcastic expression on his face. With him Vronsky was simple yet considerate.

Sviajsky accepted his defeat in the best of possible spirits.

He turned with a glass to Nevyedovsky saying that the nobility could not have found a better man to follow than himself, and that he triumphed in his triumph.

Stepan Arkadyevitch, too, was happy because he was enjoying himself and because every one else was satisfied. Sviajsky made fun of the tearful speech of the old marshal, and said that he hoped Nevyedovsky would find a better means of auditing the accounts than by tears. Another man remarked jestingly that the former marshal had instituted footmen in stockings to serve on state occasions, and that if the new marshal did not approve of them he would have to send them all back again.

Nevyedovsky was toasted all round and was addressed as " your excellency our government marshal," much in the same way as a bride is first addressed by her married name. Nevyedovsky tried to appear indifferent to it all, but was evidently happy. He refrained from giving vent to his feelings, because it would have been out of place in that new liberal *milieu* in which he happened to find himself.

After dinner telegrams were despatched to people interested in the progress of the elections. Stepan Arkadyevitch, who was in an extremely happy frame of mind, sent the following to Dolly: " Nevyedovsky elected by a majority of twenty. Congratulate. Tell the others." He dictated it aloud, adding that it would give them pleasure. But when Dolly received it she only sighed for the rouble it had cost, and knew exactly what had happened at the close of the dinner; she was familiar with Stiva's weakness to " *faire jouer le télégraphe.*"

The splendid dinner and foreign wines were elegantly served and everything was simple and jolly. Sviajsky had selected the twenty guests from among the new liberal party, and most of them were clever, brilliant men. Toasts were drunk to the new marshal, the governor, the director of the bank, and the host.

Vronsky was perfectly satisfied. He had not expected such good form in the provinces. At the end of the dinner it grew jollier still. The governor invited Vronsky to come to some concert his wife had arranged, saying that she wished to meet him.

" There is to be a ball afterwards and you will see our beauty. She is really wonderful."

" It's not in my line," Vronsky said, being very fond of the English expression, but he promised to go in the end.

They had all begun smoking and were about to leave the table when Vronsky's valet brought him a letter on a tray.

" From Vosdvejensky, by courier," he said solemnly.

" He looks rather like the prosecuting attorney, Sventitsky,"
one of the guests remarked in French, referring to the valet.

A frown spread over Vronsky's face as he read the letter.
It was from Anna. He was aware of its contents even before
he opened it. Thinking that the elections would not take longer
than five days, he had promised to be back on Friday. It was
now Saturday and he knew that the letter was full of reproaches
for being late. He had sent her a note the night before, but
she had evidently not yet received it.

The tone of the letter was precisely what he had expected
it to be. He was annoyed. " Annie is very ill," it ran. " The
doctor fears that inflammation may set in. I am losing my
head all alone; the Princess Varvara is more of a hindrance
than a help. I thought you would be back two days ago and
have sent to find out what you are doing. I had some idea of
going myself, but changed my mind, thinking it would annoy
you. Send some kind of a message that I may know what to do."

The child is ill and she wants to come here! And then that
hostile tone!

Vronsky was struck by the contrast between his present
gaiety and the burdensome love that awaited him at home.
It was necessary to go though, so he left that same night by the
first train he could take.

XXXII

BEFORE Vronsky's departure for the elections, Anna tried to
take herself in hand somewhat, feeling that the disagreeable
scenes they had had together every time he absented himself
from home only tended to cool his affections rather than
strengthen them. She bore out bravely until the end, but the
cold, stern glance he cast upon her just before leaving wounded
her to the bottom of her soul, and all her composure vanished.

Later, in her solitude, as she thought of that glance, expressing
his right to his personal freedom, the consciousness of her
humiliation increased.

" He has a right to go when and where he pleases, and not
only that, he can leave me altogether if he likes," she thought.
" He has all the rights while I have none. Knowing this he
ought not to have done it. But what did he do? He looked
at me sternly and coldly. It is nothing in itself, but it has

never happened before and means a great deal. That look proves that his love is growing weaker."

And though she felt convinced that his affection for her was beginning to cool, she could do nothing—could in no way change her relations to him. She could only retain him by her love and attractiveness. She tried to drown the terrible thoughts of what would happen if he ceased to love her by busying herself with all sorts of things in the day-time and taking morphia at night. The idea of a divorce and marriage presented themselves to her forcibly for the first time. By that means alone could she get so close to him that he would not be able to abandon her. She began to long for a divorce and decided to give her consent when next her brother Stiva happened to mention it.

In such thoughts as these she passed the five days he was to have been away from her. She took long walks, visited the patients at the hospital, talked to the Princess Varvara, and read a great deal. On the sixth day, when the coachman returned without him, she could no longer suppress her thoughts, and began wondering what he was doing there. On this day her little girl fell ill. Anna took to nursing her, but even this did not divert her attention, particularly as the illness was not of a serious nature. No matter how hard she tried, she could not bring herself to love this child, nor could she pretend to do so. In the evening when she was left alone such terror seized her on Vronsky's account that she decided to go to him, but on further reflection she wrote the contradictory letter he had received, and without even re-reading it, despatched it by a special messenger. On the next morning she received his letter and regretted her own. She waited in dread for a repetition of that stern glance he had cast on her at their leave-taking— especially when he discovered that the child had not been dangerously ill. In spite of everything she was glad she had written. Though she acknowledged to herself that he was getting tired of her, that he regretted his freedom, she rejoiced nevertheless that he was coming home again. What did it matter if he were annoyed and angry, so long as he was with her, so long as she could see him and know his every movement?

She was sitting by a lamp in the drawing-room with a new book of Taine's, reading and listening to the moaning of the wind outside and waiting the sound of an approaching carriage. Several times it seemed to her that she heard the rumble of wheels, but she was mistaken. At last there could be no mistake, the rumbling was heard distinctly, also the voice of the coachman and a dull sound in the covered drive. The Princess Varvara, who was playing solitaire, remarked that it must be Vronsky. Anna's face flushed; she rose, but instead of rushing downstairs as she had done twice before that evening, she stopped still. She suddenly felt ashamed of her deception and was afraid of meeting him. She recalled that the child had been quite well for the last two days and was almost annoyed with her for having recovered so quickly. But suddenly she remembered that he was there, the whole of him; she could hear the sound of his voice, and forgetting everything she rushed down to him.

" How is Annie? " he asked timidly as he saw her running downstairs towards him. He was sitting on a chair and a man was pulling off his boots.

" She is much better now."

" And you? " he asked, shaking himself.

She took his hand in both her own and drew his arm round her waist, not taking her eyes off him.

" I am very glad," he said, examining her coldly. He looked at her head-dress, her gown, and knew that she had adorned herself especially for him. He could not help admiring her, but he had admired her so often!

A stern, stony expression settled on his face.

" I am very glad," he repeated. " Are you quite well? " he asked, wiping his wet beard with his pocket handkerchief and kissing her hand.

" I don't care what happens, so long as he is here," she thought. " He cannot help loving me when he sees me; he dare not do otherwise."

For the rest of the evening, in the Princess Varvara's presence they were both cheerful. The latter complained that Anna had taken morphia in his absence.

" I couldn't help it; my thoughts would not let me sleep. I never take it when you are here; at any rate, hardly ever."

He began telling them about the elections. Anna knew how to draw him out with all sorts of questions, and they soon learnt of the success he had had. In her turn, she told him everything that had happened at home. Her news were very cheering and they were both getting into a happy frame of mind.

When they were left alone late in the evening Anna was seized by a desire to wipe out the unpleasant impression of her letter.

" Confess, you were sorry to get my letter and did not believe me," she said suddenly.

221

No sooner had the words left her than he realised that no matter how well-disposed he felt towards her, he had not forgiven her that.

" Yes, " he replied, " your letter was rather strange. I couldn't understand why you wanted to come when Annie was ill."

" But she was ill."

" I don't doubt it."

" Yes, you do. I can see that you are annoyed."

" Not in the least. Or if I am it is only that you will not realise that there are duties . . ."

" Duties to attend a concert! "

" Don't let us talk of it any more."

" Why not? "

" I only wished to say that some unavoidable business might crop up. For instance, I shall have to go to Moscow to see about a house. Anna! why will you be so irritable? Don't you see that I can't live without you? "

" You are getting tired of this life," she said in a different tone of voice. " You will just come home for a day and then go off again; you will act like all men. . . . "

" Anna, don't be cruel, I am prepared to lay down my life for you . . ."

But she would not listen to him.

" If you go to Moscow, then I will come too; I will not remain here. We must either part for good or live together always."

" You know quite well that that is the only thing I desire, but to make that possible . . ."

" We must have a divorce. Very well, I will write to him. I cannot live like this . . . I shall come with you to Moscow."

" It sounds rather like a threat, yet there is nothing I desire more than never to be parted from you," he said with a smile.

His glance was not only cold, but enraged, as he said these words. She noticed it and correctly interpreted its meaning.

" If that is what you feel like then no good can come of it," his glance seemed to say.

It was a momentary impression, but Anna never forgot it.

Anna wrote to her husband asking for a divorce, and towards the end of November she parted from the Princess Varvara, who had to go to St. Petersburg, and accompanied Vronsky to Moscow. They settled in a house together, quite like a married couple, and waited each day for an answer from Alexei Alexandrovitch giving his consent to a divorce.

PART VII

I

THE Levins had already been living in Moscow for three months. The time had long passed when, according to the most definite calculations of those who knew something about these matters, Kitty's confinement was expected, but there was still no more sign to show that she was nearer the end than there had been two months ago. The doctor, the midwife, Dolly, her mother and especially Levin, who could not think of the approaching event without a feeling of terror, were beginning to get impatient and anxious; Kitty alone was perfectly contented and happy.

A new feeling of love for the future, for the child within, took possession of her being, and she abandoned herself to it joyfully. The child began showing signs of leading its own independent life, and though she was frequently pained by the thought that it would no longer be part of her, she sometimes felt like laughing at this strange new joy.

She was surrounded by every one she loved; all tended her so carefully and were so anxious to shield her from the disagreeable side of things, that were she not aware that this period would soon be over, she could not have desired a more pleasant life. The only thing that spoilt the charm of it all was that her husband was no longer the same as when she had loved him in the country.

She had loved his quiet, gentle, hospitable tone at home. In the town he seemed always in a state of anxiety, always on his guard, as though he feared that some one might offend him, or what was worse, her. In his own place in the country he was never in a hurry, yet never without occupation; here he was constantly in a hurry, as though afraid of missing something, yet had absolutely nothing to do. Kitty could not help feeling sorry for him. She knew that to others he did not appear at all pitiful; on the contrary, she would sometimes look at him in society, as one often looks at a beloved person from the point of view of a stranger, and he would seem to her so desirable that she grew quite jealous of him. There was something so attractive about his old-fashioned bashfulness in the presence of women, his powerful figure, and his characteristic, expressive face. But she saw him from within rather than without; otherwise she could not have explained his condition. Sometimes she reproached him in her heart for not being able to make himself happier in the town; at others she admitted that it was difficult for him to arrange his life so that he could get any satisfaction out of it.

What could he do, really? He did not like cards, nor did he go to the club. As for going out with men, such as Oblonsky, she knew what that meant—it meant drinking and debauchery. She shuddered to think where such men often went after a night's carousal. He could go into society. But she knew that to take any interest in that it was necessary to derive pleasure from the company of young women, and she could hardly desire such a thing. He could stop at home with her, the princess, and her sisters. But their eternal conversations about the " Alins " and the " Nadins," as the old prince called them, were extremely boring to him. What could he do? He could continue working at his book. He had tried to do so, had begun by going to the library to look up certain references that he needed, but as he told her, the less work he did, the less time he had on his hands. Besides, he complained that there had been too much talk about his book in Moscow, and that consequently his ideas were all confused and he had lost interest in it.

There was one blessing about their town life—they no longer quarrelled. Whether it was due to the conditions being different or that they had both grown more sensible, the fact remained that no difference had arisen between them on account of jealousy—a thing they had dreaded so much on coming to Moscow.

In this respect an important event had happened for both of them—Kitty had met Vronsky. She had seen him quite by accident at the house of her godmother, the Princess Marya Borisovna, where she had called with her father.

The only thing Kitty could reproach herself with over this meeting was that her breath had stood still and the colour had spread over her face the instant she recognised the familiar figure in civilian clothes. But this had lasted only a few seconds. Her father had barely exchanged greetings with him, which he did in a loud tone of voice on purpose, when she recovered her composure and was prepared to look at Vronsky, and even speak with him, just as naturally as she would have done with the Princess Marya Borisovna herself. She had been most anxious to act in a way such as her husband could have approved. She felt his invisible presence hanging over her at that moment.

She exchanged a few words with Vronsky, smiled at his jokes about the elections, which he called " our parliament " (it was necessary to smile in order to show that she had appreciated the joke), then turned to the princess and did not look at him once until he took his departure. She had to look at him then out of a sense of politeness when he bowed to her.

She was grateful to her father for not referring to this meeting on their way home, but she could tell by his peculiar tenderness that he was satisfied with the way in which she had behaved. She, too, was satisfied with herself. She had not expected that she would be able to hold back her former feeling for Vronsky and not only appear indifferent, but actually be so.

Levin blushed a good deal more than she had done when he heard the news. She found it hard to tell him all the details of the meeting, particularly as he did not ask any questions, but continued looking at her with knit brows.

" I am very sorry you were not there," she said. " Not in the same room though . . . I could not have been so natural before you . . . I am blushing much more now than I did then, much more . . ." she added, the tears coming into her eyes. " I should have liked you to see me through a chink in the door."

Her truthful eyes told Levin that she was satisfied with herself, and though she blushed, he felt reassured and began asking her all sorts of questions, which was precisely what she wanted. When he had learnt everything down to the last detail, Levin cheered up entirely and declared that he was glad she had seen him, and that he would not behave a second time so stupidly as he had done at the elections, but at the very next opportunity would be as friendly with Vronsky as possible.

" It is so painful to think that there is a man, almost an enemy of yours whom it is so hard to meet," he said. " I am really very glad you have seen him."

II

" WHY not call on the Bols? " Kitty said to her husband as he came in to see her at eleven o'clock one morning previous to leaving the house. " I know papa put you down for dinner at the club, but what are you going to do all the morning? "

" I will look in at Katavasov's," Levin replied.

" Why so early? "

" He promised to introduce me to Metrov, whom I wished to talk to about my work. He is a famous St. Petersburg scholar."

" Oh, yes, I heard you praising an article of his the other day. And what will you do afterwards? " Kitty asked.

" I may go to the law-courts to see about my sister's affairs."

" Shall you not go to the concert? "

" I don't like to go alone."

" Do go! They are giving those new things you are so much interested in. I should most certainly go if I were you."

" In any case I shall come home for a few minutes before dinner," he said glancing at his watch.

" Put on your frock-coat so that you can call on the Countess Bol."

" Is it necessary to go there? "

" Of course it is! he called on us. What does it matter to you? You need only stay five minutes or so and talk about the weather."

" But you can't think how I hate that sort of thing. A perfect stranger comes in for no reason whatever, disturbs them for a few minutes, and goes away again. It is so stupid; it makes me feel ashamed."

Kitty burst out laughing.

" But you used to pay calls before we were married," she said.

" I know I did, but I was never happy, and now I've got so out of the way of it that I would rather go without my dinner for two days than pay this call. It seems to me that the people will be offended and wonder why on earth I came there."

" Oh, no, they will not. I promise you that," Kitty said, looking at him with a smile. She took his hand. " Well, good-bye . . . Do go there, please."

He kissed her hand and was about to go out when she stopped him.

" Kostia, do you know that I have only fifty roubles left? "

226

" Then I will go to the bank and get some more. How much do you want? " he asked with an expression of displeasure, so well known to her.

" Wait a moment." She held his hand. " Let us talk it over; I am beginning to feel anxious. It seems to me that I am not wasting any money and yet it melts away somehow. There is something not quite right."

" Don't worry," he said with a nervous cough, looking at her from under his eyebrows.

She was familiar with that cough. It was a sure sign that he was dissatisfied with himself. He really was dissatisfied, not because too much money had been spent, but because he was reminded about a thing he was anxious to forget, having a vague feeling that there was something wrong about it.

" I told Sokolov to sell the wheat and to get the money for the mill in advance. We shall not run short in any case."

" I am afraid we are spending too much . . ."

" Not at all! not at all! " he said hurriedly. " Good-bye, dear."

" I am sorry we listened to mamma; we should have been so happy in the country; while here I am only a nuisance to everybody and the money goes like water . . ."

" Not at all, my dear. I have never once thought since we were married that I would have anything different. . . ."

" Really? " She looked into his eyes.

He had merely said this unthinkingly to console her, but when he saw her lovely eyes fixed on him tenderly he repeated the words from the bottom of his heart. " I don't think half enough of her," he thought, and suddenly recollected what awaited them both.

" Will it be soon? How do you feel, dear? " he asked in a whisper, taking both her hands.

" I don't know. I've expected it so often that I've given up thinking about it now."

" You are not afraid, are you? "

She gave a disdainful smile.

" Not a bit," she said.

" If anything happens, I shall be at Katavasov's."

" Nothing will happen; don't worry. I shall go for a walk with papa on the boulevard and probably call in to see Dolly. I shall expect you home before dinner. By the way, I wanted to talk to you about Dolly; her position is getting impossible. She is in debt all round and has absolutely no money. Mamma and I talked it over with Arseny yesterday " (this was her eldest sister's husband) " and we decided that you and he should attack Stiva. They can't go on like that. We dare not mention it to papa . . . but if you and Arseny . . ."

" But what can we do? " Levin asked.

" You had better go and see Arseny; he will tell you what we decided on."

" Very well; I know I shall agree with Arseny. Oh, by the way, if I go to the concert at all it will be with Natalie. Good-bye."

He was stopped in the porch by his old servant Kusma, who had been with him in his bachelor days.

" Beauty has been shod, but is still limping," the old man said. " What shall we do about her? "

Beauty was the left shaft-horse that had been brought up from the country.

During his early stay in Moscow, Levin had been interested in the horses brought from home. He was eager to spend as little money as possible over them, but it turned out that keeping his own horses in town was more expensive than hiring, and that they had to hire in any case.

" Send for the veterinary surgeon; she may be a little footsore."

" But what will Ekaterina Alexandrovna do? " Kusma asked.

It no longer astonished Levin as it did in the early days that in order to go from the Vasdvejensky to the Sivtsev Vrajok, a distance of about a quarter of a mile, it was necessary to harness a pair of horses to a heavy carriage, to be dragged through the slushy snow and kept waiting there for about four hours, with five roubles to pay into the bargain. In fact, he looked upon it as quite natural now.

" Hire a couple of horses," he said.

" Yes, sir."

Thanks to his town habits, Levin solved a difficulty without the least trouble that in the country would have demanded a great deal of labour and personal attention. He left the house, took a cab, and ordered the coachman to drive to the Nikitskaya. On the way he no longer thought of money matters; his mind was full of the St. Petersburg scholar whom he was about to meet and to whom he hoped to talk about his book.

Levin had grown used to all the useless but unavoidable expenses that were demanded of him on all sides. During his early stay in Moscow he had been continually marvelling at them. In this respect a thing had happened to him that according to the old proverb is supposed to happen to drunkards. "The first glass sticks in the throat, the second flies like a falcon, and after the third they go like tiny birds." When Levin had changed his first one-hundred rouble note to buy livery for his footman and porter, he had involuntarily reflected that they were utterly useless and that they could get on very well without them, but the princess and Kitty were almost shocked at his suggestion. He could not help thinking that these liveries cost as much as two labourers would receive for a whole summer's work, that is, about three hundred working-days of hard work, from early morning till late at night. He had had qualms about that first one-hundred rouble note. The next, however, that was changed for the purposes of buying provisions to give a dinner to their relatives that cost no less than twenty-eight roubles, went easier, though according to Levin's calculations the twenty-eight roubles represented sixty-four bushels of wheat that had been mown, bound, threshed, winnowed, sifted, and put into sacks. But now he had ceased paying any attention to the bills as they were changed one after another. He had left off considering whether the labour spent on the acquisition of money corresponded to the pleasure enjoyed by what was purchased for it. In the same way he forgot the farm rule that rye ought not to be sold under a certain price. He had held back his rye, but was eventually compelled to sell it at fifty kopeks a bushel less than it would have fetched two months earlier. He was even no longer troubled by the thought that living at the rate they were doing they would not be able to go through the year without incurring debts. All that mattered was to have some money in the bank without bothering to find out where it came from, so that one might know there would be enough to buy beef with on the morrow. Just now, however, the money in the bank was all gone and he did not know exactly where more was to come from. This was the cause of his annoyance when Kitty had referred to money matters. As he drove along he tried to forget about it again and thought only of his coming meeting with Metrov.

III

DURING his stay in Moscow Levin had again come in close contact with his old college friend, Professor Katavasov, whom he had not seen since the day of his marriage. Levin liked the professor on account of the clearness and simplicity of his philosophy. He looked upon Katavasov's clearness and definiteness as a sign of a very shallow nature, while Katavasov looked upon his inconsistency as a sign of an undisciplined mind. But Katavasov's clearness was agreeable to Levin and Levin's inconsistency was agreeable to Katavasov, so they were very fond of meeting and discussing their ideas.

Levin had read several passages of his book to Katavasov and the latter had been interested. Having met Levin the day before at a lecture, he had told him that he was expecting the famous Metrov whose article he had so much admired, and that he had mentioned Levin's book to him. He also said that Metrov would be at his house the next morning at eleven o'clock and would be glad to meet Levin if he cared to come.

" I must congratulate you; you are certainly improving," Katavasov greeted him in the little drawing-room. " I could hardly believe it was you when I heard the bell. What do you think of the Montenegrins? Fighters by nature."

" What has happened? " Levin asked.

Katavasov gave him the latest news in a few words as they proceeded to his study. There, he introduced Levin to a man of middle height, squarely built, and of pleasant appearance. This was Metrov. For a while the conversation turned on politics and what the higher circles in St. Petersburg were thinking of recent events. Metrov repeated certain words supposed to have been said by the emperor to one of his ministers, saying that the information had come to him through a reliable source. Levin was trying to imagine the situation in which these words might have been uttered, and the conversation on this subject came to an end.

" Konstantin Dmitritch has nearly finished his book on the natural condition of the farm labourer in relation to the soil," Katavasov remarked. " I am not a specialist on the subject, but as a naturalist I was interested to see that he did not look upon humanity as standing outside the operation of the zoological laws. On the contrary, he sees the relation of the human being to his environment and looks for the laws of development in this relation."

" That sounds very interesting," Metrov observed.

" I began by writing a book on the science of agriculture, but involuntarily arrived at unexpected conclusions, being interested in the chief tool of agriculture—the farm labourer," Levin said, reddening. As if feeling his way, he cautiously began explaining his views. He knew that Metrov had written an article against the universally accepted doctrines of political economy, but did not know to what extent he would sympathise with his own views; it was difficult to judge from the calm, intelligent expression of the scholar's face.

" But wherein do you find the particular properties in the Russian farm labourer? " Metrov asked. " Do you consider them to be in the zoological propertie", so to speak, or in his general condition? "

The very question expressed an idea with which Levin did not agree, but he continued expounding his theory that the Russian farm labourer's relation to the soil was different from that of other nationalities. As an illustration he pointed out how the Russian peasant was frequently called upon to settle on enormous stretches of unoccupied land in the east.

" It is easy to be led into error by forming conclusions as to the general destiny of a nation," Metrov observed. " The condition of the labourer will always depend on his relation to the soil and to capital." And without allowing Levin to finish Metrov started explaining his own ideas on the subject.

What the peculiarity of his doctrine consisted in Levin did not understand; he did not even take the trouble to understand, for he saw that Metrov, like the rest, in spite of his article condemning the theories of political economy, still looked upon the condition of the Russian labourer from the standpoint of capital, wages, and interest. Though he had to acknowledge that the wages of nine-tenths of the eighty millions of the Russian population meant no more than earning their food and that capital existed only in the shape of the most primitive tools, yet he could not get away from these things, though in many respects he did not agree with the economists and had a new theory of wage-earning of his own which he tried to explain to Levin.

Levin listened reluctantly and made various objections at first. He was eager to express his own idea, which in his opinion would have made all further exposition superfluous. He soon realised, however, that their differences were so great that they would never be able to come to a common understanding; so he raised no further objections, but only listened silently. Though he was no longer interested in what Metrov was saying he nevertheless experienced a certain pleasure in hearing him speak. He felt flattered that so learned a man should condescend to explain his ideas to him. He did not know that Metrov had already worn out all his friends by talking about this subject and was delighted to have come across a new man.

"I am afraid we shall be late," Katavasov observed, glancing at his watch the moment Metrov had finished.

"We have a meeting of the Society of Amateurs to commemorate the fiftieth anniversary of Svintitch," Katavasov said in reply to Levin's question. "Peter Ivanitch and I intended going. I promised to read a paper on his zoological discoveries. Why not come too? You may find it interesting."

"Yes, it is time we were going," Metrov said. "Do come with us, and if you like we might go to my place afterwards. I should like you to read me your book."

"Oh, it is hardly finished, but I shall be glad to come to the meeting."

"Have you heard the news? I sent in a separate report," Katavasov said as he put on his coat in the next room.

And they began to discuss some university question.

The thing they were talking about had made a great stir in Moscow during the winter. Three old professors of the council had refused to accept the opinion of the younger men and the latter had sent in a report of their own. This had led to a split into two parties. The one to which Katavasov belonged saw nothing in the action of the other but base denunciation and deceit, while the party of elders regarded the affair as nothing but a piece of youthful impudence and disrespect to the authorities. Though Levin did not belong to the university, he had heard the matter discussed during his stay in Moscow and had formed his own opinion upon the matter. The three continued talking about it until they reached the university building.

The meeting had already begun. Katavasov and Metrov took their seats at a large table covered with a cloth around which six other men were seated, one of whom was reading aloud, bending closely over his manuscript. Levin sat down in one of the unoccupied chairs near the table and asked a student near him what the paper was about.

" Biography," he replied with a disapproving glance.

Though Levin was not interested in the biography of the learned man, he listened involuntarily and discovered quite a lot of interesting facts about the life of the famous scholar.

When the reader had finished, the chairman thanked him and read the verses the poet Ment had written for this particular occasion. He also thanked the poet in a few words. Then Katavasov, in his loud voice, gave his paper on the labours of the learned scholar whose anniversary was being commemorated.

When that was over Levin looked at his watch and saw that it was nearly two. He decided that there would not be time to read his book to Metrov, and besides, he had no great desire to do so. He had been reviewing their conversation during the reading and had come to the conclusion that though Metrov's ideas were original, they could be cleared up and brought into order only by individual work in the chosen field of each, and that nothing whatever could come from an interchange of ideas. At the close of the meeting he went up to Metrov who was talking to the chairman about the political news. He introduced the two to each other. Metrov was telling the chairman exactly the same thing that Levin had heard in the morning, and Levin made exactly the same remarks he had made before, with the exception of one new idea that had just entered his head. Soon they began on the university question again. As Levin had heard it all before he hastily begged Metrov to excuse him, saying that he was unable to accept his invitation, and bowing to them, he went away, straight to the Lvov's.

IV

Lvov, the husband of Natalie, Kitty's sister, had spent all his life in the capitals and abroad, where he had been educated and had served as a diplomat.

The year before he had renounced his diplomatic career (not on account of any unpleasantness, he had always been on the best of terms with everybody) and had accepted a position in the Palace Department in order to enable him to give his two boys the best education possible.

Though they were little like each other, both in their habits and views, and Lvov was much older than Levin, they had seen a good deal of each other during the winter and the closest friendship had sprung up between them.

Lvov was at home and Levin went in to him without being announced.

He was sitting in an arm-chair, dressed in a house-coat with a girdle round his waist, chamois leather slippers, and blue spectacles, reading a book supported on a reading-stand, and holding a half-smoked cigar between his beautiful fingers. His handsome, thin, still youthful face to which the silvery hair gave a still greater expression of good breeding, lighted up with a smile when he saw who his visitor was.

"How nice! I was just about to send for you. How is Kitty? Sit down and make yourself comfortable." He rose and drew up a rocking-chair. "Have you read the latest circular of the *Journal de St. Pétersbourg*? I think it excellent," he said with a slightly French accent.

Levin told him what he had heard from Katavasov, the things that were being said in St. Petersburg in high quarters, and after chatting on politics for a little time, he began telling him about Metrov and the meeting he had been to. Lvov was interested.

"I envy your being mixed up in that interesting learned world," he said. And becoming more animated, he at once passed over to the French language in which he felt more at ease. "Of course, I have no time for that sort of thing; I am too much occupied with my work and the children. Besides, I am ashamed to confess, my education has been woefully neglected."

"I don't think so," Levin said with a smile at his modesty, knowing that it was not at all feigned, but absolutely sincere.

"Really, I can't help feeling how little educated I am. For the children's sake I am constantly having to refresh my memory and learning things anew. I like to superintend their education —masters, you know, are not enough; there must be an overseer, just as you have on your farm. Here have I been reading . . ." He took up Buslaev's *Russian Grammar* from the desk. "They expect Misha to know this; it is frightfully hard; I wish you would explain it to me. It says here . . ."

Levin tried to explain that the thing could not be understood, but had just to be learned, but Lvov did not agree with him.

"You are merely making fun of it!"

"Not at all; when I look at you I begin thinking that I too will soon have to occupy myself with the education of children."

"That comes easily enough," Lvov said.

"I know of no children who are better brought up than yours," Levin said. "I only hope my own will be as good."

A smile of pleasure that he was trying to repress lighted up Lvov's face.

" I hope they will turn out better than their father at any rate," Lvov began. " You don't know all the difficulties I have had to go through and how they were spoilt by that life abroad."

" You will soon put that right; they are such clever children. The chief thing to my mind is moral education; I have come to that conclusion as a result of observing children."

" But moral education is the most difficult thing of all. You no sooner conquer one difficulty than another crops up. It is nothing but a constant struggle. Were it not for religion no father would be able to bring up his children by his own unaided strength.

They were interrupted by the entrance of the beautiful Natalya Alexandrovitch, dressed for going out.

" I didn't know you were here," she said, quite callous at having put an end to their boring conversation, as she considered it. " How is Kitty? I was going to dine with her. Arseny," she added, turning to her husband, " you had better take the carriage . . . "

And husband and wife began discussing how they would pass the day. As Lvov had to go and meet some one in connection with the service and Natalie had to go to the concert and afterwards to some public meeting of the south-eastern committee, there were a good many things to arrange. Levin, as a near friend of the house, had to take part in these plans. It was finally decided that he should accompany Natalie to the concert and the meeting, and from there they would send the carriage to the office for Arseny, who would call for them afterwards and take them to Kitty, if he got through with his work—or if not he was to send the carriage back for them.

" Kostia quite spoils me," Lvov said to his wife. " He insists that ours are the best children he has ever seen, yet I know they are far from perfect."

" Arseny goes to extremes; I've always told him so," Natalie remarked to Levin. " If you want perfection you will never be satisfied. What papa says is right. When we were children there was one extreme; we were kept in the entresol while the parents lived in the bel-étage; now there is another extreme, the parents are kept in the lumber-room while the children occupy the bel-étage. Parents have no life of their own nowadays; they only live for their children."

"Why should they not if they find it pleasanter? " Lvov

asked with his sweet smile, stroking her hand. "Anyone who did not know you would think you were a stepmother."

"No, extremes are not good in anything," Natalie said calmly, putting his paper-knife into its proper place on the table.

"Come here, you angels of perfection," Lvov said, turning to two handsome boys who were just entering the room. They bowed to Levin and walked over to their father, evidently wishing to ask him for something.

Levin wanted to talk to them and to hear what it was they wished to say to their father, but Natalie began asking him all sorts of questions. Then a colleague of Lvov's came in, a man named Mahotin, dressed in court uniform. He had come to fetch Lvov to meet some one. There began an endless conversation about Herzegovina, the Princess Korsinsky, the city council, the sudden death of the Princess Apraksin, and so on.

Levin had entirely forgotten the commission Kitty had given him. He thought of it only in the hall on his way out.

"Oh, by the way, Kitty asked me to have a talk with you about Oblonsky," he said to Lvov, who had come out to accompany him and his wife.

"Oh, yes, mamma wants us—*les beaux-frères*—to attack him," he said reddening. "But really, I don't see why I should."

"If you won't, then I will," Natalie said with a smile as she stood in her white fur coat waiting for them to finish. "Well, come along."

V

Two interesting pieces were to be given at the afternoon concert. One was a fantasia, "King Lear in the Wilderness," the other a quartette, dedicated to the memory of Bach. Both things were new and belonged to the new school, and Levin was anxious to form his own opinion about them. He conducted his sister-in-law to her seat and stopped at a column, having made up his mind to listen as attentively as possible. He did not look at the conductor of the orchestra, not wishing to have his attention diverted nor his impression spoiled, nor did he glance at the ladies in their large hats and at the mass of people who seemed occupied with all sorts of thoughts and interests—anything but that of music. He tried to avoid all connoisseurs and talkers, but stood looking down and listening.

The more he heard of the fantasia of "King Lear," the less

did he feel competent to form any definite opinion about it. There was the usual accumulation of sound at the beginning, but just as it was about to express itself in a definite motive or feeling, it wandered off into something else, at times into exceedingly complicated sounds connected in no other way than by the whim of the composer. Even the phases with any feeling in them were unpleasant, because they were so unexpected and seemed to have no relation to the rest of the piece. Joy, sorrow, despair, tenderness, and triumph appeared suddenly without any apparent reason, just like the feelings of a madman, and just as suddenly passed away.

During the whole of the piece Levin experienced the sensation that a deaf person must feel when watching others dance. He was utterly at a loss to understand what it was all about and was tired from the strained effort of listening. Loud applause was heard on all sides. People began moving from their places and talking. Anxious to know what sort of an impression the thing had produced on others, Levin walked away in search of some connoisseur, and was glad to see one of the most famous musical critics engaged in conversation with an acquaintance of his, Pestsov.

" It was wonderful! " Pestsov was saying in his deep bass voice. " How do you do, Konstantin Dmitritch? Quite statuesque so to speak, and particularly rich in colour in the passage where you feel the approach of Cordelia, where woman, *das Ewig-weibliche*, enters into conflict with fate. Don't you think so? "

" But what has Cordelia to do with it? " Levin asked timidly, having entirely forgotten that the fantasia represented King Lear in the wilderness.

" This is where Cordelia comes in; look! " Pestsov said, pointing to the programme he was holding in his hand, and giving it to Levin.

It was only then that Levin recalled the title of the fantasia and hastened to read the Russian translation of a quotation from Shakespeare, printed on the back of the programme.

" You can't follow it without the programme," Pestsov said to Levin. His other interlocutor had departed and so he had no one else to talk to.

They spent the rest of the interval discussing the merits and demerits of the Wagnerian school. Levin tried to prove that the mistake of Wagner and his followers lay in the fact that they were trying to bring music into the sphere of an art that was foreign to it, just as poetry was trying to enter the spheres of painting and sculpture into the spheres of poetry. He instanced the case of a sculptor who had endeavoured to represent poetic shadows of pictures on the pedestal about the figure of a poet. " They are so little these shadows that they seem to hover about the staircase," Levin said. He was pleased with the phrase, but recollected that he had used it before, perhaps in the presence of Pestsov, and so became confused.

Pestsov upheld the unity of art, saying that it attained its highest manifestations only when it combined the various kinds.

The second piece Levin was unable to follow, as Pestsov kept talking to him all the time, condemning it for its exaggerated simplicity, which he compared to the simplicity of the Pre-Raphaelite painters.

On his way out Levin met a number of acquaintances with whom he chatted about politics and music. Among these was the Count Bol on whom he had entirely forgotten to call.

" Why not go now? " Natalie said when he mentioned this to her. " Perhaps they are not at home, in which case you could come on to the meeting. There will be plenty of time."

VI

" PERHAPS they are not receiving to-day," Levin said to the porter as he entered the hall of the Bol's house.

" They are, sir," the porter replied, helping Levin off with his coat in a most resolute manner.

" What a nuisance! " Levin thought. He sighed, took off one glove, and smoothed his hat. " What on earth did I come for? What shall I say to them? "

At the door of the first drawing-room Levin met the countess herself, who was giving some orders to a servant, with a most anxious and serious expression on her face. When she caught sight of Levin she smiled and invited him to come into the smaller drawing-room, from whence issued the sound of voices. In this room were the countess's two daughters and a colonel. Levin exchanged greetings with them and sat down near the couch holding his hat on his knee.

" How is your wife? Have you been to the concert? We couldn't go as mamma had to attend a funeral mass."

" Oh, yes, I heard. . . . What a sudden death! " Levin said.

Just then the countess came in, and seating herself on the couch she too asked him about his wife and the concert.

Levin replied and repeated his remark about the suddenness of Princess Apraksin's death.

" She always had very poor health though."

" Were you at the opera last night? "

" Yes, I was."

" Wasn't Lucca splendid? "

" Yes, wasn't she? " Utterly indifferent as to what they might think of him, he repeated what he had heard at least a hundred times about the peculiarities of the singer's talents. The Countess Bol pretended to be listening. When he had finished, the colonel, who had so far been silent, took the field. He, too, spoke about the opera and the illuminations. Finally, after some remark about the proposed *folle journée* at Turin's, the colonel laughed boisterously, got up, and took his leave. Levin rose too, but he could see by the countess's face that it was not yet time for him to go. He had to give them at least two more minutes, so he sat down again.

He could not help thinking how stupid it all was and remained at a loss for something to say.

" Are you going to the meeting? They say it will be interesting," the countess observed.

" I promised to call for my sister-in-law," Levin said.

A silence ensued. The mother and daughters exchanged glances.

" I think it is time now," Levin thought and got up. The ladies pressed his hand and begged him to remember them kindly to his wife.

When the porter handed him his coat, he asked him where he lived and immediately wrote down the address in a large well-bound visitor's book.

" Of course, it is all the same to me, but I can't help feeling how horribly stupid it is," Levin thought, consoling himself by the reflection that every one else did the same.

When he got to the meeting the whole of society was assembled there. The minutes were just being read, which every one found very interesting. At the close people began moving about, and Levin came across Sviajsky. The latter invited him to come to another meeting, the Agricultural Society this time, where a celebrated report was to be delivered that evening. Stepan Arkadyevitch, who had just returned from the races, and various other acquaintances came up. They talked about the meeting, a new play, and some legal case that was going on. Here Levin made a very grave mistake, due perhaps to a feeling of mental weariness that had come over him. In speculating on the possible sentence that might be passed on a foreigner who was being tried in Russia, he repeated a remark that an acquaintance of his had made the day before.

" To send him out of the country would be like punishing a pike by letting it into the water," he said.

It was only later that he recalled that this thought given out by his acquaintance as original was a quotation from one of Krilov's fables, which he had come across in an article in some newspaper. Levin could not help feeling ashamed when he thought of it afterwards.

He took his sister-in-law home, and finding Kitty well and happy, he departed for the club.

VII

LEVIN got to the club just in time, when members and guests were beginning to arrive. He had not been there since his university days, when he had lived in Moscow and frequented society. Though he remembered all the external details of the club, he had entirely forgotten all the impressions he had experienced in the days when he had gone there often. But no sooner had he driven into the large semicircular courtyard and caught sight of the porter with a girdle round his waist, who came out to meet him as he ascended the porch, than he recalled everything. There was the porter's room with the members' goloshes and fur coats, there was the sound of a bell that preceded him as he went up the soft well-carpeted stairs, there was the statue on the landing, another familiar porter in uniform leisurely examining each guest as he opened the door. His former sensation of rest, contentment, and comfort returned to him.

" Your hat, please," the porter said to him, seeing that he had forgotten the club rule that hats and coats were to be left in the porter's room below. " You have not been here for a long time, sir. The prince put you down yesterday. Prince Stepan Arkadyevitch has not yet arrived."

The porter knew all Levin's relatives and connections, and immediately mentioned several people he was acquainted with.

Levin walked through the first hall with its screens and partitioned room where the fruiterer sat, and passing an old man who was walking slowly, he entered the dining-room, which was alive with people.

He passed his eye over the various tables, scanning the guests. There were a variety of men, old and young, some acquaintances, some friends. All looked contented and happy. All seemed to have left their cares and worries with their hats in the porter's room, and were leisurely getting ready to enjoy the material pleasures of life. There was Sviajsky, Shcherbatsky, Nevyedovsky, the old prince, Vronsky, and Sergei Ivanovitch.

" Ah! you are late! " the prince said with a smile, giving Levin his hand over his shoulder. " How is Kitty? " he asked, adjusting his napkin, stuck in between two buttons of his waistcoat.

" She is very well, thank you. They are all dining at home."

" There will be plenty of the Alins and Nadins, I suppose. Sorry there is no room here; go and reserve a place at that table," the old prince said, cautiously receiving a plate of soup.

" I say, Levin! " a good-natured voice called to him from some little way off. It was Turovtsin. He was sitting at a table with a military man, and near them were two upturned chairs. Levin went up to them gladly. Since the evening of his explanation with Kitty, he had always had a soft feeling for the good-natured Turovtsin, and now after all the strained and brilliant conversations, the sight of his jolly, simple face was agreeable to him.

" These places are for you and Vronsky. He will be here in a minute."

" Ah, here he comes! "

" Have you only just got here? " Oblonsky asked, coming up to Levin quickly. " How are you? Had a glass of vodka? Let us go and get some."

Levin rose and followed him to the large table on which stood all sorts of brandies and appetisers. From the large assortment there, it ought not to have been difficult to choose one, but Stepan Arkadyevitch demanded some special kind of brandy and a liveried footman immediately brought it to him. They drank a wine glass each and returned to their own table.

They had not yet finished soup when Gagin, the fourth of their party, ordered champagne and told the waiter to fill four glasses. Levin did not refuse the wine offered him, and immediately ordered a second bottle. He was hungry and ate and drank heartily; he even took part in the simple, merry conversation of the company with the greatest enjoyment possible. Gagin, lowering his voice, began relating some naughty St. Petersburg anecdote. It was so funny that Levin roared with laughter, attracting the general attention of every one in the room.

"That reminds me of the story 'I can't bear that!' Have you heard it?" Stepan Arkadyevitch asked. It's awfully funny. Bring another bottle!" he said to the waiter, and began telling his story.

"Peter Ilitch Vinovsky begs you to accept this," an old waiter interrupted him as he came up with two sparkling glasses of champagne. He handed one to Stepan Arkadyevitch and one to Levin. Oblonsky took his glass and nodded and smiled to a bald-headed, bearded man at the other end of the table.

"Who is it?" Levin asked.

"You must have met him at my house once. A very nice man."

Levin took his glass and also nodded to the man.

Stepan Arkadyevitch's anecdote was funny too, and one that Levin told was also appreciated. They began to talk about horses, about that day's races, admiring Vronsky's Atlas, which had won the first prize.

Levin did not notice how quickly the time passed.

"Ah, here they are!" Stepan Arkadyevitch exclaimed, bending over the back of his chair and extending his hand to Vronsky, who was coming towards him with a tall colonel of the Guards. Vronsky's face was beaming with the general good-humour of the club. He leant over Stepan Arkadyevitch's shoulder, whispered something to him with a smile, and extended his hand to Levin.

"Glad to meet you," he said. "I tried to find you again at the elections, but was told that you had gone."

"Yes, I left the same day," Levin said. "We were just talking about your horses. I congratulate you. It was a good record."

"But you have horses too."

"My father had, but I remember all about them."

"Where did you dine?" Stepan Arkadyevitch asked.

"At the second table by the columns."

"It was a complimentary dinner," the tall colonel remarked. "The second imperial prize! I only wish I had as much luck at cards as he has with his horses. Why waste time? " he added leaving the table. " I am off to the infernal regions."

" That is Yashvin," Vronsky replied to a question of Turovt-sin, as he sat down near them on a chair just vacated. Whether it was the influence of the general spirit of the club, or the champagne he had drunk, it was difficult to say, but Levin entered into an amiable conversation with Vronsky on cattle breeding, and was delighted to find that he no longer felt any hostility towards him. Among other things he even mentioned that he had heard from his wife that she had met him at the Princess Marya Borisovna's.

" The Princess Marya Borisovna? What a capital woman she is!" Stepan Arkadyevitch said, and began relating an amusing anecdote about her. Vronsky laughed so good-naturedly that Levin felt himself completely reconciled to him.

" Have you finished? " Stepan Arkadyevitch asked, smiling. " Then come along! "

VIII

As he left the table and accompanied Gagin to the billiard-room, Levin felt that his arms were swaying particularly lightly and easily. In the large hall he came across his father-in-law.

" Well, how do you like our temple of idleness? " the prince asked, taking his arm. " Come, let us walk round a bit."

" I wanted to examine the place myself, it is rather interesting."

" It may be for you, but my interest is of a different character. Do you see these old men? " he said, indicating a stooping old man with an over-hanging lip, who was shuffling along towards them in his soft boots. " Do you think they were born such dowdies? "

" How do you mean? "

" That is our club term for such men. You go about laughing and enjoying yourselves, while we are merely waiting to become like that. Do you know Prince Chechensky? " he asked, and Levin could see by the twinkle in his eye that he was going to tell him something funny.

" No, I don't."

" How is that? But it doesn't matter. The celebrated prince always plays billiards. Three years ago he was still bright and sprightly, and amused himself by calling other men dowdies. One beautiful day he comes to the club, and our porter—you know, Vassily, the fat one; very smart he is. Well, Prince Chechensky asked him, ' Vassily, who is here? Are there any dowdies? ' and Vassily replies, ' Two, sir, and you are the third! ' "

Talking and exchanging greetings with any acquaintances they met on the way the prince and Levin made the tour of the club. They passed through the large room where the tables were already placed and the usual partners were playing a small game; through the divan-room where a few members were playing chess and Sergei Ivanovitch was engaged in conversation with some one; through the billiard-room, where at one corner a jolly crowd had gathered round Gagin, drinking champagne and talking merrily; they even took a peep into the infernal regions where Yashvin was already seated at a table with a crowd of adherents. Stepping very cautiously so as not to make any noise they entered the reading-room, where under the shaded lamps sat a cross-looking young man, fingering one periodical after another, and a bald old general who was buried in a book. From there they passed into what the prince called the " intellectual room." Here three men were engaged in a heated discussion on politics.

" We are ready, prince," some acquaintance said to him, coming in. They had formed a card party and were waiting for the prince to join them. Levin sat and listened to the political discussion when the prince had gone, but after the conversations of the morning he found it frightfully boring, and got up to find Oblonsky and Turovtsin with whom it was much jollier.

Turovtsin was sitting on a couch in the billiard-room, drinking, while Stepan Arkadyevitch and Vronsky were talking together by a door in a distant corner of the room.

" She does not feel exactly lonely, but the indefiniteness, the vagueness of her position . . ." As Levin caught these words he was about to turn away, but Stepan Arkadyevitch called to him.

" Levin! don't go away! " Stepan Arkadyevitch said, and Levin could see that his eyes were not exactly tearful, but humid, as was always the case with him when under the influence of wine or sentiment. Just now he was under the influence of both. He pressed Levin's arm firmly, evidently intent on not letting him slip away.

" This is my oldest and almost dearest friend," he said to Vronsky. " And you, too, are for some reasons even nearer and dearer to me. I only wish you could be close friends, because you are both such excellent men."

" There seems nothing left for us to do but to embrace," Vronsky said jestingly, in his good-natured way, extending his hand to Levin.

The latter pressed the hand offered him warmly.

" I should be very glad, " he said.

" Waiter! A bottle of champagne! " Stepan Arkadyevitch called.

" And I too," Vronsky said.

But in spite of Stepan Arkadyevitch and their own mutual desire to be friendly, they felt that they had nothing to say to each other.

" What do you think? he has never met Anna," Stepan Arkadyevitch said to Vronsky. " I am most eager to introduce him to her. Shall we go, Levin? "

" Really? She will be delighted to see you," Vronsky said, " I would go home at once, but feel uneasy about Yashvin. I shall have to stay until he gets through."

" Is he doing badly? "

" He is losing all the time, and I'm the only man here who can hold him in check."

" Shall we have a game at pyramids? Will you play, Levin? That's right! Place the pyramids, please," Stepan Arkadyevitch added, turning to the marker.

" Everything is quite ready," the man replied. He had already placed the balls in the triangle and was rolling the red one to amuse himself.

" Come, let us begin."

After the game Vronsky and Levin seated themselves at the table with Gagin, and Levin, upon Stepan Arkadyevitch's advice, began to bet on aces. Vronsky would turn every now and then to an acquaintance who came up to him, or run down into the infernal regions to see how Yashvin was getting on. Levin experienced a pleasant relief from the mental fatigue of the morning. He was happy that the hostility he had felt for Vronsky was at an end, and the impression of the club comfort and calm never left him for a moment. When they finished the game Stepan Arkadyevitch took his arm.

" Shall we go to Anna's now? She is at home, and I promised to bring you. You were not going anywhere else this evening, were you? "

" Nowhere in particular. I told Sviajsky that I might go

to the meeting of the Agricultural Society, but I shall be pleased to come with you."

"All right, come along. Find out if my carriage has come," Stepan Arkadyevitch said to one of the club servants.

Levin went up to the table and paid the forty roubles he had lost; then he paid the club bill to the old waiter who was standing at the door post, and in some mysterious manner knew precisely what it was, and swaying his arms in a peculiar way crossed all the halls on his way out.

IX

"PRINCE OBLONSKY'S carriage!" the porter called in an angry voice. The carriage drew up to the door and both took their seats. The moment they drove out into the streets, and the agreeable impressions of the club were left behind, Levin began to reflect on what he was doing, and wondered whether Kitty would approve of his going to see Anna. Stepan Arkadyevitch, however, gave him no time to meditate; as though divining his thoughts, he tried to dispel them.

"I am so glad you are going to meet her!" he said. "You know Dolly has been wanting this for a long time. Lvov calls on her sometimes. She is a remarkable woman, though she is my sister. But you will see for yourself. Her position is a very difficult one, especially now."

"Why now?"

"We are trying to persuade her husband to divorce her. Though he is willing, the matter has been dragging on for three months over some difficulty concerning her son. As soon as she gets a divorce she can get legally married to Vronsky. How stupid that old custom is of 'Rejoice, Isaiah!' which nobody believes in and is only in the way of people's happiness!" Stepan Arkadyevitch observed. "When it is all over their position will be defined, like yours and mine."

"But what is the difficulty?"

"Oh, it's a long story. Everything is so vague with us. Here she is, living in Moscow where everybody knows her, waiting for the divorce. She never goes out and sees no women except Dolly; she does not wish people to call on her merely for pity's sake. That stupid Princess Varvara would not stay with her here, because she considered it improper. Any other woman in Anna's place would not have known what to do with herself, but she. . . . You will see for yourself. Her life is all repose and dignity. The lane on the left, opposite the church!" Stepan Arkadyevitch shouted to the coachman as he leaned out of the carriage window. "How hot it is!" h'e exclaimed, throwing open his fur coat, in spite of the twelve degrees of Réaumur.

"I hear she has a little girl who, I suppose, takes up a good deal of her time," Levin observed.

"You seem to look upon every woman as nothing but *une couveuse*," Stepan Arkadyevitch remarked. "If a woman is occupied then it must be with children. She brings her up excellently I believe, but you will hear nothing about the child. She is busy writing for one thing. I see you smile, but reserve your judgment. It is a book for children she is busy upon; she never speaks of it to any one, but she read it to me. I gave the manuscript to Vorknev—you know, the publisher—he writes himself, I believe. At any rate he is a good judge, and he declares it is a remarkable book. But don't imagine that she is the typical authoress. Not in the least. First and foremost she is a woman with a heart. Just now she is interested in an English girl and a whole family."

"In the philanthropic line I suppose."

"You always try to see the worst side of everything. I assure you it is more than that. Vronsky had an English trainer, a very good man at his work, but an awful drunkard. He drank himself into delirium tremens and the family are left destitute. Anna takes an interest in them and helps them all she can. She does not patronise them merely, but is taking a great deal of trouble over them, besides giving them money. She is preparing the two boys for school and has taken the girl into her own house. But you will see for yourself."

The carriage drove into the yard and Stepan Arkadyevitch gave a loud ring at the bell. Without asking the servant who answered it whether his mistress were at home, he entered the hall. Levin followed, doubting more and more whether he had done right in coming. Catching sight of his own face in the mirror, he noticed that it was very red, but he felt sure he had not drunk too much, and followed Stepan Arkadyevitch up the carpeted stairs. A footman at the top bowed to Stepan Arkadyevitch as to a near friend of the house and informed him that Anna Arkadyevna was with Vorknev.

"Where are they?"

"In the study."

Crossing a small dining-room with dark panelled walls, they walked over a soft carpet into a little study, lighted by a lamp with a large dark shade. Another lamp with a reflector hung on the wall, throwing its light on to a full-sized portrait of a woman, to which Levin involuntarily directed his attention. It was the portrait of Anna done by Mihailov in Italy. While Stepan Arkadyevitch stepped behind the screen, Levin continued looking at the portrait, unable to tear himself away from it. He had forgotten where he was and did not hear what was being said around him, but kept his eyes fixed on the picture. It was not a portrait, but a living woman, charming with her wavy black hair, bare arms and shoulders, and the pensive smile on her soft lips, as she looked down at him gently, with those bewildering eyes of hers. She was not alive only because she was more beautiful than a living woman could be.

"I am very glad," he suddenly heard a voice near him, evidently addressing itself to him—it was the voice of the very woman whose portrait he was admiring. Anna came out from behind the screen to meet him, and Levin saw in the semi-obscure light of the room the very woman of the portrait, in a dark blue striped gown, not in the same position, nor with the same expression, but with the same beauty the artist had caught in the picture. She was less brilliant in reality, but there was something new and attractive in her living form that was absent in the portrait.

X

SHE rose to meet him without concealing her joy at seeing him. And in the calm, dignified way in which she extended her small, energetic hand and introduced him to Vorknev and the pretty, red-haired English girl, whom she called her charge, Levin saw the natural, agreeable manners of a grand society lady.

"I am delighted to see you," she welcomed him again, and coming from her, these words assumed a special significance for him. "I have known and liked you for a long time, both on account of your friendship for Stiva, and your wife. . . . I knew her only for a short time, but she left on me the impression of some charming flower. She is a flower indeed, and I hear she is soon to be a mother!"

She talked freely and easily, transferring her glance every

now and again from Levin to her brother. Levin felt that he
had produced a good impression and was remarkably at ease
in her presence. She was so simple that it seemed to him as
though he had known her from childhood.

" Ivan Petrovitch and I have come into Alexei's study for
the very reason that we might smoke," she said in reply to
Stepan Arkadyevitch, who had asked if he might smoke. She
glanced at Levin, drew a cigarette-case towards herself, and
took out a cigarette.

" How do you feel to-night? " her brother asked.

" Oh, fairly well. My nerves are as usual."

" Isn't it fine? " Stepan Arkadyevitch said as he noticed
Levin looking at the portrait again.

" I have never seen a better portrait."

" A very good likeness, don't you think? " Vorknev remarked.

Levin glanced from the portrait to the original. Anna's face
lighted up as she felt his gaze upon her. Levin blushed, and
anxious to conceal his embarrassment he wanted to ask how
long it was since she had seen Darya Alexandrovna, but Anna
was the first to speak.

" Ivan Petrovitch and I have just been talking about Vashchenkov's latest pictures; have you seen them? "

" Yes, I have," Levin replied.

" Pardon me, I believe I interrupted you. You were about
to say . . ."

Levin asked his question about Dolly.

" She was here yesterday. She seemed upset about the way
they are treating Grisha at school. The Latin master it appears
was very unjust to him."

" I was very much taken with Vashchenkov's pictures,"
Levin remarked, anxious to bring the conversation back to the
subject she had begun upon.

Levin no longer talked with the same indifference to things with
which he had spoken all the morning. Every word he uttered
was carefully weighed. It was pleasant to talk to her and still
more pleasant to listen to what she had to say.

Anna spoke naturally, ascribing little value to her own
thoughts, and a great deal to those of her interlocutor.

The conversation turned on the new tendency in art, and they
began discussing a French artist who had just finished a set of
illustrations of the Bible. Vorknev accused the artist of realism,
carried to the point of coarseness. Levin maintained that it
was a wholesome reaction against the extreme conventionality

of the French school. He declared that the realistic artist saw poetry in the fact that he did not lie.

Levin was satisfied with this remark, and Anna's face lighted up as she took in its meaning. She laughed.

" I am laughing as one laughs when one sees an excellent likeness," she said. " What you say is so characteristic of modern French art, both in painting and literature; take Zola and Daudet for example. But I suppose conceptions have always been constructed from conventional, imaginary figures. When all possible combinations of the imaginary had been made, the artist grew tired of them and had to turn to the more natural, more realistic figures."

" That is quite true," Vorknev observed.

" Have you just come from the club? " Anna asked, turning to her brother.

" Now this is a woman! " Levin thought, oblivious to everything, as he gazed intently at her beautiful, animated face, the expression of which had suddenly changed. He did not catch what she was saying to her brother as she bent over him, but he marvelled at the change of her whole expression. Her features, so exquisite a moment ago in repose, suddenly expressed curiosity, anger, and pride. But this lasted only a moment. She half-closed her eyes as though trying to recall something.

" However, this does not interest any one," she remarked, and turned to the English girl. " Please order tea in the drawing-room."

The girl rose and went out.

" Did she pass her examination? " Stepan Arkadyevitch asked.

" Yes, and very well too. She is an extremely capable girl and has a sweet disposition."

" You will probably end by loving her more than your own child."

" That is a man's way of looking at things. There is no such thing as more or less in love. I love my child in one way and her in another."

" I have been telling Anna Arkadyevna," Vorknev remarked, " that if she spent one-hundredth part of the energy she is spending on this English girl on the common cause of the education of Russian children, she would be doing a greater and more useful work."

" Say what you please, but I couldn't do that. When I was in the country, Count Alexei Kirillovitch tried to encourage me to busy myself with the school there." (As she pronounced

Vronsky's name she cast a timid look at Levin, who replied to her with a respectful glance.) " I tried to do what I could; the children were very sweet; but I confess I could not interest myself in the matter. Work must be based on love, and love can neither be purchased nor commanded. Now I have come to love this girl, though I don't myself know why."

Again she looked at Levin. Both her smile and her glance told him that she addressed herself exclusively to him, esteeming his opinion only and knowing in advance that they understood each other.

" I quite agree with you," Levin said. " You can't put your heart into schools nor into institutions of that kind; that is the reason why nearly all philanthropic establishments yield such poor results."

Anna smiled.

" I never could do that sort of thing," she said. " *Je n'ai pas le coeur assez large* to fall in love with an asylum full of plain little girls. *Cela ne m'a jamais réussi.* There are a great many women who have made their social position out of it. Even now, when some kind of occupation is essential to me, I cannot do it," she said addressing herself outwardly to her brother, but inwardly to Levin. Suddenly she frowned, and Levin understood that she was annoyed for having talked so much of herself.

" I have heard about you," she said to him. " They say you are not a good citizen, but I have defended you to the best of my ability."

" What did you say in my defence? '

" It depended on the attack. Wouldn't you like some tea now? "

She rose and took up a book bound in morocco leather.

" Do give it to me, Anna Arkadyevna," Vorknev said. " It is really very good."

" Oh, no, it's so unfinished."

" I told him about it," Stepan Arkadyevitcb remarked, indicating Levin.

" Why did you? My writing reminds me of the little baskets and carvings made by the prisoners that I bought from Liza Merkalova," she added turning to Levin. " She used to visit the prisons, and the unfortunate creatures were executing marvels of patience "

Levin saw a new feature in this woman who had pleased him so much. In addition to her intellect, grace, beauty, she possessed truthfulness. She had no desire to conceal from him the gravity of her position. Saying this, she sighed and her face suddenly assumed a proud, stern expression. She looked even more beautiful than she had done before, but the expression was strange, unlike the one the artist had caught in the portrait that seemed to diffuse happiness all about her. Levin glanced at the portrait again, then back at her, as she took her brother's arm and walked with him through the high doorway. He felt a peculiar sense of tenderness and pity for her that were surprising to him.

She begged Levin and Vorknev to go into the drawing-room and herself remained behind to have a few words with her brother. " They will be talking about the divorce, about Vronsky, about what is going on in the club, and possibly about me," Levin thought. He was so full of speculations as to the subject of their conversation that he scarcely listened to Vorknev, who was telling him something about Anna's story for children.

At tea the same pleasant, interesting conversation was continued. They were never at a loss for a subject to talk about, and each felt that they had not time enough to say all they wanted to, but gladly restrained themselves in order to listen to each other. For Levin, everything that was said, thanks to her attention and remarks, assumed a special significance.

While following the conversation he kept admiring her beauty, her culture, her simplicity, and above all her kindness. He listened and talked, yet all the time thought only of her and tried to divine her inner life, her feelings. Though he had condemned her formerly, he now pitied her from the bottom of his heart, and began fearing that Vronsky did not fully understand her.

At eleven o'clock when Stepan Arkadyevitch got up to leave (Vorknev had already gone) it seemed to Levin that they had only just come. He rose regretfully.

" Good-bye! " she said, holding his hand and looking at him appealingly. " I am glad *que la glace est rompue*."

She let go his hand and half-closed her eyes.

" Tell your wife that I love her as much as ever, and that if she cannot forgive me on account of my position then I don't wish her ever to forgive me. It is necessary to go through what I have done to be able to forgive, and God forbid that she should do that! "

" I will tell her by all means. . . ," Levin replied, reddening.

XI

" Poor thing! what a wonderfully sweet woman she is!" Levin thought, as he and Stepan Arkadyevitch stepped out into the frosty air.

" What did I tell you? " Stepan Arkadyevitch said enthusiastically, observing the strong impression Anna had produced on him.

" Yes, she is an extraordinary woman; not only clever, but kind-hearted as well. I'm awfully sorry for her."

" I hope matters will come out right for her," Stepan Arkadyevitch remarked. " It just shows that one should never judge hastily." He opened the carriage door. " Good-night; I'm sorry I'm not going your way."

As he reviewed his conversation with Anna and recalled the fleeting changes of expression that had swept over her features, Levin grew more and more in sympathy with her situation and felt really sorry for her. In this frame of mind he reached his own house.

When he entered, Kuzma informed him that Katerina Alexandrovna was well and that her sisters had just gone. He gave him two letters which Levin read then and there in order to avoid being disturbed later. One was from his steward, Sokolov, telling him that it was impossible to sell the wheat just then as no more than five and a half roubles were offered for it, and that there was no other way of raising money. The other letter was from his sister, who reproached him because her affairs were still unsettled.

" I suppose we must sell it for that price if we can't get more," Levin thought, instantly settling a thing that had formerly appeared to him so difficult. " It's astonishing how one's time is taken up here," he reflected, in reference to the other letter. He felt a little conscience-stricken that he had not seen after his sister's affairs better. " Here is another day gone and I haven't been to the court. There is not a moment to spare." And deciding to attend to the matter to-morrow, he proceeded to his wife's room. On the way he briefly reviewed the events of the day. He thought of all the conversations to which he had listened and in which he had taken part; all were concerned with matters that would never have interested him had he been living in the country; but here they seemed of immense importance.

He found his wife rather sad and bored. All three sisters had grown tired of waiting for him; the other two had gone and Kitty was left alone.

" Did you have a good time? " she asked, looking straight at him. His eyes were uncommonly bright. Fearing that she might hinder him from telling his own story, she concealed her suspicions and with a smile of approval listened to his account of the way in which he had spent the evening.

" I really was glad to meet Vronsky," he said. " I was not in the least embarrassed. Of course I shall avoid him as much as I can, but I am glad the ice has been broken between us." He blushed as he said this, recalling his visit to Anna's. " We always imagine that the common people are drunkards," he continued; " but I am really not sure whether they drink more than we do. It is true they get horribly drunk at holiday times, but . . ." Kitty was entirely indifferent as to when and how the common people indulged in liquor; she had noticed him blush and wanted to know the cause of it.

" Where did you go after the club? " she asked.

" Stiva was very anxious for me to meet Anna Arkadyevna." He blushed still more and was now quite certain that he had done wrong in going.

Kitty's eyes flashed when he mentioned Anna, but she controlled herself and tried to hide her emotion from him.

" Oh! " was all she said.

" You don't object to my going there, do you? Stiva was anxious to take me there, and Dolly, too, wanted me to meet her."

" Not in the least," she replied; but the expression in her eyes had betrayed her effort to conceal her displeasure.

" She is really a very nice woman and ought to be pitied," he said when he had told her about Anna's life and occupations and delivered the message she had given him.

" Of course she is to be pitied," Kitty remarked when he had finished. " From whom were your two letters? " she asked.

He explained, and deceived by her calmness went out to change his clothes.

When he returned he found Kitty in the same chair. At his approach she looked up and burst into a flood of tears.

" What is it? What is the matter? " he asked, though he knew quite well what it was.

" You have fallen in love with that dreadful woman! I know you have! She has bewitched you; I can see it in your eyes! You had too much to drink at the club and played cards . . . and then went to visit . . . No, we must go away from here . . . I shall go to-morrow. . . . "

It was long before Levin could calm her. He began by agreeing with her, saying that it was probably the wine and the pity he felt for Anna that had influenced him, and he had consequently fallen under the spell of her cunning, but promised to avoid her in the future. He was perfectly sincere in a certain part of his confession when he said that having been for so long in Moscow with nothing to do but to eat, drink, and gossip, he was beginning to lose his common sense. They talked until the small hours of the morning, and it was only after three o'clock that they became somewhat reconciled and dropped off to sleep.

XII

AFTER her visitors had gone, Anna began pacing the room restlessly.

Though it was only unconsciously that she had tried to attract Levin that evening—a thing that rarely happened in her relations with young men—she confessed to herself that she had succeeded, in so far as an honourable married man could be attracted to another woman at first sight. She, too, was attracted to him. In spite of the immense outward differences between him and Vronsky, with a woman's intuition she had discovered a likeness between the two—a certain quality that had attracted her in both; but no sooner had he gone than she completely dismissed him from her thoughts. One idea alone possessed her. " If others are attracted to me, like this quiet married man for instance, then why is *he* so indifferent? It may not really be indifference, because I do not even know whether he loves me at all. Something has come between us. Why does he stay away the whole evening? Stiva says that he stayed behind to watch over Yashvin, but surely Yashvin isn't a child! Even if it were true, that could not be the only reason. He is glad of an opportunity to show me that he has other duties, though I know that quite well. Why does he persist in trying to prove it to me? He wishes me to understand that his love must not stand in the way of his liberty; but I do not want his liberty; love alone is sufficient for me. He ought to see how miserable it is for me living in Moscow, if it can be called living. Waiting for a solution that never comes is not living. There is no answer yet and Stiva declines to go to Alexei Alexandrovitch. I can't write again. I can't do anything or change anything. I have just to go on waiting patiently and invent all sorts of ways of passing the time . . . the English family, for instance. I try to read and write, but it is only deluding myself like taking morphia. If only he showed some sympathy!" Tears of self-pity stood in her eyes.

At this moment she heard Vronsky's nervous ring at the door, and hastily drying her tears she took a book and sat down near the lamp, trying to look unconcerned. But she had to show him that she was displeased because he had not kept his word, only in such a way that he should not see her misery, nor her own self-pity. She had a perfect right to pity herself if she liked, but he must not see it. She did not wish to quarrel with him, but involuntarily assumed a hostile attitude.

" You were not lonely, were you? " he asked cheerfully as he entered the room. " Really, gambling is an awful vice!"

" Oh, no, I have long schooled myself against feeling lonely. Stiva and Levin called."

" They told me they were coming. How did you like Levin? " He sat down beside her.

"Very much; they've only just gone. How did Yashvin fare?"

" He won seventeen hundred roubles at first; I wanted him to leave off, but he would go on, and is losing dreadfully now."

" Then why did you leave him? " she asked, looking into his face. Her expression was cold and unfriendly. " Stiva told me that you intended looking after him, and now you go and leave him to his fate."

Vronsky's face darkened.

" In the first place, I never asked Stiva to tell you anything; in the second, I never lie. I wanted to stay and I stayed," he said frowning. " Anna, Anna! Why will you be so impossible? " he said to her after a pause, trying to take her hand. She was glad of this tender appeal, but some strange force seemed to harden her, as though the conditions of the contest prevented her from giving in.

" You wanted to stay and you stayed! Of course, you always do as you wish, but why should you say that to me? Why? " she exclaimed, her agitation increasing. " I do not dispute your rights."

He closed the hand she had refused to take and leaned back. His face had assumed a determined look.

" It is nothing but obstinacy on your part," she said as she looked at him and instantly discovered a name for the expression that annoyed her. " Sheer obstinacy! All you want to do is to conquer me, while I . . ." Again the same feeling of self-pity took possession of her and the tears rose to her eyes. " If you only knew what it means to me when I feel how antagonistic you are; if you only knew how near to ruin I am at such moments, how I fear for myself . . ." She turned away to hide a sob.

" What is it? " he asked, alarmed at the expression of despair on her face. He bent over her and raised her hand to his lips. " What have I done? Am I looking for outside amusements? Do I not avoid the society of other women? "

" I know you do," she said.

" Then tell me what I ought to do to make you happy. I would do anything I could," he added, touched by the look of suffering on her face. " I hate to see you suffering like this."

" I'm all right now," she said. " I don't know what makes these moods come over me. It may be my loneliness, or perhaps my nerves; at any rate, let us say no more about it. Tell me about the races; how did you get on? " she asked, trying to conceal her triumph.

He asked to have supper served and told her all about the races, but his coldness of manner and voice showed that he had not forgiven and that she had not conquered that obstinacy against which she was trying to contend. He seemed to have grown indifferent to her, as though he repented of his submission.

As Anna recalled the words that had given her the victory, " if you only knew how near to ruin I am at such moments, how I fear for myself," she realised that she had wielded a dangerous weapon, that she would be unable to make use of a second time. She felt that along with the love that bound them, a spirit of strife had appeared that they could not banish from their hearts.

XIII

THERE are no conditions to which a man may not become accustomed, particularly if he sees that they are accepted by those about him. Levin would hardly have believed it possible three months ago that he could sleep soundly in the conditions in which he found himself to-day, and yet here he was leading a senseless, purposeless life, beyond his means, and taking it all as a matter of course. How could he sleep calmly and peacefully after the excesses of the evening at the club (could he think of it in any other way?), after his strange friendship for a man his wife had once loved and his still stranger visit on a fallen woman (she could not be called by any other name), after his infatuation with her that had so angered his wife? Yet strange to say he slept as soundly as it was possible for a man to sleep. His fatigue and the wine had done their work.

At about five o'clock in the morning he was awakened by the sound of an opening door. He sat up in bed and looked about him. Kitty was no longer by his side; behind the partition that divided the room he saw a light and heard her footsteps.

" Kitty, what is it? What is the matter? " he asked, only half awake.

" Nothing," she replied coming towards him with a candle in her hand. " I was not feeling very well," she added with a sweet, expressive smile.

" Is it beginning? " he asked in a tone of anxiety. " We must send for the doctor at once." He began to hurry into his clothes.

" Oh, no," she said with a smile, trying to stop him. " It was only a false alarm; I just felt a little unwell, that is all; I am all right again now."

She extinguished the candle and got into bed again. Though the calm way in which she breathed was in itself suspicious, and the peculiarly suppressed excitement in her voice when she had said " nothing " was rather alarming, still Levin felt so sleepy that he dozed off again. It was only later when he recalled her quiet breathing that he realised what must have taken place in her soul as she had lain there beside him in the expectation of the greatest possible event in a woman's life.

At about seven o'clock she touched his shoulder gently, undecided whether to wake him or not.

" Kostia, don't be frightened, dear," she said softly, " it is nothing . . . but I think we had better send for Lizaveta Petrovna."

She had lighted the candle again and was sitting up in bed knitting something she had been busy on for the last few days.

" Don't be alarmed; it is nothing; I am not in the least afraid," she said, as she noticed the frightened look on his face. She kissed his hand and pressed it against her heart.

He jumped up hurriedly, almost beside himself, and watched

her attentively as he got into his dressing-gown. He had to go,
yet could not tear himself away; he stood there gazing at her.
Her sweet, lovely face, so familiar to him, wore an expression that
he had never seen there before. How he hated himself when he
recalled the suffering he had caused her the night before. Her
flushed face, with the little stray curls escaping from under her
night-cap, was radiant with joy and determination. Levin was
overcome by what it revealed to him now that all other emotions
were absent, and he saw her soul, so to speak, shining out in her
eyes. There she was, chaste and unveiled—she, the woman he
loved. She smiled, but suddenly her brow contracted; she
sighed, and looking up into his face took his hand and clung to
him. He saw that she suffered and knew that she was asking
for his sympathy. He somehow felt a sense of guilt for her
suffering, but the tenderness that shone out of her eyes told him
that her love for him was unchanged and that she did not
reproach him.

"Who then is to blame for her suffering if I am not?" he
thought, feeling that the culprit ought to be found and punished.
But there was no culprit; she merely suffered and wanted
sympathy; she rejoiced in her suffering. A wonderful change
was going on in her soul, but he did not understand its nature;
it was beyond him.

"I have sent for mother. You must go and fetch Lizaveta
Petrovna; I am all right just now." She walked away from
him and rang the bell. "You can go now, Pasha is coming;
you need not be afraid of leaving me."

And to Levin's great surprise she went on with her knitting.
The maid entered just as he was about to go out. He heard
Kitty giving her all sorts of directions and help her move the bed.

He dressed while the horses were being harnessed (it was
impossible to hire anything at that early hour), and before going
looked into the bedroom once more, walking not on tip-toe, but as
though on wings. Two maids were busy moving the furniture,
while Kitty paced up and down giving orders and doing her
knitting.

"I'm just off for the doctor; they've already sent for Lizaveta
Petrovna, but I shall call there myself. Do you want anything else? I can look in on Dolly, too."

She glanced at him, but had evidently not taken in what he
had said.

"Yes, yes, all right," she said with a frown, motioning him
away hurriedly.

On his way to the drawing-room he was arrested by a low pitiful moan.

" My God! " he said to himself, and pressing his head between his hands, he rushed out of the room. " Lord help us and have mercy upon us! " he kept repeating. The words had come unexpectedly to his lips. He, the unbeliever, was praying fervently. At that moment neither doubt nor his habit of subjecting faith to a critical analysis prevented him from praying. Arguments were of no avail. He addressed himself to Him who held in His power his soul and his love.

His agitation grew beyond bounds while he was waiting for the carriage, and unable to contain himself any longer, he decided to set out on foot and ordered Kusma to follow him.

As he turned the corner of the street a sleigh came hurrying past, and he caught a glimpse of Lizaveta Petrovna in her velvet cloak and her head wrapped in a shawl.

" Thank God! " he said with a sigh of relief as he recognised her pale, serious face, and turning about he ran abreast of the sleigh.

" About two hours, did you say? " Lizaveta Petrovna asked. " You are sure to find the doctor in, but don't hurry him, and call at the chemist's to get some laudanum."

" You think it will be all right? " he asked, but she had gone. " The Lord help us and have mercy upon us! " he said to himself. His own sleigh drove out of the gate. He took his seat beside Kusma and told him to drive to the doctor's.

XIV

THE doctor was not yet up, and the servant informed Levin that he had retired very late last night and did not wish to be disturbed, saying that he would soon be up of his own accord. He seemed so absorbed in the task of cleaning lamp-chimneys as to be utterly indifferent to what was going on in Levin's house, much to the latter's amazement. He realised that no one could possibly understand the state of mind he was in and decided to act with more calm and decision. " I must be more circumspect and deliberate," he said to himself, feeling his energy to be equal to the occasion.

When he learned that the doctor was still in bed, he cast about in his mind for the best thing to do, and resolved to despatch Kusma for another doctor, while he himself ran to the chemist's for the opium. Should the doctor still be asleep when he returned, he would either bribe one of the servants to wake him or do so himself if need be.

At the chemist's a gaunt young apprentice was making up some powders for a coachman with as much deliberation as the servant at the doctor's had used in cleaning the lamp-chimneys. When Levin asked for the laudanum, he refused to give it to him. Controlling himself with an effort, Levin told him what he wanted it for and named the doctor and midwife, whereupon the young man called out to some one in German at the other side of the partition, asking if he should let him have the drug. Receiving a reply in the affirmative, he reached down a small phial and a funnel, carefully poured some laudanum into it, put on a label, sealed it, and in spite of all Levin's entreaties to the contrary, began to wrap it up in a piece of paper. Levin's patience was at an end; he snatched the bottle from the man's hand and rushed out of the shop.

When he returned for the doctor, he found him still in bed. The servant who was busy spreading a rug, again refused to call him. Levin took a ten-rouble note out of his pocket and gave it to the man, at the same time explaining that the doctor (how great and important he seemed to him at this moment!) had promised to come any time he was called and that he would not mind being awakened in the least.

The man relented, and ushering Levin into the waiting-room, went upstairs.

Levin could hear the doctor's footsteps, his voice, and the sound of running water. Though but a few minutes had elapsed it seemed to Levin that he had been waiting for hours.

" Peter Dmitritch! Peter Dmitritch! " he cried imploringly, opening the door. " For God's sake let me see you as you are! I've been waiting for about two hours! "

" All right, coming," the doctor replied, and Levin was amazed to hear him laugh.

" Only for a moment! "

" All right."

Two more minutes passed while the doctor pulled on his boots and another two while he put on his coat and brushed his hair.

" Peter Dmitritch! " Levin called again in despair just as the doctor, who had finished his toilette, entered the room. " Really these men have no consciences," Levin thought. " Here he is brushing his hair while some one is dying! "

" Good morning! " the doctor greeted him calmly, shaking hands. " There's no hurry. How is she? "

His calmness exasperated Levin, but he implored him to come at once and described his wife's condition as best he could with many unnecessary details.

" Try not to get so excited. I don't suppose I shall be needed at once, so sit down and let us have a cup of coffee."

Levin stared at him and wondered whether he were joking, but the doctor was quite serious.

" Yes, I know," he said with a smile, " I'm a married man myself. We husbands cut but poor figures at such a moment. I have one patient whose husband always hides in the stables at these times."

" Do you think she will be all right, Dmitry Petrovitch? "

" There is no reason to think otherwise."

" You'll come at once, won't you? " Levin implored, casting an angry look at the servant who was bringing in the coffee.

" I'll come in about an hour."

" For Heaven's sake make it sooner! "

" Just let me have a cup of coffee." He began sipping it in silence. " The Turks have had a bad defeat," he remarked after a minute or two. " Did you read last night's despatches? " he asked, munching a roll.

" I can't stand this! " Levin cried jumping up. " You will come in a quarter of an hour without fail, won't you? "

" In half an hour."

" On your honour? "

When Levin got back he met the princess at Kitty's bedroom door. Her hands were trembling and her eyes were full of tears. When she saw him she fell on his neck and burst out sobbing.

" How is she, my dear? " she asked, laying her hand on Elizaveta Petrovna's arm, as the latter came out of the room with a busy, cheerful air.

" She is going on quite satisfactorily," she replied, " but I wish you could persuade her to lie down; it would be easier for her."

Ever since Levin had got up and come to understand how matters stood he had prepared himself to bear everything that might come, without any reflection, without any anticipations, by tightly shutting up all his thoughts and feelings, and without making his wife nervous. Without allowing himself to think of what would happen and how it would all end, nor how long it would last, he had steeled himself to suffer for the next five hours, imagining that it would all be over by then. But when he returned from the doctor's and saw Kitty's suffering once more, he raised his eyes to heaven and kept on repeating inwardly, " Lord help us and have mercy upon us ! " He began to be assailed by terror that he would not be able to endure it and would burst out crying or run away. An hour passed in this agony. But after three more had gone and then five, that he had fixed upon as the outside limit, he went on suffering because there was nothing else to be done, thinking each minute that his heart would break.

But minutes and hours passed and still there was no change. Levin's nerves were strained to the utmost. The ordinary conditions of life had ceased to exist for him ; he had lost all sense of time. The minutes he spent at her side when her moist little fingers closed over his own convulsively, or when she pushed him aside, seemed to him hours, while again hours seemed no more than minutes. When Lizaveta Petrovna asked him to light a candle, he realised that it was five o'clock, but was not at all surprised. He hardly knew where he was nor what had happened ; he only saw Kitty's face at one moment convulsed in agony, at another with a smile about her lips. In a little while he distinguished the woe-begone figure of the princess with her hair dishevelled and eyes full of tears, and Dolly and the doctor, who was smoking, and the calm, energetic face of Lizaveta Petrovna, and the old prince, pacing up and down the hall. But how they came in and went out, where they were, he did not know. The princess was now with the doctor in the bedroom, now in the study, where a table had appeared, spread for supper, now with Dolly. Levin recalled that he had been sent somewhere, asked to move a table and a couch. He fulfilled these errands with alacrity, imagining that he was doing them for Kitty's comfort, only to learn later that he had been preparing his own bed for the night. Then he remembered being sent into the bedroom to ask the doctor for something, and how the latter replied and continued his discussion with some one on some scandal in the town council. Next he remembered being sent to the princess's room to help an old maid-servant fetch an ikon in a gold chasuble, and how he had climbed on to a small cabinet to reach it down and had broken the shrine. He recalled how the maid had consoled him and how he had carried the ikon into Kitty's room and carefully hidden it behind the pillows at the head of her bed. But he could not give an account of how, why, and when it had all happened. Nor did he understand why the princess grasped his hand and begged him to be calm, nor why Dolly tried to persuade him to eat something and to get rid of him, nor why the doctor was anxious about him and offered him a soothing drug. His feelings were exactly the same as those he had experienced a year ago in the provincial hotel where his brother had died. But that had been sorrow and this was joy. And both were outside the usual plane of existence, a revelation, as it were, into some higher sphere. The present moment was hard and incomprehensible, and in its contemplation the soul rose to heights it had never attained before, where the reason was unable to follow.

"Lord help us and have mercy upon us!" he kept on repeating, addressing himself to the Almighty with the same faith and simplicity he had felt in his childhood and youth.

Two conflicting emotions swayed him; one was outside her presence, with the doctor, who was smoking one fat cigarette after another, or with Dolly and the prince, who were talking about dinners, politics, Marya Petrovna's illness, and so forth, when for a moment he forgot what was happening and fancied he had been awakened from some dream; the other was at her bedside, where his heart was torn with pity and compassion, and he prayed incessantly. Each momentary spell of oblivion was speedily destroyed by a cry of agony that came from Kitty's room. He would start from his seat, rush out, he knew not where, try to justify himself, but instantly realised that he was not to blame, and that he was only anxious to console and assist her. But when he looked at her, he understood that he could not help; he was seized with a sense of horror and unconsciously repeated his prayer, "Lord help us and have mercy upon us!" And the longer this state of mind lasted the sharper grew the dividing line between these two conflicting emotions. When he was not with her, he seemed to forget her and grew calm, yet somehow the sense of her suffering and his own helplessness became keener. In a second or two he would start up as though to escape from it and rush to her room. When she called him he blamed her in his own mind, yet when he saw her submissive smile and heard her say, "I am sorry to torment you," he cursed himself and invoked God's mercy in one breath.

XV

HE did not know whether it was early or late. The candles had burned low. Dolly entered the room and suggested that the doctor might take a rest. Levin, who had been listening to the latter's story about the trickery of some magnetic healer and watching the ashes of his cigarette, had already rested for a short while. He was just able to grasp the meaning of the doctor's words, when suddenly a terrible shriek echoed through the house. It was so heartrending that he remained petrified, staring at the doctor with bated breath. The latter also listened, his head on one side and a smile of approval on his lips. The unusual had become so commonplace that it no longer surprised Levin. "It must be all right, but who shrieked like that?" he thought without stirring. The next moment he was tip-toeing into the bedroom. He took up his post at the head of the bed; the princess and Lizaveta Petrovna stood at the side watching. Things seemed to him different now, though he could not explain exactly why. Lizaveta Petrovna, pale and solemn, with quivering lips, had her eyes fixed on Kitty. He saw Kitty's flushed, agonised face, with a stray lock of hair clinging to her moist forehead. Their eyes met. She extended her hands to him and pressed his against her burning cheeks.

"Don't leave me, don't go away! I am not afraid now," she murmured. "Mamma, do take these ear-rings away; they're a nuisance. You're not frightened, are you?" she asked him. "It won't be long now, will it?" she added, turning to Lizaveta Petrovna. She spoke quickly, almost cheerfully, but suddenly her face became distorted with pain and she pushed him away.

"My God, my God, I shall die! Go away, go away!" she cried, and the same unearthly shriek resounded through the house.

Levin clasped his head in both his hands and rushed out of the room.

"It's all right! it's all right!" he heard Dolly calling after him. But no matter what was said, he felt that the end had come. Leaning against the door-post in the adjoining room, he was startled by a new cry, a wail he had never heard before —it was the cry of the child. He had long ceased wishing for it, and now he hated it. He no longer even prayed for Kitty's life—all he wished for was that her agony might come to an end.

"Doctor, why don't you help her? Why do you let her suffer?" he cried, seizing the doctor's hand as the latter entered the room.

"It's all over," the doctor said, but Levin misunderstood him. He thought that it was all over with Kitty, and that she was dying.

Beside himself he rushed into the bedroom again and at first could distinguish only Lizaveta Petrovna, whose face looked paler and sterner than ever. Kitty's features were completely changed; they seemed more like a mask. She was still moaning piteously. He leaned his head on the rail of the bed; his heart stood still. The shrieks came quickly one after another, but soon ceased altogether. There was no doubt of it, though Levin could hardly believe his own ears. Not a sound was to be heard except a quiet bustling and the deep breathing of the people about her. "It is all over," she whispered softly and tenderly.

He raised his head and saw her lying there, beautiful and peaceful, with one hand resting on the counterpane. She gave him a long, wistful look.

From the awful, mysterious world in which Levin had been living for the last twenty-two hours, he was transported to the world of reality, filled for him at that moment with a flood of happiness that completely overcame him. He could not utter a word for the sobs that choked him. He fell on his knees by the bed, took Kitty's hand and covered it with kisses, while she replied by a gentle pressure.

Meanwhile, at the foot of the bed, a human life trembled in the hands of Lizaveta Petrovna like a flickering flame—a life that had not existed a moment ago, but now claimed its separate existence with the rest of humanity.

"Alive, alive! and a boy! Don't worry!" he heard the voice of Lizaveta Petrovna, who was patting the baby on the back with her trembling hand.

"Is it true, mamma?" Kitty asked.

The princess's only reply was a sob. And in the stillness, as an indubitable answer to the mother's question, came a voice, entirely different from the repressed voices in the rcom, bold and insistent—the cry of the newly-born babe.

Had Levin been told but a short time ago that Kitty had died, that he had died with her, and that their children were

angels in heaven and that they were in the Lord's hands, he would not have doubted anything. But now that he had returned to the world of reality, he found it difficult to believe that Kitty was still alive, and would soon recover, and that the screaming little mass was his son. That she had been spared and her sufferings were at an end filled him with joy. But the child? Whence and wherefore did it come, and who was it? For a long time he could not get used to the thought that it was there.

XVI

AT ten o'clock the next morning the prince, Stepan Arkadye-vitch, and Sergei Ivanovitch were sitting with Levin chatting about the young mother and other matters. Levin listened to them, involuntarily recalling the events of the past day. A hundred years seemed to have passed since then. He felt as though he were dwelling on some higher sphere from which he descended every now and again so as not to hurt those about him. As he spoke he thought only of his wife, of her present condition, and of his son, to whose existence he was trying to accustom himself. The meaning of a woman's life which had only dawned on him after his marriage now rose so high in his estimation that he was almost unable to comprehend it.

" I wonder what she is doing now? " he thought as he listened to the others talking about last night's dinner at the club. " Perhaps she is asleep; perhaps Dmitry is crying." He rose suddenly and left the room.

" Let me know when I can see her," the prince called after him.

" All right," he replied, without stopping to look round.

Kitty was awake talking with her mother about the christen-ing. She looked very sweet as the lay on her back with her pretty cap and blue ribbons and her white hands resting on the counterpane. She welcomed him with a glad smile. Her face wore an expression of heavenly bliss such as one sometimes sees on the faces of the dead, but with them it signifies a farewell, with her a greeting. As he thought of the emotions he had experienced during her hours of agony, his heart stood still. She pressed his hand in hers and asked him if he had rested, but he did not reply. He turned away from her to hide his emotion.

" I've had such a nice sleep, Kostia, and feel quite rested now."

As he looked at her he noticed for the first time how her expression had changed.

" Give him to me, Lizaveta Petrovna," she said when she heard the baby cry. " I want his papa to see him."

" Oh, yes, papa shall see him directly," the nurse replied, as she lifted a strange, squirmy little thing. " We must make our toilet first," she added as she deposited the wriggly little creature on the bed, supporting its tiny body with one finger as she applied the powder puff.

As Levin watched this pitiful specimen of humanity, he searched around in vain for the smallest symptom of paternal love in himself; the only feeling that possessed him was one of aversion. But later, when he saw its bare little body with its tiny arms and legs, still somewhat yellow, and its funny little fingers and toes, the big one distinct from the others, as Lizaveta Petrovna was swathing them with linen garments, a feeling of pity for the weird little creature came over him. Fearing that the nurse might hurt it, he unconsciously put out his hand to protect it.

Lizaveta Petrovna laughed.

" You need not be afraid! " she said.

When the child was dressed and changed into a firm little doll, Lizaveta Petrovna tossed him from one hand to the other as though proud of her work, then drew back for Levin to admire him in all his glory.

Kitty could not take her eyes off him.

" Give him to me, give him to me! " she said, trying to raise herself in bed.

" No, no, Katerina Alexandrovna; you mustn't do that; wait until I bring him. Let his papa see him first! "

And Lizaveta Petrovna lifted the baby with one hand, using the other to support its little head. The squirmy, red creature tried to hide its face under the swaddling clothes. Levin caught a glimpse of something that looked like a nose, two squinting eyes, and smacking lips.

" Isn't he fine! " the nurse exclaimed.

Levin gave a deep sigh.

This " fine " specimen inspired him only with a feeling of disgust and pity. It was not in the least what he had anticipated. He turned away. A sudden laugh made him look round again. It was Kitty laughing with joy as Lizaveta Petrovna handed her the baby and he took the breast.

" He has had enough now," Lizaveta Petrovna said a few minutes later, but Kitty would not have him moved and he fell asleep in her arms.

" Look at him now! " she said turning him round for her husband to see. At this moment the little creature screwed up its face still more and sneezed.

Smiling and with difficulty repressing the tears of emotion, Levin kissed his wife's hand and left the room.

His feelings for the little creature were not at all what he had expected. There was not an atom of pride or joy in his sentiments; on the contrary, he was oppressed by a sense of fear and added responsibility. The desire to protect the feeble little thing was so strong that it deadened any other feeling.

XVII

STEPAN ARKADYEVITCH'S affairs were in a bad state. The money he had received for two-thirds of the timber had all been spent, and, moreover, he had allowed the merchant a discount of ten per cent. for the ready money. For the last third the latter refused to pay as Darya Alexandrovna had for the first time asserted her rights to her own property and declined to sign the contract. Stepan Arkadyevitch's salary was mostly used up in paying petty debts, so that they were literally without any money whatever.

The situation was horribly disagreeable, and in Stepan Arkadyevitch's opinion ought not to be allowed to continue. The whole trouble, as he understood it, lay in the fact that he received too small a salary. The post he occupied might have been considered good five years ago, but things had changed since then. There was Petrov, the director of a bank, receiving twelve thousand roubles a year, and Sventitsky, a member of the council, seventeen thousand, and Miton fifty thousand. " Evidently I fell asleep and was forgotten," Stepan Arkadyevitch thought. He began to listen and look about him, and towards the end of the winter he espied a very good place and directed his attack on it, first from Moscow through the influence of uncles, aunts, and friends, and later, when matters had matured, he himself went to St. Petersburg. It was one of those places of which the salaries varied from one thousand to fifty thousand roubles a year, more numerous now-a-days than the snug places that had formerly flourished on bribes. It was the position of a commissioner of the Consolidated Agency of Mutual Credit Balance of Southern Railways and Banks. This post, like all similar positions, demanded enormous knowledge and activity, such as was difficult to find united in one man. As it was impossible to secure such a man it was thought expedient to entrust the post to an honest one at any rate. Now Stepan Arkadyevitch's honesty was above question. He was not only honest in the ordinary sense, in which one says an " honest " writer, an " honest " public servant, an " honest " institution, an " honest " aim, but he was honest to the degree of maintaining his own principles against the government.

The particular post yielded from seven to ten thousand roubles a year, and Oblonsky could hold it without giving up his government office. The power to confer it lay in the hands of two ministers, a certain lady, and two Jews. Though they had all been approached on his behalf, it was still necessary to pay a personal visit to St. Petersburg to solicit the post for himself. Moreover, he had promised Anna to see Karenin and get a definite answer from him about the divorce. And so he begged Dolly for fifty roubles and took his departure.

He sat in Karenin's study listening to his theory on the causes of the bad state of Russian finance, waiting for an opportunity to approach him about his own and Anna's affairs.

" Yes, that is quite true," he said, when Alexei Alexandrovitch, taking off his eye-glasses without which he could not read now, looked interrogatively at his brother-in-law. " That is true in detail, but still the principle of our time is liberty."

" That may be, but I indicate another principle that embraces liberty as well," Karenin remarked, emphasising the word " embraces " and adjusting his eye-glasses in order to read the passage he had mentioned.

He turned over the leaves of his beautifully written manuscript and re-read the convincing passage.

" I am not advocating protection for the benefit of private individuals, but for the welfare of people of all classes. But *they* cannot understand it; *they* are busy only with their personal interests and are carried away by words."

Stepan Arkadyevitch knew that when Karenin began to talk about what *they* did and thought, that is, those who did not wish to accept his projects and were the cause of all Russia's misfortunes, the end was in sight, and so he at once relinquished his argument in favour of the principle of liberty, and agreed with him. Alexei Alexandrovitch paused as he turned over the leaves of his manuscript.

" By the way," Stepan Arkadyevitch began, " I wanted to talk to you about a little matter of my own. Should you happen to see Pomorsky do influence him on my behalf in connection with a post that is about to become vacant on the commission of the Consolidated Agency of Mutual Balance Credit of Southern Railways and Banks. The name of the commission was so near his heart that he pronounced it without the least mistake.

Alexei Alexandrovitch asked what the aims of this new commission were, but did not commit himself either one way or the other. He was trying to think whether its activity was at all likely to clash with his own projects. As its functions were rather complicated and his own projects were vast, he was unable to grasp the situation all at once.

" Of course I will do what I can," he said; " but why do you want the post? "

" It is fairly remunerative; the salary is nine thousand, and you know my means are rather . . ."

" Nine thousand! Really? " Karenin frowned. The high figure of the salary reminded him that in one respect Stepan Arkadyevitch's proposed activity would be antagonistic to his projects, which were always of an economical nature.

" In my opinion (I have explained this in a report I have written on the subject) these liberal salaries are in themselves symptoms of the false aims of our bureaucracy."

" But what would you have? " Stepan Arkadyevitch said. " To my mind if the director of a bank gets ten thousand a year, he earns it; or if an engineer gets twenty thousand, it is the business that demands it, say what you will."

" I assume that salary is a payment for goods and should be subject to the law of supply and demand. When the apportionment of salaries departs from this law, it is a mistake bearing grave consequences. Take the case of two engineers, for instance, both possessed of the same knowledge and capacity and one gets forty thousand while the other is satisfied with two; or when hussars and graduates of the law schools are appointed bank directors and are given large salaries, regardless of the fact that they have no special knowledge and are not suited for the posts. Of course these salaries are not determined by the law of demand and supply, but simply by favouritism. This is a grave abuse that has an injurious effect on the government service, and I am inclined to think . . ."

271

At this point Stepan Arkadyevitch interrupted him.

" What you say may be true, but a new and useful institution is about to be established, and you will agree with me that an *honest* man is needed to conduct it."

The Moscow *nuance* of the word *honest* was lost on Karenin,

" Honesty is a negative quality," he said.

" Still, you would be doing me a great favour in dropping a hint to Pomorsky, unintentionally, so to speak."

" These things depend more on Bolgarinov," Alexei Alexandrovitch remarked.

" I am sure Bolgarinov will have no objections," Oblonsky said, reddening at the mention of his name. He had called on him that morning and had come away with a disagreeable impression.

He, Oblonsky, a descendant of the Ruriks, had been kept waiting for two hours in the Jew's waiting-room with a lot of other petitioners. The thought was enough to make him blush! Besides, for the first time in his life had he deviated from the ways of his ancestors, who had always served the government, and was seeking a new field. He had reflected much on this as he had paced the waiting-room, chatting with the other visitors, stroking his whiskers, trying to think of a pun on the word " Jew," and to appear indifferent. When Bolgarinov had at last come out with exaggerated politeness and a look of triumph over his discomfort, and had dismissed him after a time without binding himself to anything, Stepan Arkadyevitch had grown uneasy. It was the thought of this that had made the blood rush to his face,

XVIII

" THERE is another thing I wish to speak to you about; I dare say you can guess what it is," he said, after a pause. " It concerns Anna," he added, trying to banish from his mind the unpleasant recollections of his morning visit.

At the mention of Anna's name Karenin's face suddenly changed. All his animation vanished and a weary look came over him.

" I can't understand what you want of me," he said, turning uneasily in his chair and closing his eye-glasses with a snap.

" We should like a decision of some sort, Alexei Alexandrovitch. I turn to you " (" not as to an injured husband," he was about to add, but fearing that he might prejudice his own cause, he substituted the word " statesman " which sounded rather irrelevant). " I address you as a good man and a Christian; you ought to take pity on her, " he said.

" What do you mean? " Karenin asked softly.

" Exactly what I say. Had you seen her as I have seen all this winter, I am sure you would agree with me. Her condition is frightful, simply frightful."

" I was under the impression that Anna Arkadyevna had everything she wanted," Karenin replied in a shrill, piercing tone.

" For God's sake, let us not go into recriminations! What is past is past. You know quite well that she wants a divorce."

" But I concluded that she refused the divorce if the custody of the boy was to be left to me. I told her that I could not divorce her on any other conditions and believed the matter was settled," he replied in the same shrill voice.

" Do be calm," Stepan Arkadyevitch implored, touching his brother-in-law's knee. " The affair is not settled by any means. If you will permit me to remind you the matter stood like this: when you separated you were great, as magnanimous as one could be; you were prepared to give her everything— her freedom and even a divorce. She appreciated your generosity, believe me; so much so that during those first moments she did not consider everything and could not consider everything. She refused the divorce then, but now, time and reality have shown her that her situation is impossible as well as painful."

" Anna Arkadyevna's life is of no interest to me," Alexei Alexandrovitch interposed, raising his eyebrows.

" I cannot believe that," Stepan Arkadyevitch said gently. " Her situation is painful to her and without any advantage to any one. You may say she deserves it. She knows that and does not ask you for anything. But I, we, her relatives who love her, ask and implore you to put an end to her sufferings. Who is the gainer by it? "

" Excuse me, you are putting me rather in the position of a defendant," Alexei Alexandrovitch muttered.

" No, no, not at all," Stepan Arkadyevitch remonstrated hastily, laying his hand on Karenin's arm as though hoping to soften him by his touch. " I am only saying that her position is unbearable, and that it lies in your power to relieve it, and that you will lose nothing by doing so. I should be most happy to arrange it all for you. You promised, you remember . . ."

" Oh, yes, I know I did, but that was before the question concerning my son arose. Besides, I presumed that Anna Arkadyevna would have enough generosity left to . . ." Alexei Alexandrovitch turned pale and his lips trembled.

" She relies on you; she implores you to grant her but one thing, to relieve her from her intolerable position. She no longer asks for her son. Alexei Alexandrovitch, you are a good man, consider her situation. The divorce is like a question of life and death for her. Had you not made your promise she might have become reconciled to her life and gone on living in the country. She came to Moscow on the strength of your promise. She has been there for six months waiting each day for an answer from you. Every time she meets an acquaintance it is like a knife in her heart. It is as though you were keeping a criminal in suspense with a rope around his neck between the hope of pardon or a sentence of death. As I have said, I will arrange everything for you, so that your scruples . . ."

" I was not thinking of my scruples," Alexei Alexandrovitch interrupted him with a look of disgust. " I promised what I had no right to promise."

" Do you mean that you retract it? "

" I never refuse to do what is in my power, but I must have time to consider whether the promise I made is possible."

" No, Alexei Alexandrovitch! " Oblonsky exclaimed, jumping up; " I cannot believe it of you! She is as miserable as it is possible for a woman to be, and you have no right to refuse . . ."

" I will keep my promise in so far as it is possible. *Vous proffessez d'être un libre-penseur*, but I am a believer and find it difficult to act in the matter contrary to the Christian teaching."

" But divorce is allowed in Christian communities and the Church permits it. We even see that . . ."

" May be, but not in a case of this kind."

" I can hardly recognise you, Alexei Alexandrovitch," Oblonsky said after a pause. " Did you not forgive everything? And were you not ready to sacrifice everything, guided by that same Christian spirit? You said yourself, ' If a man take thy coat, then give him thy cloak also,' and now . . ."

" I beg you to put an end to this conversation! " Alexei Alexandrovitch exclaimed as he rose to his feet, pale with anger.

" I am sorry if I have hurt your feelings," Stepan Arkadyevitch said, extending his hand with a timid smile. " Forgive
me. I merely came as a messenger, that is all."

Alexei Alexandrovitch pressed his hand.

" I must think it over," he said after a moment's reflection.
" I will give you a final answer the day after to-morrow."

XIX

STEPAN ARKADYEVITCH was just about to go, when Korney
entered the room and announced, " Sergei Alexaevitch ! "

" Who is Sergei Alexaevitch . . . " Stepan Arkadyevitch began, but immediately recollected. " Why, of course, Serioja ! "
he exclaimed. " I was confusing him with Sergei Alexandrovitch, the head of our department. " Anna asked me to see
him," flashed across his mind. And he recalled the timid,
pitiful expression with which Anna in taking leave of him had
said, " You will see him, won't you ? Find out who his tutor
is and what school he attends. And, Stiva, if it is possible . . .
It is possible, is it not ? "

Stepan Arkadyevitch knew that she was referring to the
possibility of retaining her son in the event of the divorce being
granted. Though he knew that such a thing was out of the
question, still he was very pleased to see his nephew.

Alexei Alexandrovitch cautioned him not to mention his
mother in the boy's presence

" He was very ill after the last interview he had with her,"
he said ; " so much so, that we feared for his life. But a rational
treatment and sea-baths have improved his health wonderfully.
The doctor advised me to send him to school, thinking that the
influence of other boys would be good for him. He is quite
well now and is getting on excellently with his studies.

" A fine boy indeed ! and no longer Serioja, but Sergei
Alexandrovitch ! " Stepan Arkadyevitch said with an affectionate smile, as a broad-shouldered, handsome lad, in long
trousers and a dark blue jacket, entered the room looking the
picture of health. He greeted his father and his uncle, the
latter as he would a stranger, but on recognising him, blushed
and turned away. He went back to his father and handed
him his school report.

" That's all right," his father said ; " you may go now."

"How tall and slender he has grown; no longer a baby, but a boy! Do you remember me?" Stepan asked him.

The boy threw a hasty look at his father.

"Yes," he replied with a confused glance.

Oblonsky called him to his side and took his hand.

"Well, how are you?" he asked, not knowing exactly what to say to him.

Serioja blushed; he did not reply, but cautiously drew his hand out of his uncle's. No sooner was he released than he cast a questioning look at his father and fled from the room.

A year had passed since Serioja had last seen his mother. Her name was never mentioned before him. That same year he was sent to school and made a great many friends. The dreams and reminiscences he had treasured about her no longer interested him. If they did haunt him now and again he would shake them off as a weakness unbecoming in a boy. He knew that there had been a misunderstanding between his father and mother, and that he must get used to the thought of living alone with his father. His uncle's strong resemblance to his mother had startled him, calling forth memories of which he was ashamed. From their confused expressions and the few words he caught as he had entered the room, he gathered that they had been talking about his mother and was annoyed. He did not wish to blame his father and still less to be sentimental—a thing he regarded as beneath his dignity—so he had decided to avoid his uncle who had come to disturb his peace. But when Stepan Arkadyevitch met him on the staircase a few minutes later, and began questioning him about how he spent his time out of school, Serioja, no longer in his father's presence, became quite communicative.

"We sometimes play at railways," he said, in answer to his uncle's question. "You see, it is like this: two boys sit down on a bench—they are the passengers, you know; one stands up, and the others hold on with their hands or belts and we gallop through all the rooms, the doors having been opened beforehand. It is very hard to be the guard."

"Is he the one standing up?" Stepan Arkadyevitch asked.

"Yes; you have to be on the look-out, particularly if some one happens to fall."

"It's quite a serious business I see," Stepan Arkadyevitch said with a sad look at the boy's bright eyes, so like his mother's. Though he had promised Alexei Alexandrovitch not to mention Anna, he could not resist doing so

" Do you remember your mother? " he asked suddenly.

" No," Serioja replied, lowering his eyes and blushing to the roots of his hair; and his uncle could not get another word out of him.

When his tutor met him on the stairs half an hour later he could not make out what had happened to him.

" Did you fall and hurt yourself? " he asked. " I told you not to play that dangerous game. They ought to forbid it at school."

" If I had hurt myself nobody would have known it, you may be sure of that."

" What is it then? "

" Let me alone! What difference does it make whether I remember or not? It's none of his business! I wish they would leave me in peace!" he exclaimed, addressing himself not to his tutor, but to the whole world.

XX

STEPAN ARKADYEVITCH, as usual, did not pass his time uselessly in St. Petersburg. In addition to the two matters of business he had to attend to—his sister's divorce and the possible post for himself—he had come to shake off some of the Moscow mustiness, as he put it, for in spite of its *café-chantants* and buses, Moscow was, after all, a stagnant pool. Stepan Arkadye-vitch had always felt it. A prolonged residence with his family in Moscow invariably made him apathetic; he would even grow sensitive to his wife's ill-humour and reproaches, would worry about her health and, unheard of thing, allow his debts to trouble him. But no sooner did he get to St. Petersburg, where people did not vegetate as in Moscow, but lived, than he made himself at home among his intimate circle of friends, and all these disagreeable thoughts instantly melted away.

His wife? . . . He had just had a talk with Prince Chechensky who had a family too; some of the children were nearly grown up and the boys were pages. And in addition he also had an illegitimate family. Naturally, the first family was well enough, but somehow Prince Chechensky felt himself happier with the second. He had even introduced his eldest son to them, and told Stepan Arkadyevitch that he considered it good for the boy's education. What would Moscow have said to that?

The children? In St. Petersburg children did not act as obstacles to their fathers. They were educated in schools, not on the Moscow principle, which holds that children should have all the luxuries of life and the parents nothing but the burden and care, as in the case of Lvov. Here they understood that a man had to live for himself, as an educated man ought to do.

As for the government service, that, too, was different in St. Petersburg. Instead of a tedious, monotonous routine, it was rather interesting to belong to the official world. A meeting, an obliging act, a word well put, the ability to perform all kinds of tricks—and behold a man's career was made, as was the case with Briantsev, whom Stepan Arkadyevitch had met yesterday and who was now at the top of the bureaucratic ladder.

But more than anything else the ideas current in St. Petersburg regarding money matters had a soothing effect on Stepan Arkadyevitch. Bartniansky, who was spending at least fifty thousand a year, judging by the way he lived, had told him some remarkable witticism about it the night before. In the course of their conversation Stepan Arkadyevitch had said to him—

" I believe you are on intimate terms with Mordvinsky and should be glad if you would say a word or two to him on my behalf. It is in connection with a post I should rather like to get . . . a member of the agency . . ."

" Not another word, because I shall forget it all the same. Why do you want to mix yourself up with railways and Jews? "

Stepan Arkadyevitch had not stopped to explain that he considered the business of vital importance, as Bartniansky would not have understood him.

" I must have something to live on."

" How is that? Don't you live now? "

" In a way, but I'm in debt."

" Really? How much do you owe? " Bartniansky had said sympathetically.

" Ever so much; about twenty thousand roubles."

" Lucky mortal! " Bartniansky had exclaimed with a merry laugh. " I am in debt to the extent of a million and a half; I have nothing, and here I am living."

And Stepan Arkadyevitch realised that these were not mere words but facts. There was Jiviakov, who was in debt to the extent of three millions with not a kopek to his name, and yet he lived, and well too! Then Count Krivtsov, who had been given up long ago—and yet he could afford to keep two mistresses. Petrovsky had squandered five millions and was still going on; he was even in charge of finances and received a salary of twenty thousand roubles a year.

St. Petersburg had certainly a most delightful influence on Stepan Arkadyevitch. In Moscow he worried about his baldness, took a nap after dinner, got breathless when walking upstairs, was bored in the society of young women, no longer went to dances, whereas in St. Petersburg he felt himself ten years younger.

He fully sympathised with what old Prince Pierre Oblonsky had said to him on his return from abroad—

" We don't know how to live here. I spent the summer in Baden, you know, and felt like a young man again. Whenever I met a pretty woman, I would . . . With a couple of glasses of wine after dinner I felt as vigorous and strong as possible. But when I went down to my wife in the country, in less than two weeks I donned a dressing-gown and gave up dressing for dinner. I assure you I never think of pretty women now; I am an old man once more. There is nothing else to think about but the salvation of my soul. Yet I know that a fortnight in Paris would shake it all off again."

Stepan Arkadyevitch felt precisely the same as old Prince Oblonsky. Life in Moscow made him feel so old that he began to fear that he, too, would have to turn his thoughts to the salvation of his soul. St. Petersburg, however, made him feel a man of the world again.

The strangest relations had always existed between Stepan Arkadyevitch and the Princess Betsy Tversky. They had known each other for a very long time, and Stepan Arkadyevitch had half jestingly paid her attentions and told her many naughty stories because he knew that she liked them. Stepan Arkadyevitch went to call on her the day after his visit to Karenin. He felt so young and gay that his levity carried him to such an extreme that he did not know how to extricate himself, for to tell the truth he was not in the least attracted to the Princess Betsy; on the contrary, he disliked her exceedingly. This tone had been established between them because he had noticed that his attentions had pleased. He was consequently glad of the arrival of the Princess Mahky who interrupted their *tête-à-tête*.

" Ah, here you are!" she greeted him. " How is your poor

sister? You need not look so surprised," she added. " Ever since everybody has been down on her, and some who are a thousand times worse than she is, I have felt very sorry for her. I can't help feeling that she has acted nobly. I shall never forgive Vronsky for not letting me know when she was in St. Petersburg. I should most certainly have called on her and accompanied her anywhere. Do give her my love when you see her. Come, tell me all about her."

" Her position is not an enviable one," Stepan Arkadyevitch began, believing, in the simplicity of his heart, that the princess' interest in Anna was genuine, but she immediately interrupted him and began chattering herself.

" She did no more than everybody else does except me, only she did not conceal it. That is precisely what I admire about her. I am glad she left that fool of a brother-in-law of yours. I always maintained that he was a fool, though every one would insist that he was clever. Now that he has leagued himself with Lydia Ivanovna and Landau every one is beginning to agree with me. I hate to think the same as other people and would gladly go over to the opposite side, but I cannot find it in my heart to do so."

" Do tell me what it all means," Stepan Arkadyevitch said. " I called on him yesterday, on my sister's behalf, to demand a definite answer about the divorce. He told me that he wanted to consider the matter and would let me know in a day or two, but instead of a reply I receive an invitation to spend the evening at the Countess Lydia Ivanovna's."

" That's exactly what I expected! " the Princess Mahky exclaimed joyfully. " They will consult Landau."

" But who is Landau, and why should he be consulted? "

" What! Don't you know *Jules Landau, le fameux, Jules Landau le clairvoyant?* He is also a fool, but on him depends your sister's fate. That's what comes of living in the provinces; you don't know a thing. Landau, you see, was a clerk in a shop in Paris who happened to go and see a doctor one day and fell asleep in his waiting-room. In his sleep he began giving advice to the other patients—miraculous pieces of advice! Do you remember Juri Medinsky? He was always ill, you know. His wife heard about this Landau and took him to her husband. The man has been trying to cure him. In my opinion Medinsky is no better than he was before, but they hung on to Landau and took him everywhere they went. That is how he happened to come to Russia. Every one has taken him up here. He has cured the Countess Bezubov, who took such a liking to him that she has adopted him as her son."

" Really? "

" Yes, really. He is no longer Landau now, his name is Count Bezubov. But that is another matter. As for Lydia Ivanovna, though I am very fond of her, I can't help admitting that she's a crank. The poor thing has also become infatuated with him, and now neither she nor Alexei Alexandrovitch decide on anything without his sanction. So you see your sister's future depends on this Landau—alias Count Bezubov."

XXI

AFTER an excellent dinner and plenty of cognac consumed at Bartniansky's, Stepan Arkadyevitch drove up to the door of the Countess Lydia Ivanovna's house.

" Is any one else with the countess? " he asked the porter, as he noticed two overcoats on the rack, one, a strange looking garment with clasps, the other which he recognised as Karenin's.

" Alexei Alexandrovitch Karenin and Count Bezubov," the porter replied in a tone of disapproval.

" The Princess Mahky was right," Stepan Arkadyevitch thought as he walked up the stairs. " It does seem funny! However, it would be well for me to cultivate her acquaintance. She has plenty of influence at her command. A word from her to Pomorsky and my affair would soon be settled."

It was still daylight, but when he entered the drawing-room the blinds were already lowered and the lamps lighted. The countess and Karenin were seated near a round table with a lamp on it, talking in low tones. A pale, thin man, of medium height, with broad hips and somewhat bowed legs, was standing at the other end of the room examining the portraits on the walls. He had a fine face, bright expressive eyes, and hair falling over the collar of his coat. Stepan Arkadyevitch greeted the hostess and involuntarily turned to have another look at the stranger.

" Monsieur Landau! " the countess introduced him graciously. Landau turned quickly, put his moist hand into Oblonsky's, then turned his attention to the portraits again without a word. Alexei Alexandrovitch and the countess exchanged glances.

" I am very glad to see you, especially to-night," the countess

said, motioning him to a seat beside Karenin. " I have introduced him to you as Landau," she added, lowering her voice
and glancing at the Frenchman, " but in reality he is Count
Bezubov, as you may have heard. He does not like to use his
title."

" Oh, I quite understand," Stepan Arkadyevitch said. " I
have heard about his curing the Countess Bezubov."

" She came to see me to-day," Lydia Ivanovna said to
Karenin. " His departure will be such a blow to her, poor
thing."

" Is he really going? " Karenin asked.

" Yes, he is going back to Paris," she replied. " He heard
a voice last night," she added with a glance at Stepan
Arkadyevitch.

" Ah! indeed! " the latter said feeling that he must be on
his guard in that company, in which all sorts of mysterious
things were happening.

There was a pause, after which the countess turned to Oblonsky
with a meaning smile as though she were about to broach the
subject he had come about.

" I have known you for some time and am glad of this opportunity of getting to know you better. *Les amis de nos amis
sont nos amis.* But to be a friend one must try and enter into
a friend's heart, and you have not always done that in regard
to Alexei Alexandrovitch. You understand my meaning, I
trust," she added, looking at Oblonsky with her deep, pensive
eyes.

" Partly, countess; I understand that the position of Alexei
Alexandrovitch . . ." Oblonsky began. He did not quite
realise what she was driving at and resolved to confine himself
to generalities.

" The change has no reference to his external situation,"
the countess interrupted him, following Karenin with an affectionate glance as he rose and joined Landau. " I fear you have
given but little thought to the change that has taken place in
his heart."

" Well, in a general sort of way I can imagine the change.
We have always been very friendly and even now . . ." Stepan
Arkadyevitch replied with a tender glance at her, at the same
time wondering with which of the two ministers she was on
better terms, so as to get her to speak to him.

" The change that has taken place in him cannot diminish
the love that he has for his fellow men; on the contrary, it can

only strengthen it. But I am afraid you don't understand me. Will you have some tea? " she asked as a footman approached with a tray.

" Not quite, countess. Of course, his misfortune . . ."

" A misfortune that has grown to be his highest joy now that his heart has become renewed," she said with a loving look at Karenin.

" I dare say she might mention it to both if I asked her," Stepan Arkadyevitch thought.

" Quite so, countess," he said, " but these changes are of such an intimate nature that one does not care to disclose them to one's nearest friends."

" That is not right; we should open our hearts and help each other."

" I quite agree, but sometimes people's convictions are so different . . ." Oblonsky gave an ingratiating smile.

" There can be no difference in matters of Sacred Truth."

" Of course not, but . . ." Stepan Arkadyevitch stopped in confusion; he realised that she was talking of religion.

" I think he will soon fall into a trance," Alexei Alexandrovitch said in a whisper approaching the countess.

Stepan Arkadyevitch turned round. Landau was sitting by the window with drooping head, his hands resting on the arms of his chair. When he perceived the others looking at him, he raised his eyes and gave a bland smile.

" Please take no notice of him," the countess said, drawing up a chair for Alexei Alexandrovitch. " I have frequently been struck by the fact . . ." A footman entered the room and handed the countess a letter. She ran through its contents quickly, wrote a few lines in reply, and came back to the table. " I have often noticed," she continued, " that you Moscovites, especially the men, are most indifferent to religion."

" Oh, no, countess! I always understood that we Moscovites had the reputation of being staunch believers," Stepan Arkadyevitch remarked.

" You, I am sorry to say, are of the indifferent kind," Alexei Alexandrovitch said with a weary smile.

" How can one be indifferent? " the Countess Lydia exclaimed.

" My position is one of expectancy more than indifference," Stepan Arkadyevitch said with a sweet smile. " I am not prepared to discuss these problems."

Karenin and the countess exchanged glances.

" We should hardly consider whether we are prepared or not," Karenin remarked. " Grace is not guided by human motives; it descends on the lowly and unprepared ªlike, as in the case of Saul, for instance."

" No, not yet, I think," the countess said, who during this time had been watching the Frenchman.

The latter rose and walked over to them.

" May I listen? " he asked.

" Certainly, but I hope we shall not disturb you. Please sit down," she said with a tender look into his face.

" We should keep our eyes open so as not to shut out the ght," Alexei Alexandrovitch continued.

" If you but knew the joy we experience when we feel His eternal presence in our souls! " Lydia Ivanovna exclaimed with an ecstatic smile.

" But a man may feel himself incapable of rising to such a height," Stepan Arkadyevitch ventured. He had not the courage to confess his liberal religious views to a lady who might be so useful to him in the matter of securing the desired post.

" Do you mean that sin may prevent him? " the countess asked. " That is the wrong way to look at it. A true believer cannot sin, for his sins are already pardoned. Excuse me," she said as a footman came up to her with another note. " It will be to-morrow at the grand duchess's," she said to him after she had read it. " For a true believer there is no sin," she continued, addressing herself to Stepan Arkadyevitch.

" Yes, but faith without deeds is dead," Stepan Arkadyevitch observed, recalling these words from the catechism, and asserting his independence with a smile.

" He is quoting the Epistle of James," Alexei Alexandrovitch remarked with a note of reproach in his voice, turning to the countess, as though referring to a subject they had often discussed before. " What a lot of harm the false interpretation of that passage has caused! It is more dangerous to faith than anything; people always twisted it to an opposite meaning."

" To save our souls by work and fasting," the Countess Lydia said contemptuously, " are the wild conceptions of our monks. We do not find it written anywhere. It is all much simpler and easier," she added with the smile she always used to encourage inexperienced maids of honour at court.

" We are saved through Christ and through faith," Karenin put in.

"*Vous comprenez l'anglais ?*" the countess asked as she rose and selected a book from a shelf. "Shall I read *Safe and Happy*, or *Under the Wing ?*" she asked, addressing herself to Karenin. She resumed her seat and opened the book. "It is quite short," she said. "The author describes the way one may acquire faith and the heavenly bliss that it brings. A true believer can never be unhappy because he is never alone." She was about to commence reading, but was again interrupted by a servant. "Madame Borozdin?" she asked. "Say we meet to-morrow at two o'clock. Yes," she continued with a sigh, as she found the passage she had marked and looked up with her beautiful, dreamy eyes; "let me tell you how true faith affects people. Do you remember Marie Sanin? Well, she had the misfortune to lose her only child. She was in despair at first until she found this Friend, and now she thanks heaven for the death of her child. Such is the joy that faith can give!"

"It is wonderful, indeed," Stepan Arkadyevitch said, delighted that the reading was about to commence, so that he could get an opportunity of collecting his scattered thoughts. "It would be better not to mention business matters to-day," he thought. "In fact it would be better to say as little as possible upon anything to avoid getting myself into a muddle."

"It will be dull for you, as you don't know English," the countess said to Landau; "but it won't take very long."

"Oh, I shall understand," Landau said with the same smile, closing his eyes.

The countess and Karenin exchanged significant glances, and the reading began.

XXII

STEPAN ARKADYEVITCH was completely baffled by the strange conversation in which he had taken part. The complexity of St. Petersburg life in general had an exciting effect upon him after his Moscow stagnation. He liked this complexity when in a familiar circle; but in this strange sphere he was perplexed and puzzled and did not know what to make of it all. As he listened to the reading and felt Landau's eyes (naïve, fascinating, roguish, he did not know which) fixed upon him, his head was in a whirl.

The most varied thoughts floated through his brain. " Marie Sanin is glad because her child is dead. It would be nice to have a smoke! One can be saved only by faith. The monks are unable to show us the way to salvation, but the countess is . . . I wonder why my head feels so heavy? Is it the cognac or these strange surroundings? I think I've behaved all right so far, still it wouldn't do to ask any favour of her now. I've heard it said that they make you pray; it would be too absurd if they made me! What twaddle that reading is! but she has a good English accent. Why should Landau be called Bezubov? Suddenly Stepan Arkadyevitch felt his lower jaw dropping into a yawn. He hastily smoothed his whiskers to conceal it, and pulled himself together. In a minute or two he began dozing and felt that he would snore. He could hear the voice of the countess saying, " He is asleep." He started up with a guilty conscience, but was delighted to see that her words referred to Landau, who like himself had fallen asleep during the reading. If he had gone to sleep, it might have offended them, but the fact that Landau was dozing seemed to give them some special pleasure.

" *Mon ami*," the countess said to Karenin, as she raised the folds of her silk dress to prevent it rustling, " *donnez lui la main. Vous voyez ?* In her excitement she had forgotten to address Karenin as Alexei Alexandrovitch and had used the intimate words *mon ami*. " Sh-h! " she said to a servant who had just entered. " Admit no one! "

The Frenchman was asleep or pretending to be. His head was leaning against the back of the chair and his clammy hands, resting on his knees, were making feeble gestures as though wanting to grasp something.

Alexei Alexandrovitch rose cautiously, not without hitting his foot against the table, and put his hand into the Frenchman's. Stepan Arkadyevitch rose too, and opening his eyes as wide as he could looked incredulously from one to the other, wondering whether he were asleep or awake. His head was in a whirl.

" *Que la personne qui est arrivée la derniere, celle qui demande, qu'elle sorte. Qu'elle sorte !* " the Frenchman muttered without opening his eyes.

" *Vous m'excuserez, mais vous voyez . . . Revenez vers dix heurs encore mieux demain.*"

" *Qu'elle sorte !* " the Frenchman repeated impatiently.

" *C'est moi, n'est ce pas ?* " And having received a reply

in the affirmative, Stepan Arkadyevitch tip-toed out of the room forgetting to ask for the countess's intercession in his own affair as well as his sister's, impelled only by the thought of rushing away from that house as from a pest. It was only when he got out into the street and engaged a cab and chatted and joked with the driver, that he regained his equilibrium.

In the French theatre, where he arrived in time for the last act, and afterwards at the Tartar restaurant over his champagne, Stepan Arkadyevitch became himself again. But in spite of it all the memory of the evening was an unpleasant one.

On his return to old Prince Oblonsky's, where he was staying, he found a note from Betsy. She invited him to come and see her the next day to finish their interrupted conversation. He was just making a grimace over the note when downstairs he heard the clumsy tread of men, carrying something heavy.

Stepan Arkadyevitch came out to see what it was and discovered that it was the rejuvenated Peter Oblonsky. He was so drunk that he was unable to walk up the stairs and had to be carried. When he recognised Stepan Arkadyevitch, he ordered the men to set him down, and leaning on Stepan's arm went with him into his own room, and while relating the events of the evening fell fast asleep.

Stepan Arkadyevitch felt low spirited, a thing that rarely happened with him. For a long time he could not fall asleep. The disagreeable impressions of Lydia Ivanovna's house haunted him.

On the following morning he received a letter from Alexei Alexandrovitch definitely declining to grant Anna a divorce, saying that his decision had been based on the prophecies of the Frenchman.

XXIII

In order to accomplish anything in any given home, two opposite conditions are necessary—either a perfect harmony between husband and wife or a complete antagonism. With both these conditions lacking nothing can be decided upon. Thus it is that many families live on without any sort of change for no other reason than that its members are not sufficiently united to agree upon anything or sufficiently disunited for one of them to take things into his or her own hands, irrespective of the others.

This very misfortune had befallen Anna and Vronsky. Though life in Moscow, with its heat and dust, was becoming intolerable, they still stayed on instead of going to Vosdvejensky, as neither of them could decide upon any definite step.

The irritation that separated them had no external cause, and all attempts at explanations, instead of decreasing it, only made it worse. It arose on her side from the fact that she feared he was beginning to love her less; on his, from the fact that he found himself in an uncomfortable situation on her account—a situation which she was by no means trying to ameliorate. Neither the one nor the other gave expression to the causes of this irritation, for each believed the other to be in the wrong and seized upon every opportunity to prove it.

To her, Vronsky, with all his habits, thoughts, and wishes, was summed up in one characteristic—his love for women, and this love as she felt should be centred entirely on herself. If his love waned in the least degree, she suspected him of giving part of it to other women and was jealous. In reality she was not jealous of any particular woman, but of his love. As she had no subject for her jealousy, she tried to find one, and at the smallest provocation transferred her jealousy from one subject to another. Now she was jealous on account of those coarse women, with whom, thanks to his bachelor connections, he could easily enter into relations; now she was jealous of any society women he was likely to meet, now of some imaginary girl whom he would marry after breaking with her. The latter supposition tormented her more than anything else, particularly as Vronsky, in one of his confidential moods, had told her that his mother understood him so little as to suggest his marrying the Princess Sorokin.

Her jealousy made her unjust, and she sought for causes for her suspicion everywhere. She blamed him for her painful situation, for her miserable time in Moscow, for her wasted expectations, for his indecision, for her loneliness. Had he loved her, she thought, he would have realised the misery of her life and tried to bring her out of it. It was his fault that she was still in Moscow and not in the country. He hated country life. He absolutely needed society, and he had placed her in that terrible position, the gravity of which he did not want to understand. And again it was his fault that she was for ever separated from her son.

Even those rare moments of tenderness that occurred between them did not calm her. A kind of assertiveness had crept into his manner towards her that she had not observed before, and this was offensive to her.

It was dusk. Anna, awaiting Vronsky's return from a bachelor dinner, was pacing up and down his study, where the noise of the street traffic was least heard, going over in her mind the details of their last quarrel. She recalled the words that had most offended her, and finally traced them back to the thing that had caused them. It seemed incredible that their difference should have started from such a harmless, insignificant conversation, and yet it was so. It had all begun with his ridiculing the girl's gymnasia, while she defended it. He had spoken disrespectfully of women's education in general, and had said that Hannah, Anna's English *protégé*, did not need to know physics.

This had irritated Anna. She saw in it a contemptuous reference to her occupations, and brooded over a sentence that would repay him for the pain he had caused her.

" I did not expect you to consider my feelings as a lover would, but I did expect a certain amount of delicacy from you," she had said.

Vronsky had blushed with annoyance and made some disagreeable retort. She could not remember her reply, but she recalled how he had said, with the evident purpose of offending her—

" You are right; I am indifferent to your infatuation with that girl, because it seems to me nothing but affectation."

The harshness and injustice with which he had demolished her little world, created under such difficult conditions and consoling to her in her miserable position, angered her.

" I am sorry that only the coarse and material things are comprehensible and natural to you," she had said as she swept out of the room.

When he had come to her in the evening, they had not mentioned the quarrel, but both felt that it had merely been smoothed over, not forgotten.

Now he had been away from home the whole day and she felt so lonely, and was so oppressed at the consciousness of the quarrel, that she was ready to forget everything, only so as to make her peace with him.

" It was all my own fault," she thought. " I am irritable and unpardonably jealous. We must make it up together and then we can go into the country where I shall be more at peace."

" Affectation," the word itself, and the offensive meaning

he had intended it to convey, flashed across her mind. " I think I know what he meant; he wanted to say that it was unnatural for me to love the child of a stranger more than my own. What does he know about love for children? Have I not sacrificed Serioja for his sake? And he meant to hurt me! He must be in love with some other woman or he would not have said that." Suddenly she realised that she was only making the round of the circle she had traversed so many times before and grew frightened at herself. " Can I believe otherwise? Am I to blame? " she asked herself, and again she began from the beginning. " He is honest and straightforward; he loves me and I love him. In a day or two we shall get the divorce and all our difficulties will be over. What more can I want? I must be calm and have more faith in him. I will tell him that it was my fault. I shall say how sorry I am, even though I still believe that I was not to blame. We must go into the country."

Vronsky returned home at about nine o'clock.

XXIV

" DID you have a good time? " she asked, going out to meet him with a guilty look on her face.

" As usual," he replied, guessing by her expression that she was in one of her good moods. He had become accustomed to these changes and was pleased to see her happy to-day, for he was himself in the happiest frame of mind.

" What do I see? That is nice! " he said, indicating some trunks that were standing in the ante-room.

" We really ought to go away. I went out for a drive and the air was so delightful that I began to long for the country. There is nothing to keep you here, is there? "

" There is nothing I want more. I shall not be a minute and we can have a talk; I just want to change my clothes. Do order some tea, please."

Vronsky went into his study.

His remark " that is nice " had jarred on her. It was the sort of remark that is made to a capricious child. And then his self-confident tone compared to her guilty one was so striking that a desire for further strife arose within her, but conquering herself by a supreme effort she met Vronsky as merrily as she had done before.

When he came back, she told him of the incidents of the day and of her plans for their departure.

"You know, I was almost inspired to-day," she began; "why should we go on waiting for a divorce? It doesn't really matter in the country one way or the other. I can't wait any longer. It's no use hoping for or expecting anything; I have decided that it shall no longer influence my life. Don't you agree with me?"

"Certainly I do," he replied, noticing her agitation with uneasiness.

"What did you do at your dinner? and who was there?" she asked after a pause.

Vronsky named the guests.

"The dinner was splendid, and the boat-races and all that was quite nice, but you know in Moscow they can't do anything without becoming ridiculous. A woman appeared, the swimming mistress to the Queen of Sweden, and gave a display of her art."

"Do you mean to say that she swam?" Anna asked with a frown.

"In a kind of costume *de natation*—a hideous old woman she was too. When do you propose leaving?"

"How absurd! Does she swim well?" Anna asked without replying to his question.

"Not a bit. It really was absurd. When do we go?"

Anna shook her head as though to drive away an unpleasant thought.

"The sooner the better. We can't get off to-morrow I'm afraid, but we may the day after."

"Yes, but . . . The day after to-morrow will be Sunday and I must see *maman*," Vronsky said, but instantly grew uneasy, for no sooner had he mentioned his mother than he felt Anna's eyes fixed on him suspiciously. Her face grew crimson and she turned away from him. Now it was not the swimming mistress, but the Princess Sorokin staying with the Countess Vronsky that began to haunt her.

"Can't you go to-morrow?" she asked.

"Not very well. The business that takes me there—powers of attorney and money matters—cannot be attended to to-morrow."

"In that case we will never go."

"Why not."

"It must be Monday or never!"

" But why? That's simply absurd."

" It may be absurd for you, because you don't care for me. You seem unable to understand my position. The one thing that interested me here was Hannah, and you told me plainly it was affectation on my part. You accused me of not loving my own daughter and of being unnatural, but I should like to know how I can possibly be natural here."

For a moment she was appalled at not having remained true to her intentions, and though she knew she was only harming herself, she lost all self-control and was only anxious to make him see that he was in the wrong, and that she would not submit to him.

" I never said anything of the kind; all I said was that I did not sympathise with that sudden kind of love."

" You might as well tell me the truth; you are always boasting of your truthfulness."

" I never boast of my truthfulness, nor do I tell lies," he said quietly, repressing his anger. " I am sorry you do not respect . . ."

" Respect has been invented to conceal the lack of love. If you no longer love me, it would be more honest to say so."

" This is getting unbearable! " Vronsky cried, rising and facing her. " Why do you try my patience? " he asked, deliberately, in a tone as though he could say a great deal more, but was on his guard. " It has its limits."

" What do you mean by that? " she cried, looking with terror at the expression of unconcealed hatred in his face and in his eyes.

" I mean to say . . ." he began, but stopped. " What is it that you want of me? " he asked after a pause.

" All I want is that you should not abandon me as you think of doing," she said, comprehending what he had left unsaid. " Not that though . . . that is of no importance. I want your love and it is gone. Everything has come to an end! " She turned to the door.

" Wait a moment! " Vronsky said, detaining her. " What is it all about? I merely suggested that the journey should be put off for three days and you accused me of lying and being dishonest."

" Yes; and I repeat that a man who reproaches me by saying that he has given up everything for my sake is worse than dishonest, he is heartless."

" There are limits to everything! " Vronsky cried, dropping her hand that he had taken.

"He hates me, that is certain," she thought as she walked out of the room with an unsteady step. "He must be in love with another woman," she said to herself as she entered her own room. "I want his love, but that is gone. All is over now; I must make an end of everything. But how?" she asked herself, dropping into a chair by the mirror.

She began making all sorts of plans. First she would go to the aunt who had brought her up, or to Dolly's, or abroad by herself. She tried to imagine what he was doing alone in his study and whether this quarrel was final or reconciliation was still possible. She wondered what her St. Petersburg acquaintances would think and what Alexei Alexandrovitch would say. A dim thought was lurking somewhere at the back of her brain, but she was hardly conscious of it. As she recalled Alexei Alexandrovitch she thought also of her illness after childbirth and of the feeling that had possessed her at that time. "Why did I not die?" she remembered the words she had uttered then and the sensation they had brought with them. And suddenly she comprehended what was in her soul. It was a desire for death. Yes, death would solve everything.

"The disgrace I have brought upon Alexei Alexandrovitch and Serioja and my own disgrace—everything would be wiped out by my death. If I die, he, too, will be sorry; he will love me and suffer for me." She gave a smile of compassion for herself as she sat in the chair, fingering the rings on her fingers and trying to picture his feelings after her death.

The sound of approaching footsteps roused her. She pretended to be putting away her rings and did not turn to him. He came up close to her and took her hand.

"Anna," he said gently, "let us go to-morrow if you wish it; I am quite willing."

She made no reply.

"Well?" he asked.

"You know best," she said, and unable to restrain herself any longer she burst out sobbing.

"You had much better leave me!" she said between her sobs. "I could go to-morrow. Who am I? A lost woman; nothing but a stone round your neck. I will not torment you any longer! I will set you free. You do not love me, you love another woman!"

Vronsky implored her to be calm and assured her that there was not the slightest ground for her jealousy, that he had never ceased loving her, and that he loved her now more than ever.

"Anna, why will you torment us both?" he asked, kissing her hand. There was a look of tenderness in his face, and it seemed to her that she detected the sound of tears in his voice and that she felt their moisture on her hands. Passing quickly from anguish to passion, she threw her arms about him and covered his head and neck and hands with kisses.

XXV

THE next morning, feeling the reconciliation complete, Anna began making preparations for the journey. It was still undecided whether they would leave on Monday or Tuesday as each was anxious to yield to the other, but Anna went on making active preparations quite indifferent over a day more or less. She was standing in her room over an open trunk when he came in, completely dressed for going out though it was rather earlier than was his wont.

"I am going to *maman* now," he said. "I can get her to send the money through Yegorov and we can leave to-morrow."

Though she was in a good humour the mention of his mother annoyed her.

"I will hardly be ready myself," she said, and immediately thought, "So it was possible for him to go when I wanted him to, after all!—No, you mustn't upset your plans. Wait for me in the dining-room, I shall join you directly, as soon as I've put these things away."

Vronsky was eating his beef-steak when she entered the dining-room.

"You can't imagine how I loathe these rooms," she remarked, seating herself near him to drink her coffee. "There is nothing quite so detestable as these *chambres garnies*. They have absolutely no individuality. The clocks, hangings, and above all the wall-papers are a perfect nightmare to me. I am longing for Vosdvejensky as for the promised land. Have you sent back the horses yet?"

"No, they are coming on after us. Are you going out?"

"I wanted to go down to Mrs. Wilson to take her some garments. We are going for certain to-morrow, aren't we?" she asked cheerfully.

A sudden change came over her features as Vronsky's valet came to ask for a receipt of a telegram from St. Petersburg.

There was nothing extraordinary about the fact of Vronsky's having received a telegram, but from the hurried way in which he told the man that the receipt was in his study, it seemed to her that he wished to conceal something from her.

"I shall have everything settled by to-morrow."

"Who was your telegram from?" she asked, taking no notice of what he had said.

"From Stiva," he replied reluctantly.

"Then why did you not show it to me? What secrets can there be between you and Stiva?"

Vronsky called the man back and asked him to bring the telegram.

"I thought it best not to tell you, because Stiva has a passion for wiring without any reason."

"Is it about the divorce?"

"Yes. He says that nothing has yet been decided, but that he expects an answer in a day or two. You may read it for yourself."

Anna took the telegram with trembling hands and read what Vronsky had told her. It ended with the words: "There is little hope, but I will do everything possible and impossible."

"I told you last night that I was completely indifferent about the divorce," Anna said flushing. "There was no need to conceal it from me.—If he conceals this, he can also conceal his correspondence with women," she thought.

"Yashvin wanted to call this morning with Voitov," Vronsky said. "I think he has won everything from Pevtsov, even more than he can pay—about sixty thousand."

"Really!" she said, irritated at the sudden change of subject. "What makes you think that I am so interested in the contents of the telegram that you must needs conceal it from me? I told you that I did not wish to think of it and should be glad if you gave as little thought to it as I do."

"I am interested because I like clearness."

"Clearness is not essential, but love is," she said, her agitation increasing, not so much at his words as at his calmness. "Why should you care about the divorce?"

"Oh, Lord! again about love!" Vronsky thought, frowning. "You know very well why, for your sake and for the sake of our future children," he said.

"There will be no future children," she said.

"That is a pity."

"You want it for the sake of the children, but you do not

think of me," she said, forgetting his words ": for *your sake* and for the sake of our children."

The question of her having any more children had long ago become a cause for quarrels, and irritated her always. She put down his desire to have children as a lack of appreciation of her beauty.

" But I said for your sake; mostly for your sake," he replied with annoyance. " I am sure that your irritability is largely due to the uncertainty of your position."

" Yes, he has now thrown off the mask and I can see his coldness and his hatred," she thought, paying no heed to his words, but gazing in terror at the cold, cruel look in his eyes that were fixed upon her.

" That is not the reason," she said. " I am at a loss to understand how my irritation, as you are pleased to call it, can possibly be the reason. I am completely in your power, so where does the uncertainly come in? On the contrary . . ."

" I am sorry that you do not want to see it," he interrupted her deliberately, bent on expressing his thought. " The uncertainty is due to your imagining that I am free."

" You may be at ease on that score," she said, and turning away from him began drinking her coffee.

She raised the cup to her lips and drank a few drops. As she glanced at him she could see by the expression of his face that he was irritated by her gesture and by the sound she made in drinking.

" I am quite indifferent as to what your mother thinks and how she wants to get you married," she said, putting down her cup with a trembling hand.

" We were not talking of that."

" Precisely about that. A perfectly heartless woman, be she old or young, your mother or a stranger, can have no interest for me; I do not want to know her."

" Anna, I beg of you not to speak disrespectfully of my mother."

" A woman who is unable to see wherein lies the honour and happiness of her son has no heart."

" I beg you again not to speak disrespectfully of my mother," he said sternly, raising his voice and looking her straight in the eyes.

She made no reply. Looking fixedly at him, at his face, his hands, she recalled all the details of last night's reconciliation, his passionate kisses and caresses. " Just such caresses

he has been lavishing and wishes to lavish on other women!"
she thought.

"You don't love your mother! those are merely words,
words, words!" she said, looking at him with hatred.

"If so, then it is necessary . . ."

"To make up our minds; I have already made up mine,"
she said, wishing to leave the room; but just then Yashvin
entered. Anna stopped and exchanged greetings with him.

Why she should have to feign before a stranger who would
sooner or later find out everything she did not know, but
though a storm was raging in her heart, a storm that might
produce terrible consequences, she mastered herself and began
talking to their guest.

"How are your affairs?" she asked. "Have you received
the money?"

"Oh, that's all right; I may not get it all, but you see I
must leave here on Wednesday. When are you going?" he
asked, glancing at Vronsky and feeling that he had come at
an unpropitious moment.

"We are going the day after to-morrow," Vronsky replied.

"Yes, I know you had decided on going."

"This time it is final," Anna said with a hostile look at
Vronsky, as though warning him that reconciliation was
impossible.

"Aren't you sorry for poor Pevtsov?" she said to Yashvin.

"I never stop to think about it, Anna Arkadyevna. My
whole fortune is here," he said, touching his pocket. "I am
a rich man now, but I am going to the club and may come out
a beggar. Whoever plays with me has no more compunction
than I have. We enter into the contest freely; that is what
makes it so exciting."

"But supposing you were married, how do you think your
wife would feel?" Anna asked.

"That is why I never wanted to marry and never shall,"
Yashvin replied with a laugh.

"What about Helsingfors?" Vronsky asked, watching Anna's
smile. When their eyes met her expression changed at once,
as though she seemed to say, "I have not forgotten; it is still
the same."

"Have you ever been in love?" she asked Yashvin.

"Oh, yes, numberless times. You see, some men sit down to
cards and always get up in time for the *rendez-vous*, but I can
play the love game and leave off in time for cards in the evening."

"I did not mean that exactly; I meant really in love." She too wanted to ask about Helsingfors, but did not wish to repeat Vronsky's words.

When Voitov (who had come to buy the stallion) was announced, Anna left the room.

Before going, Vronsky went in to see her. She pretended to be searching for something on the table, but ashamed of her deceit, she looked up at him with a cold glance.

"What do you want?" she asked in French.

"I want Gambetta's certificate; I have sold him," he said in a tone that implied more clearly than words, "I have no time for explanations that lead to nothing."

"I am not to blame before her," he thought; "if she wants to punish herself, *tant pis pour elle.*" As he was leaving the room it seemed to him that he heard her say something and his heart was wrung with pity.

"What is it, Anna?" he asked.

"Nothing," she replied with her former coldness.

"If nothing, *tant pis,*" he thought, growing indifferent. As he turned to leave the room, he caught sight of her face in the mirror; it was deadly pale and her lips trembled. He wanted to stop and console her, but was already outside the door before he could think of anything to say.

He was out all day, and when he returned at night Anna's maid told him that her mistress had a headache and did not wish to be disturbed.

XXVI

THIS was the first time that a quarrel between them had lasted all day. It was not exactly a quarrel; it was a manifest admission of a complete estrangement. Was it possible to look at her as he had done when he came in to ask for Gambetta's certificate? How could he have left her indifferently when he saw that her heart was bursting from despair? He was not merely indifferent to her, but he hated her, he loved another woman; she was now certain of that.

She recalled all the cruel words he had said to her and added others that he might have wanted to say.

"I do not keep you; you are at liberty to go whenever you like. You do not want to be divorced from your husband so that you may be able to return to him. I shall not object if you do. I can let you have some money if you want it. How much do you need? "

The most cruel words that only the coarsest kind of man might have employed she imputed to Vronsky in her imagination and forgave him no less than if he had really said them.

" And only yesterday he declared that he loved me! he, the man of honour! Have I not often tormented myself in vain? " she thought a moment later.

Except for the two hours she took in going to Mrs. Wilson's, Anna spent the whole day at home pondering as to whether everything was at an end, whether there was still any hope for a reconciliation, whether she should leave at once or see him once more. When she retired to her own room in the evening after having ordered the maid to tell him that she had a headache, she said to herself, " If he comes in spite of that, I shall be sure that he loves me still, if not, then it means that the end has come and I must decide what to do."

Later she heard the rumble of his carriage, his ring at the door, his step, his conversation with the maid. He had taken the maid's word and had not come to see her, consequently all was at an end.

And the idea of death presented itself to her as the only means of regaining his love, of punishing him, of vanquishing the evil spirit that had taken up its abode in her heart and was waging war with him.

It was all the same to her now whether they went to Vosdvejensky or not, whether they got the divorce or not—the only essential thing was to punish him.

When she poured out her usual dose of opium and thought how easy it would be to swallow the whole bottleful and be no more, she began to picture to herself with delight how he would suffer, how he would cherish her memory, how he would long for her when it would be too late. She lay on her bed in the light of a candle with wide open eyes staring at the moulded cornice of the ceiling, at the shadow cast on it by the screen, trying to imagine how he would feel when she was no more. " How could I have said those cruel things to her? " he would say. " How could I have left her without a word? She is dead; she has left us for ever. She is there . . ." Suddenly the shadow of the screen began to quiver and covered the whole cornice, then spread over the ceiling; shadows from the other side darted across to meet it; for a moment they rushed back, then moved up with increasing rapidity, quivered, blended together, and all grew dark. "Death!" she thought. Such terror seized her that she could not make out where she was, and for a long time her trembling hands could not find a match with which to light another candle in the place of the one that had gone out.

"No, anything but death! He loves me and I love him. All this does not matter; it will pass," she said to herself as tears of joy at her return to life flowed down her cheeks. She rose, and to escape from her fancies she fled to Vronsky's study.

Vronsky was sound asleep. She held the candle over him and remained for a long time looking at him. A feeling of tenderness for him came over her, yet she knew that if he were to wake he would gaze at her coldly, conscious of his own righteousness, and that before she could talk to him of her love, she would have to prove to him how guilty he had been towards her. She went back to her room without disturbing him, and taking a second dose of opium, fell into a heavy troubled sleep.

Towards the morning she was roused by a terrible nightmare that had frequently come to her in the early days of her liaison with Vronsky. An old man with a matted beard, muttering some unintelligible French words, was busy adjusting a piece of iron over her. What constituted the most terrible part of the nightmare was that he seemed to take no notice of her, but went on fumbling with the iron as if she were not there. She awoke in a cold perspiration and dimly recalled the events of last night.

"We had a quarrel, but that has happened before. I told them to say that I had a headache and he did not come in. To-morrow we shall leave . . . I must see him and get ready for the journey." She asked one of the servants where he was, and on hearing that he was in his study, went out to him. As she crossed the dining-room she heard the sound of an approaching vehicle, and looking out of the window she saw a young girl in a lilac hat sitting in a carriage and giving some directions to a footman who was ringing the front door bell. After some exchange of questions in the ante-room, some one went upstairs, and then she heard Vronsky's step coming down. She looked out again and there he was, hatless, standing by the carriage window. The young girl handed him a packet with a smile. Vronsky smiled too and said something to her. The carriage drove off and he ran upstairs again quickly.

The mist that had weighed on Anna's soul suddenly lifted.

The painful feelings of yesterday returned, only with greater force. She could not understand how she could have stooped to remain under the same roof with him, and resolved to inform him of her decision at once.

" It was the Princess Sorokin and her daughter," he said when she went in to him. " They brought me the money and papers from *maman*. I couldn't get them yesterday. How is your headache? better? " He spoke quite naturally, taking no notice of the severe, solemn expression of her face.

She stood in the middle of the room, looking intently at him in silence. He glanced up at her for a moment, frowned, and continued reading his letter. She turned slowly and walked towards the door. He might have stopped her, but he was silent. All that could be heard was the rustling of the letter as he turned it over.

" By the way," he said, when she was already at the door, " we are going to-day, aren't we? "

" You, but not I," she said, turning towards him.

" Anna, it is impossible to live like this . . ."

" You, but not I," she repeated.

" This is getting intolerable! "

" You . . . you will be sorry for this," she said as she left the room.

Alarmed by the desperate expression with which these words had been uttered, he jumped up and was about to run after her, but changing his mind, he sat down again and ground his teeth. Her impossible threat irritated him. " I have tried everything," he thought, " the only thing that remains is to take no notice." He got ready to go out to his mother's whose signature was required for the deed.

She heard his step in the study, then in the dining-room. He paused at the drawing-room door, but did not enter her room. He gave some orders to a servant to let Voitov have the horse when he called for it, then she heard the sound of the carriage, a door was opened and he went out. There he was again in the ante-room and some one ran upstairs. It was his valet who had gone to get the gloves he had forgotten. She looked out of the window and saw him take the gloves, and without looking up, he touched the coachman on the back and gave him some directions. Then, still without looking up, he took his seat, crossed his legs in his usual way, and pulling on a glove, disappeared round the corner.

301

XXVII

"Gone! All is ended!" Anna said to herself, standing at the window, and in response to the exclamation, the impressions of the darkness when the candle had gone out blended with those of her nightmare and filled her heart with terror.

"No, it is impossible!" she exclaimed, and crossing the room she rang the bell. She was so terrified at her own thoughts that she could not remain alone a moment longer and went out to meet the servant.

"Find out where the count has gone."

The servant told her that he had gone to the stables.

"He left orders that you were to be informed that the carriage would return at once in case you wished to go out."

"Very well. Wait a moment. I want to write a note. Send Mihail to the stables with it at once."

She sat down and wrote the following:—

"It is all my fault. Come back; we must talk things over. For God's sake come! I am afraid of myself!"

She sealed the note and gave it to the servant.

Still afraid to be alone, after the servant had gone she went into the nursery.

"No, that is not he! Where are his blue eyes, his sweet, timid smile?" was her first thought when she saw her rosy-cheeked little girl with her black, curly hair instead of Serioja, whom, in the confusion of her thoughts she had expected to find in the nursery. The child, engaged in pounding the table with a cork, looked up at its mother with its round vacant eyes. In reply to the Englishwoman's question, Anna said that she was quite well and that they were going into the country to-morrow. She seated herself beside the little girl and began twirling the stopper of a decanter in front of her, but her loud, ringing laugh and a certain motion of the eyebrows so vividly reminded her of Vronsky that she was hardly able to keep back her sobs. She rose hurriedly and went out of the room.

"Is it all ended? No, it is impossible! He will come back. But how will he explain away the smile with which he had spoken to her? I shall believe him even if he fails to explain it satisfactorily. If I do not believe him there is only one thing for me to do, and that I will not do."

She looked at the clock. Twelve minutes had passed.

"He must have received my note and is now on his way

home. He won't be long now, ten minutes at the most. . . .
But supposing he does not come? No, that is impossible! I
mustn't let him see that I've been crying; I must go and bathe
my eyes. Have I brushed my hair? " She touched her head.
" Yes, I must have, but when did I do it? " She could not
believe her touch and went to the mirror to see. " Who is
that? " she thought as she caught sight of her own feverish
face reflected therein, with the scared look in the glistening
eyes. " That is I," and she shuddered as she suddenly seemed
to feel his kisses upon her shoulders. She raised her own hand
to her lips and kissed it.

" Am I going out of my mind? " she asked herself and went
into her bedroom, where Annushka was cleaning up.

" Annushka," she began, stopping in front of her without
knowing what to say.

" Are you going to Darya Alexandrovna's? " the maid asked
as though to anticipate her meaning.

" To Darya Alexandrovna's! Yes, of course! "

" Fifteen minutes there and fifteen minutes back," she thought.
" He is on his way and will be here directly." She took out
her watch. " How could he have gone and left me in this state
of mind? How can he live without being friends with me? "
She went up to the window and looked out into the street. It
was time for him to be back. But her calculations might have
been wrong and she began counting the minutes all over again
from the time he had left the house.

Just as she walked over to the clock to verify her watch
a carriage drove up to the door. She looked out of the window
and saw that it was his. She heard voices below, but no one
came upstairs. She went down to speak to the messenger who
had come back in the carriage.

" I could not find the count; he had just gone to the Nijni-
Novgorod station."

" What did you say? What is that? " she asked of the
merry, rosy-faced Mihailov as he handed her back her note.

" Oh, he did not get it," she recalled.

" Take this note at once to the Countess Vronsky's; the
count is there. You know where she lives, don't you? Bring
back an answer," she said to the messenger.

" And what shall I do with myself meanwhile? " she thought.
" I must go to Dolly's else I shall go mad. I can send him a
wire of course! " She immediately wrote out the following
telegram:—

"I must speak to you; come at once."

Having sent it off she went upstairs to dress. As she was putting on her hat she looked at plump little Annushka whose calm grey eyes were fixed on her with compassion.

"Annushka, dear, what am I to do?" she cried, dropping helplessly into an arm-chair and bursting into tears.

"You should not worry so, Anna Arkadyevna. Such things will happen! You had better go out; a change will do you good," the maid advised her.

"Yes, I think I will. If a telegram comes in my absence, send it to Darya Alexandrovna's . . . but no, I shall be back soon."

"Yes, I must not think, I must do something, I must get away from here," she said to herself in terror as she felt the throbbing of her own heart. She hurried out of the house and took her seat in the carriage.

"Where do you wish to go?" Peter asked as he climbed on to the box.

"To the Oblonskys, on Snamenka."

XXVIII

It had been misty and rainy in the morning, but now the weather had cleared. The roofs of the houses, the pavements, the wheels, the leather, the brass trimmings of the carriage— all shone brightly in the May sunshine. It was three o'clock in the afternoon and the streets were full of people.

Sitting in a corner of the carriage that barely swayed on its flexible springs at the rapid trot of the greys, Anna, to the accompaniment of the rumble of the wheels and the incessant noises in the open, went over the events of the last few days, and saw her position in an entirely different light from what it had appeared to her at home. The thought of death no longer appeared to her so terrible, yet it now seemed no longer inevitable. She rebuked herself for the degradation to which she had descended. "I have implored him to forgive me. I have submitted to him, confessed myself in the wrong. Why? Can I not live without him?" And not stopping to think how she would live without him, she began reading the signs they passed on the way. "'Office and Stores. Dentist.' Yes, I will tell Dolly everything. She does not like Vronsky. It will be humiliating to tell her, but I will. I shall follow her advice because I know she loves me. I will not submit to him; I will not allow him to teach me. ' Philipov, Pastry Cook.' They say that they take his dough to St. Petersburg. The Moscow water is so good. ' A. Mitischensky, Pancakes.' " She recalled how long, long ago, when she was seventeen, she used to drive with her aunt to the Troitsa. " It was on horseback, too. Could it have been I with those red hands? How many things have become insignificant since then—things that used to appear so beautiful and unattainable? Now it is the other way about; the things I used to despise then are now for ever unattainable. Could I have believed then that I would come to this degradation? How proud and satisfied he will feel when he gets my note! But I will prove to him . . . What a horrid smell that paint has! Why are they always building and painting? ' Dressmaker and Milliner,' " she read. A man bowed to her. It was Annushka's husband. " Our parasites," she recalled the words Vronsky had once used. " Ours? Why ours? The awful part of it is that you can't tear out the past by the roots. Yes, but I can try not to think about it. I must do that." She suddenly remembered Alexei Alexandrovitch and how she had eradicated him from her memory. " Dolly will think that I must be in the wrong, because I am leaving my second husband. I don't care! I don't want to be in the right; I can't! " She was almost on the point of tears. Two girls passed laughing. " I wonder what they are laughing about? " she thought. " They must have been talking about love. They do not know that it is not cheerful, but humiliating. . . . Here is the boulevard and children. There are three boys playing at horses. Serioja! I shall lose everything, yet I will not get him. Yes, I shall lose everything if he does not come back. Why do you want to humiliate yourself again? " she asked herself. " No, I will go to Dolly and tell her everything. I will say to her: I am unhappy; I know I deserve it and that it is all my fault, but still I am unhappy . . . help me. These horses, this carriage—how contemptible I am in it! they are all his, but I will not see them again."

Going over in her mind what she would say to Dolly and purposely lacerating her own heart, Anna ascended the steps that led to the front door of the Oblonskys' house.

" Are there any visitors with Darya Alexandrovna? " she asked in the ante-room.

" Katerina Alexandrovna Levin is with her," the porter replied.

"Kitty! The same Kitty with whom Vronsky had once been in love!" Anna thought. "He always thinks of her with love; he is sorry that he did not marry her. But of me he thinks with hatred, and is sorry that his life is united with mine."

While Anna was walking up the stairs Dolly and Kitty were holding a conversation on the subject of nurseries. Hearing of her arrival, Dolly went out to meet her.

"Oh, you have not gone yet? I wanted to go to you," she said; "I've just received a letter from Stiva."

"We had a wire from him," Anna replied, looking around for Kitty.

"He writes to say that he can't understand what it is that Alexei Alexandrovitch wants, but that he will not go away without some definite reply."

"I thought there was somebody here. May I read the letter?"

"Yes, Kitty," Dolly said, rather confused; "she is in the nursery. You know she was very ill."

"So I've heard. May I read the letter?"

"I will get it at once. There is no refusal yet and Stiva still has hopes . . ." Dolly said from the door.

"I have no hope and I don't want it."

"I suppose Kitty considers it degrading to meet me," Anna thought when she was left alone. "Perhaps she is right. But it is not for her, who has been in love with Vronsky, to let me see it. I know that not a single decent woman would receive me in my present position. I know that I sacrificed everything for him from the first moment. And this is my reward! Oh, how I hate him! Why did I come here? It is even worse than at home." She heard the two sisters talking in the next room. "What shall I say to Dolly now? Shall I give Kitty the pleasure of knowing that I am unhappy and let her patronise me? No, Dolly will not understand. I have nothing to tell her. It would have been interesting though to see Kitty and show her how I despise everybody and everything, and how it all makes no difference to me now."

Dolly came in with the letter. Anna read it and returned it to her.

"I knew that before," she said; "I am not in the least interested."

"Why? On the contrary I hope . . ." Dolly looked at her intently. She had never seen her in such a strange state of agitation. "When are you going away?" she asked.

Anna half-closed her eyes, but made no reply.

" Why does Kitty hide herself from me? " she asked, looking towards the door and flushing a deep red.

" What nonsense! She nurses the baby and things are not going right, so I have advised her to . . . She will be glad to see you . . . She is coming in a minute . . . " Dolly was confused. " Here she is! "

When Kitty first heard of Anna's arrival, she did not wish to go out to her, but Dolly had persuaded her to do so. Collecting all her strength she came out, and going up to Anna, extended her hand with a blush.

" I am very glad to see you," she said in a trembling voice.

Kitty was torn between her hostility to this bad woman and the desire to be condescending to her, but the moment she saw Anna's sad, sympathetic face all these feelings vanished.

" I should not have been at all surprised had you not wanted to meet me; I am accustomed to that," Anna said. " I am sorry to hear you have been ill. You have changed a great deal."

Kitty felt that Anna was hostile towards her, but put this down to the awkward position in which she was placed before her, and pitied her.

They talked about Kitty's illness, about the baby, about Stiva, but Anna was listless all the time.

" I came to bid you good-bye," she said, rising.

" When are you going? "

Anna turned to Kitty without replying.

" I am very glad to have seen you," she said with a smile. " I have heard so much of you from all sides, even from your husband. He came to see me once and I liked him very much," she said with a rather spiteful intention. " Where is he now? "

" In the country," Kitty replied with a blush.

" Please give him my kindest regards."

" I shall be delighted," Kitty said simply, looking compassionately into her eyes.

" Well, good-bye, Dolly! " She kissed her, and pressing Kitty's hand went out of the room.

" She is just the same and still as attractive," Kitty said when Anna had gone. " But there is something pitiful about her; terribly pitiful! "

" Yes, there is something strange about her to-day," Dolly said. " When I took her to the door, it seemed to me as though she wanted to cry."

XXIX

ANNA took her seat in the carriage in a worse state of mind than when she had left home. To her former torments was added a feeling of insult and renunciation, which she had clearly felt at her meeting with Kitty.

The coachman asked her where he was to drive to.

"Home," she replied, not even thinking where they were going.

"They looked at me as at something strange and incomprehensible," she thought. "I wonder what they are talking about?" she asked herself as two pedestrians passed engaged in animated conversation. "Can one tell another person of one's feelings? How glad I am that I did not tell Dolly! She would have rejoiced at my misfortune, not openly perhaps, but she would have been glad because I was punished for the very pleasures she envied me. Kitty would have been still more pleased. I can read her through and through. She knows that I was unusually nice to her husband and hates and despises me. In her eyes I am an immoral woman. Had I been that I could have made her husband fall in love with me . . . it would have been easy had I but wanted to. And in a way I did then. How self-satisfied that man looks!" she thought as a portly, red-faced man, who drove past her, mistaking her for an acquaintance, raised his shiny hat from his shiny, bald head. He thought he knew me, but he knows me as little as anybody in the world does. I do not know myself; I only know my appetites as the French say. I suppose they want that filthy ice-cream," she thought as she noticed two boys stop an ice-cream vendor, who took his vat down from his head and wiped his perspiring face with the end of a towel. "We all of us want something sweet, something that tastes nice. If there are no chocolates then we content ourselves with dirty ice-cream. Kitty too; if not Vronsky, then at least Levin. She envies and hates me. And we all hate each other; I Kitty and she me. That is a fact. ' Tutkin, *Coiffeur.*' *Je me fais coiffer par* Tutkin . . . I shall tell him so when he comes home," she thought with a smile. But at that moment she recalled that she could no longer tell him anything funny. "Besides there is nothing funny any way; everything is horrid. Those bells must be for the evening service; how conscientiously that merchant is crossing himself! Why that ringing, these churches and lies? Only in order to conceal the fact that we despise each other, like these cabmen who do nothing but abuse each other all day. Yashvin was right when he said, ' He wants to leave me a beggar and I him.' "

With such thoughts as these she arrived at her own house, and it was only when she saw the porter that she recollected herself and remembered the note and telegram she had sent to Vronsky.

" Is there any answer? " she asked.

" I will go and see," the porter replied, and looking in his desk he produced a telegram. " I cannot come before ten o'clock.—Vronsky," she read.

" Has the messenger come back? "

" No, madame," the porter replied.

" If that is so, then I know what I must do," she said to herself, anger and a desire for revenge rising within her as she ran quickly up the stairs. " I will go to him myself. Before leaving him for good I will tell him what I think of him. I have never hated any one so much as I do him!" She shuddered with horror as she caught sight of his hat on the rack.

She did not realise that his wire had been a reply to hers and that he had not yet received her note. She imagined him talking calmly to his mother and the Princess Sorokin, and rejoicing at her suffering. " Yes, I must go there at once," she said to herself, not knowing exactly how. She was seized by an overwhelming desire to escape from the sensations she experienced in that house. The servants, the walls, the furniture—everything in the house disgusted and oppressed her.

" I must go to the station, and if he is not there, then I shall go to the house and surprise him." Anna looked at the time-table. " There is a train at 8.2. Yes, I could just catch it." She ordered fresh horses to be harnessed and packed a few things such as she might need for several days into a travelling-bag. She was determined not to come back again. She decided in a vague sort of way, after the numerous plans that had floated through her brain, that after what would happen at the station or at the countess's house, she would travel on the Nijni-Novgorod line and stop at the first town she happened to come to.

Dinner was on the table. She sniffed at some bread and cheese, and convincing herself that she could eat nothing, ordered the carriage and went out. The shadow of the house already lay across the street, but it was still warm and clear. Annushka, who took down her things, Peter, who put them into the carriage, the coachman who seemed dissatisfied, all displeased her, and irritated her by their words and motions.

" I shall not want you, Peter."

" But how about the ticket? "

" As you please; it's all the same to me," she said angrily.

Peter jumped on to the box and told the coachman to drive to the station.

XXX

" THERE it is! Again I understand everything," Anna said to herself as the carriage rumbled over the cobblestones. Impressions came quickly one after another.

" What was the last good thought I had? " she tried to recall. " Tutkin, *Coiffeur ?* No, not that. The thing that Yashvin talked about . . . that the struggle for existence and hatred are the only things that bind people. You are going there in vain," she said mentally to a party of people who were driving a four-in-hand, evidently going somewhere with the object of enjoying themselves. " The dog you are taking with you will not help you. You can't run away from yourselves." Following the direction in which Peter was looking, she saw a drunken workman who was being led along by a policeman. " That one is more likely," she thought. " Vronsky and I did not find that pleasure either, though we had expected much from it." And Anna for the first time saw her relations with Vronsky in an aspect that she had never dared to face before. " What did he hope to find in me? Not so much love as the gratification of his ambition." She recalled his words, his submissive expression that had reminded her of a devoted dog during the early days of their liaison. And everything now confirmed that. " Yes, he was triumphant over a successful ambition. He was proud of me. Now it is past; there is no longer anything to be proud of. He has taken from me everything he could and no longer needs me. He is tired of me and does not wish to be dishonest. Only yesterday he blurted out that he merely wanted the divorce so as to burn his own ships. He loves me, but how? The zest is gone. How satisfied that man looks! " she thought, glancing at a clerk who rode by.

"Yes, the zest is gone. In the bottom of his heart he will be glad if I leave him."

This was not a supposition—she seemed to see it clearly in the dazzling light that now illuminated the meaning of life and of human relations.

"My love is growing more passionate and selfish and his is cooling off more and more. That is why we are drifting in different directions. And it can't be helped. He is all in all to me, and I demand that he should give himself up entirely to me, while he wants to get farther and farther away from me. That is it; at the beginning we were irresistibly drawn to each other; and now we are irresistibly drawn apart. And it can't be changed. He tells me that I am absurdly jealous and I keep on telling myself that I am, but it isn't true. I am not jealous; I am dissatisfied. But . . ." She was so agitated by the thought that came to her that she could scarcely sit still. "If I could be anything more than his mistress, passionately loving his caresses! but I cannot and do not wish to be anything else. And by this desire I arouse his disgust and he my resentment, and it cannot be otherwise. Do I not know that he would never think of deceiving me, that he has no intentions on the Princess Sorokin, that he is not in love with Kitty, that he will not betray me? I know it all, but that does not make it easier for me. To be treated kindly and gently out of a sense of duty, not love, is worse than unpleasant, it is hell. And that is precisely what has happened. He has ceased loving me for some time. When love ends hatred begins. I don't know these streets at all. How hilly it is, and there are houses and houses . . . and the houses are full of people; there is no end to them, and they all hate each other. Supposing I discover what I want in order to be happy? Well, I get a divorce and Alexei Alexandrovitch gives me Serioja and I marry Vronsky."

As she thought of Alexei Alexandrovitch she immediately saw him before her with extraordinary vividness. She could see his lifeless, near-sighted eyes, the blue veins on his white hands, hear the intonation of his voice, the cracking of his finger joints, and recalling the feeling that had existed between them—a feeling that had also been called love—she shuddered with disgust.

"Well, I get a divorce and become Vronsky's wife. Will Kitty cease looking at me as she looked at me to-day? No. And will Serioja stop asking or thinking of my two husbands? What new sentiment will grow up between me and Vronsky?

311

Can I possibly hope if not for happiness, at least for peace? No and no!" she replied to herself without the least hesitation. "Impossible! We diverge along different ways; I am the cause of his unhappiness and he of mine, and it is impossible to change either of us. Every attempt has been made . . . There is a screw loose somewhere. There goes a beggar woman with her child. She thinks she ought to be pitied. Have we not all been put into the world for no other purpose than to hate and torment one another? There go some schoolboys, laughing. Serioja? I thought I loved him and used to be sentimental over my tenderness for him, but I exchanged him for another love and never complained so long as that love pleased me." She shuddered in disgust at what she had called love. The clearness with which she saw her own life and that of other people gave her a sense of pleasure. "Such am I, and Peter, and Fiodor, the coachman, and that merchant, and all those people who live near the Volga where all these advertisements tell us to go. It is the same everywhere and always." She was just nearing the Nijni-Novgorod station and several porters rushed out to her carriage.

"Do you want a ticket to Obiralovoka?" Peter asked.

She had entirely forgotten where and for what purpose she was going and only understood the question with difficulty.

"Yes," she replied handing him a purse, and taking a small red bag on her arm, she left the carriage.

As she made her way through the crowd to the first-class waiting-room, she slowly reviewed all the details of her situation and all the plans between which she was wavering. And again now hope, now despair, took possession of her aching heart. She sat down on a couch to wait for the train, and looked with disgust at the people about her. She began picturing to herself how she would arrive at the station and send him a note, of how she would enter the room, and what she would say to him. She imagined him complaining to his mother about his situation without in the least understanding her. Then again she thought of how she might still have been happy, of how terribly she loved and hated him, and how violently her heart was beating.

XXXI

Тне bell rung; some impertinent young fellows came hurrying by, then Peter in his livery and gaiters went up to Anna to take her to the train. The noisy young fellows grew silent as she passed them on the platform, and whispered among themselves. Anna entered the carriage and sat down on the dirty seat that had once been white. Her little bag gave a jump as she sank into the cushions, then lay still beside her. Peter, with a stupid smile, raised his hat at the window as a sign of farewell, and the impudent conductor slammed the door and pulled down the latch. An ugly woman came hurrying up (Anna mentally divested her of her clothes and shuddered at her ugliness) with a young girl, laughing unnaturally, behind her.

" Katerina Andraevna has it all, *ma tante !*" the girl shouted.

" The girl too is hideous and deformed," Anna thought.

To avoid seeing people she got up and seated herself at the opposite window in the empty carriage. A dirty, ugly peasant in a cap, beneath which peeped his matted hair, passed by the window, bending down to the wheels of the carriage. " There is something familiar about that peasant," Anna thought, and as she recalled her dream, she shuddered and walked over to the opposite door. The conductor opened the door to let in a married couple.

" Do you wish to go out, madame? "

Anna made no reply. Neither the conductor nor the passengers getting in noticed under her veil the expression of terror on her face. She went back to her corner and took her seat. The married couple seated themselves on the opposite side and began examining her gown. They both appeared disgusting to Anna. The husband asked her for permission to smoke, not because he wanted to, but in order to get into conversation with her. Having received her consent he began talking to his wife in French though they had absolutely nothing to say to each other, and spoke of the silliest possible things, only so that Anna might hear them. She saw clearly that they were bored and hated each other; nor could such miserable creatures be anything else but hated.

The second bell was heard; there was a moving of luggage, a terrific noise, and some one's laughter. It was so clear to Anna

313

that nobody had any cause for joy that this laughter grated on her ears, and she put her hands over them in order to shut it out. The third bell was rung; there was a shrill whistle, the engine screeched, the chain clanked, and the man opposite made the sign of the cross.

" It would be interesting to ask what he means by it," Anna thought, giving him an angry look. She glanced out of the window; the people on the platform seemed to be gliding backwards though they were only standing still to see the train off. The carriage in which Anna was sitting swayed evenly at the junction of the rails and glided past the platform, past a wall, past other cars; the noise of the wheels sounded softer, emitting a slight metallic sound; the window was lighted up by the gorgeous evening sun and the breeze swayed the curtain gently to and fro. Anna forgot about her fellow passengers, and inhaling the fresh air, continued her thoughts.

" What was it I stopped on? Oh, yes; on the reflection that I could not imagine a situation in which life would not be a torment. We were all created in order to be tormented; we all know it, yet only contrive means for deceiving ourselves. But what would we do if we saw the truth? "

" Man has been given reason that he may be able to free himself from what worries him," the woman opposite remarked in French, apparently satisfied with the phrase.

These words seemed an answer to Anna's thoughts.

She glanced at the red-cheeked man and at the emaciated looking woman and understood at once that the woman considered herself unappreciated, that the husband was deceiving her and maintaining her in her opinion about herself. Anna seemed to read their history and penetrated to the innermost corners of their souls. As she found nothing of interest in them, she returned to her own thoughts.

" Yes, I am worried, and reason is given me that I may free myself. Why not put out the candle when there is nothing more to look at, when it is revolting to see it all? But how? Why did the conductor run by, holding on to the rail. Why do those young men in the next carriage make such a noise? Why do they talk, why do they laugh? Everything is false, everything is evil! "

When the train stopped at the station, Anna got out with a crowd of other passengers, and moving away from them as from the plague-stricken, she stood still on the platform, wondering why she had come there, and what it was she had intended

to do. Everything that had seemed so possible to her before was now horribly difficult to imagine, especially among that noisy, disgusting crowd that gave her no peace. Porters ran up to her offering their services, young men stamped on the planks of the platform, talking in loud voices and staring at her, people were coming towards her in every direction. Recalling that she had intended to travel on should there be no answer, she stopped one of the porters and asked him if Count Vronsky's coachman was anywhere about.

"Count Vronsky? His men were here a short time ago. They met the Princess Sorokin and her daughter. What sort of a man is the coachman?"

As she was talking to the porter, Mihail the coachman, red-faced, merry, smartly dressed, came up proudly and handed her a note. She tore it open and her heart was compressed even before she read it.

"I am sorry, your note did not reach me. Shall be back at ten," was the answer, written in a careless hand.

"Yes, I expected it!" she said to herself with a malicious smile.

"All right; you can go home," she said quietly to Mihail. She spoke softly, for the violent beating of her heart interfered with her breathing. "No, I will not allow you to torment me," she thought. She turned and walked down the platform, past the station.

Two housemaids, who were walking up and down, turned back to look at her and made some loud remarks about her toilet. "Real," one of them said, referring to the lace trimmings of her dress. Young men, too, stared at her and laughed as they passed her. The station-master, walking by, asked her if she was going to take the train. A boy, selling kvas, did not take his eyes off her.

"My God! where shall I go?" she asked herself walking farther and farther down the platform. At the end of it she stopped. Some ladies and children, who had met a man in glasses, and were laughing and talking merrily, grew silent and scanned her as she passed by them. She increased her speed and walked away to the very edge of the platform. A goods train was approaching. The platform shook, and it seemed to Anna that she was in the train again.

In a flash she recalled her first meeting with Vronsky and the man who had been run over, and comprehended what she had to do. Descending with a light rapid gait the steps that led from the water tower to the rails, she stopped close to the moving train. She looked at the bottom of the carriages, at the linchpins, the chains, and the iron wheels of the front carriage, and measuring with her eye, tried to determine the point midway between the front and hind wheels and the exact moment when it would be in front of her.

"There!" she said to herself, looking in the shadow of the carriage at the sand and coal dust with which the ties were covered; "there in the very middle . . . and I will punish him and be freed from it all and from myself."

She wanted to drop down in the middle of the first carriage that came up, but the red bag, which she began to pull off from her arm, retarded her; it was too late, the middle had passed. She had to wait for the next one. A sensation similar to the one she had always experienced when bathing, before she took her first plunge, came over her; she made the sign of the cross. This gesture called forth in her a whole series of girlish and childish memories, and suddenly the darkness that had enveloped everything lifted, and for a moment life presented itself to her with all its past joys. But she did not take her eyes off the wheels of the approaching carriage. And at the very moment when the middle was opposite her, she threw aside the red bag and, drawing in her shoulders, dropped down under the carriage on her hands, and with a light motion, as though preparing to rise at once, got on her knees. At that moment she became horrified at what she was doing. "Where am I? What am I doing? What for?" She wanted to get up, to throw herself back, but an enormous, relentless mass knocked her on the head and dragged her by the shoulders. "Lord, forgive me everything!" she murmured, feeling the futility of the struggle. A peasant, working on the line, was muttering some incomprehensible words. And the candle by which she had been reading the book filled with pain and sorrow, deceit and evil, flared up with a brighter light, illuminating for her everything that had been enshrouded in darkness, then flickered, grew dim, and went out for ever.

PART VIII

I

Two months had passed. It was now the middle of a hot summer and Sergei Ivanovitch had only just got ready to leave Moscow.

Certain events had also happened in Sergei Ivanovitch's life. A little over a year ago he had finished his book on the *Outline of the Principles and Forms of Political Life in Europe and Russia*, the fruit of six years' labour. Several parts of it and the introduction had already been published in reviews and read to men of his circle, so that its ideas were not absolutely new to the public; none the less Sergei Ivanovitch had expected that the work would create a sensation, if not a complete revolution in the scientific world.

The book, after having been carefully polished up, was published and sent out to the booksellers.

He never asked any one about it and answered all questions reluctantly; he did not even inquire of the booksellers how it was selling; nevertheless, he was watching eagerly for the first impression the book would produce on the public and on literature in general.

But a week passed, a second, a third, and the public remained absolutely indifferent. Even his friends, especially those who were not interested in scientific subjects, scarcely mentioned it to him, apart from a few, including specialists and scholars, who merely spoke to him of it out of a sense of politeness.

Sergei Ivanovitch watched in great trepidation for the first review, but a month passed and then another, and still there was silence. Only in the *Northern Beetle*, in a humorous article about the singer Drabanti, whose voice was cracked, was there an accidental reference to Kosnishev's book, showing in a few contemptuous words that it had long been condemned and turned over to the public ridicule.

Finally, after the third month after publication, there appeared a criticism in some serious periodical. Sergei Ivanovitch knew its author, having once met him at Golubtsov's.

317

He was an extremely young man, a clever journalist, but a man of little culture and timid socially.

In spite of his contempt for the author, Sergei Ivanovitch read the review respectfully. It was terrible.

The young journalist had comprehended the book in the most impossible sort of way, and had cleverly quoted certain passages that made the whole work appear as nothing but a conglomeration of high-sounding words, and the author a very ignorant man. It was all so cleverly done that Sergei Ivanovitch could not help admiring it, and it was precisely that that made it so terrible.

In spite of the sincerity with which Seregi Ivanovitch justified the critic's arguments, he was not for a moment taken aback, but instantly began recalling all the details of his meeting with him and wondering whether he had offended him in any way.

He suddenly remembered that he had corrected the young man in some ignorant statement he had made, and at once concluded that that was the explanation of the article.

Nothing further was either said or written about the book, and it at last dawned on Sergei Ivanovitch that the six years of labour, spent with so much love and care, had passed by unnoticed.

Sergei Ivanovitch's situation was the harder, because after finishing his book he found himself without an occupation, having formerly spent the greater part of his time on it.

Sergei Ivanovitch was clever, cultured, healthy, energetic, and did not know what to do with his energy. Drawing-room discussions, sessions, meetings, committees, took up a good deal of his time, but always living in the town as he did, he did not permit himself, like his brother, to waste all his time in endless conversations, and so had much leisure and mental powers to spare.

The one bright spot of that oppressive time was that the Slavonic question had come to the front, pushing all other problems and questions into the background, and as Sergei Ivanovitch had always taken an interest in it he now abandoned himself completely to it.

In the circle in which Sergei Ivanovitch moved, no one could speak or write about anything except the Serbian war. Everything that the idle crowd usually does to kill time was now being done for the benefit of the Slavs. Balls, concerts, dinners, matches, ladies' gowns, beer, inns—everything bore evidence of the public sympathy for the Slavs.

318

Sergei Ivanovitch agreed with very little of what was being said and written at that period. He saw that the Slavonic question had become merely a fashionable pastime, which served as an amusement for society, and also that many men interested themselves in it purely for selfish, ambitious motives. The papers printed much that was unnecessary and exaggerated, for the sole purpose of attracting popular attention and to outcry one another. He saw that those who cried loudest of all were the failures, people who had been overlooked, such as generals without armies, ministers without congregations, journalists without periodicals, leaders of parties without followers. He saw, on the one hand, much that was frivolous and ridiculous; on the other, unquestionable, ever growing enthusiasm, uniting all classes, with which it was impossible not to sympathise. The massacre of co-religionists, the Slavs, called forth sympathy for the oppressed and indignation against the oppressors. And the heroism of Serbians and Montenegrins, fighting for a great cause, bred in the whole nation a desire to help them not only in words but in deeds.

At the same time another phenomenon rejoiced Sergei Ivanovitch's heart. The public had expressed a definite opinion, the national soul had at last expressed itself, as Sergei Ivanovitch put it. The more interested he grew in this matter, the more he became convinced that it was an epoch-making period. He devoted himself entirely to the cause and forgot to think about his book. He was now so occupied that he had no time to answer all his letters or to fulfil the numerous demands made on him. Having worked all the spring and part of the summer, in July he got ready to go into the country to his brother's. He looked forward to a couple of weeks' rest and the pleasure of seeing the popular spirit in the heart of the country that had rejoiced him so much in the town. Katavasov, who had long promised to pay Levin a visit, went with him.

II

SERGEI IVANOVITCH and Katavasov had barely reached the unusually animated station of the Kursk railway when a crowd of volunteers drove up. They were met by ladies with bouquets and entered the station amid a surging crowd. One of the ladies turned to Sergei Ivanovitch.

"Have you also come to see them off?" she asked in French.

"No, princess; I am going down to my brother's place for a rest. And do you always come to see them off?" Sergei Ivanovitch asked with a faint smile.

"That would be hardly possible," she replied. "I hear that eight hundred have already gone; Malvinsky would not believe it."

"More than that, I think. Counting those who did not go direct from Moscow, there must be more than a thousand," Sergei Ivanovitch said.

"That's just what I said!" the lady broke in joyously. "Is it true that a million roubles have been collected?"

"More, princess."

"What do you think of to-day's telegram? It appears the Turks have been beaten again."

"Yes, I read it," Sergei Ivanovitch replied.

This telegram confirmed the news that three days ago the Turks had been badly beaten and that a decisive battle was to be expected on the morrow.

"Oh, by the way, such a nice young man wanted to volunteer, but I don't know why, certain difficulties were put in the way. Could you write a note for him? He comes from the Countess Lydia Ivanovna."

Having learnt all the necessary details about the young man, Sergei Ivanovitch went into the first-class waiting-room, wrote a note to the proper person, and took it to the princess.

"Do you know, Count Vronsky, the famous one . . . is on this train," the princess said with a significant smile, as Sergei Ivanovitch handed her the note.

"I heard that he had volunteered, but did not know when he was going. Is he on this train?"

"I saw him a moment ago, accompanied by his mother. Under the circumstances it was the best thing he could do."

"I quite agree."

While they were talking, the crowd moved past them to the refreshment room. They, too, moved on. A man was standing with a wine-glass in his hand, addressing the volunteers in a loud voice. "To serve for our faith, for humanity, and for our brothers," he was saying, his voice rising more and more. "Mother Moscow will bless you for this great work. *Jevio !* "[1] he concluded almost in tears.

[1] The Serbian word for *Hurrah*.

There was a general cry of " *jevio !* " and the crowd surged
into the hall and almost knocked the princess off her feet.

" Ah! glad to see you, princess!" Stepan Arkadyevitch
exclaimed with a joyous smile, suddenly appearing from among
the crowd. " He spoke well, don't you think? Ah, and here
is Sergei Ivanovitch! You ought to have spoken too, just a
few words of encouragement; you do it so well." He gave
a respectful, cautious smile as he took Sergei Ivanovitch's arm.

" I'm afraid I mustn't; I'm just going."

" Where to? "

" Down to my brother's."

" My wife is there. Do please tell her that you have seen me
and that I am all right; and if you would be good enough, you
might also mention that I've been appointed a member of the
Commission of the Consolidated . . . but she will understand.
You know, *les petites misères de la vie humaine*," he added,
turning to the princess as though to excuse himself. " Did I
tell you that Mahky, not Liza, but Bibish, is sending a thousand
rifles and twenty nurses? "

" So I've heard," Kosnishev replied reluctantly.

" What a pity you are going away!" Stepan Arkadyevitch
said. " To-morrow we are giving a dinner to two volunteers,
Dimir-Bartniansky and our Veslovsky. You know he has
married lately. A capital fellow I think, don't you, princess? "
he asked, turning to the lady.

The princess gave a glance at Kosnishev and did not reply.
The fact that both she and Sergei Ivanovitch were anxious to
get rid of him did not in the least embarrass Stepan Arkadyevitch. He looked smilingly, now at the feather of the lady's
hat, now sideways as though he were going to pick something up.
Whenever a lady passed him with a collecting-box, he called her
up and dropped a five-rouble note into it.

" I can never allow these boxes to pass so long as I have any
money left," he remarked. " Have you seen to-day's telegram?
The Montenegrins are splendid fellows."

" Really!" he exclaimed when the princess informed him
that Vronsky was going by that train. A look of grief passed
over Stepan Arkadyevitch's face, but a moment later, when he
entered the room where Vronsky was, he entirely forgot the tears
of despair he had shed over his sister's body, and saw in Vronsky
only a hero and an old friend.

" With all his faults we must do him justice," the princess
remarked to Sergei Ivanovitch the moment Oblonsky had

gone; "he has a thoroughly Russian, Slavonic nature. Only I am afraid it will be unpleasant for Vronsky to see him. Say what you please, but I am touched by the fate of that man. Do talk to him on the way!" the princess said.

"I will, if the opportunity occurs."

"I never liked him, but this expiates everything. He is not only going himself, but is taking a whole squadron at his expense."

"So I've heard."

A bell was rung. All hurried towards the door.

"There he is!" the princess said, indicating Vronsky, who, in a long coat and broad-brimmed hat, was walking along arm-in-arm with his mother. Stepan Arkadyevitch was by his side, talking in an animated way.

Vronsky looked straight in front of him with knit brows, as though he did not hear what Stepan Arkadyevitch was saying.

At a hint from Oblonsky, he looked in the direction of the princess and Kosnishev and raised his hat. His worn face that looked aged was full of pain and suffering.

On reaching the platform Vronsky let his mother pass by him in silence and disappeared into one of the carriages.

On the platform were shouts of "God save the Tsar! Hurrah!" and "Jivio!" One of the volunteers, a young man with a flat chest, bowed and waved his felt hat and a bouquet above his head. Two officers came after him and an elderly man with a long beard, who was wearing a soiled cap.

III

TAKING leave of the princess Sergei Ivanovitch, followed by Katavasov, who had just come, entered the crowded carriage, and the train started.

At the Tsaritsin station the train was met by a fine choir of young men singing, "To Glory." Again the volunteers thrust their heads out of the windows, but Sergei Ivanovitch paid no further attention to them. He had had so much to do with them and knew their types so well that he was no longer interested. Katavasov, on the contrary, who had been so busy with his learned labours as not to have time for anything else, watched them attentively and asked Sergei Ivanovitch all sorts of questions.

Sergei Ivanovitch advised him to go into a second-class

carriage and talk to the heroes in person. At the next station Katavasov followed his advice and went into a second-class carriage. A group of volunteers were sitting in one corner talking loudly; they were obviously aware of the fact that the attention of the other passengers, as well as that of Katavasov who had just entered, was directed to them. The tall young fellow with the hollow chest spoke the loudest of all. He was obviously drunk, and was telling some incident that had happened in their establishment. Opposite him sat a still taller young officer in a military coat of the Austrian Guards' uniform. He smiled as he listened to the story, and stopped the speaker every now and again. A third, in an artillery uniform, was sitting on a trunk near by. A fourth was fast asleep. Entering into conversation with the youth, Katavasov learned that he was a rich Moscow merchant who had squandered a large fortune before he was twenty-two. Katavasov did not like him, because he was spoiled, weak, and effeminate. He seemed to be under the impression that he was doing something very heroic, and boasted in the most disagreeable manner possible.

The second, an ex-officer, also produced an unpleasant impression on Katavasov. He was a man who seemed to have tried everything. He had worked on the railway, had been a superintendent, and had even established factories. He talked about everything, and used all sorts of unnecessarily long words in and out of place.

The artilleryman, on the contrary, pleased Katavasov very much. He was a modest, quiet man, who seemed to bow down before the knowledge of the ex-guardsman and the heroic self-sacrifice of the merchant, and did not say anything about himself.

"Well, everybody is going," he replied, when Katavasov asked him the reasons that had induced him to go to Serbia. "One must help the Serbians; they are to be pitied."

"Yes, they lack artillerymen," Katavasov observed.

"I have only been in the artillery a short time; perhaps they will attach me to the infantry or cavalry."

"Why should they, since they need the artillery most?" Katavasov said, judging from his years that he must be of fairly high rank.

"I have not served long in the artillery; I am only a retired under-officer," he said, then began explaining why he had not passed his examination.

The whole thing produced a most disagreeable impression on Katavasov, and when at the next station the volunteers went out to get a drink, he felt as if he must talk to some one about it. He turned to another passenger, an old man in a military uniform, who had been listening to Katavasov's conversation with the volunteers.

"What different kinds of men all these volunteers are," he observed, vaguely wishing to express his own opinion and at the same time to elicit that of the old man.

The latter was a soldier who had gone through two campaigns. He knew what a soldier was, and judging by the dashing way in which these young fellows applied themselves to the bottle, he formed but a poor opinion of them. However, he feared to give expression to any unfavourable opinion, it being rather dangerous in the present mood of society, and so was anxious to find out Katavasov's ideas first.

"Well, men are wanted there," he said, with a twinkle in his eye. They began discussing the latest news from the front, concealing their mutual surprise that a battle was to be fought on the morrow when the Turks were supposed to have been beaten at all points. Thus the two parted without really disclosing their ideas to each other.

When Katavasov returned to his carriage he made a compromise with truth and gave Sergei Ivanovitch a glowing account of the young volunteers whom he had seen.

At the next town the volunteers were again met with singing and cheers. Here, too, there were men and women with collecting boxes and provincial ladies with bouquets, but it was all much quieter than at Moscow.

IV

WHEN they stopped at the principal town of the province, Sergei Ivanovitch did not go to the refreshment room, but walked up and down the platform. Passing Vronsky's carriage he noticed that the blinds were drawn. When he walked by it a second time the old countess was at the window. She made a sign for him to come to her.

"I am seeing him off as far as Kursk," she said.

"Yes, so I've heard," Sergei Ivanovitch said, looking in at the window. "I think it very noble of him," he added, noticing that Vronsky was not in the carriage.

" What else was he to do after his misfortune? "

" It was a terrible event! " Sergei Ivanovitch remarked.

" You can't think what I've gone through! Won't you come in? You can't think what I've gone through! " she repeated when Sergei Ivanovitch had entered and taken a seat beside her. " For six weeks he did not speak to any one and only took food when I implored him to do so. We couldn't leave him alone for a minute; we had to take away everything from him with which he would be likely to kill himself; we even had to live on the lower story, for it was impossible to foresee what he might not do. You know he shot himself once on her account," she added, and her old brows wrinkled as she recalled this. " She ended as such a woman ought to have ended; she even chose a low, disgusting kind of death."

" It is not for us to judge, countess," Sergei Ivanovitch ventured with a sigh; " I can quite understand how hard it must have been for you, though."

" Oh, don't speak of it! I was on my estate at the time, and he had come to see me. A note was brought to him. He wrote an answer and sent it off. We did not know that she was at the station. In the evening, when I had just retired, my maid told me that a lady had thrown herself under a train at the station. I can't tell you how it was, but I somehow knew it was she. My first thought was of him; I wanted to prevent them telling him, but it was already too late; his coachman had seen it all. When I ran into his room, he was no longer himself; it was terrible to look at him. He rushed away to the station without a word. I don't know what happened there, but they brought him home half dead. I could scarcely recognise him. *Prostration complète* the doctor declared. He was almost mad for a time, but why speak of it? " the countess said with a wave of the hand. " It was a terrible time! Say what you please, but she was a bad woman. What is the use of these desperate passions? It seems as though they only indulge in them for the sake of being original. Well, she has been that, and has ruined two good men, her own husband and my unfortunate son."

" What is her husband doing? " Sergei Ivanovitch asked.

" He took the child. you know. At first Alexei agreed to everything, but now he is horribly tormented at the thought of having given his daughter to a stranger. He can't take back his word though. Karenin came to the funeral and we did all we could to prevent Alexei meeting him. For the husband it was the best way out of the difficulty; she has set him free at any rate, but my poor son gave himself up to her entirely. He threw up everything, his career and us, and she did not pity him; it seemed as though she wanted to ruin him on purpose. Say what you please, her death even was that of a bad, unprincipled woman. May God forgive me, but I can't help hating her memory as I look at my poor, unfortunate son."

"How is he now?"

"This war seems to have come as a blessing. I am an old woman and understand nothing about these matters, but God must have sent it for his sake. Of course, being his mother, I feel terribly about it; the main thing is, they say, *ce n'est pas bien vu à Pétersbourg*. But what is to be done? This was the only thing that could lift him up. His friend Yashvin, you know, lost all he possessed and was getting ready to go to Serbia. He came to see him and persuaded him to go too. This occupies his attention somewhat. I wish you would go and talk to him a little; it would divert him; he is so miserable. Added to his other woes he has a toothache. I am sure he will be glad to see you. Do go and talk to him; he is walking about on that side."

Sergei Ivanovitch said that he would be delighted, and walked over to the other side of the train.

V

In the slanting evening shadows of the sacks piled up on the platform, Vronsky, in his long overcoat, his hat drawn over his forehead, and his hands in his pockets, was pacing up and down like some caged animal. It seemed to Sergei Ivanovitch as he was walking towards him that he pretended not to notice him, but he paid no attention to that. His relations with Vronsky were above personal considerations. In Sergei Ivanovitch's eyes Vronsky was at that moment an important factor in a great cause, and he considered it his duty to say a few words of encouragement to him. He went up to him boldly. Vronsky looked up and, recognising him, extended his hand.

"Perhaps you would rather not have seen me," Sergei Ivanovitch began, "but I thought I might be able to be of use to you."

"There is no one whom it would be less unpleasant to meet

than you," Vronsky replied. "Excuse me! there is nothing pleasant for me in life."

"I understand; I merely wanted to offer you my services," Sergei Ivanovitch said, looking closely into Vronsky's suffering face. "Wouldn't you like a letter to Ristich or Milan?"

"No, thank you," Vronsky replied, only with difficulty comprehending what was said to him. "Let us walk up and down if you don't mind; it is so close in the carriage. It's very good of you, but to die, no letters of recommendation are needed; unless it be a letter to the Turks. . . ." He gave a grim smile.

"Still it would be easier for you to enter into relations with a man to whom you had been introduced; one must live, anyhow. I was glad to hear you had decided to go. So many attacks have been made on the volunteers that the fact of a man like you going cannot help raising them in the public opinion."

"I have this advantage over other men, that I attach little importance to life," Vronsky said. "I have enough vitality left to rush into the fray and crush them or fall myself; that I know. I am glad to be able to give up my life for a cause, a life that is not only useless to me, but a burden. Somebody will be the gainer by it." He ground his teeth impatiently. The pain prevented him from saying what he had wished to.

"You will come back regenerated, I feel sure," Sergei Ivanovitch said, touched by Vronsky's words. "The liberation of our brothers is a cause worth living for as well as dying for. May God grant you success and inward peace," he added, extending his hand to him. Vronsky pressed it firmly.

"I may be of some use as a tool, but as a man I am a wreck," he said hesitatingly.

The agonising pain of his tooth made it difficult for him to talk. He grew silent, and gazed at the wheels of the tender as they glided slowly and softly over the rails. Suddenly an inner torment made him forget his toothache. The sight of the tender and rails, the conversation, Sergei Ivanovitch, whom he had not seen since Anna's death, brought her vividly back to his mind, or as much as there had been left of her when, like a madman, he had rushed into the station and had seen her lifeless, blood-stained body, shamelessly stretched out among strangers. The unmarred head with its heavy braids and hair over the temples was thrown back, and her lovely face, with its half-open mouth, wore a strange, steely expression, pitiful about the lips, and terrible in the arrested gaze of the open

327

eyes, as though she were uttering that terrible threat she had used during their last quarrel. And he tried to recall her such as she had been when he had first met her at the station, charming, mysterious, loving, seeking and giving happiness, not cruel and revengeful as he had last seen her. He tried to think of his best moments with her, but they were poisoned for ever. He remembered only her solemn threat about his repenting, and that it was now accomplished. He no longer felt his toothache; his face was contorted by sobs.

When they had passed the sacks twice, and he regained his composure, he turned calmly to Sergei Ivanovitch.

"Has there been no telegram since yesterday? They have been crushed for the third time. but to-morrow a decisive battle is expected."

They talked about the proclamation of Milan as king, and of the enormous consequences this might lead to, until the second bell was rung, when each returned to his own carriage.

VI

UNCERTAIN when he would be able to leave Moscow, Sergei Ivanovitch had not telegraphed to his brother to send some one to meet him. Levin was not at home when Sergei Ivanovitch and Katavasov drove up to the house at about twelve o'clock in a vehicle hired at the station. Both were covered with dust and looked like negroes. Kitty, who was sitting on the balcony with her father and sister, instantly recognised her brother-in-law, and ran downstairs to meet him.

"Why didn't you let us know?" she greeted him, offering him her forehead to kiss.

"We got here quite well without troubling you," Sergei Ivanovitch replied. "I am so dusty that I daren't touch you. I was so busy that I did not know when I should be able to get away. You, as usual, are enjoying your quiet happiness beyond the current, in your calm pool," he added, with a smile. "Here is our friend Vassily Fedotitch, come to see you at last."

"I am not a negro; I only want a wash to make myself look like a man," Katavasov said in his jocular way, extending his hand with a smile. His black face had a peculiar sparkle in it.

"Kostia will be delighted. He is out on the farm, but I expect him back quite soon."

" Still attending to his farm? We townspeople can think of nothing but the Serbian war. What does our friend think of it? Quite differently from other folk, I suppose."

" No, he is just like the rest," Kitty replied, somewhat confused, looking back at Sergei Ivanovitch. " I will send for him. Papa is with us; he has only just returned from abroad."

She despatched some one for Levin, gave orders for the two dust-covered men to be conducted to their rooms, and ran quickly up the balcony stairs.

" It's Sergei Ivanovitch and Professor Katavasov," she said when she got to the top.

" Rather heavy in this heat! " the prince observed.

" No, papa; the professor is a very nice man, and Kostia is very fond of him," Kitty said with a smile, noticing the look of sarcasm on her father's face.

" I didn't mean any harm."

" Do go down to them, dear," Kitty said, turning to her sister. " They saw Stiva at the station, and say that he is well. I must run down to Mitia. Unfortunately, I haven't nursed him since breakfast. He is awake by now and must be crying." And she made for the nursery with a rapid step.

She knew that the child was crying even before she got there, and indeed she had not been mistaken. It was a good hungry cry.

" Has he been awake long, nurse? " Kitty asked, seating herself on a chair and undoing the bodice of her dress. " Give him to me quickly. How tiresome you are, nurse! Can't the cap be tied later? "

The child yelled loud and louder.

" It won't do at all, Katerina Alexandrovna," Agafia Mihailovna said, who was nearly always present in the nursery, " he must be made to look decent. There, there, little one," she said, trying to soothe the child, and paying no further attention to the mother.

The nurse carried the child over to Kitty; Agafia Mihailovna walked behind, her face full of tenderness.

" I declare he knows me! he knows me! " she shouted louder than the baby.

Kitty paid no heed to her words; her impatience, like that of the child's, was increasing.

Owing to their mutual impatience things did not go smoothly at first; the child had some difficulty in taking the breast, and grew angry.

Finally, after a desperate cry, matters were satisfactorily arranged between them, and mother and child grew quiet simultaneously.

" He seems all in a perspiration," Kitty said, feeling the boy. " What makes you think that he knows you? " she asked Agafia Mihailovna, looking sideways at the child's eyes, which seemed to her to peep out roguishly from beneath his cap. " It's impossible! If he recognised any one at all it would be me."

She smiled to herself. In her heart she knew that he not only recognised Agafia Mihailovna, but comprehended a whole lot of things that nobody ever knew, and that she was only just beginning to find out, thanks to him. For Agafia Mihailovna, for the nurse, for his grandfather, and even for his father, Mitia was only a weak little creature who demanded material attention, but for her he was already a human being, with a whole history of moral relations.

" When he wakes up, you will see for yourself," Agafia Mihailovna said. " When I do this, he beams, the darling. His little face looks as bright as the sky on a clear day."

" All right, we shall see," Kitty said in a whisper. " You can go now; he is falling asleep."

VII

AGAFIA MIHAILOVNA went out on tiptoe; the nurse pulled down the blinds, drove out the flies from underneath the netting of the baby's crib, sat down, and began waving a birch branch over mother and child.

" How hot it is! If only the Lord would send us a little rain! " she said.

" Sh . . . sh . . . sh . . . " Kitty said, rocking gently to and fro. She was pressing Mitia's chubby little hand, that looked as though it had been cut by a string at the wrist, afraid to kiss it for fear of waking him. The nurse stopped fanning them and fell fast asleep. From upstairs came the sound of the old prince's voice and Katavasov's loud laughter.

" They seem all right without me," Kitty thought. " What a nuisance it is that Kostia is not yet back! He must have gone to the apiary again. Though it is lonely to have him away so often, I am glad of it. It keeps him occupied. He is much happier than he was in the spring. How gloomy and miserable he was then! He is so funny!" She smiled to herself. She knew what it was that made her husband unhappy; it was his unbelief. Though she held that for an unbeliever there could be no salvation, still, his unbelief did not disturb her in the least. She loved her husband's soul more than anything else in the world, yet his unbelief merely amused her.

"Why does he keep on reading those philosophies of his all the year round?" she thought. "If they merely contain untruth what is the use of reading them? He says himself that he would like to believe, then why doesn't he? Because he thinks too much, I suppose. And he thinks too much because he is nearly always alone. He can't talk to us about everything. Our newly-arrived visitors will be a pleasure to him, especially Katavasov. He likes to discuss all kinds of questions." She began wondering where she should put Katavasov for the night, whether by himself or together with Sergei Ivanovitch, when suddenly she grew so agitated by a thought that came to her that she even disturbed Mitia, who looked up at her reproachfully. "Why, the washing has not yet come home, and I shall have no clean bed-linen for the guests! I must make haste, else Agafia Mihailovna may give Sergei Ivanovitch sheets that have been used!" At this thought alone the blood rushed to Kitty's face.

"I can see to it later, though," she decided, and tried to recall what it was she had been thinking about. "Oh, yes, Kostia is an unbeliever." She smiled. "And if he is? I would rather have him such as he is than see him like Madame Stahl, or as I wanted to be when I was abroad. Kostia would not pretend!"

There could be no doubt of his goodness. A recent instance of it rose up before her. Two weeks before Dolly had received a letter from her husband imploring her to save his honour by selling her estate in order to pay his debts. Dolly had been in despair. She despised and hated her husband, and wished to be separated from him. She refused his request at first, but finally agreed to dispose of a part of the estate. Here Kitty recalled with a tender smile how embarrassed her husband had been in offering his help, and finally, having discovered a means of doing so without offending Dolly, he had suggested to Kitty that she should give up the portion of the estate that belonged to her. It had never even occurred to Kitty herself.

"I don't see where the unbelief comes in. He has a heart of

gold, and would not hurt a soul. He does everything for others and nothing for himself. Sergei Ivanovitch seems to think that it's Kostia's duty to be his manager; and so does his sister. Now he has Dolly and the children as well. And these peasants come to him every day as though he were obliged to serve them. If only you would be like your father, just like him!" she murmured, as she touched the child's cheeks with her lips, and handed him over to the nurse.

VIII

FROM the moment when, at the sight of his dying brother, Levin had for the first time looked at the questions of life and death through his new convictions, as he called them, convictions which, in the period between his twentieth and thirty-sixth year had imperceptibly taken the place of his childish beliefs, he had become horrified, not so much at death, as at life, without the least conception whence it came, what it was for, and what it meant. The organism, its dissolution, the indestructibility of matter, the law of the conservation of energy, evolution, were the words that had taken the place of his former beliefs. These words and the conceptions they stood for satisfied his mental requirements, but they gave him nothing for life, and he suddenly began to feel himself in the position of a man who has given up his fur coat in exchange for a gauze garment, and at the first approach of the frost realises that he is little better than naked, and must inevitably die a painful death.

Levin continued to live as before, but was constantly tormented on account of his ignorance. He had a vague feeling that what he called his convictions was not only ignorance, but that it actually stood in the way of the knowledge that he needed.

In the early days of his marriage his new joys and duties had completely drowned these thoughts, but latterly, after his wife's confinement, when he had lived in Moscow without occupation, the question began to present itself more and more frequently, demanding a solution.

It presented itself in this way: "If I do not accept the explanation offered me by Christianity on the problem of my existence, where shall I find others?" He scrutinised the whole arsenal of his scientific convictions and found no answer whatsoever to this question. He was in the position of a man who seeks to find food in a toy shop or a gun shop.

Involuntarily and unconsciously he sought now in every book, in every conversation, in every person he met, some sympathy with the subject that absorbed him.

What surprised and puzzled him most was the fact that the majority of men of his circle, who had, like himself, substituted science for religion, did not experience the least moral suffering, and were perfectly contented and happy. Were they insincere, or did science give them a clearer answer to these troublesome questions? And he took to studying these men and books that might contain the solution that he desired.

He discovered that he had made a gross error in taking up the idea of his university friends, that religion had outlived its day and no longer existed. The best people he knew were believers—the old prince, Lvov, for whom he had taken such a liking, Sergei Ivanovitch, all the women, including his wife, who believed, just as he had done when he was a child, nine-tenths of the Russian people—the part of the nation whose lives inspired him with the greatest respect, were believers.

Another strange thing was that, as he read many books, he became convinced that the materialists whose opinions he shared did not attach any importance to these questions. Far from explaining them, they set them aside and took up others of no interest to him, such, for instance, as the evolution of organisms, the mechanical explanation of the soul, and so forth.

Moreover, during his wife's illness an extraordinary event had occurred. He, an unbeliever, had prayed fervently, in full faith. But as soon as the danger was over he was unable to give that spiritual experience any place in his life.

He could not admit that he had known the truth then and was mistaken now, for the moment he began to think of it calmly everything went to pieces. Nor could he admit that he had been mistaken then, for he thought too highly of that experience, and if he assumed it to have been a weakness, he was defiling those precious moments. He was in painful discord with himself, and strained all his mental powers in order to put himself right.

IX

THERE were days when these thoughts tormented him more than others, but they never left him entirely. The more he read and thought, the further he felt himself from the aim he was pursuing.

Having convinced himself that he could get no answer from the materialists, he turned to Plato, Spinoza, Kant, Schelling, Hegel, Schopenhauer—all those philosophers who did not give a material explanation of life.

The ideas seemed to him fruitful, particularly as a refutation of the material teaching, but the moment he reflected on the solution of the important question, he found the same thing repeated again and again. Following the definition given to obscure words such as spirit, will, freedom, substance, and purposely allowing himself to be caught in the word-trap, he seemed to understand something, but he need only forget the artificial chain of thoughts and return to what satisfied him, than the whole edifice fell to pieces like a house of cards.

When reading Schopenhauer one day he substituted the word " love " for " will," and for a short time this new philosophy consoled him, but even that fell like the rest when dissected and brought into the domain of real life.

His brother advised him to read the theological works of Horniakov, and the second volume, in spite of its polemical, brilliant, elegant style, which at first repelled him, impressed him deeply by its Church doctrine. He was struck by the idea that the attainment of divine truth was not given to one man, but to the totality of men, embodied in the Church. He rejoiced at the thought that it was easier to believe in an existing, living Church embracing all the creeds of men with God at its head, than to begin with some distant, mysterious, unknown God.

Later, when he read a history of the Church by a Catholic writer, and another by a Greek Orthodox writer, and saw that both Churches, infallible in their essence, denied each other, he was again disappointed in Horniakov's doctrine, and this structure, too, fell to pieces just as the philosophical teachings had done.

The spring was a most difficult time for Levin, and he lived through some terrible moments.

" Without knowing who I am and why I am here life is impossible. And I cannot know it, consequently I cannot live," he would say to himself.

" In endless time and space, in the infinitude of matter, an organic bubble separated itself, will hold together a while, and burst. And that bubble am I."

It was an agonising untruth, but it was the result of centuries of labour of the human mind in that direction.

It was the last belief on which was reared all human inquiry, in all its branches. It was the reigning conviction, and Levin had involuntarily adopted it out of all other explanations, as being the most clear.

But it was only an untruth—a cruel sarcasm of some evil power, impossible to submit to.

It was necessary to free oneself from that power, and each man held his liberation in his own hands. There was only one means to do this, and that was death.

And though in good health and happily married, Levin was several times so near to killing himself that he had to hide a rope so as not to hang himself, and would not go out with a gun for fear of shooting himself.

But he did neither the one nor the other, and still continued living.

X

WHEN Levin puzzled over what he was and where he came from, he found no answer and fell into despair, but when he ceased worrying about it he seemed to know definitely why he was there, and acted accordingly. Latterly his life had even assumed a more definite purpose than before.

On his return to the country at the beginning of June, he returned also to his customary occupations. The farm, his relations with the peasants and the neighbouring gentry, his home affairs, his brother's and sister's affairs, his relation with his wife and her relatives, his care for the child, the new bee-keeping that had fascinated him since the spring, and a hundred other things, absorbed all his time.

These matters interested him not because he justified them by some general principle as he had done formerly; on the contrary, having become disenchanted by the failure of his various undertakings for the common good, he now busied himself for no other reason than because it seemed to him that he could not do otherwise.

Formerly, whenever he had tried to do anything for the good of humanity, for Russia, for the village, he had observed that the idea itself was agreeable, but the work senseless. There was no full conviction that it was absolutely necessary, and from at first appearing great, it grew smaller and smaller, until it reached the point of impossibility. Since his marriage, however, he had begun to confine his life more strictly to himself, and though he no longer experienced the same joy at the thought of his activity, he felt more certain of its usefulness, saw that it proceeded much better than before, and that it grew larger instead of smaller.

Almost against his will he buried himself deeper and deeper into the soil, so that he could not get out of it without opening a furrow.

To live as his father and grandfathers had lived, to carry out their work so as to hand it on to his children, seemed to him a plain duty. It was as necessary as eating when one is hungry. And for that, just as one had to prepare a meal, one had to keep the farm at Pokrovsky in such a manner as to make it profitable. Just as it was necessary to pay one's debts, so it was necessary to manage the estate in such a manner that when his son inherited it from him, he would be as grateful as Levin himself had been when he had received it from his grandfather. And so he looked after his cows, fields and manures, and planted forests.

He could not help attending to the affairs of Sergei Ivanovitch and his sister, and the peasants had become so accustomed to coming to him for advice that he had not the heart to cast them off. Then he had to see to the comforts of his sister-in-law and her children, whom he had invited to stay with them, and to that of his wife and child; he had to be with them at least a small part of the day.

Taken all together, Levin's life was fully occupied, yet it had no meaning for him whenever he thought of it.

Not only did Levin see clearly what it was he had to do, but he saw also how he must do it, and what part was of paramount importance.

He knew that it was necessary to hire labourers as cheaply as possible, but that he ought not to enslave them by advancing them money in order to get them below the market price. There was no harm in selling peasants straw when they had no food for their cattle, but the wine and the dramshop had to be abolished, even though they brought in an income. Wood-stealing he would punish most severely, but he would take no fines for cattle driven on to his land, much to the disgust of his own herds.

Peter, who was paying a moneylender ten per cent. a month, was to get a loan in order to save him, but no mercy was to be shown to those peasants who did not pay their rents. His bailiff was not to be forgiven for having delayed mowing a small meadow and thus losing the grass for nothing; on the other hand, the eighty acres where a wood had been set were not to be mowed at all. No mercy was to be shown to a labourer who went away during working time because his father had died, no matter how much he was to be pitied, and he was to be paid less for the valuable time he had lost; at the same time, he could not refuse giving a monthly allowance to old, worthless servants.

Upon returning home he knew that he had to go to his wife even though some peasants had been waiting for him for hours, yet he would forego the pleasure of settling a swarm of bees to talk to the peasants who came to find him at the apiary.

He did not know whether he was doing right or wrong, indeed he had ceased thinking about the question. He dreaded any reflection that would have given rise to doubts and obscured the clear and accurate view he had taken of his duties. But an infallible judge was ever present in his soul who decided which of two possible acts was the better one, and instantly let him know the moment he did not act as was proper.

Thus he lived, not knowing and not seeing the remotest possibility of knowing what he was and for what purpose he had been placed in the world. He was tormented by this ignorance to the extent of fearing suicide, yet at the same time was laying out for himself a definite path in life.

XI

THE day on which Sergei Ivanovitch reached Pokrovsky was one full of torment for Levin. It was at that hurried, busy season of the year when the peasantry put forth an extra-ordinary amount of effort and show an endurance quite un-known in any other conditions of life—an endurance that would be prized more highly were it not repeated every year, and did it not produce such very simple results. Digging, sowing, mowing, reaping, harvesting, threshing—these are labours that seem simple and commonplace, but to accomplish them in the short time accorded by nature, every one, old and young, must set to work. For three or four weeks they must be content with the simplest fare, such as black bread, garlic, and kvas, and must haul the ricks at night and not get more than two or three hours' sleep a day. And this is done every year throughout the whole of Russia.

Having lived the greater part of his life in the country in close relations with the people, Levin always felt the electric feeling of this particular time communicate itself to him.

Early in the morning he went out to see the first sowing of the rye and the oats that were being hauled to the lofts, and returning home, he drank his coffee with his wife and sister-in-law, and afterwards departed on foot to the out-farm, where they were to start a newly erected threshing-machine for the preparation of the seeds.

All that day while talking with his bailiff, the peasants, or at home with his wife, Dolly, the children, and his father-in-law, Levin kept thinking of the one and only thing that interested him at that time, in spite of all his farm cares. "What am I? where am I? and why am I?" he asked himself.

Standing in the cold-room of the newly thatched kiln, he watched the dust thrown off by the threshing-machine flying about in the air, the chaff settling down on the sunny grass, while the swallows took refuge under the roof and the labourers hurried about in the dark interior. A strange idea came into his head.

"What is all this done for?" he thought. "Why do I stand here compelling them to work? What makes them bustle so and try to show their zeal in my presence? Why does that old woman Matriona work so hard? I remember curing her once when she was struck down by a beam during a fire." He was looking at the haggard old woman who was trotting about on her sunburnt feet over the rough, uneven threshing floor, turning the grain over with a rake. "She recovered then, but to-day, or to-morrow, or in ten years, she will be dead and buried, and nothing will be left of her. And that pretty woman in the red blouse, who is so nimbly separating the grain from the chaff, will share the same fate. She, too, will be buried, and so will that horse," he thought, as he gazed at the piebald gelding that was breathing heavily through its dilated nostrils as it walked in the tread-mill. " The horse will be buried and so will Fiodor, the feeder, with his curly beard full of chaff and the shirt that is torn over the shoulder. And I, too, will be buried and nothing will be left. What is it all for? "

During these thoughts he kept a steady watch in order to calculate how much work they would do in an hour. He had to know that in order to fix the task of the day.

" An hour has nearly gone and they are only on the third rick," Levin thought. He walked over to the feeder, and raising his voice above the rumble of the machine, ordered him to feed it more evenly.

" You put in too much at a time, Fiodor! You see, it catches and goes more slowly. Try and make it more even! "

Fiodor, his face black from perspiration and dust, shouted something in reply, but still did not do what Levin wanted him to.

Levin walked over to the drum, and pushing Fiodor aside began feeding himself.

He worked until the peasant dinner hour, then went out of the kiln with the feeder, and stopped talking to him at the yellow stack of cut rye.

The man came from a distant village, where Levin had once let land on the company system. Now it was let to the innkeeper.

Levin questioned Fiodor about this land, and asked whether Platon, a rich merchant of that village, would not take it for the coming year.

" The price is high, Konstantin Dmitritch; Platon cannot make it pay," the peasant replied, picking out the ears from his perspiring bosom.

" But how does Kirillov make it pay? "

" Oh, Mityuha could make anything pay! " (Mityuha was a nickname the innkeeper was known by in the village.) " He will squeeze a fellow and get what he wants. He will not spare a Christian. As for Uncle Fokanitch " (thus he called Platon), " he is different. To some he gives on credit, and on others he loses. Sometimes he does not get back his own. He is a good man."

" But why doesn't he insist on getting his own? "

" People are different; one man lives for himself alone, like Mityuha, who only thinks of filling his belly, but Fokanitch is an honest man; he lives for his soul. He thinks of God."

" What do you mean by that? How does he live for his soul? " Levin almost shouted.

339

" It's quite simple, according to the truth, according to God's word. There are all kinds of people. Take yourself, for example, you would not hurt any one . . . "

" Yes, yes, good-bye! " Levin said, hastily, and turned away. He took his cane and walked rapidly towards the house, in a state of great agitation. The peasant's simple words about Fokanitch living for his soul, according to God's word, set a whole chain of thoughts whirling in his brain, blinding him with their light.

XII

LEVIN walked along the highway with long strides, excited, not so much by his thoughts, as by his strange mental condition— a condition he had never experienced before.

The words uttered by the peasant were like an electric spark, that suddenly transformed and blended into a whole series of heterogeneous, impotent, disconnected thoughts, that had never ceased interesting him. They had been with him even when he had spoken to the peasant about the land.

He felt that something new was taking place in his soul, and though he did not yet know what it was, he felt a pleasurable excitement in the feeling.

" Not to live for oneself, but for God. For what God? Could any one have said anything more stupid? According to Fiodor one must live not for one's own needs, that is, for what we want, what we understand, but for some incomprehensible God whom nobody knows or can define. Well? Did I not understand the meaning of Fiodor's words? Did I doubt their justice? Did I find them senseless, incomprehensible, insignificant? I understood them just as Fiodor understood them. I understand them more clearly and fully than anything in life, and never have I doubted them, or could have doubted them. Not I alone, but everybody, the whole world understands them fully; in this alone men have no doubts, and are in complete accord. Fiodor said that Kirillovitch the innkeeper lives only for his stomach. That is comprehensible and sensible. All sensible people cannot help but live for their stomachs. And suddenly this same Fiodor says that it is bad to live for one's stomach, that one ought to live for truth, for God, and I understand him. And the millions of people who lived centuries back, and those who are living now, peasants, the poor in spirit, and the wise, those who have thought and written about it, those who say the same in their own simple language—all are agreed on this one point, and know what it is we should live for, and what is good. With all people in common, I have one firm, indubitable piece of knowledge—a knowledge that cannot be explained through reason, because it is beyond the sphere of reason, a knowledge that has no causes and can have no effects. If good has a cause, it is no longer good; if it has an effect—rewards—it is again not good. Consequently good must be beyond the law of cause and effect.

" I know this and we all know it.

" I wanted a miracle to convince me. But here it is, the only possible, existing miracle, surrounding me on all sides, and I did not even observe it! What greater miracle can there be?

" Is it possible that I have found the solution to everything? Is it possible that all my sufferings have come to an end? " Levin asked himself, as he continued on his way along the dusty road, oblivious to heat and fatigue, with a sensation as though an old pain had suddenly left him. The sensation was so joyous that it seemed almost incredible to him. He was so overcome by emotion that he was unable to proceed, and leaving the road, he turned aside into the forest. He took off his hat and sank down on the rich, luxurious grass, under the shade of the aspens.

"Yes, I must consider it carefully," he thought, gazing at the untrodden grass in front of him, and watching the movements of a little green caterpillar that was climbing up a blade of couch-grass. " What is it I have discovered? " he asked himself, bending another blade of grass for the caterpillar to crawl on. " Why am I so pleased? What have I discovered?

" Formerly I used to say that in my body, in this grass, in this caterpillar, a transmutation of matter takes place according to physical, chemical, and physiological laws. And in all of us, in these aspens, in the clouds, evolution is going on. Evolution from what, to what? An eternal evolution and struggle? As if there could be any direction and struggle in the infinite! And in spite of all the efforts of my reason in that direction, until now, the meaning of life, the meaning of my own impulses and strivings were not revealed to me. Now I know that life consists in living for God, for the soul.

" I have not discovered anything; I have merely found what I knew already. I have come to understand the power that gave me life in the past, that gives me life in the present. I have freed myself from deception and found the master."

He reviewed briefly the whole progress of his thoughts of the last two years, thoughts that had first been aroused by the sight of his sick, dying brother. Then, for the first time, had he clearly comprehended that for every man, and himself too, there was nothing ahead but suffering, death, eternal oblivion. He had decided that it was impossible to live thus, that it was necessary to explain life in a more sane way or else shoot himself. But he had done neither the one nor the other; he had continued to live, think, and feel. He even married during that time, experienced many joys, and was happy so long as he tried to shut his eyes to the meaning of life.

What did it mean? It meant that he was living well and thinking badly.

He had been living unconsciously on the spiritual truths he had imbibed with his mother's milk, yet in his thoughts he had not only refused to acknowledge them, but had cautiously avoided them altogether.

Now it was clear to him that he could only live according to the beliefs in which he had been brought up.

"What should I have been, how should I have passed my life had it not been for those beliefs, had I not known that one must live for God and not for one's own needs? I might have robbed, lied, and killed. What are now the chief joys of my life would never have existed for me." And try as he would he was unable to picture to himself the bestial creature he would have been had he not known what he was living for.

"I have been seeking an answer to my question, but reason could not give it to me. It was life itself gave me the answer, through my knowledge of good and bad. This knowledge I have not acquired in any way; it was given me from the beginning, given me because I could not get it anywhere.

"Where did it come from? Was it reason that told me it was necessary to love my neighbour? It was told to me in my childhood, and I gladly believed it, because it was already in my soul. Who discovered it? Not reason; reason discovered the theory of the struggle for existence and the law demanding that I should gratify my own desires at the cost of others. To love my neighbour could not have been discovered by reason, because it is unreasonable."

XIII

LEVIN recalled a recent scene between Dolly and her children. When left alone one day the children began amusing themselves by making raspberry jam in a tea-cup over a lighted candle, and throwing milk into each other's faces. Their mother, catching them in the act, began scolding them before Levin. She tried to impress on them the idea that what they were destroying had cost their elders a large amount of labour, performed for their sakes, also saying that if they broke the cups they would have nothing from which to drink their tea, and that if they spilled the milk they would have nothing to eat, and would have to go hungry.

Levin was struck by the indifference and scepticism with which the children listened to their mother's words. They did not believe what she said, and were merely sorry to have their interesting game interrupted. They did not believe because they did not know the value of what they were playing with, and did not understand that they were destroying their own means of subsistence.

" That is all very well," they thought, " but these things are not so important, for they have always been and always will be. We needn't worry about that, that is all ready for us. We want to invent something new. It was quite a nice idea to make raspberry jam in a cup over a candle, and to pour milk into each other's mouths as from a fountain. It was very jolly, and not in any way worse than drinking it out of a cup.

" Are we not doing the same? " Levin thought. " Have I not done it by trying to discover the meaning of the forces of nature and human life through reason? And is not the same done by all philosophical theories that lead us by strange paths to the knowledge that we already have? Can we not see clearly in the development of the theory of any philosopher that he knows in advance, just as much as Fiodor did, what is the real meaning of life?

" If we were to let the children get things for themselves, make the dishes, milk the cows, and so forth, what would happen? They would starve, probably. In the same way if we were let loose with our passions and ideas, without any conception of a God, a Creator, of what is good or evil, we

343

should only destroy just as the children do. For without the idea of a God we cannot build up anything.

"From whence did this joyful knowledge come to me, a knowledge that I have in common with the peasant Fiodor, which alone gives me peace of mind? Here am I, a Christian, brought up in the faith, surrounded by the blessings of Christianity, living upon these spiritual blessings without being conscious of them, and failing to understand them, destroying that by which I live. And the moment anything important in life occurs I run to Him as children run to their mother when they are cold and hungry.

"Yes, what I know has not come to me through reason, it has been given to me, revealed to me; I know it with my heart, by my faith in the teachings of the Church.

"The Church? The Church?" Levin repeated to himself as he rolled over on his other side and, leaning on his arm, looked away into the distance, beyond the cattle going down to the river.

"But can I believe in all that the Church teaches?" he said, in order to test himself, and bring up everything that might destroy his present feeling of security. He purposely brought to mind the part of the Church teaching that had seemed to him strange and had most alienated him. "Creation? Yes, how did I explain existence? By existence? By nothing? The devil, and sin? But dow did I explain evil? The Redeemer? . . .

"But I know nothing, nothing, and cannot know other than what I have been told with the rest."

It seemed to him now that not one of these Church dogmas was inimical to the great objects of life—faith in God and goodness. On the contrary, all tended to produce the greatest of miracles; enabling the world with its millions of human beings, young and old, Lvov, Kitty, peasants, and kings, to comprehend the same great truths, so as to live the life of the soul—the only life that is worth living.

Lying on his back he looked up into the high, cloudless sky. "Do I not know that that is endless space and not a vault of blue stretching above me? But however much I may strain my sight I can only see a vaulted dome; and in spite of my knowledge of infinite space I am unquestionably right when I see it like that, far more right than when I try to probe into the beyond."

Levin stopped thinking, and listened intently to the mysterious joyful voices that seemed to be talking about him.

344

" Is it faith? " he thought, afraid to believe his own happiness
" My God, I thank thee! " he cried, swallowing the sobs that
rose within him, and brushing the tears from his eyes.

XIV

LEVIN looked in front of him and saw the cattle, then a cart
drawn by one horse and his coachman on it. The coachman
drove up to the shepherd and said a few words to him; afterwards Levin heard the sound of wheels near him and the snort-
ing of the well-fed horse, but he was so absorbed in his thoughts
that he did not even wonder why the coachman was coming
towards him.

" Madame has sent me for you; your brother and another
gentleman have come," the coachman called to him as soon as
he was near enough.

Levin shook himself got into the cart, and took the reins.

He felt as though he had just awakened from a deep sleep
and had not yet fully regained his senses. He stared at the
horse, at Ivan, the coachman, and vaguely recalled that he had
been expecting his brother, and that his wife would be worried
by his long absence; he also conjectured as to who the other
guest might be. And his brother, and wife, and the unknown
guest—all appeared to him in a different light.

" There will no longer be that estrangement that has always
existed between Sergei and myself—no more quarrels; as to
the other guest, I shall be kind and amiable to him, whoever he
may be. And with the servants, and Ivan too, I will be different."

Levin pulled the reins tightly and looked at Ivan, who was
sitting beside him, and did not know what to do with his unoccupied hands. Levin wanted to enter into conversation with
him, and was about to remark that the saddle-strap was raised
too high, but as that sounded too much like a reprimand, he
held his peace, not being able to think of anything else to say.

" Please bear to the right: there is a stump here," Ivan
cautioned him with a tug at the rein in Levin's hand.

" Don't touch it; I know quite well how to do it without
you," Levin said, annoyed. Interference from anybody always
made him angry, and he could not help thinking with a feeling
of sorrow that his new spiritual mood had not yet changed him
in that direction.

When they were about a quarter of a mile from the house, Levin saw Tania and Grisha running towards him.

"Uncle Kostia! Mamma is coming and grandpapa and Sergei Ivanovitch and another man," they shouted in one breath, as they climbed into the cart.

"Who is it?"

"A terrible man! He throws his arms about like this," Tania said, standing up in the cart and imitating Katavasov.

"Is he old or young?" Levin asked, with a laugh, for Tania's gesture had reminded him of some one. "I hope it's not some disagreeable person," he thought.

At the bend of the road Levin caught sight of the whole party and recognised Katavasov in his straw hat, swaying his arms as he walked along precisely in the way Tania had described.

Katavasov was very fond of discussing philosphy, and during his last stay in Moscow he and Levin had had many disputes. The first thing Levin recalled as he saw him was one occasion when Katavasov was supposed to have vanquished him.

"Under no conditions will I dispute or express my ideas with levity," Levin thought.

He got out of the cart, exchanged greetings with his brother and Katavasov, and asked how Kitty was.

"She has taken Mitia into the wood, because it was so hot in the house," Dolly said.

"She insists on carrying him from place to place," the old prince said with a smile. "I advised her to take him down to the ice-cellar."

"She wanted to go to the apiary, thinking you were there," Dolly said. "As a matter of fact we were all going there."

"Well, what are you doing now?" Sergei Ivanovitch asked, as he and Levin got ahead of the others.

"Nothing in particular; occupied with the farm as usual," Levin replied. "Shall you stay for some time? We have long been expecting you."

"About a fortnight; there is such a lot to do in Moscow."

At these words Levin, in spite of his strong desire to be friendly and natural with his brother, felt a sense of discomfort in his presence.

He thought of everything he might say that would be agreeable to Sergei Ivanovitch, so as to draw his attention away from the Serbian war and the Slavonic question he had hinted at in his reference to Moscow.

346

" Have you seen any reviews of your book? " he asked.

Sergei Ivanovitch smiled. Levin's pointed question amused him.

" No one is interested in it, and I least of all," he replied. " I think it is going to rain, Darya Alexandrovna," he added, turning to Dolly and indicating some black clouds that had made their appearance over the tops of the aspens.

And these words again established that cold, almost hostile relation between the two brothers—a relation that Levin had so much wished to avoid.

Levin went up to Katavasov.

" I am so glad you made up your mind to come at last," he said.

" I have long wanted to. We shall now have an opportunity of talking together. Have you read Spencer? "

" I haven't finished him yet, but I don't think I need him now," Levin replied.

" Why? That sounds rather interesting."

" I have merely come to the conclusion that he cannot offer me a solution to the questions that interest me. Now . . . "

But Katavasov's calm, jolly face suddenly brought back his recent mood, and recollecting his intention, he broke off. " We can talk later," he added. " If you want to go to the apiary we must turn down this path," he said, turning to the whole company.

Levin conducted his guests through a clearing covered with wild pansies until they reached the shade of a young aspen wood, where he asked them to wait while he himself went into the apiary to feed the bees.

He tried to move as slowly as possible and listened to the bees as they flew past him over the path leading to the hut. As he reached the porch a bee got caught in his beard, but he freed it cautiously.

On entering the porch, he took down his net, hanging on a peg in the wall. He put it on, thrust his hands into his pockets, and went into the enclosed apiary. On a mown plot the old hives were standing, each with its own storey, while along the wicker fence were the young ones.

Levin was glad to be left alone for a moment, to escape from the reality that had already depressed his spirits. He recalled that in quite a short space of time he had been angry with Ivan, shown coolness to his brother, and spoken with levity to Katavasov.

" Can it have been only a momentary mood that will pass without leaving any trace? " he thought.

But that very moment it came upon him again and he felt with joy that something new and important had taken place within him. The spiritual peace he had found was still unharmed, though reality had shrouded it for a moment.

Just as the bees, circling and buzzing about him, deprived him of his full physical calm and compelled him to shrink and evade them, so also did the cares that had beset him from the moment he had taken his seat in the cart deprive him of his spiritual freedom. But it had only lasted so long as he was in the midst of them. And just as, in spite of the bees, his physical strength was unharmed, even so was his newly born spiritual power.

XV

" KOSTIA, do you know with whom Sergei Ivanovitch was travelling? " Dolly asked, dividing up the cucumber and honey among the children. " With Vronsky; he was on his way to Servia."

" He is taking a whole company out at his own expense," Katavasov put in.

" That is just like him," Levin said. " Are the volunteers still going out? " he asked, glancing at his brother.

Sergei Ivanovitch did not reply. He stuck the blunt side of a knife into the cup in which lay a white honey-comb, and tried to extricate a bee that had got caught in the flowing honey.

" I should say so! You ought to have seen them at the station yesterday! " Katavasov remarked, crunching some cucumber.

" I really fail to understand it all," the old prince observed. " For Heaven's sake, Sergei Ivanovitch, explain it to me! Where are all these volunteers going, and whom they are going to fight."

" The Turks, of course," Sergei Ivanovitch replied, with a smile, extricating the helpless bee and putting it on an aspen leaf.

" But who declared war against the Turks? Ivan Ivanitch, the Countess Lydia Ivanovna, and Madame Stahl? "

" Nobody has declared war; people feel compassion for their fellow-creatures and desire to help them," Sergei Ivanovitch said.

" The prince is not talking of help, but of war," Levin put in,

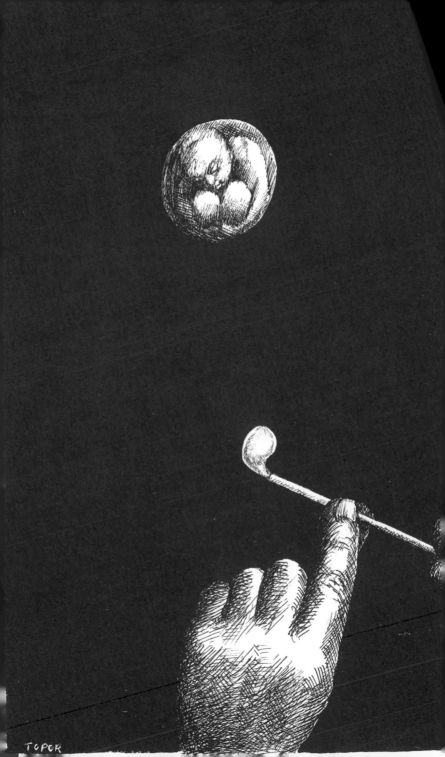

TOPOR

taking the side of his father-in-law. "The prince means that individuals have no right to participate in this war without the sanction of the government."

"Kostia, look, here is a bee! I'm afraid it will sting us," Dolly said, warding off a wasp.

"It's not a bee; it's a wasp," Levin said.

"Well, come along, what is your theory?" Katavasov asked with a smile, evidently anxious to provoke a discussion. "Why have individuals no right to go to the war?"

"To my mind war is such a beastly cruel thing that not a man, one need hardly say a Christian, can take upon himself the responsibility of beginning one; war must be left to the government, whose business it is to look to these things. Besides, both science and common sense say that in matters of state, especially in matters of war, citizens should renounce their personal will."

Sergei Ivanovitch and Katavasov began to speak at once.

"That is where the trouble comes in," the latter said; "there may be cases when the government does not carry out the will of the people, and then society must declare its own will."

Sergei Ivanovitch did not approve of these words.

"You do not put the question rightly," he said with a frown. "There has been no declaration of war, but simply the expression of a Christian sentiment. Brothers of one blood and one faith are being slaughtered. Supposing you were walking in the street and saw a drunkard striking a woman or a child, you would not stop to ask whether war had been declared on that man, you would simply go for him and defend the assaulted person."

"Yes, but I should not kill him," Levin said.

"You would if necessary."

"I don't know about that. I should probably give way to my immediate feelings; it is difficult to say what one would do under the circumstances, but there can be no immediate feeling in the case of the oppression of the Slavs; the thing is too remote."

"It may be for you, but others feel more keenly about it," Sergei Ivanovitch said, frowning impatiently. "There still exists among the people the tradition about the orthodox suffering under the yoke of the 'infidel Hagarites.' The people have responded to the sufferings of their brothers."

"Perhaps," Levin said evasively, "but I do not see it. I, too, form part of the people, and I do not feel it."

" I confess I feel as Kostia does," the old prince remarked. " When I lived abroad I used to read the papers and wonder why the Russians had suddenly fallen so deeply in love with their Slavonic brothers, when I did not care for them in the least. It used to grieve me horribly and made me think that I was some kind of a monster, or that Karlsbad was having a bad effect upon me, but when I came home I was quite consoled. I could see that other people besides myself were interested only in Russia, and did not care for our Slavonic brothers. There is Kostia, for example."

" Personal opinions hardly count," Sergei Ivanovitch observed. " They can have little weight when the whole of Russia, the nation, has expressed its will."

" Excuse me, I don't see that. As far as one knows, the people care nothing about it," the prince said.

" What makes you think so, papa? Don't you remember Sunday in church? " Dolly said to her father. " Can you let me have a towel, please? " she turned to an old peasant who was standing by with a cup of honey, looking at the children with a smile. " It can't be that all . . . "

" What was there so particular in church on Sunday? The priest was commanded to read it and he did," the old prince said. " They did not understand a single word, and sighed just as they do at any sermon. When they were told that a collection was to be taken for some soul-saving affair, they produced their purses and gave their kopeks, but what it was for they did not know."

" The people can't help knowing; they are always conscious of their fate, and at such moments as these it is doubly clear to them," Sergei Ivanovitch observed with a glance at the old bee-keeper.

The handsome old man with his long black beard, turning grey, and his silvery hair, stood there motionless, looking down at his masters from the height of his stature with a kindly smile, not understanding and not wishing to understand what they were talking about.

" That is so," he said with a significant shake of the head at Sergei Ivanovitch's words.

" You had better ask him," Levin said. " He knows nothing and thinks nothing. Mihail, have you heard about the war? " he asked, turning to the old peasant. " What do you think about the reading in church? Ought we to fight for the Christians? "

"Why should we trouble ourselves about that? Alexander Nicholaevitch, the emperor, takes care of us, and we trust him in these matters too. He knows best. Shall I bring some more bread? Would the boy like some?" he asked, turning to Darya Alexandrovna and pointing to Grisha, who was finishing a crust.

"I have no need to ask," Sergei Ivanovitch said; "we have seen hundreds and hundreds of men throw up everything in order to serve the cause—men coming from all ends of Russia and openly declaring their thoughts and purposes. Some bring their small contributions, others go themselves; that surely signifies something!"

"It merely signifies that in a nation of eighty millions there will always be found, not hundreds, but thousands of people who have lost all social standing—a restless crew, ready to go anywhere, to join Pugatchev's robber band, or to Hiva, or to Serbia!" Levin said, beginning to grow excited.

"They are not a restless crew, but the best representatives of the nation," Sergei Ivanovitch said severely. "Besides, there are the contributions. In that way the whole nation directly expresses its will."

"The word 'nation' is so very indefinite," Levin objected. "Of the peasantry, I don't suppose one in a thousand knows what is going on. The great majority of our eighty millions, like Mihail, not only do not express their will, but have not the slightest conception what to express their will about. It seems to me we have no right in saying it is the nation's will."

XVI

As an experienced dialectician, Sergei Ivanovitch did not reply to Levin's words, but attacked the question from another side.

"It would be very difficult to discover the national spirit in an arithmetical way. Voting has not been introduced into our country, and cannot be, because it is not an expression of the popular will; there are other ways of ascertaining that. It is in the air, and you can feel it with the heart. I am not alluding to those undercurrents that have begun to move in the stagnant sea of the people—currents that are plainly visible to any unprejudiced person. Look at society in the narrower sense! All the most varied intellectual parties, so hostile before, are now united. All dissensions have stopped, all public organs speak of one and the same thing, all have come to feel the elementary force that has seized them and is carrying them in one direction."

"Yes, the papers all say the same thing," the prince put in; "I agree with you there. They all croak alike just as frogs do before a storm. You can't hear anything else for their croaking."

"Frogs or no frogs; I am not an editor of a newspaper and do not wish to defend them; I am talking about the unity of ideas in the intellectual world," Sergei Ivanovitch said, turning to his brother.

Levin was about to make some retort, but the old prince interrupted him.

"As to the unity of ideas, a great deal might be said on that score," he said. "I have a son-in-law, Stepan Arkadyevitch—you know him quite well; he is about to be appointed a member of some commission or other, I don't exactly remember what. All I know is that there is no work to be done . . . well, what does it matter, Dolly? it is no secret! and he is to get eight thousand roubles a year. If you were to ask him whether his service was useful or not, he would prove to you without the smallest doubt that it was the most useful work on the face of the earth. He is a truthful man too; but how can one believe otherwise of eight thousand roubles a year?"

"That reminds me, Stepan Arkadyevitch asked me to inform Darya Alexandrovna that he has already received the appointment," Sergei Ivanovitch said, impatient at the prince's irrelevant remark.

"It is just the same with the newspapers too. When a war breaks out their incomes are doubled. How can they help being sympathetic over the fates of nations, over the Slavs and all that?"

"I agree that most of the newspapers are unscrupulous, but that is hardly just," Sergei Ivanovitch said.

"I would only make one condition," the prince continued. "Let all those who preach war be sent out in a special legion to lead the attack!"

"What funny figures the editors would cut!" Katavasov said with a loud laugh, as he recalled some of those he knew, and tried to imagine them at the front.

"They would run away; they would only be in the way," Dolly objected.

"If they run, fire canister shot at them, or send Cossacks after them with horsewhips!" the prince said.

"Excuse me, it is a very poor joke," Sergei Ivanovitch remarked.

"I don't see that it's a joke at all, it is . . . " Levin began, but Sergei Ivanovitch interrupted him.

"Every member of society has to do his own particular work, and the men of ideas do theirs by expressing public opinion. We ought to be very thankful for the press. Twenty years ago we should have kept silent, but to-day the voice of the Russian people is heard like one man, ready to sacrifice themselves for their oppressed, down-trodden brothers. That is a great step in advance, I think."

"They not only sacrifice themselves, but they kill the Turks as well," Levin observed, timidly. "The people sacrifice themselves and are prepared to go on doing so for the sake of their souls, but not for the purpose of wholesale slaughter," he added, involuntarily connecting the present conversation with the ideas that had been interesting him.

"For the soul? A most difficult conception for a naturalist. What is a soul?" Katavasov said with a smile.

"You know quite well."

"I assure you I don't," Katavasov said with a loud laugh.

"Christ said, 'I am come to bring, not peace, but a sword,'" Sergei Ivanovitch interposed in a simple manner.

That particular quotation from the Gospel always irritated Levin.

"That is so," the old peasant said again, in reply to Sergei Ivanovitch's glance, accidentally cast at him.

"You are beaten! completely beaten!" Katavasov called out merrily.

Levin blushed with annoyance, not because he considered himself beaten, but because he had not been true to his resolve, and had mixed himself up in a discussion.

"No, I must not dispute with them," he said to himself. "They have an impermeable coat of mail and I am naked."

He saw that it was impossible to convince either Katavasov or his brother, and that it was still less possible to agree with them. What they were preaching was the very same mental pride that had ruined him. He could not agree with the statement that a few dozen men, even though they included his brother amongst them, had the right of saying that they and the newspapers were expressing the thought of the people—a thought that found its expression in bloodshed and murder. He knew full well that the masses among whom he was living, of whom he felt himself a part, could not wish for war, or advocate it for any general purpose. He upheld Mihailitch and the people who had expressed their thought in the tradition about the invitation tendered to the Varegs: " Rule and direct us; we gladly promise full submission. We take all the labour, humiliations, and sacrifices upon ourselves, but we do not wish to judge or decide." And now the nation, according to Sergei Ivanovitch, renounced the right that had been purchased so dearly.

He also wanted to say that if public opinion was an infallible judge, a revolution, the Commune, could be every bit as much justified as the movement in favour of the Slavs, but seeing that the discussion irritated Sergei Ivanovitch, he thought it best to put an end to it. He drew the attention of his guests to the gathering clouds, and advised them all to get back home before the rain.

XVII

THE prince and Sergei Ivanovitch seated themselves in the cart and drove off; the rest of the company walked home.

The clouds gathered so rapidly that they had to increase their pace the last part of the way. A few yards from the house a high wind rose and the clouds grew blacker than ever. The children ran on ahead screaming with fear and delight. Darya Alexandrovna followed them as quickly as she could, her skirts clinging to her legs. The men held their hats on with their hands and took long strides. They had no sooner reached the porch than a large drop of rain splashed against the edge of the iron gutter. The children, followed by the elders, ran quickly under the roof for protection.

" Where is Katerina Alexandrovna? " Levin asked Agafia Mihailovna, who met them in the hall with a bundle of rugs and shawls.

" I thought she was with you."

" And Mitia? "

" In the wood with the nurse."

Levin seized the shawls and ran out.

In the short interval the sky had grown blacker and more threatening than ever. The wind blew in strong gusts, tearing the leaves and blossoms off the lime-trees, baring the birch branches, and bending everything, acacias, flowers, burdock, grass, and tree-tops all in one direction. The girls working in the garden ran screaming into the house. The fields and the wood disappeared behind a curtain of rain.

Bending his head and fighting vigorously against the gale, Levin advanced as best he could. He was already in the wood and thought he saw something white beyond an oak-tree, when suddenly a glare of light seemed to burst from the ground before him, and the vault of the sky above seemed to fall with a loud crash. When he opened his dazzled eyes, he peered through the thick curtain formed by the rain, that cut him off from the woods, and saw to his horror that the green top of a well known oak had disappeared. "Was it struck?" The thought had barely time to cross his mind, than the oak came down with a crash, bringing other trees along with it.

"My God! My God! Keep them safe!" Levin murmured, rigid with fear; and though he instantly felt the absurdity of the prayer, since the harm would have been done already, he repeated it again and again, for he knew that, absurd though it was, he could do nothing else to help them. He hastened to the spot where they generally went, but did not find them there. They were in another part of the wood under an old lime-tree, and were calling to him. Two figures in dark dresses were standing there, bending over something. It was Kitty and the nurse. The rain was beginning to stop and it was growing lighter when Levin came up to them. The lower part of the nurse's dress was dry, but Kitty's garments were drenched through and through and clung to her body. Though it had stopped raining they were still standing with a large green umbrella over the baby-carriage.

"Alive! unharmed! thank God!" he muttered, splashing through the puddles as he ran towards them.

Kitty's rosy wet face wore a timid smile as she peeped up at him from beneath her ruined hat.

"How could you be so careless!" he exclaimed in his annoyance.

"It was not my fault, really. We were just going home when a fit of naughtiness seized him. He had to be changed. We just . . . " Kitty began excusing herself.

Mitia was quite dry and had slept through the storm.

"Well, thank God you are all safe and sound! I didn't know what I was saying!"

They gathered up the wet napkins; the nurse took the baby

in her arms and started; Levin walked beside his wife, a little conscience-stricken on account of his indignation, and pressing her hand stealthily so that the nurse might not see.

XVIII

FOR the rest of the day, in all the varied conversations in which Levin took part with his reason only, he was joyfully conscious of the fulness of his heart, in spite of the disenchantment about the change that had taken place within him.

It was too wet to go out walking after the rain; besides, the storm clouds did not leave the horizon, so the whole company remained at home.

There were no more discussions, and after dinner every one was in the happiest of moods.

Katavasov amused the ladies with his funny stories, and later, incited by Sergei Ivanovitch, he told them of his interesting observations on the character of the house-fly. Sergei Ivanovitch, too, was as merry as could be, and at tea he expounded his views on the Eastern question in such a very simple manner that all listened to him with pleasure.

Kitty was the only one who did not hear him to the end; she was called away to give Micia his bath. A few minutes later, Levin, too, was called to the nursery. Though somewhat anxious to know why he was thus summoned to the nursery—a thing that only happened on special occasions—he went out reluctantly, sorry to cut short such a very pleasant conversation. But his anxiety, as well as the curiosity aroused by his brother's ideas, disappeared as soon as he found himself alone for a moment. His secret happiness came back to him, clear and strong as in the morning. He had no need to arouse it by reflection; the feeling had become independent of thought.

As he walked across the terrace he saw two stars glowing in the sky.

" Yes," he said to himself, " as I looked at the heavens I thought there was a truth in the delusion that what I saw was a solid vault. I did not finish my thought and concealed something from myself. Now what was it? One has only to consider and everything becomes clear."

It was only when he had entered the nursery that he recalled what it was he had concealed from himself. It was this:

" If the chief proof of the existence of God lies in the inward revelation of good and evil He has given to each of us, why should this revelation be limited to the Christian Church? How about those millions of Buddhists and Mohammedans who are also seeking for the truth? "

It seemed to him that there must be an answer to this question, but he could not find and express it to himself before entering the room.

Kitty, with her sleeves rolled up, was bending over the bath in which Mitia was kicking and splashing. When she heard her husband's footsteps she turned her face towards him and beckoned him with a smile. She was supporting the baby's head with one hand and sponging him with the other.

" Just look at him! " she said when her husband came up. " Agafia Mihailovna is right; he is beginning to recognise people."

An experiment had to be made. Levin bent over the bath, and the child seemed to know him. The cook was then called; she, too, bent over him and the child frowned and screwed up its face. Next Kitty bent over him and his face lighted up with a smile. He pressed his little hands against the sponge and made such a strange, satisfied sound that not only Kitty and the nurse, but even Levin was transported with joy.

The child was taken from the bath, wrapped in a sheet, rubbed down as it yelled lustily, and turned over to his mother.

" I am glad you are beginning to love him at last," Kitty said to her husband, as she sat down in her customary place with Mitia at her breast. " You always said you had no feeling for him, and it used to worry me."

" Did I say that, really? I only meant that I was disappointed in him."

" What! disappointed in him! "

"Not exactly in him, but in my feeling for him; I had expected more. I had expected some new, pleasant feeling, but instead there was only a sensation of pity, disgust . . ."

Kitty listened to him as she put on her rings, that she had taken off before bathing the baby.

" There was more fear and pity than satisfaction. I never knew until to-day, during the storm, how I loved him."

Kitty's face grew radiant.

" Were you very much frightened? " she asked. " I was too, but I feel even more frightened now; I must go and look at the oak to-morrow. What a dear Katavasov is! The whole day has been such a pleasant one. I am glad to see you so friendly with Sergei Ivanovitch. You can be when you like. . . . But you had better go to them. It is always hot and close in here after the bath."

XIX

On leaving the nursery, Levin at once reverted to the thought that had not been very clear to him. Instead of returning to the drawing-room he remained on the terrace, and leaning over the balustrade he gazed up at the sky.

It was beginning to grow dark; to the south not a cloud was to be seen, but it was still threatening on the other side. Every now and again there was a flash of lightning and a distant rumble of thunder. Levin listened to the drops that fell rhythmically from the trees in the garden, and looked up at the stars and the Milky Way. At each flash of lightning they all disappeared, but the moment the lightning vanished they shone out again, brighter than ever.

"What is it that troubles me?" he asked himself, feeling that the solution of his doubts was already in his soul. "Yes, the laws of good and evil revealed to the world are the only proofs, the evident, unimpeachable proofs of the existence of a God. These laws I recognise in the depths of my heart, whether I will or no. I am united to all those who recognise them like myself. It is this union of souls sharing a common belief that calls itself the Church. But Jews and Mohammedans, Confucians and Buddhists, what are they?" he asked himself, recurring to the dilemma that had threatened him before. "Can these millions of human beings be deprived of the greatest blessing—deprived of the only thing that invests life with meaning?" He paused for a while. "What is it that I want to know?" he asked himself. "I am seeking to find the relation of all the different forms of human belief to the Divinity. It is the relation of God to the universe with all its stars and planets that I am presuming to fathom. The knowledge has already been revealed to my heart, so why do I persist in trying to express it by means of reason, and through the medium of words that are foreign to it?

"Do I not know that the stars do not move?" he asked himself, looking at a bright planet that had already changed its position over the top of a birch-tree. "But seeing the stars change place and being unable to imagine the rotation of the earth, I am right in saying that the stars move. And the astronomers, could they have understood or calculated anything if they had taken into account all the varied motions of the earth? Have not their marvellous conclusions as to the distances, the weight, the motions, the revolutions of the celestial bodies, all been based upon the apparent movements of the stars round a motionless earth? They were based on these same movements that I now witness, that millions of men have witnessed for centuries, and that can always be verified. And just as the conclusions of the astronomers would have been inaccurate and false had they been based on the observation of the visible heavens in relation to one meridian and one horizon, so all my conclusions as to the knowledge of good and evil would be false if I did not connect them with what has been revealed to me through Christianity, and can always be verified in my own soul. I have no right to try to solve the relation of other faiths to the Divinity; that must remain unfathomable for me."

"Haven't you gone in yet?" he suddenly heard the voice of Kitty, who was on her way back to the drawing-room. "You are not worried about anything, are you?" she asked, looking fixedly into his face in the starlight.

A flash of lightning suddenly illuminated it for her, and she could see that it was calm and joyful. She smiled at him.

"She understands," he thought; "she knows what I am thinking about. Shall I speak to her or not? Yes, I think I will." But just as he was about to begin she turned to him first.

"I say, Kostia, do run into the corner room and see whether Sergei Ivanovitch will be comfortable there; I can't very well go myself, and I want to know if they've put in the new wash-stand."

"Certainly, if you like," Levin said, kissing her.

"No, I shall not tell her," he thought, as she passed out before him. "This secret is only important to me, and cannot be expressed in words.

"This new feeling has not changed me, made me happy, enlightened all at once; it is rather like the first feeling that I had for my son. It did not take me by surprise either. Through suffering it has entered my heart imperceptibly, and taken up its abode there. I shall probably get angry with Ivan, the coachman, the same as ever, embark upon useless discussions, express my thoughts irrelevantly just as before; there will always be the same dead wall between my soul and that of others, even with my wife; I shall probably go on accusing her in my anxiety and repenting of it afterwards. I shall continue to pray without being able to explain to myself why, but my life, my whole life, independently of what may happen to me, every minute of it, will no longer be senseless as before, but every moment, every action will be invested with meaning.